La
Seduction

MARIE FERRARELLA

GAIL BARRETT

CINDY DEES

All rights reserved including the right of reproduction in whole or in part in any form. This edition is published by arrangement with Harlequin Books S.A.

This is a work of fiction. Names, characters, places, locations and incidents are purely fictional and bear no relationship to any real life individuals, living or dead, or to any actual places, business establishments, locations, events or incidents. Any resemblance is entirely coincidental.

This book is sold subject to the condition that it shall not, by way of trade or otherwise, be lent, resold, hired out or otherwise circulated without the prior consent of the publisher in any form of binding or cover other than that in which it is published and without a similar condition including this condition being imposed on the subsequent purchaser.

® and ™ are trademarks owned and used by the trademark owner and/or its licensee. Trademarks marked with ® are registered with the United Kingdom Patent Office and/or the Office for Harmonisation in the Internal Market and in other countries.

Published in Great Britain 2014
by Mills & Boon, an imprint of Harlequin (UK) Limited,
Eton House, 18-24 Paradise Road, Richmond, Surrey, TW9 1SR

LAS VEGAS: SEDUCTION © 2014 Harlequin Books S.A.

Special thanks and acknowledgement to Marie Ferrarella, Gail Barrett and Cindy Dees for their contribution to the Love in 60 Seconds mini-series.

The Heiress's 2-Week Affair, His 7-Day Fiancée and *The 9-Month Bodyguard* were first published in Great Britain by Harlequin (UK) Limited.

The Heiress's 2-Week Affair © 2009 Harlequin Books S.A.
His 7-Day Fiancée © 2009 Harlequin Books S.A.
The 9-Month Bodyguard © 2009 Harlequin Books S.A.

ISBN: 978 0 263 91181 7
eBook ISBN: 978 1 472 04476 1

05-0414

Harlequin (UK) Limited's policy is to use papers that are natural, renewable and recyclable products and made from wood grown in sustainable forests. The logging and manufacturing processes conform to the legal environmental regulations of the country of origin.

Printed and bound in Spain
by Blackprint CPI, Barcelona

THE HEIRESS'S 2-WEEK AFFAIR

BY

MARIE FERRARELLA

Marie Ferrarella, a *USA TODAY* bestselling and RITA® Award-winning author, has written more than one hundred and fifty books for Mills & Boon, some under the name Marie Nicole. Her romances are beloved by fans worldwide. Visit her website at www.marieferrarella.com.

To
Shana Smith.
Welcome
aboard.

Prologue

The burst of joy that bathed over her like warm summer rain when Natalie Rothchild opened her eyes began to recede as the reality of the situation slowly penetrated her consciousness.

The spot beside her on the bed was empty.

Empty and cool to the touch when she ran her fingers over it.

"Matt?" She called out his name, but only the echo of her voice answered her. There was no sound of running water from the bathroom, no indication that there was anyone else in the hotel room but her.

Her heart began hammering hard, so hard that it physically hurt her. It felt as if someone had shot arrows through it.

He couldn't have gone.

But if he was here, where were his clothes? The ones

that he'd torn off so carelessly last night, throwing them on the floor along with hers? The first time they'd made love last night, she'd all but caught on fire.

The ache within her chest grew.

"Matt?" she called out again. Fear and bewilderment filled her voice as she sat up. A chill ran down her spine. Something was wrong.

Last night, he'd told her that he loved her, told her that they'd be together forever. He'd said he wanted to marry her. She *knew* he'd meant it. Knew it wasn't just something expedient to say because he wanted to make love to her. He'd said it after, not before. After was when it carried weight.

So where was he?

And why did she have this awful, sick feeling in the pit of her stomach, this uneasy sensation that something was very, very wrong?

As Natalie shifted to swing her legs out of bed, she saw it. Just beneath his pillow—*his* pillow—there was a bit of paper peeking out.

Natalie froze.

She wanted to leave it there. To ignore it. Because the moment she acknowledged it was the moment she had to read it. And the moment she read it, she knew that the euphoric state she'd allowed herself to slip into would burst apart like a soap bubble that had floated on the breeze a second too long, done in by the very thing that had made it float.

But she was Natalie Rothchild. Natalie, the sensible one. The one who faced her problems and life in general head on and fearlessly. Natalie, the rebel who refused to allow her family's vast fortune to keep her from living a life of purpose.

Matt told her that was one of the things he loved about her.

He *loved* her.

Didn't he?

Pressing her lips together, steeling herself, Natalie pulled the note out from beneath the pillow. She held it in her trembling hands and forced herself to read it.

Her eyes clouded with tears, nearly blinding her before she finished.

Balling up the paper, she threw it across the room and then buried her face against her raised knees. Her heart broken, Natalie did what she rarely did. She surrendered to despair.

Quiet sobs filled the silence within the room.

She was really alone.

Chapter 1

Excitement vibrated through Candace Rothchild's veins.

She could literally *feel* her adrenaline accelerating. Creating a rush. It was always this way when she stepped out in front of the cameras. Being the center of attention—even *anticipating* being the center of attention created a high that few drugs, legal or otherwise, could equal. Ever since she could remember, Candace thrived on the limelight, ate it up as if it was a source of energy for her.

Unlike her twin sister, Natalie, whom she considered a dull, placid being with little imagination or flair, Candace positively bloomed when attention was thrown her way. The bigger, the better had always been her motto.

To this end, she always made sure that she was picture perfect. She wore the latest fashions, had the kind of figure women would kill for and men remembered long after she had passed out of their lives. If, at times, that necessitated starving herself and spending outrageous amounts of money, well, so be it. It was all worth it. She wasn't cut out for the tranquil, humdrum life. Which meant the role of doting mother, to sons she hardly knew and had less time for, wasn't for her. The only plus from that end was that the tabloids were forever attempting to guess who had fathered them and if, indeed, it had been the same man in both cases.

Beyond that, the children—Mick and David, named after her favorite singers—held no interest for her. Far more important was that there was always another premiere, another function, another occasion to be photographed and fawned over. At times, she would imagine average, desperate women hungrily devouring the tidbits of her life, fantasizing about the men she'd bedded, all in an effort to leave, however briefly, their own drab lives behind.

She was doing a public service living this way, Candace told herself, a smirk twisting her ripe, collagen-full lips. She gave those poor, hopeless women something to dream about.

Why, she was positively noble, if you gave it any thought, Candace silently congratulated herself as she gracefully slid out of the backseat of the limousine and onto the red carpet that was unfurled before The Janus. This opulent casino, where tonight's charity gala was being held, was Luke Montgomery's most extravagant enterprise to date. Never mind that Luke and her father were rivals the way only the nouveau riche could be in Las Vegas, where the stakes that ran highest were not always found on a blackjack table.

The gala Luke was hosting centered around an international jewelry convention. On display was a breathtaking collection of gems that had been donated by various members of the rich and famous, all in the name of charity. The price of admission was high but only in terms of what the average person could afford.

The sum meant nothing to Candace. Money had never been a problem for her. Sustaining her high had been—because she needed to stay in the spotlight in order to survive. Without it, the insecurities that lingered in the background began to encroach, darkening her world and threatening to sink her into a nether region fraught with madness.

So she did what she could to ensure that she would never descend to those levels. She surrounded herself with glamorous people and basked in the glow of the limelight the way no one else could.

Charity or not, Candace had no gems she was willing to part with. She never met an expensive bauble she didn't immediately love. And tonight, she was sporting the best of the best, a legendary diamond that, according to a rumor she'd heard, had been in her family for several decades. The Tears of the Quetzal. Only gems of quality had names, she thought with a smug grin.

Her father, Harold Rothchild, thought the ring was safely under lock and key. But then, he had no idea how determined she could be. Or how clever. Like everyone else, he had underestimated her. His problem, she thought carelessly.

Besides, what good was jewelry if you couldn't wear it? Couldn't flaunt it and make others look at it enviously? None, that's what. Jewelry had to be seen to be appreciated.

And its owner envied.

Candace looked down now at the ring on her hand. The incredible multifaceted diamond captured all the light in the immediate vicinity and flashed it back onto her in bursts of green and purple. It was as if she had a star on her ring finger. Rumor had it that there was a curse attached to it.

All nonsense, she was certain. The so-called curse was started by her father, or maybe Grandpa Joe before him to keep people from making off with the gem. But she wasn't ignorant like the rest of her pathetic family.

She had no concerns about a curse, only about the attention wearing the priceless gem could garner her. She stood for a moment as the limousine pulled away, letting those in the immediate vicinity drink in the sight of her. She gave the appearance of being taller than she was, helped, in part, by stiletto heels. The long, clinging scarlet gown she wore would have been eye-catching under any circumstances. On her it was doubly so, and she knew it. Cascading platinum hair completed the picture. She was a knockout.

She was alone tonight. Deliberately so. She wanted to be unencumbered as she scanned the sea of men this gala had lured. She wanted to be free to scan them and to bring the one that pleased her most back to her condo. Her sons had been packed off with the nanny for an overnight visit with the nanny's sister and nephews—which left the terrain open for her. There would be no disapproving nanny, no annoying children popping up at inopportune times to ask even more annoying questions.

She was in the mood for something new tonight. Something different. Exotic, perhaps.

Exotic, yes.

A smile slipped over her lips as she slowly made her way along the carpet, her pace timed to the flashes that were going off, marking her passage. Photographers called out her name and vied for better positions in order to snare the "perfect" photograph.

In a pinch, Candace mused, she might not mind reverting back to the tried and true. Like Luke Montgomery. In his time, he'd been very hot in bed. Hot enough to leave an impression on her in his wake, even now. Not an easy feat considering the number of lovers she'd had over the years. Her collection had begun at the precocious age of fourteen when she'd surrendered her virginity, already rather compromised, to the family chauffeur. Paolo, as she recalled, had been poor, but beautiful.

And very, very skilled in the ways of lovemaking.

She wondered where Paolo was these days. Her father had gotten rid of the driver the moment he'd found out about the affair. Harold Rothchild had indignantly threatened the man with prison, but even she'd known that the threat was empty. Ever conscious of their reputation, her father wanted nothing more than to avoid any sort of public scandal that reflected poorly on the family.

She'd given him quite a run for his money, she thought, turning her face up so that the lighting caught her just so.

"Poor Dad, you should have raised prize-winning roses, not daughters," she mused under her breath.

Recognizing them, she paused to pose for several national magazine photographers. One hand on her hip, the other—the one with the ring—delicately placed just beneath her collarbone and above the deeply plunging neckline that left only the tiniest speck to the imagination. Of the two of them, she wondered which was more of a disappointment to her father, she with her penchant of attracting every photographer within a fifty-mile radius, or Natalie, who worked as a police detective, for God sakes. How mundane and common can you get?

"This way, Candace. Look this way!" a deep male voice called out urgently.

The voice, she noted, sounded vaguely familiar to her, although she doubted she could place it as she turned in the direction it had come from.

And then she smiled more brilliantly. She was right. She *had* recognized the voice. Recognized the man as well, although she couldn't remember his name.

Something beginning with a *P*, she thought, although she couldn't be sure. Or maybe it began with a *B*. But then, it didn't matter if she remembered them, only that they remembered her, and by the look on this one's face, he most certainly did remember her.

They'd slept together, hadn't they? she thought. He looked like her type. Tall, muscular, with an olive complexion, thick black hair and high cheekbones that gave him almost an aristocratic look. She might have mistaken him for one of the invited guests—if not for the camera he was clutching.

But he was exotic looking and she really was in the mood for someone exotic.

"What have you got for us, Candace?" he called out, elbowing his way forward ahead of the gaggle of photographers. Grumbling and curses marked his forward progress.

"A lot of sugar," she answered in a breathless voice that made her sound as if she were channeling the spirit of the late Marilyn Monroe at her zenith. "And, of course, this."

"This" was the ring that she now held up like a courtesan in the court of King Henry VIII waiting to have her hand kissed. A satisfied smirk graced her lips again. A flurry of cameras went off, capturing the image and the moment.

But her attention was only focused on the photographer with the aura of danger about him. Winking, she bent forward, giving him, she knew, ample view of her endowment.

"Didn't we...?" Candace deliberately let her voice trail off even as her eyes held him prisoner in their blue gaze.

His smile, she caught herself thinking, was incredibly sexy as he answered in a low voice, "Yes, we did. I'm flattered that you remembered."

It was the perfect thing to say to her and he knew it, even as he maintained his innocent expression.

Candace did her best to recall the details of their coupling—and failed. "I'm afraid your name..." She shrugged playfully, a laugh escaping her carefully made up lips. "I was never good with names."

"Patrick," he supplied politely, snapping another photograph. She preened. "My name's Patrick Moore."

"I *knew* it was something that started with the letter *P*," she declared triumphantly.

It took effort for the photographer to keep his true feelings from showing on his face. It took even more effort to keep from telling this two-bit slut what he thought of her and her whole degenerate family. But then, that would have been counterproductive to his plan. He hoped that by supplying her with the name he was going by these days, it would keep her from thinking too much. From remembering.

But then, he comforted himself, her brain usually oscillated between being fried or being pickled. Neither state was conducive to remembering pertinent details, like the ones that would blow his cover.

"Is the ring yours now?" someone else, obviously at least mildly familiar with the ring's chain of ownership, called out to Candace.

She didn't bother trying to hide the condescending glance she sent toward the photographer. Her laughter echoed with victory.

"It's always been mine," she announced.

Out of the corner of her eye she caught a glimpse of Luke just within the entrance. Six foot two, lean and muscular, with dark hair she remembered running her fingers through, he looked incredible. A touch of nostalgia surfaced. He always did look good in a tux.

Looked damn good out of one, too, she thought with a lascivious smile.

"If you gentlemen'll excuse me," she murmured to the reporters. And then, because she hated the prospect of facing the night in an empty bed, she glanced back at the exotic reporter. It never hurt to have an ace in the hole. "Maybe we can get together later. I'll fill you in on what I've been doing lately. For your tabloid," she added with a wink as she patted his face, her ring sparkling and throwing off beams of light with every movement.

"I'd like that," he told her.

She expected nothing less. "Yes, I'm sure you would. I'm staying at—"

"I know where you're staying," Patrick Moore cut her short.

She smiled, inclining her head. "Clever boy," she murmured.

With that, she sashayed off to the casino, every step a calculated movement guaranteed to make men's mouths water.

Once inside, Candace began to move just a tad faster. If she'd retained her present pace, the object of her pursuit, Luke Montgomery, would have put too much distance between them. She very much wanted to hook up with the gala host. Men of power were like an aphrodisiac for her, and Luke Montgomery, despite his humble beginnings, was now regarded as one of Vegas's movers and shakers. Nothing she liked more than being on the winning team.

She had, she liked to think, a lot to bring to the table.

"Luke," she called out to him. When he didn't appear to hear her, Candace raised her voice, temporarily abandoning Marilyn Monroe's sexy, throaty whisper for pragmatic reasons. There was still no response.

The third time she called out his name, Luke stopped walking. He could feel his shoulders tensing. He'd heard her the first time and had hoped that she would just give up.

He should have known better.

Damn that shrew anyway. He wanted the focus of this gala to be on him, his newest casino and the charity he was sponsoring, in that order. Nowhere in that hierarchy did he want to include a vapid, superficial bleach-blonde.

But if he didn't acknowledge her, he knew she was going to cause a scene, and that was the last thing he wanted tonight.

So Luke turned around, a perfunctory smile of civility on his lips worn for the benefit of anyone who might be passing by.

"Hello, Candace," he said as soon as he crossed back to her. Towering over the woman, he all but quietly growled, "I don't seem to remember sending you an invitation."

A careless laugh met his statement. "I'm sure it was just an oversight." Candace possessively threaded her arms through his. Being so close to Luke vividly reminded her of the last time they'd been together. Though she'd never said anything, she'd considered settling down with him. At least for a while. A lady-killer who lived up to his reputation, he was a magnificent lover who always left her wanting more.

Because she sensed that this gala meant a lot to him, she tried to get on his good side by saying, "This certainly has the looks of being quite a successful event."

He certainly hoped so. Luke had undertaken hosting this event and pulling together all the beautiful people from the four corners of the world not just to benefit the charity he was sponsoring but also because hosting such an event, where all the rich and famous showed up in droves, would garner him an enormous amount of goodwill. Good publicity was crucial since he was on the verge of building yet another casino and hotel—this one on the exact spot where the tenement building he'd lived in as a child had stood.

The Phoenix, as the new establishment would be

called, was very near and dear to him, and he wanted nothing to hamper its success. Someone like Candace Rothchild and the kind of attention she attracted could do a lot of harm to all his good intentions.

He wanted her out of here, and he had no time to be polite about it. Moving over to a more private corner of the casino, he asked in a controlled, low voice, "What is it you want, Candace?"

Her eyes raked over his body, blatantly undressing him as she looked up into his eyes. "Why, darling, that should be very evident to someone as smart as you." Tightening her hold on his arm, Candace raised her face up to his. Her mouth was barely inches away from his lips. "You."

Gone were the days when he would have been flattered. He knew her for what she was. A woman with no soul on her way out, living in a town that didn't care. She was swiftly becoming a punch line to a good many insulting jokes.

"Not now, Candace."

A pout appeared on her moist lips. "Then when?" she wanted to know.

What had he ever seen in her? he couldn't help wondering. Granted, there'd been a time when he would have gladly taken her up on her offer, but he'd been younger then and far more impressionable. He'd like to think he was too smart now to be tempted to lie down with a black widow.

He shook his arm free and then grasped hers. He began directing her toward the front entrance. "Some other time, Candace," he said forcefully.

Instantly, her face clouded over. "I don't like being

rejected, Luke. Your little party won't go so well if I make a scene. That's what they'll remember, *me,*" she emphasized, "not you or this little jewelry store display of yours."

It was a threat with teeth, and they both knew it.

He didn't react well to threats. "I think you'll be happier elsewhere, Candace," Luke told her coldly. He snapped his fingers over her head at someone across the floor.

She didn't bother looking to see who Luke was summoning. She wasn't interested.

"And I think I'll be happier here," she insisted. Accustomed to getting her way, it infuriated her to be contradicted.

The next moment, they were joined by a third party. Matt Schaffer, the head of security for Montgomery Enterprises, was at her elbow. But rather than look at her, his attention was completely focused on his employer. Matt waited silently for instructions.

Candace always perked up when in the company of a good-looking man, and this time was no exception as recognition entered her eyes.

"Why, hello handsome," she purred.

Candace had already had too much to drink, Matt realized. He could smell it on her. But he was careful not to allow his disdain to register on his face. Instead, he raised his eyes to Luke's face.

"Mr. Montgomery?"

"Schaffer, please escort Ms. Rothchild out of the casino," Luke requested, his voice flat and devoid of emotion. "She was just leaving."

Candace became incensed. "No, I wasn't," she insisted heatedly. She gave every impression that she was about to dig in her heels, and if Matt intended to remove her, it was going to have to be by force.

But rather than take hold of her arm and drag her from the premises, cursing and screaming, Matt leaned over and whispered into her ear. "There are a bunch of photographers outside asking about you," he told the Rothchild heiress smoothly. "You wouldn't want to disappoint your public, would you?"

Her blue eyes flashed, reminding him of another pair of blue eyes. Matt banked down the memory and the feelings it threatened to usher in with it. He'd made his choice, and he had to live with it...*had* been living with it these last eight years.

"*I* don't want to be disappointed," Candace told him haughtily.

There was another, more logical approach to this. "You'll save face if you make it look as if leaving is your idea. Ms. Rothchild," Matt told her quietly. "But make no mistake, one way or another, you *are* leaving the casino."

Candace exhaled angrily, then, right before his eyes, she managed to get herself under control. There was a squadron of cameras waiting to capture her beautiful likeness, she thought, and she knew that when she frowned, she looked closer to her own age. Thirty was a horrible number.

As she moved toward the door, Candace thought she could see that reporter—the sexy one—looking in her direction. Patrick Moore.

Something told her that the evening was not going to be a total waste after all.

She flashed a radiant smile. "I'll have your head," she

promised Matt through lips that looked as if they were barely moving.

They were almost at the entrance, but Matt knew better than to release her. If he did, she might just double back, and he needed her on the other side of the door.

"From what I hear," he told her conversationally, "that's not the part that interests you when it comes to men."

They made brief eye contact. Just like that, her fury was gone. The smile on Candace's lips was genuine. "I know you, but I can't seem to remember your name."

He saw no point in refusing to answer. From what he knew, she and Natalie hadn't spoken in a long, long time. She wouldn't tell Natalie about this. "Matt Schaffer."

Candace nodded her head, as if absorbing the name. "Right. Of course you are."

Matt pushed the door open for her. He watched the woman saunter away and swiftly become engulfed by the crowd hanging around the casino entrance. She was in her element.

As he walked back into the casino, Matt could only shake his head. The woman he'd just escorted out was light years away from Natalie. Hard to believe they were actually sisters, much less twins.

The next moment, he forced himself to think of something else. Thinking about Natalie would do him no good. That part of his life was over.

By choice.

Chapter 2

She had to be out of her mind, Anna Worth Rothchild thought.

It was past eleven o'clock, and by all rights, she should have been in bed. The all-night parties that Vegas was so famous for no longer interested her. They never really had, but she'd pretended they did for his sake. Now, instead of curling up in her queen-sized bed, sleeping peacefully, here she was pulling up into her old driveway. Summoned by the distraught note in her ex-husband's voice when he'd called her less than an hour ago.

She was an idiot for doing this.

What she should have said to him, Anna silently lectured herself as she got out of her ice-blue sports car, was "Tell it to your little bimbo, Rebecca Lynn. Whatever's wrong in your life isn't my problem anymore."

But that was just it—it *was* still her problem. Her

problem because she chose it to be. And that, sadly, was because reasonable, independent woman that she was, she nevertheless still loved the man. Loved him despite the fact that he had, as the old jazz songs went, "done her wrong."

There was a term for women like her, Anna mused, and if she had half a brain, she'd turn around, get back into her car and drive back home. There was no reason for her to be here.

Yes, between the two of them, they had four daughters in common. Anna's natural child, Silver, was her ex-husband's daughter whom Harold later adopted. Silver grew up in the vicinity of three stepsisters from Harold's first marriage—twins Natalie and Candace and their younger sister Jenna. Raising these girls together would forever bind Anna and Harold to one another. But he had made it perfectly clear he wanted to spend the rest of his life with that gold-digging slut who was only four years older than his twin daughters. He deserved everything that happened to him for being such a fool. For throwing away their marriage after all the years she'd stood by his side, taking care of every detail, leaving him free to handle his businesses and his hotels.

So why was she here? Why did she even *care* if Harold was distraught?

Because she did, Anna thought with a sigh, wrapping her ermine stole tighter around her shoulders against the April evening chill. It was as simple as that. She just did.

About to ring the doorbell, she was caught off guard when the door suddenly swung open and Clive, Harold's butler for the past twenty-five years, firmly ushered out a tall, dark-haired man with an olive complexion. The well-built, exotic-looking man was far from happy to be leaving the premises. Although he was wearing formal attire, it appeared somewhat rumpled.

The intruder nearly knocked her down as he was being hustled out of the mansion. The unexpected close contact allowed Anna to catch the faintest whiff of a sweet scent. It was vaguely familiar and nudged something distant in her consciousness, but she couldn't place it.

The next moment, the memory was gone. The thought that the scent was something a woman might wear whispered through her mind as she regained her balance. The latter was accomplished largely due to Clive's swift action. Seeing her predicament, he quickly caught the former mistress of the mansion by the arm and kept her from falling.

"Sorry, ma'am, didn't mean to be forward," he apologized, withdrawing his hands the moment she regained her footing.

Anna smiled. After all these years with the family, Clive was still incredibly formal. She sincerely doubted that they made people, much less butlers, like him anymore.

"Apology more than accepted, Clive. If you hadn't caught me, that oaf would have mowed me down." She glanced over her shoulder and saw the stranger was retreating through the gate. She decided the man had to belong to the car that was parked down the street. "What was that all about?"

"I'm sure I don't know, ma'am. He's one of those ruthless reporters, I believe." Anna was certain that Clive knew far more than he was saying. Nothing happened in this house or to this family that the gray-haired man was not aware of. "So nice to see you again, ma'am," he said warmly, deftly changing the topic. "Mr. Harold is expecting you. He's in the den."

The butler dutifully escorted her to the room. Along the way she noted some changes. There were expensive, somewhat showy, paintings gracing the walls. Rebecca Lynn's handiwork, no doubt, she mused. If there was a spare dime lying around, the woman would find something to spend it on.

Opening the den's double doors for her, Clive unobtrusively backed away and withdrew, moving as silently as a shadow.

Harold, his back to her, was alone in the room. When he turned around, she was struck by how drawn he looked. His hand was wrapped tightly around a chunky scotch glass. The glass was almost empty.

Her first thought was that something had happened with the eye candy he referred to as his third wife. Had she been a lesser woman, she might have secretly gloated at the thought. But Anna was made of better stuff than that, and she found her heart aching for him, aching despite the fact that he had been less than kind during the final days of their marriage.

"All right, Harold, I'm here," she declared, crossing to him. Removing her wrap, she carefully draped it over the back of the cream-colored leather sofa. "What's the big emergency that couldn't wait until morning?"

On his best day, Harold Rothchild was never one of those men who exuded power. What power he had he inherited from a father who had been almighty, leaving no room for a son to emerge and become his own man, even if he was handsome enough to turn a few heads. All his life, Harold had searched for a way to do that, to become his own man. Years after Joseph Rothchild's death, Harold was still searching.

Draining his glass, he placed it on the desk and cleared his throat before finally giving her an answer. He felt a tightness in his chest. "It's gone."

He wasn't making any sense, and there was panic evident in his blue eyes. Anna put her hand on her ex-husband's, as if to silently reassure him that she was there for him. "What's gone, Harold?"

"The ring." His voice seemed to crackle with the stress he was experiencing. "My father's ring. The Tears of the Quetzal. Candace kept asking me questions about it. When she asked to see it, I said no. I thought she'd get angry, but she just said, 'All right.' After she left, I had this feeling that something was wrong," he confessed, almost talking to himself. "So I went to the safe to look at it—and it was gone," he wailed. "And now something bad is going to happen. I can feel it. Something awful."

Anna didn't follow him, but then, Harold had always been secretive when it came to the ring and its origins. All she had ever gotten out of him was that, in the right hands, it brought true love to its owner within sixty seconds. In the wrong hands, dire things came to pass. Personally, she'd always thought it was all just empty talk, something to glorify the ring, nothing more. She'd only seen it once herself, and it was far too gaudy for her taste.

"Worse than the ring disappearing?" she asked.

Harold seemed to go pale right in front of her eyes. A line of sweat formed on his forehead. He sounded almost breathless when he said, "Much worse."

Natalie Rothchild felt sick to her stomach. It took all she had to keep the light breakfast down that she'd consumed this morning.

After working her way up within the Las Vegas Police Department to the rank of detective in a relatively short amount of time, there weren't many things that still got to her. She'd learned to harden herself, to separate herself from her work. She kept a firm, if imaginary, line drawn in the sand for herself. Her professional life was not allowed to cross over into her personal life—what little there was of it.

Natalie was well aware that if she began to take her work home with her, she would burn out within six months—the way Sid Northrop, one of the homicide detectives on the force when she'd first joined it, had.

But this was different. This *was* personal. And she hadn't been summoned to the scene because it was personal. She'd come because she'd overheard the dispatch put the call out on the police scanner. According to the information, a hysterical nanny had come home with her two charges only to find the children's mother dead on the living room floor. Natalie was about to ignore it because two other detectives were being called in to handle the homicide and God knew she had enough on her plate already without being Johnny-on-the-spot for yet another murder.

But the address that the dispatch rattled off stopped her cold. The address belonged to Candace.

A wave of fear mingled with disbelief washed over her. Her hands felt icy as she held onto the steering wheel. Even though she and her sister lived in two different worlds and didn't interact, she still felt an obligation to keep tabs on Candace. Her twin sister had cotton candy for brains, not to mention that Candace's self-esteem was like a giant champagne bucket with a hole in the bottom. She seemed in desperate need of adulation and found it living her life on the wild side.

If anyone needed a keeper, it was Candace. And even though they no longer had anything in common but blood, Natalie secretly had appointed herself her sister's protector, keeping Candace out of harm's way whenever she possibly could.

Damn, but she'd really dropped the ball this time, Natalie upbraided herself grimly.

In Candace's condo now, she fought back anguished tears as she looked down at her sister's battered face and body. The room looked like a battlefield, and Candace was lying on the floor next to the marble coffee table, her limbs spread out in a grotesque, awkward fashion like a cartoon character that hadn't been drawn correctly. The scarlet dress that Candace had undoubtedly paid a fortune for accented the pool of blood that encircled her head lying on the ivory rug.

"You shouldn't be here," a gruff voice behind her admonished.

She blinked twice, banishing her tears before she glanced over her shoulder at Adam Parker, one of the two detectives who had been called in.

"Yeah, well, neither should she," Natalie bit off angrily.

Reaching out, she adjusted the right side of the front of Candace's dress to cover her exposed breast.

"Hey, you know better than to touch anything," Miles Davidson, the other detective, pointed out, crossing over to her.

Yes, she knew better. But this was her sister, and at least in death, Candace needed a little respect.

"I just wanted to cover her," Natalie answered quietly, rising to her feet. It didn't matter that, at one time or another, half of Vegas had probably seen Candace naked; she didn't want this being the final impression those processing the scene came away with. Taking a cleansing breath, Natalie looked over toward Parker, the older and far more heavyset of the two detectives. "What have you got?"

His frustrated expression answered before he did. "You got here fifteen minutes after we did. Nothing so far," he replied somberly. "The ME can answer a few basic questions for us once he gets her on the table." Natalie continued to look at him expectantly. The ME had been on the scene when she arrived. Parker exhaled sharply. "Right now, it looks like time of death was around eight, maybe nine o'clock last night. We looked around and robbery doesn't seem to have been a motive. Nothing's been taken." He pointed toward Candace's throat. "She's still wearing a diamond necklace." A weary sigh escaped his lips. "Judging by her bruises and the state of this room, I'd say this was personal."

Squatting down again, Natalie looked at her twin's right hand. Last night, while heating up a frozen dinner, she'd kept the TV on for background noise. A program devoted to fawning over celebrities had been on, and they had gushed over live film clips from the gala in progress at The Janus.

She hadn't been surprised to see Candace on camera. Candace had a penchant for showing up anywhere that a camera was rolling. What had surprised her was that her twin was flashing the Tears of the Quetzal, holding it up for the camera to capture. Natalie knew for a fact that her father kept the ring under lock and key, refusing even to allow any of them to see it, much less flaunt it in public.

How had Candace managed to get it away from their father?

And who had taken it off Candace's finger?

"The ring's gone," she told Parker quietly.

"Ring? What ring?" Davidson blinked, suddenly looking more alert.

Parker didn't need to ask. Natalie knew he was already aware of what she was referring to. "You mean that big golf ball-sized rock that your dad's got hidden away in some faraway safe?" When his partner looked at him in surprise, Parker shrugged the wide shoulders beneath his worn all-weather coat. "What? I read *People* magazine. Sue me."

"That's the one," Natalie replied with a sigh, standing up again. Her grandfather, Joseph, had owned the diamond mine from which the multifaceted, near priceless gem had emerged, or so she had heard from her stepmother. Her father's fortune was partially built on it.

Did he kill you for it, Candace? Did whoever did this to you try to take the ring only to have you fight him off? You should have let him have it. It was a stupid rock...it wasn't worth your life.

A thought suddenly hit her, and she looked up at the two detectives. "Anyone notify my father yet?"

Parker and Davidson exchanged looks. She had her answer. Notification of a loved one's death was never high on anyone's to-do list.

"Not yet," Parker answered grimly.

Natalie nodded, already resigned to her part in this. "I'll do it. Let me know what the ME comes up with as soon as there's a report."

Parker frowned, but his tone was kind as he tried to make her understand his position. "Natalie, we can't have you—"

She stopped him before he could finish voicing his protest. "Unofficially," she emphasized. "Notify me unofficially." There was no room for argument in her voice. She looked around. "Where are the kids?"

"Kids?" Davis echoed.

"Kids," she repeated. "Candace's kids. Mick and David. My sister has—had—two children. Dispatch said the nanny found her and called this in. Where are they?"

"Take it easy. She took them back to her sister's house. Don't worry, Sanchez went with her," Parker said, mentioning another detective. "Um, correct me if I'm wrong, but from what I heard, your sister really didn't keep close tabs on her kids."

"No, she didn't." She needed to get in touch with the nanny, Natalie thought as she left.

She had the woman's name and number programmed into her cell phone. She'd already checked out Amelia Pintero's background to satisfy herself that her young nephews were in good hands—and not because Candace had asked her to. Candace, as she recalled, was just glad to have someone else take care of them for her. She would have used Gypsies if they'd crossed her path before Amelia had.

Natalie knew that it was a given that she wouldn't be allowed to investigate her sister's murder, but there was no law that said she couldn't look into it on her own when she was off duty. And even if there was, there was no way she was about to abide by the restriction. She and Candace hadn't gotten along in a long time, but blood was blood and after all was said and done, Candace was still her sister. More, she'd been her twin. A part of her was dead.

She deserved some answers—and the killer deserved to be put away for the rest of his life. It was as simple as that. And she planned to kick off her investigation by going to The Janus, the casino where Candace was last seen. She was going to have to find a way to get a look at the security tapes, to see if someone had followed her sister when she left the casino—or if, and this scenario was far more likely, Candace had elected to leave the casino with someone new.

In her heart, Natalie had always known that men would be her sister's downfall.

And that makes you different how? a mocking tone in her head queried. For her, it hadn't taken a squadron of men; all it had taken was one. One man who had sworn his love for her, given her an engagement ring and then pulled a disappearing act.

It had made her back away from the entire species.

Damn, she hadn't thought about Matt in, what? A couple of months or so.

Now was not the time for a stroll down memory lane, Natalie chided herself as she pulled up in her father's winding driveway.

Natalie took a deep breath, bracing herself for the ordeal ahead. It didn't really help.

With effort, she got out of her car.

The walk from the driveway to the front door felt exceptionally drawn out and almost painful, a little like a prisoner walking the last mile before his execution, she mused.

Clive answered the door. He smiled at her, looking both formal and kind at the same time. It was a feat she never quite understood how he accomplished. A pleased light entered his hazel eyes. "Miss Natalie, what a pleasant surprise."

She knew he meant it. For a second, she allowed herself to absorb his words, and then she set her mouth solemnly. "Not so pleasant I'm afraid, Clive. Is my father home?"

To his credit, Clive displayed no curiosity, asked no questions. "Yes he is, Miss, but I fear that he doesn't seem to be himself today."

Natalie looked at the butler in surprise. Had her father heard about Candace? But how? The police were keeping everything under wraps for now. Their main logic behind this was to stave off the media vultures for as long as possible. They could feed on this kind of fodder for six, nine months at a time. And they would. But right now, they weren't supposed to know.

Had there been a leak?

"Why?" she pressed. "What's wrong, Clive?"

She knew that the man was very closemouthed, but

she also knew that while she'd lived in this cold mausoleum of a house, she had been his favorite. So she looked up at the tall man and waited for a response.

It came. "It's the Tears of the Quetzal, Miss. I'm afraid that someone seems to have made off with it."

An image of Candace, flaunting the ring in front of the cameraman, flashed through her mind. It was immediately followed by the sight of her lifeless body lying on the rug, her hand denuded of the legendary ring.

"You can say that again," she murmured under her breath. "Where is he?"

"He's on the terrace, Miss. He's been there for most of the night. I tried to get him to come in, but…" His voice trailed off.

"You're a good man, Clive. But some people won't allow themselves to be helped." She was talking about Candace—not her father—but for now, it was applicable to him as well.

Turning, Natalie made her way to the back of the house, no small feat. As far as houses went, she'd always felt that this one could have provided shelter to a small third world country. Neither she nor her stepmother, Anna, had cared for its enormity, but Candace had loved it and her father's current wife, Rebecca Lynn, the world's only living brain donor, had actually been lobbying for something even bigger and more ostentatious.

Maybe the Taj Mahal was up for sale, Natalie thought sarcastically. She could remember thinking when they first moved to this house that she needed to drop bread crumbs to mark her way or be forever doomed to wandering the halls, looking for the way out.

She'd found the way out years ago.

Finally reaching the back of the building, she walked out onto the terrace. She was immediately struck by her father's profile as he sat at the table. He was still a handsome man, Natalie caught herself thinking. But right now, he looked gaunt and incredibly weary, as if he had the weight of the world on his shoulders.

That was Rebecca Lynn's fault, no doubt. He was trying to keep up with a woman half his age who was determined to "do it all." Either that, or become a young widow. God knew she wouldn't put it past Rebecca Lynn.

She didn't say anything until she was almost at his elbow. "Hi, Dad."

She'd startled him. He sucked in his breath, his body tense and rigid. "Natalie, what are you doing here?"

There was no point in beating around the bush. It only prolonged the inevitable, and that wasn't her style. "I have some terrible news, Dad." Natalie sat down at the table and placed her hand over his. Her father wasn't the touchy-feely type, but this time, she thought some contact might actually help. "Candace is dead."

He visibly paled but didn't look nearly as surprised as she thought he would. She supposed that, given Candace's lifestyle, all of them had been expecting this day now for a long time. "When?"

"Last night."

He slowly nodded his head, as if that helped him take in the information. "Where?"

"They found her body at her condo. The nanny came home with the kids after a sleepover and discovered her. She called the police." She enunciated the words slowly, refusing to allow her voice to break, her emotions to leak through. Her feelings were private, even from her father. "Candace was murdered."

It took Harold a moment to process the information she'd given him, and then he looked up at her, his expression devoid of emotion. "Did she have the ring on her?"

"Ring?" Natalie repeated, stunned. She remembered what Clive had said about her father's distress because the ring was missing. Candace was dead. Didn't that trump a missing ring? Didn't he care? "Is that what you're concerned about?" she cried, struggling to keep her temper under control. "The damn ring?"

He grew more upset in the face of her reaction. "Natalie, please understand, of course I'm devastated about Candace, but that ring...that ring can mean the difference between our family's financial collapse and success."

How could he even think about money at a time like this? "What are you talking about?"

Harold nervously ran his tongue along his dry lips. "I made some shaky investments," he confessed. "I'm spread rather thin right now, and I had to borrow some money from—" He paused for a moment before finally blurting out a name. "The Schaffer family."

He'd been desperate at the time; there was no other explanation for his doing what he'd done. He didn't have his father's flair for making money, so he'd turned to a family known to have underworld connections. Men who broke legs as easily as matchsticks and with less thought. He wouldn't put it past Matt Schaffer to try to ruin him.

His eyes grew bright. "Matt Schaffer's the one who has the ring. I'd bet my life on it," he concluded heatedly.

She hadn't thought she'd ever hear that name again.

"Matt Schaffer's in California," she heard herself saying hoarsely.

And then her father blew her world apart by saying, "No, he's not. He's right here in Vegas. Working for Luke Montgomery. Or at least that's the story he gives out."

Matt Schaffer.

Here. In Vegas.

Natalie suddenly felt as if the ground beneath her feet had turned to quicksand.

Chapter 3

Harold continued to talk, but Natalie could no longer make out the words.

Her father's voice became a buzzing sound in the background as she grappled with the information he'd just carelessly flung out at her. Coming on the heels of Candace's murder, learning that Matt Schaffer was now living back in Vegas was almost too much for her to process. Or bear.

But she had to, Natalie told herself fiercely. What choice did she have? There was no one around to run interference for her, no one to try to smooth out the choppy waters so she could navigate them without going under and drowning.

All that was on her shoulders. But then, she'd more or less been on her own for the last eight years.

Natalie raised her chin proudly. Okay, she'd deal

with Matt being here in Vegas. Deal with having to see him.

But despite the way things had ended between them, she knew Matt Schaffer would never kill anyone. If he had the ring in his possession, then he'd gotten a hold of it while Candace was still alive. She'd make book on it.

You also thought he'd never leave you, remember? Called that one wrong, didn't you? her annoying little voice taunted.

Still, just because the man didn't have the guts to commit and lacked the backbone to tell her so face-to-face didn't mean he would kill someone over a ring no matter how valuable it was. He wasn't a killer or a thief, if she discounted his stealing her heart.

"Matt wouldn't kill Candace," she told her father firmly.

Her father looked like a cornered man desperately fighting to survive. He vacillated, not sure of anything anymore.

"Maybe not, but someone in his family would." Everyone knew that the Schaffers had underworld ties, connections to people who did things that could not bear scrutiny. He grasped her hand as if that would make her understand better. "I *owe* them, Natalie. I owe them." Harold struggled to keep his voice from cracking. "The Schaffers know people. And those people," he insisted, "have killed for pocket change."

She glared at him. "Then *why* would you have knowingly gotten mixed up with them?" she demanded.

It made no sense to her. There were lending institutions. Yes, money was hard to come by, but Harold Rothchild was a reputable businessman with a great deal of collateral. Going to a loan shark, if that was indeed what he'd done, was like agreeing to play Russian roulette with not one but half the chambers loaded with bullets.

"Because…" He began to explain, then stopped abruptly. "Oh, it doesn't matter why. I did, and now Candace is dead and the ring's gone."

Her father seemed to have forgotten one very important element in this horrible tale. So typical of him, she thought.

"Your nephews are fine, thanks for asking," she told him sarcastically. She'd checked on the boys on her way over here. She'd stopped by the nanny's sister's home and asked Amelia to tell her in her own words what she'd seen. She had to wait until the young woman stopped throwing up. The details were sketchy, the nanny's reaction honest. She'd asked the young woman to watch the boys until she got back to her.

"The boys." Harold stared at her for a moment, a lost look in his eyes. And then he seemed to come to. "Where are they?"

"I left them with their nanny." She rattled off the address. It was far off the beaten path of both the casinos and the better residential areas, but it was still a decent-enough neighborhood, thanks to a renovation effort on the part of the city.

"I'll send a car for them," Harold said, thinking out loud.

"Good idea."

She didn't mean that to sound as caustic as it did. But she was on edge. The toughest part of her day was still ahead of her. She was going to have to go and interface with the one man she didn't want to ever see again.

Some days it just didn't pay to get up out of bed, Natalie thought wearily.

About to say goodbye, something in her father's expression stopped her. She knew it would drive her crazy for the rest of the day if she didn't ask. "Is there something else?" she wanted to know. "You look like you want to tell me something."

"No." Denial was always his first choice, but then Harold thought better of it just as his daughter began to leave. "There was a note."

Natalie turned around. What was he talking about? And why hadn't he said anything when she'd first come in? "A note?"

He nodded his head. "I didn't understand what it meant until you told me that Candace was dead." He sounded breathless as he said, "We're all in danger. The curse is real."

Natalie looked at her father as if he'd lost his mind. It took considerable effort to remain patient. "You're talking in riddles, Dad. Start at the beginning. *What* note?"

Rather than continue trying to explain, Harold took a folded piece of paper out of the pocket of his robe and handed it to her. She noticed that his hand shook a little.

"This was in the mailbox this morning. Clive found it when he went to put in the outgoing mail."

Using her handkerchief, Natalie took the note from him and carefully unfolded it. She didn't want to get any more fingerprints on it than there already were.

There was a single line typed in the middle of the page: *One down, many to go.*

The words had been typed by a laser printer, and she was willing to bet a year's salary that once the LVPD lab tech finished analyzing it, he would find nothing remarkable about the paper or the printer that had been used.

"We're all in danger, Natalie," her father repeated insistently.

She folded the note. Leaving it within the folds of her handkerchief, she placed it in her purse. She didn't have time to hold her father's hand—she had a murderer to track down.

"Try to think positive for once, Dad," she advised crisply. "I'll get back to you when I have more information," she said by way of parting.

She left him the way she found him, sitting on the terrace, staring off into space.

Though she did her best to talk herself out of it, Natalie could feel the adrenaline rush through her veins as she left the Rothchild grounds and made her way to The Janus.

It was coming in waves, she realized, a little like when she knew there was going to be a showdown. One that might leave her wounded.

There were few things in her life that Natalie had believed to be a certainty, but one of them was that she'd thought she would never see Matt Schaffer again. Eight years ago he'd vanished out of her life, leaving behind a one-line note tucked under a pillow that had grown cold. All the note had said was: *I'm sorry, but this just isn't going to work.*

That was it. No explanation, no real indication of remorse, no mention of the possibility that whatever it was that was taking him away from her could, in time, be resolved. The note had been as clinical, as removed and compassionless as an eviction notice, which, in effect, it was, she thought as she navigated through the morning traffic. Matt had written the note to evict her from his life.

She'd spent the next two weeks crying, breaking down without warning as she walked down the street, talked on the phone or sat, staring at a meal she couldn't bring herself to eat.

Candace, she remembered with a bittersweet pang, had tried to get her to go clubbing in order to get her to forget about Matt.

She'd turned her twin down, but she *did* get her act together. If Matt didn't think enough of their relationship to try to get in contact with her, to try to make her understand why he'd changed so radically from lover to stranger, then the hell with him. He was dead to her, she resolved. And he'd remained that way.

Until twenty minutes ago.

The adrenaline in her veins kept mounting.

Natalie focused on her driving. Vegas in the daylight wasn't nearly as alluring as it was after dark. Like an aging woman best seen in soft lighting, Vegas's imperfections were all visible in the daylight. Natalie supposed that was why people like her sister didn't like to get up until well past noon. They lived for the night.

Except that Candace could no longer do that.

The thought brought a fresh, sharp ache with it.

"Damn it, Candy, what a waste," Natalie murmured under her breath, calling her sister by the nickname she hadn't used in years. "What an awful, awful waste."

Reaching her destination, she pulled up before The Janus. As she did so, Natalie saw one of the three valets currently on duty make a beeline for her vehicle.

The lanky young man was quick to hide the frown that had begun to curl his lips.

He was undoubtedly used to parking a higher class of vehicle, Natalie thought. Unlike her twin, she was determined not to touch any of the family fortune or the trust fund that her grandfather had set aside for them on the day they were born. Instead, she lived on and spent only what she earned. Perforce, that limited her lifestyle. The salary of an LVPD detective didn't stretch very far, restricting her to the basic necessities of life. Consequently, her automobile was a six-year-old Honda Accord, but it proved to be more reliable than most of the people she knew.

"Welcome to The Janus," the young attendant said cheerfully as he opened the driver's side door for her with a flourish.

"We'll see," she replied solemnly.

As he pulled away with her car, Natalie looked up at the casino's logo. Janus was the Roman god with two faces, one pointed toward the past, the other facing the future. It struck her as rather ironic, given what she was doing here, seeking out someone from her past in order to get answers so that the future could be settled.

The moment she entered the casino, the Vegas phenomena took hold.

It was like stepping into a world where time did not matter or even make an appearance. Though there were cameras everywhere, capturing and time-stamping every movement that was made by the casino's guests, there were no clocks displayed throughout the actual casino, no measurement of time passing in any form. All there was was a sense of "now."

The feeling of immortality was created out of this sort of fabric, Natalie thought.

Because, in her experience, she'd discovered that bartenders knew the inner workings of any establishment they worked for better than anyone else, Natalie made her way to the first bar she came across.

The bartender in attendance was a gregarious man who looked to be in his early forties. He had premature gray hair and a quick, sexy smile, which was probably one of the main reasons he'd been hired. That, and his dexterity when it came to mixing drinks. She noted that he had fast hands.

His name tag identified him as Kevin.

Moving to her end of the bar, Kevin asked, "What'll it be, pretty lady?"

Slipping her hand between the bottom of the glass and the bar, Natalie stopped him from placing it down. "Information." She saw a dubious look cross his brow. To counter that, she took out her badge. Granted she wasn't here in an official capacity, but "Kevin" didn't need to know that. "Were you on duty last night?"

Because there was no one else at the bar seeking his services, Kevin began to wipe the gleaming black surface, massaging it slowly. "You mean during the gala?"

"Yes."

The smile gracing his lips was a satisfied one. Last night had obviously been profitable for him, she figured. "I caught an extra shift."

She took out Candace's photograph and carefully placed it on the bar, turning it around so that he could look at it head-on. "Did you happen to see this woman there?"

The bartender glanced at the picture. Mild interest

turned to recognition. "You mean Candace Rothchild? Yeah, she was here, loud and brassy as always. But not for long," he added, looking rather disappointed. There was always a circus when Candace was around, Natalie thought. People came along for the entertainment. "The boss and she had at it, and then he had Schaffer 'escort' her out."

She latched on to the first part of his statement. "They argued?"

"Yeah."

"About?"

He shook his head. "Couldn't tell you. Too far away for anything but body language," he confessed.

"And Schaffer?" she repeated.

"He got her to leave."

She leaned in over the bar. "Tell me about him."

"Don't know much," the bartender admitted. "Just that his name's Matt Schaffer, and he's Montgomery's head of security for the casino. Boss flew him in from L.A., where he's head of security for Montgomery Enterprises."

There was no avoiding it, she thought darkly. She was going to have to talk to Matt. The thought left her cold. "Do you know where I can find him right now?"

Kevin glanced at his watch. "He should be in his office."

She rarely frequented casinos, and when she did, they weren't ones that belonged to her father's rivals. Luke Montgomery had made no secret that he wanted to be the King of Vegas, a position that her father had once aspired to.

"And his office would be—?" She waited for the bartender to enlighten her.

"On the second floor, toward the rear." He pointed her in the right direction.

Taking out a twenty, she placed it on the bar. "Thanks for your help."

In a practiced, fluid motion, Kevin slipped the bill into his vest pocket. "Any time, lovely lady," he called after her. "Any time."

She debated going up the stairs, then decided on the elevator. The car that took her up to the second floor was empty. Natalie stepped out of the elevator, looked around to get her bearings and then walked toward the rear of the floor.

The office where the monitors and the people who watched them were housed was encased in dark, tinted glass walls. It gave her an opportunity to scan the room and its occupants before she entered.

None of them were Matt. But then, as head of security, he'd probably have his own area, she thought, most likely removed from the others.

Into the Valley of Death rode the six hundred, she silently recited, digging deep for a line from a poem by Tennyson. Wrapping her hand around the brass handle, she opened one of the glass doors and walked in.

The woman whose desk was closest to the door looked up and then began to cross to her. "I'm sorry, but you can't come in here. This is a restricted area."

Natalie already had her ID in her hand and held it up. "I'm looking for Matt Schaffer," she told the woman.

God, even saying his name made her mouth go dry. She was supposed to be over him, had moved on with her life. What happened?

The woman began to answer her. "He's—"

"Right here."

The deep voice came from behind her. Natalie felt every single nerve ending go on tactical alert at the same moment that all the hairs at the back of her neck stood up.

Despite the fact that it had been eight years, she would have recognized his voice anywhere.

"What can I…do for you?" The break in the question came because she turned around in the middle of his inquiry.

Natalie.

For a fraction of a heartbeat, Matt Schaffer stopped breathing. He'd known that, most likely, it would be just a matter of time before their paths crossed. Knew when he had reluctantly agreed to Luke Montgomery's proposition that he transfer to Vegas to oversee security at The Janus because there'd been a problem with the last man who'd been in charge. His only condition had been that the transfer be temporary, lasting only until someone reliable could be found to fill the slot.

If luck had been with him, he might have been able to avoid this.

But deep down in his bones, he'd known all along that this was destined to happen. Maybe even unconsciously he'd actually wished that it would. Now that it had, that same old feeling he'd always had around Natalie slipped over him.

If anything, Natalie had gotten more beautiful, not less. Her straight brown hair was still lustrous, still silky, and her eyes were that incredible shade of blue that could pull him in without warning. Maturity sat well on her, like a rosebud that had bloomed into a breathtaking flower. He felt that old magic, that crackle of chemistry humming between them.

The reasons he had walked away from her all those years ago were still valid, still in play. Leaving hadn't been a mistake. He'd done it for her, but God, he'd missed her all these years. So much so that it almost hurt to look at her. To look at her and realize all that he had missed. All that he would continue to miss, because nothing had changed.

"Natalie." He said her name warmly.

She raised her chin in that way he'd always found both endearing and amusing. More than once he'd wanted to give in to impulse and just nibble on it. He'd refrained, knowing the action would have earned him an indignant right cross because when she raised her chin like that, she wanted to be taken seriously. It was her tell, he thought, a sign that gamblers looked for in other gamblers because it was used to clue them in on what was to come next.

"Hello, Matt." Her voice was formal, devoid of any emotion, her body almost rigid. He could remember how fluid she felt in his arms. It made him ache. "It's been a long time."

And he'd been acutely aware of every moment of that passage of time without her. More than once he had thought about the way things could have been, if he had only been able to go back and change things, be someone different…

But he'd always come to the same conclusion—that it was useless to waste time wishing. Things were the way they were and that was that.

"Yes, it has," he agreed quietly. "What can I do for you?"

She made it cut and dried. All she wanted was to get this over with. "You can answer some questions and give me access to all of last night's surveillance tapes."

Whatever he was expecting, it wasn't this. "I don't understand—"

It was then that Natalie took out her badge again and held it up for him to look at. When they'd last been together, she'd just graduated college. Being a policewoman hadn't even entered her mind. All she wanted to do was spend her days and nights loving Matt. Just showed how naive and stupid the very young could be, she thought cynically.

"Candace Rothchild was here last night," she told him crisply.

"Yes, she was." Was this about his making her sister leave?

"She was also found dead in her condo early this morning. Time of death was sometime last night."

He stared at her, trying to process what she was telling him. "Your sister's dead?" he asked incredulously.

"Yes." The answer came out in a hiss between her teeth. Their paths hardly ever intersected anymore, but it was hard imagining a world without Candace in it. There'd be no more promises to make in fleeting moments of remorse only to break again the very next day. No more publicity-fraught attempts at trying to be a better mother to Mick and David. All that was gone now.

"I'm sorry for your loss, Natalie."

"Thanks." The single word was said without any emotion.

She saw the look of concern that came over his face. He'd become an accomplished actor since she'd last seen him, she thought cynically. One would have even thought he cared—except that she knew better. The only one Matt cared about was himself.

"Let's go to my office," he said in a low voice, turning on his heel to lead the way.

She had no choice but to follow.

Chapter 4

The moment Matt pushed the door open and walked into his spacious glass-enclosed office, the phone on his desk began ringing.

Talk about timing. An exasperated sound escaped his lips, and he looked over his shoulder at Natalie. "Do you mind if I get that?"

She gestured toward the multilined console on his desk. "Go ahead."

His being on the phone would give her a few more seconds to pull herself together, she thought. She hadn't realized seeing him again would affect her like this, shaking her to the core. If anything, his physique seemed more buff, harder, somehow. And looking into his blue eyes had her reliving bits and pieces of the past that made her feel so vulnerable. So much for being over him.

"Schaffer," Matt said as he put the receiver to his ear.

Natalie caught the shadow of a frown forming on his lips just before he turned his back to her. Matt lowered his voice, and even though she couldn't actually make out all the words, there was no missing the annoyed undercurrent.

"I don't have time for this, Scott," Matt finally said, cutting his older brother short on the other end of the line. He'd been in town less than two weeks and already Scott was seeking him out, dumping his problems in his lap. He wasn't about to allow himself to get sucked back into this kind of a rut again. He was done with all that. *Done.* "This time, you're going to have to bail yourself out of trouble."

The voice on the other end of the line begged indulgence.

Because this was his brother and because, God-only-knew-why but family still meant something to him despite all the turmoil it had caused in his life, Matt spared his older brother a minute more.

He sighed again, weary. "All right, I'll call you later. Until then, don't do anything stupid." Matt broke the connection before Scott could add another layer to the tale of woe that he'd been spinning.

Replacing the receiver in its cradle, Matt turned back around to look at Natalie. She looked stern, he thought. And beautiful despite her frown. "Sorry."

Her eyes met his. Hers were unfathomable. "Of course you are."

He would have had to have been deaf not to hear the sarcastic edge in her voice.

He had it coming, Matt thought, and he couldn't blame her, not after the way they had parted company. But he still felt in his heart that he had done the right thing.

Even if it hurt like hell at the time.

He wasn't exactly feeling terrific right now, he realized. Eight years and he still wanted her. Maybe even more than ever. He'd often wondered over the years, in isolated moments when he found himself alone, if he would ever get over her. He had his answer now. And it was a resounding "No."

She didn't need to know that, either, he thought, doing his best to appear impassive.

The next thing out of Natalie's mouth threw him for a loop.

"Did you have my sister killed?"

It took him a second to find his tongue. "What?" The implication behind the question had him reeling. How could she even *think* that? "Do you actually believe that I would be capable of something like that?"

Though she was certain that she gave no indication of it, she was struggling against her attraction to him. The fact that she could feel that, after all that had happened, disgusted her. She was supposed to be a stronger person than that. Right now, Natalie felt as if her emotions had been dumped into a blender, the button set on "high."

"I discovered a long time ago that I'm not exactly a great judge of character."

He had that coming, too, Matt thought. He refrained from commenting on her words. Instead, he answered her unsettling question.

"No, I didn't kill Candace." And then he hit her with a question of his own. "What could have possibly been my motive?"

She'd asked because her father had planted the idea

in her head, but she didn't want to bring him into the conversation just yet. "When they found her, Candace's ring was missing."

He stared at her, stunned. "Robbery?" he asked in disbelief. All right, his family had had some shady dealings in the past, but he himself had never been found guilty of anything. Had never traveled on the wrong side of the law. "You think I killed her to rob her?" Even as he said it, it sounded ludicrous. Matt looked at her for a long moment. "I don't believe you believe that," he told her quietly.

She didn't know what to believe. Her heart told her that Matt had nothing to do with this, but her heart hadn't exactly been batting a thousand.

"I really don't care what you believe," she informed him coldly. "The ring is worth millions. People do a lot of things for a lot less."

"People, maybe," he allowed. "But not me." And then the import of what she was saying hit him. "You're talking about the Tears of the Quetzal? *That* was the ring that was stolen?"

"As if you didn't know. Someone saw you escort Candace out."

They were attracting attention despite the closed door. Some of the people in the outer office kept glancing in their direction. Matt walked over to glass walls and one by one lowered the blinds, giving them privacy.

It also created a sense of intimacy that he really didn't want. Right now, it only complicated things. But he wanted prying eyes even less, so he left the blinds where they were. "A lot of people saw me escort Candace out."

"How far out?" Natalie challenged heatedly. "To

your car? Maybe you decided to take her for a little drive and wound up at her place?"

Candace and Natalie might have been twins but he had never met two sisters who were so utterly different, not just in looks but in personality. He had never experienced the slightest attraction, not even momentarily, to Candace.

"I walked her to the entrance," he told Natalie. "Where she went from there and with whom, I have no idea." She looked unconvinced. "I can show you the tape that verifies that." Although, he thought, he shouldn't have to.

"Tapes can be doctored," she countered. "As I remember, you were pretty good at that sort of thing. 'Enhancing' I think you called it."

That both wounded and irritated him, but he let it go. Instead, he appealed to her logic. Her logical mind was one of the things he'd loved about her.

"Natalie, think about it. What could I do with the ring if I did take it? I can't fence it. It's not some little piece of glitter. This rock is famous. Pieces have been written about it. A lot of people know what it looks like."

Everything Matt said made sense, but she wasn't willing to let him off the hook just yet. She needed more answers. "My father says he's into your family for a lot of money."

He was surprised her father had admitted that. Arrangements had been made secretly, so no one would know that Rothchild was in financial trouble.

"The family lent him money, yes."

Matt couldn't help thinking how ironic that was. Eight years ago, Harold Rothchild had come to him for the express purpose of buying him off. The man had offered him a quarter of a million dollars if he promised to disappear and never get in contact with Natalie again. Angry and offended because he knew that in Rothchild's eyes, he wasn't good enough for Natalie, he'd told her father what the man could do with his money and his offer.

And then, days later, his brother had succeeded in doing what Rothchild couldn't. He'd succeeded in making him leave Natalie, but for completely different reasons.

Natalie was looking at him suspiciously. They both knew what her father thought of the Schaffer family. "Why would your family give him a loan?"

Because Rothchild had told Natalie about the loan, he didn't feel bound by the initial promise of secrecy surrounding the deal. "Your father overextended himself. A note was due on his casino, and he stood to lose everything." He shrugged carelessly, his custom-made jacket rustling. "I was in a position to help." He'd been the one who had brokered the deal, acting as a go-between with his family and Rothchild.

That didn't answer her question. She pinned him with a look. "Again, why?"

He'd asked himself the same thing. This was a man who, eight years ago, would have gladly seen him run out of Vegas on a rail. But then he rethought his position. "Because he was your father, and I thought that what happened to him affected you. If he had to file for bankruptcy, your inheritance might be in jeopardy as well." He smiled at her. "Let's just say I thought I owed it to you."

Damn it, his smile wasn't supposed to affect her anymore, wasn't supposed to make her knees feel weak. She was a cop, for God's sake.

"You don't owe me anything, Schaffer," she told him, her voice edged with steel. "Except for straight answers."

"I gave you that," he told her. "I didn't kill Candace. I didn't *have* her killed, either," he added, covering all his bases. That, hopefully, out of the way, he had questions of his own. "How did she die?" he wanted to know.

She didn't answer him immediately. Instead, she looked at him for a long moment, debating whether or not she believed him. God help her, she did. Did that make her a fool?

After a beat, she decided there was no harm in answering. The papers would be carrying the story soon enough, and the media always had a way of ferreting things out.

"My guess is that the blow to the back of her head did it. And whoever was there got in a few licks on her face as well." Natalie shuddered. Had Candace suffered before she died? Lord, she hoped not. "Revenge, hatred, I don't know."

His eyes held hers. "And you thought I would do that?"

She gave him a nonanswer. "I had to ask."

He had a lot coming to him for the way things had ended between them, but not that. "No, you didn't."

Her temper flared. "Yes, I did," she insisted, struggling to keep her voice under control. "Because *I don't know you*."

Yes, you do, Natalie. In your heart, you know me, he thought. And then another thought hit him. "Let me ask you a question."

"All right." Not knowing what to expect, she braced herself. "Ask."

He sat down on the edge of his desktop, crossing

his arms before him. "Have the rules changed since I left Vegas?"

He looked relaxed all of a sudden. Why? Where was he going with this? She became suspicious. "Depends on what kind of rules you're talking about."

He watched her expression as he spoke. "The rules that say a detective with a personal stake in a case isn't supposed to be allowed to investigate said case."

He should be the last one to talk about rules, she thought angrily. "No, they haven't changed," Natalie replied stoically.

Matt spread his hands in a silent question. "Well then, why—?"

She stopped him before he could go any further. "My captain put me on bereavement leave."

"That doesn't answer my question."

Well, not only did she not know him but he obviously didn't seem to know her, either she thought bitterly. "Do you honestly expect me to sit with my hands folded and not even *try* to find my sister's killer?" she snapped.

"No," he admitted, "I expect you to do exactly what you're doing. We have that in common, you and I." Their eyes met, and she wanted to look away, but found she couldn't. "We're both loyal to our families—even when they don't deserve it."

She took offense for her sister. "You're a fine one to pass judgment."

"I was talking about my own family," he clarified quietly, and with those few words, he effectively took the wind out of her sails.

"Oh." For a second, she was completely at a loss as to how to respond.

Sensing her discomfort, Matt changed the topic. He always had been in tune with her. "So, you're a police detective."

She looked at him warily. "Yes."

He smiled. It went straight to her belly. "Can't say that's something I saw in your future."

"I don't think there was anything you saw about my future." She couldn't refrain from making the dig. It kept her from demanding to know why he had walked out on her all those years ago without so much as a word of explanation.

There were so many things he wanted to say to her, but he didn't. They would all sound like excuses. And he knew she was better off this way. And safer. That had always been his goal, the motive behind his actions, to keep her as safe as possible. And that meant they couldn't be together. But if he'd told her the truth back then, she wouldn't have allowed it to keep them apart.

It was better this way. If he'd begun to waver in his decision, Scott's phone call had convinced him otherwise.

"I'd like to see those surveillance tapes from last night if you don't mind," she said crisply, her tone indicating that even if he did mind, she would still find a way to view them.

There were an awful lot of tapes to go through. They had a hundred different cameras just on the ground floor alone. That made for a great deal of viewing time. "What exactly is it that you're looking for?"

She wanted to say "anything suspicious" but she kept it succinct. "I want to see if Candace went home with anyone, or if anyone followed her."

There, at least, he could be of some help. "Well, I don't know for certain if anyone followed her, but I can tell you that when she left here, she was alone. I stood at the entrance and watched her for a few minutes to make sure she didn't double back."

He made Candace sound like some sort of undesirable. Granted her sister had been loud and tended to be outlandish at times, but she'd never been barred from any place. Casinos vied for her attendance.

"Exactly why was she escorted off the premises?"

"You'd have to take that up with Luke Montgomery," he told her.

His answer wasn't good enough. "You have no thoughts on that?" she wanted to know. "No impressions as to why he'd ask you to remove her?"

He told her what he knew. "They looked like they were quarreling when Montgomery signaled for me to come over."

The bartender had said the same thing. "Quarreling? Quarreling about what?" Maybe Montgomery sought Candace out later in her condo, to pick up in private where they had left off. She needed to know the nature of the argument.

Matt made an educated guess, based on what he knew about Candace. "I think your sister wanted to cause a sensation with her ring, and Montgomery wanted the focus to remain on the gems at the gala. Montgomery went to a lot of expense to get celebrities to donate the jewelry and get them all under one roof and, well, Candace always had a way of making love to the camera, to the exclusion of everyone else."

Natalie's eyes narrowed. "I guess you would know

about the lovemaking part." The retort was out before she could prevent its emergence.

She'd managed to catch him completely off guard. "Excuse me?"

Oh, he was good, Natalie thought. He really looked as if he didn't know what she was talking about. "Give it up, Matt. Candace told me that she thought you were really good in bed. One of her 'better' lovers, I believe she said."

For a moment, he was speechless. "Candace would have no way of knowing that."

She wasn't about to be taken in by his act, no matter how much part of her wanted to believe it. "Oh, don't bother playing innocent with me, Matt. Why would my sister lie?"

"The last thing I am is innocent," he informed her. "But I *never* made love to your sister and as for why she would lie to you, I could think of a dozen reasons. Her being a pathological liar would be at the top of the list." He saw that made Natalie angrier, but he stood by his statement. "I think, between her lifestyle, the booze, the drugs and the men, your sister lost her grasp on reality a long time ago."

Incensed, heartbroken and still in shock at seeing Matt after all this time, Natalie found herself in a very fragile state. Far more fragile than she ever thought she would be. Without thinking, she reacted, defending a sister who could no longer defend herself. She took a swing at Matt.

He caught her by the wrist, stopping her fist from making contact and then quickly caught the other when she switched hands.

Furious, she tried to pull free. "Let me go," she fumed.

"Only if you stop making a fist," he told her. When he saw her uncurl first one hand, then the other, he released her wrists.

And promptly received a stinging slap to his cheek. Without registering surprise—he really should have seen that coming, he upbraided himself—Matt merely looked at her as he rubbed his face.

"Feel better?"

She wanted to say yes, but nothing had been solved, nothing had been released. She still felt this pent-up anger, and it had nowhere to go. "No."

"I didn't think so." He wanted to take her hands in his, not to restrain her, but to make contact. He refrained, relying on his words instead to bridge the gap. "Look, I'm sorry about Candace, but unless you want to be next, I think you should leave this alone and let someone else handle it."

"Is that a threat?"

"That's an observation. Maybe the ring was just icing on the cake. You said she had bruises on her face. She didn't when she left here. Whoever killed your sister might have done so in a blind rage. Maybe revenge, not theft, was the motive."

"Revenge?" Natalie echoed. Candace had been thoughtless and had rubbed a great many people the wrong way, but she was harmless. She'd never done anything to anyone that would make them want to kill her. "You think whoever killed her was trying to teach her a lesson?"

He had a somewhat different theory to back up his thought. "No, maybe they were trying to get back at your father."

"My father?" she repeated. "Why?" But even as she asked, it made sense—if she thought of the note he'd shown her.

"All rich men make enemies along the way. What better way to get back at him than to kill someone in his family? One of his beloved daughters?"

She was still trying to turn this around on him. "You sound as if you're familiar with that kind of a life."

"Just speculating," he replied. "And if I'm right, you could be in danger."

"I'm a cop," she reminded him, deliberately resting her hand on the hilt of the weapon that was exposed beneath her jacket. "Being in danger kind of goes with the territory."

God help him but he suddenly had a very real urge to see her wearing her holster and a pair of stiletto heels—and nothing else.

"The territory," he advised, "might just have gotten a little rougher. I don't want anything happening to you."

If she could believe that...

But she couldn't. She knew better. "You have nothing to say about that," she informed him tersely. "You lost the right to have a say a long time ago, remember?"

He exhaled. It didn't help, didn't make the ache in his chest go away. "Yeah, I remember."

Chapter 5

"You know I can't release the tapes to you without a court order," Matt told her. There was protocol to follow, and even if things hadn't ended the way they did between them, technically his hands were tied. "And I'm guessing," he went on, "you can't get one because this isn't your case."

Her temper flared quickly, and it took effort to bank it down. She might have known he'd stonewall her. *Did* he have something to hide?

Natalie narrowed her eyes. She was not in the mood to be waved away like some annoying insect. "Look, Schaffer—"

Schaffer. She was calling him by his last name, the way a law enforcement agent would, he thought. The chasm between them was widening.

Good for her, he thought. She was moving on, or had moved on.

Bad for him, of course, but he'd resigned himself eight years ago that this was the way things had to be. Her father had been right all those years ago—he wasn't good enough for Natalie. Not because he didn't love her more than anything in the world but because his family would, in the end, drag him down. And if she were with him, they'd drag her down, too. He couldn't have that happen.

"However," he continued as if she hadn't interrupted him, "there really is nothing to stop you from looking over my shoulder as I review the tapes."

That stopped her in her tracks. "You're going to review the tapes?"

She couldn't read his expression. "The only responsible thing for a good citizen to do, don't you think?"

Natalie was surprised when a tinge of amusement whispered through her. "Is that what you are, a good citizen?"

"I do my best. Come with me," he said as he opened his office door.

The moment he did, there was a quick shuffling of bodies and rustling of chairs moving back into place. The techs in the surveillance room were returning to their posts, he thought. No doubt curiosity had gotten the better of them, with more than a few of the people who manned the monitors trying to get closer to his office in order to hear what was being said. Despite the fact that he was head of security for Montgomery Enterprises, he was, in effect, the "new kid on the block," at least in this location.

Until two weeks ago, he'd been based in Los Angeles, where he would have rather remained. But Montgomery had been adamant that he wanted him at The Janus, and the man did pay a damn good salary. Too good to refuse.

Making no comment about the temporary break that had been taken, Matt walked over to the computer tech seated just outside his office.

"Wilson—it is Wilson, right?" he asked the tall, painfully skinny, barely-out-of-adolescence young man.

Surprised at being singled out and obviously somewhat nervous because of it, the young man bobbed his head up and down. "Yes sir, Stuart Wilson."

Matt could see Wilson's Adam's apple moving up and down like a runaway golf ball. He'd looked into all their backgrounds his first day here. Wilson was the best of the best when it came to computers. What he couldn't make a computer do *couldn't* be done.

But the young technician's considerable proficiency didn't make him any less gawky, Matt thought. Wilson really needed to have someone take him under their wing, he mused.

Too bad he wasn't going to be here long enough for that. Matt had already made up his mind that he was going to be in Vegas just long enough to give The Janus's security system a once-over and babysit it until Montgomery hired a suitable replacement for him.

"Wilson, I need you to pull up the surveillance tapes that we have of Mr. Montgomery's gala last night."

Wilson's mouth dropped open as his jaw slackened. His small eyes widened as far as they could go. "All of them?" he repeated, stunned. Nervously, he added, "That's an awful lot of footage, sir."

He should have been more specific, Matt thought.

"Let's start with what we have between eight and nine o'clock. For the time being, I'm only interested in the first floor." He narrowed it down even more. "Make it the entrance and the casino floor between that and Ballrooms B and C."

The two ballrooms had been combined for the evening in order to accommodate all the people who had RSVPed that they were attending. By the middle of the evening, the two rooms were teeming with celebrities. He knew that Montgomery had pulled in a sizable amount for the charity he was sponsoring. In addition he had earned himself a great deal of goodwill and thereby excellent publicity, which he knew had been Montgomery's underlying goal.

Right now, the man was golden, Matt mused. Luke Montgomery had come a long way from the poor boy who'd been ridiculed for wearing the same clothes to school day after day. And, to his vast credit, Montgomery had risen far above his poverty-stricken roots without resorting to any deals with the devil.

In this case, Matt thought, that would be the other members of his family, from whom he would have enjoyed maintaining a continuing estrangement. However, his brother kept insisting on calling him, asking for help. It wasn't in him to say no.

He was working on that.

Wilson's long, thin fingers were flying across the keyboard. The resulting staccato rhythm, coming fast and furious, sounded not unlike rapid gunfire from a small handgun.

As Natalie watched the technician's monitor, the first of many tapes began to play across the screen. "Here's the tape of the entrance," Wilson announced.

Matt nodded. He rethought his offer to Natalie about having her look over his shoulder. He had things to attend to, and if he wound up spending any length of time sitting so close to her, well, he'd just rather not put himself to that sort of test.

Turning to Natalie, he indicated a nearby empty desk. One of the computer techs had called in sick this morning.

"Why don't you pull up a chair beside Wilson?" he suggested. "He'll be able to go through all the pertinent tapes for you."

Wilson stopped typing, anxiously darting his eyes between the two of them. "Is there anything specific that you're looking for?" he asked Natalie nervously.

It was easy to see that the tech was far more comfortable with computers than he was with people, Natalie thought. She pulled the chair over from the other desk and sat down beside Wilson, then took out the photograph she had of Candace and placed it beside the keyboard.

"I'm looking for any footage you have of this woman." She looked at the tech's face, expecting to see some sort of indication that he recognized her sister. Candace had attended every wild party, frequented all the casinos and in general had done her level best to turn herself into a household name.

Candace, Natalie couldn't help thinking, would have been bitterly disappointed with Wilson. There was absolutely no sign of recognition. He merely nodded at what he took to be his assignment. "Okay, let's see if I can find her."

As the tech began typing again, Matt withdrew. Natalie was aware the exact second that he stepped away and went back to his office.

Damn it, eight years and her Matt-radar was as keen as ever. The very *air* seemed to change when he was close by.

Get a grip, she sternly reminded herself. *You're here to find Candace's killer, not reignite something that was doomed from the beginning.*

With concentrated effort, Natalie settled in and focused on the images that were going by on Wilson's screen.

More than an hour had passed. Her neck was getting stiff, and she felt as if she was going to go cross-eyed. Tape after tape had been accessed and screened. A lot of the "beautiful people" came and went, each and every one of them had been greeted by Montgomery with enthusiasm.

The man certainly looked the part of a casino mogul, she couldn't help thinking. It was almost as if he'd been sent over from Central Casting. Suave, six foot two, muscular, dark-haired and handsome.

Almost as handsome as Matt.

Where the hell had that come from? she silently lamented. Looks weren't everything. As a matter of fact, looks were nothing, absolutely nothing if there was no heart. She'd learned that the hard way, thanks to Matt Schaffer.

Her mind wandering, she was suddenly jolted back to the present. Alert, she straightened in her seat. "Wait, go back," she ordered Wilson.

The tech jumped in surprise. Quickly, he rewound the footage.

"Stop!"

"This her?" he wanted to know. He'd just accessed footage from the front of the casino. The time stamp on the tape was 8:47 p.m. A sultry Candace, her scarlet gown clinging to her curves with every step she took, filled the monitor. Natalie thought she heard Wilson murmur an appreciative, "Wow."

That was the best word to use when summing up Candace, Natalie thought. *Wow.*

As she watched her sister walk down the red carpet, she felt a lump suddenly forming in her throat. Her eyes were moistening.

Damn it, where were all these stampeding emotions coming from?

She usually had better control over herself than this. But then, she supposed in her own defense, she wasn't usually confronting videos of a slain family member while sitting in the office of a former lover who had turned her heart into Swiss cheese.

Blowing out a breath, Natalie forced herself to watch the screen and analyze what she saw. This was no time to give in to tears.

From all indications, Candace appeared to be alone. And then, as Natalie watched, her sister's face lit up as if she saw someone she knew. Not unusual in a town that her sister had regarded as her personal playground, Natalie mused wryly. Whoever she spotted was off camera, part of the reporters elbowing each other out of the way for an outstanding shot.

As she continued to view the tape, she saw Candace begin to head directly over toward Montgomery.

Unlike his gracious behavior toward all the other attendees, the casino owner actually looked annoyed to see Candace. There wasn't even the pretense of cordiality, she noted.

Candace, on the other hand, looked delighted to see him. She was animated, and with every word she uttered, she would wave her left hand around. It was almost as if she was attempting to cast a spell.

Natalie slid to the edge of her chair. "Can you pull in on that?" she asked Wilson. "On her hand," she specified when he looked at her quizzically.

"Sure." The next moment, her left hand had all but filled the entire screen.

Natalie blinked. The image was somewhat grainy, but unmistakable. Her father was right. Candace had taken the ring, and she'd had it on when she walked into the casino. But not when they found her body in the condo.

Was the motive just robbery? Then why leave the necklace?

And just how had Candace gotten her hands on the ring in the first place? She would have bet anything that her father was the only one with the combination to the safe. He didn't trust anyone else with it. But then, maybe the ring hadn't been in the safe in the first place. Maybe her father had only alluded to it being there to throw everyone in the family off.

Maybe that eye candy he'd married had given him cause for concern and he'd moved the ring. Without realizing that Candace had observed him.

It was all just pure speculation. She needed facts. Fact, Candace had the ring on at 8:47 p.m. Fact, she didn't when they found her body the next morning. *This* morning, she thought grimly. *What was I doing while you were fighting for your life, Candy? Was I sleeping? Watching that old movie on TV?* She couldn't even remember the title.

A pervasive feeling of deep sorrow filled her.

Wilson, she noted, was waiting for her to tell him what to do.

She waved him on. "Okay, go back to the regular image," she requested.

When he did, she instructed him to keep going and then watched in silence as an obvious argument erupted between her sister and Montgomery. It escalated quickly. Within a few minutes, the casino owner gave up trying to reason with Candace and was signaling to someone.

Natalie didn't need to guess who. She pressed her lips together as she watched Matt come on the scene. Very politely, he took hold of Candace's arm.

Her stomach churned as she saw her sister turn up her charm. She was obviously playing up to Matt. Had she been right after all? Had there been something between the two of them?

There'd been rumors circulating that he had been one of Candace's lovers. There'd even been some talk that he had fathered one of her sons. Given the boys' ages, that would have meant that he had returned to Vegas, at least for a little while, six years ago. It didn't make any sense.

Trying to sort through her feelings, Natalie's head began to ache. She didn't know what to believe. All she knew was that she'd never felt as alone—and lonely—as she did right at this very moment.

Her hand to her forehead, she went on watching. Matt brought her sister to the casino's front entrance, just as he had told her that he had. And, also as he had said, he then stood there for several minutes, looking out. Presumably watching Candace walk away and making sure that she didn't attempt to come back.

All right, from all appearances, Candace left the casino. Did she hook up with someone just outside? Or did someone, captivated by that damn ring she kept sticking in people's faces, follow her home? All these questions nagged at her. She needed answers.

"Can we get a shot of the outside of the casino?" she asked Wilson.

He hesitated. "I'd have to access the footage from the valet area," he explained.

She didn't want excuses. "Just do it," she instructed.

"Yes'm," Wilson mumbled into his disappearing chin. Again, his fingers flew across the keyboard almost like independent digits. They seemed to be going at just under the speed of light. Natalie could feel her impatience mounting as the tempo increased.

And then Wilson accomplished his goal. He got the right footage. Candace was seen from another angle, this time from the outside of the building. She was moving away from the entrance.

She was pouting like a child who had been refused the toy she desired. And then, just like that, her face lit up again.

A beat later, she'd moved offscreen.

Natalie half rose in her seat. "Where is she going?" she demanded. When Wilson didn't answer her, she looked at the computer technician expectantly. "Get me the tape from the next camera." To clarify, she pointed at the screen. "The one to the right of this one."

"I—I can't," Wilson stuttered.

"What do you mean, you can't?"

The tech looked completely intimidated. "I—I would if I—I could, ma'am, but that one is—is down." As he spoke, his stutter became more pronounced.

God, now she was scaring geeky technicians, Natalie thought, feeling guilty.

She took a breath, then released it, trying her best to sound less threatening. Inside, she was tied up in knots. She was *certain* that whoever killed her sister was just offscreen.

"What do you mean it's down?"

"As in not working," Matt told her easily, coming up behind her chair. She swung around to face him. "It happens."

She didn't believe in coincidences. Someone had put that camera out of commission. "Conveniently," she bit off.

Matt moved so that his back was to the computer and he could see her better. "As a matter of fact, very inconveniently."

All right, whoever Candace had seen wasn't on camera. But that didn't mean she couldn't find out who it was. "I want to talk to all the valets who were parking cars last night," she told him.

Matt inclined his head. "That can be arranged," he told her. And then he smiled at her and said, "Ask me nicely."

She gritted her teeth together. Maybe this was entertaining him, but she meant business.

"I want to talk to the valets who were parking cars last night or you're going to suddenly find yourself a guest of the city for impeding a homicide investigation." She shot him a warning look. "And I promise you, Schaffer, you really won't like the accommodations."

He crossed his arms before him. "That wasn't asking nicely, Natalie," he observed.

She jumped up to her feet. "Look—" But she got no further.

Because, just then, Adam Parker and Miles Davidson pushed open the door and walked into the surveillance room.

Both men looked as surprised to see her as she was to see them.

Parker frowned at her. "You wouldn't be conducting an investigation into your sister's death after the captain gave you explicit orders not to and put you on bereavement leave, would you Rothchild?" he asked.

Natalie didn't know if the question was tongue in cheek or not. She was pretty certain the men would turn a blind eye to her pursuing leads as long as it wasn't right in front of them. This put all three of them in an awkward position.

"As a matter of fact, Natalie's here visiting me," Matt informed the detectives genially. Both men looked rather dubious. "We used to be close," he went on. "I invited her in here so that I could keep an eye on the monitors while we caught up on old times." As he talked, he approached the detectives. Passing Wilson's desk, Matt pressed a key on the board so swiftly that the movement was all but imperceptible.

Except that Natalie saw him.

A long, narrow bar appeared on the bottom of the screen, indicating that something was currently being saved.

Matt deliberately placed his body before the two detectives and in front of Wilson's computer, effectively blocking it.

He looked from one man to the other. “I’m Matt Schaffer, head of Montgomery Enterprises security.” He shook each detective’s hand in turn. “Is there anything I can do for you?”

“Yeah.” Parker nodded toward the computers in general. “You can hand over all your surveillance tapes from last night.”

Matt remained unfazed. “That’s a tall order, detective. Do you have a subpoena?”

Parker reached into his inside pocket and took out an envelope. “Right here.”

Natalie felt her heart sink.

Chapter 6

He smiled to himself as he watched the news on the flat-panel TV in his dreary apartment. Another building blocked sunlight from entering through the window, but that didn't dampen his spirits. Today, he felt on top of the world.

Didn't take long, did it? he thought, tossing away the greasy wrapper that had held his fast-food lunch. But then, the media was full of nothing but sharks these days no matter what venue they reported in. The moment they smelled blood—in this case, a story about a tabloid queen who'd led an in-your-face life since she put on her first pair of thong underwear—there was a feeding frenzy.

The story had broke early this morning, and there'd been nothing but a recycling of details, ad nauseam, since then.

No matter, it would be a long time before he got tired of hearing them.

"There'll be more to join her soon enough," he promised the attractive blonde whose turn it was to interrupt the scheduled morning programming with this "Breaking news."

A wicked smile curved his mouth, marring his handsome features. One by one, he was going to make all the Rothchilds pay for what had been done, both to his father and, consequently, to his mother.

"Think he can clear his conscience by throwing a few dollars our way?" he seethed, addressing the words to the air. "Was that supposed to make up for robbing us of Poppi *and* what was his? Well, Rothchild's in for one hell of a surprise if that's what he thinks."

The laugh that echoed within the dim room sounded more like a demonic giggle.

He slipped his hand into his pocket and curled his fingers around the prize he'd secured last night. It comforted him not because of what it was but because he knew that Harold Rothchild grieved over its absence probably even more than he grieved for his daughter's demise. The newscaster was saying something about robbery being the motive.

Let them think that, he thought. Stealing the dazzling ring had just been the cherry on top of the sundae. Hitting Rothchild where it hurt most. Besides, he wasn't stealing; he was reclaiming. The gem belonged to his family, not Rothchild's. And his aim was to go on eliminating family members until old man Rothchild was the last man standing.

Once Rothchild's entire family was gone, then and

only then, would he move in to bring an end to the old man's misery. Slowly, he decided. Very, very slowly. He was going to enjoy hearing Rothchild beg for mercy.

His father had never had the chance, he thought bitterly. Joseph Rothchild had been his father's judge and executioner—and Harold Rothchild had stood in the shadows and watched, shaking like a little girl, too afraid of his own father to do the right thing and intervene.

Well, this was going to teach that spineless bastard to mess with his family, the young man promised himself with mounting glee.

Knowing he needed to go out, he looked around the small, airless apartment, searching for a place to leave the priceless ring. But there was nowhere within the three untidy rooms that he, as an accomplished thief, wouldn't have looked in his search for goods. Thieves were rampant in this city of glitter and sin.

The safest place, for now, he decided, was with him. So he left it in his pocket.

His smile widened. It was the kind of malevolent look that made a man's blood run cold, he thought proudly, catching a glimpse of himself in the cracked, smoky mirror that he passed on his way to the door.

Besides, in the right hands, the hands of the family who were the rightful owners of the diamond, wasn't it supposed to bring some kind of good luck? Since his father had been the one to have originally found the gem in that godforsaken mine, that meant the multicolored diamond with its hypnotic gleam belonged to *his* family. And that, in turn, meant that it was supposed to bring *him* luck.

In a way, he mused philosophically, it already had.

He'd killed Candace Rothchild and no one was the wiser. No one had seen it coming, not even Candace until the late few moments. The lying, empty-headed bitch thought she was going to have a blood-pumping roll in the sack, not receive a one-way ticket for a trip on the River Styx.

Surprise!

Curling his fingers around the ring, he walked out of his apartment whistling. He took care to lock the door behind him.

Natalie watched in silence as the two men she worked with cleared out the last of the surveillance tapes. They packed the lot of them into a box that one of Matt's people had provided. Parker had the decency to look contrite as the other detective hefted the box.

"Sorry, Nat," the older man apologized, and then he paused because he didn't want working relations to deteriorate between them. "But we'll get him—or her," he augmented since the killer had left no indication as to gender. There was always an outside chance that Candace had been done in by a jealous wife or girlfriend who had been thrown over by her man because the partying heiress had come on the scene.

Natalie sighed and nodded her head. It was clear to Matt that passive was not a role she played well. He waited until the two detectives had left with their booty, then looked expectantly at the young technician. Without a word, Wilson began typing, his fingers flying again.

Natalie had caught the look that had gone between the two. Caught, too, the swift sleight of hand that had occurred when Matt had passed the technician's keyboard. She doubted if either Parker or Davidson had noticed. If they had, something would have been said. Matt was still that good.

"What did you do?" she asked him.

His intensely blue eyes looked at her with amusement. "Excuse me?"

There was a time when she would have found this charming. But that naive girl had grown up years ago.

"Don't try to sound innocent, Schaffer. It's far too late for that. When Parker and Davidson came in, before they even asked you for the tapes, you did something on the keyboard as you walked by. Don't bother denying it," she cautioned. "I saw you."

"My hand slipped," Matt deadpanned. He knew that it was just a matter of seconds before the computer was finished going through its paces and he had what he needed.

Who the hell did he think he was kidding? Natalie thought.

"That might fly with Parker. He doesn't know computers—or you—the way I do." Her eyes narrowed, pinning him. "Now, what did you do?"

He would have thought she would have figured it out by now. "I backed up the tapes that were just handed over to your buddies."

Even though she'd viewed the pertinent ones, she'd still wanted to have the tapes so that she could look them over more closely. She looked at him in surprise. "You made me a copy?"

"I made *me* a copy," he corrected, then added loftily. "And, if you're very nice to me, I just might let you have them—"

She was not in the mood to play games—and even if she was, it wouldn't have been with him. "You're obstructing justice—" she began.

"On the contrary," he contradicted her in a mild, easygoing voice that she found infinitely irritating. "I cooperated with law enforcement. Law enforcement just took the tapes with them. You, in this case, are a private citizen, remember?"

She pinned him with a look. "I also have a temper, remember?"

Matt grinned then, recalling how volatile she could be—and how much fun making up afterward always was. It was hard to believe that he had once been that young, that devoid of a sense of impeding consequences to have considered allowing her to remain in his life. He knew better now.

"How could I forget it?" And then he added, "Don't worry, I still remember how to share and play well with others." He looked toward the tech. "Are you finished?"

"Just about." Wilson pushed his glasses up his noise, something she noticed he did every few minutes. "Just gotta put it on a disk."

"Make it a jump drive," Matt told him. He took what looked like a key chain advertising Montgomery Enterprises out of his pocket and handed it to the tech. "Easier to carry around." He said the words to the tech, but he was pointedly looking at Natalie as he said them.

He was going for "hide in plain sight," she thought. "Thank you," she said grudgingly.

Matt was already walking away, and he shrugged in response. "I owe you."

Natalie saw no reason to dispute that. "Yes," she agreed emphatically. "You do."

Three minutes later, the newly uploaded key chain in hand, she walked into Matt's office without bothering to knock first. There was a TV on the side of the office, and he had it on, giving it his attention for the moment. But he was aware of her entrance. She still wore the same fragrance.

Matt turned around in his chair. "Leaving now?" he asked.

She was about to say no, but the words temporarily evaporated from her lips. Her eyes were drawn to the TV on the back wall despite the fact that he had the sound lowered. Along the bottom of the screen was a banner announcing "Breaking news." Candace's photograph, taken at some other recent function, was in the upper right-hand corner as a newscaster read words off a teleprompter announcing to the few who hadn't yet heard that Candace Rothchild, the darling of the paparazzi set, had been found dead in her condo. Because the room where she was found had been ransacked, the banner continued, foul play was suspected.

"Foul play," Natalie echoed incredulously, spitting the term out. "What an innocuous term for murder."

He was well aware that news reporting was an art form. They had to tantalize the public, taking care not to put them off so much that they couldn't bear to hear the details.

"Keeps the public coming back for more and still separates them from the horror of it." Something protective kicked in within him. Leaning over, he deliberately turned off the TV. She didn't need to be subjected to that.

"Otherwise, if you showed all the gruesome details, the only ones who'd tune in would be serial killers in the making. And ghouls," he added. He rose from his desk, guessing why she'd sought him out. "Leaving?"

Natalie shook her head. "Just getting started," she contradicted.

He'd forgotten how stubborn she could be. Like a junkyard dog once she got hold of something—except a lot prettier. Still, he knew he had to give appealing to her common sense a shot. "Natalie, I really think you should leave this to the others."

Was he serious? "And I really think you should help me."

He thought that his part was over with the tapes. "What?"

Damn, she hated sounding as if she was asking for favors, but he was right. She had no official capacity here, couldn't rely on her badge, so this placed it in the realm of favors.

"Believe me, this is not something I'm asking lightly, but you were the last one to see Candace alive," she reminded him.

"Correction, a whole plaza full of people were the last ones to see your sister alive—not to mention whoever killed her," he added.

She intended on asking questions until someone remembered something, or said something that would point her in the right direction. For that, she needed him, because he could pave the way for her. And, as he had already mentioned, he owed her.

"I need to talk to Luke to find out what the argument was about, and I need to talk to the valets on duty to see if any of them noticed anyone leaving with Candace," Natalie told him. "She was obviously smiling at *someone* off camera."

As she paused, she realized that Matt looked as if he was going to refuse her. She wasn't about to give him the chance. She intended on hammering at him until he surrendered.

"Now, I'm going to do this with you or without you," she said, "but it would go a whole lot easier for me if you were there to smooth the way for me."

"Natalie—"

He still looked dubious. Did having her around repulse him so much that he would deny her the right to find her sister's killer?

She guessed at the reason behind his reluctance. It had been eight years. She hadn't expected time to freeze for him—the way it had for her. "Don't worry. As soon as I have my answers, I'll be gone. You won't need to explain me to your wife or girlfriend or whatever."

"I'm not worried about that," he told her. She didn't realize how much of a hole her absence had left, but then, why should she? "And for the record, there's no wife or girlfriend or 'whatever.'"

He wasn't married, wasn't involved with anyone. Natalie could feel her heart do a little leap in her chest and she tried in vain to pay no attention to it.

"Good," she responded crisply, "then you're free to help."

He pointed out the obvious. "I'm working," but even as he said it, he knew it wasn't an excuse. She was determined, and he was afraid that she would push too hard and get herself killed as well.

"We're not going to Mars. We're staying on the premises." She frowned at him. "Now, are you going to help me?" She drew closer to him, as if her proximity would draw the words out of him. "Or do you have something to confess?"

Her scent filled his head, triggering memories. Nostalgia brought a side order of yearning with it.

Yes, I have something to confess. I never got over you. You're a fever in my blood, Natalie Rothchild. And seeing you now has just made me realize that I was a fool to ever think I could put you behind me.

But he kept all of this tightly wrapped inside of him. If he said anything at all, then he'd wasted the last eight years trying to make a life for himself without her. So he kept his face impassive and glanced at his watch. "I can give you an hour."

Eight years ago, he called the shots. This time around it was her turn. "You'll give me as much time as I need," she countered.

Amusement curved his lips. "You've gotten tougher since I last saw you."

Her eyes met his for a long moment. "I've had to," was all she said.

There had been five valets on duty last night. Because of the double duty they'd pulled, they were all off now and had to be summoned back to the casino.

"This is where your part comes in," Natalie told him as he had the head attendant place calls to all five valets. Matt made no comment as he gave the attendant instructions.

One by one, the valets—all young, lean men in their

twenties, came straggling in. They looked bleary-eyed and somewhat bewildered. The gala hadn't ended until two in the morning.

Natalie decided that questioning them en masse would be simpler. In response, she heard the same story over and over again. Between regular guests of the casino and its accompanying hotel, and the attendees at the gala, all five valets had been kept hopping. They were far too busy parking and retrieving cars to take any kind of notice of the comings and goings of the attending celebrities for more than a fleeting second, if that long.

What it boiled down to was that they all assured Natalie that they hadn't seen who Candace might have left with. Her optimism was flagging when the last valet suddenly remembered that he had seen the flamboyant young woman exchanging words with another woman.

"She didn't exactly look pleased," the valet confided to her.

She took a guess as to who the pronoun referred to. "Candace?"

The young man shook his head. "No, the woman Miss Rothchild was talking to."

Excitement instantly sparked. "Could you describe her?"

The valet, Blake, looked at her sheepishly. "No," he confessed. It took him a moment to continue. When he did, he avoided looking into Natalie's eyes. "I was watching Ms. Rothchild. She was um, gesturing so hard that, um…" And then, because he seemed to suddenly realize he was talking to the dead woman's sister, he abruptly stopped, red-faced.

It took no effort for Matt to read between the lines. "You were watching to see if her dress would stay put or fall off."

The words sounded antiseptic, but the valet still looked somewhat embarrassed by what he'd accidentally admitted to. Still, he seemed aware that she was waiting for him to answer. So he made the admission to his shoes. "Yeah, that's it."

Natalie couldn't begin to describe the frustration she felt. She grabbed hold of the valet's arm and tugged, forcing him to look up at her. "You have to remember *something,*" she insisted. "Blonde? Brunette? Redhead? Tall? Short?"

The valet pressed his lips together and screwed his face up, hard. It looked as if he was straining his brain. Any second, Natalie was certain she was going to see steam coming out of his ears. Finally, he said, "She wasn't old."

"Great," Natalie murmured. "I'll put out an APB for half of Vegas."

The valet looked genuinely contrite. "Sorry," he apologized.

Matt put his hand on the young man's shoulder. "It's all right, Blake," he told him. "You can go back home now." Matt looked at the other valets still gathered there. "That goes for the rest of you—unless anyone remembers anything else."

"No."

"Sorry."

"Not me."

"It was a busy night, Mr. Schaffer."

Matt nodded. "I know. Get some sleep, you'll be back on duty soon."

The valets immediately cleared out, obviously relieved to be dismissed.

Natalie turned on Matt, her hands on her hips. He'd usurped her authority, just like that. "Maybe I wasn't finished with Blake," she said, struggling to rein in her irritation.

"What were you planning on doing?" he challenged. "Performing exploratory surgery on his brain to see if he was hiding something? The kid told you all that he remembered."

Something was nagging at her. In Natalie's opinion, Matt had been much too lax with the valets, almost eager to send them on their way—especially the last one. Was he covering for this Blake guy?

Or was he covering for someone else? She hated this feeling, but she just didn't trust him. "And have you told me all you know, or are you hiding something?"

He could only shake his head. How many times were they going to go through this? "I'm the one who called the valets in, remember? And the one who got you a backup of the tapes." He would have thought that the latter would have gotten him some goodwill. "When did you get so suspicious of everyone?"

There was no hesitation on her part. She fired back, "The day I found a note tucked under the pillow next to mine."

What could he say to that? That he had done it for her own good? That it had killed him to leave her? That he'd looked back at her sleeping face, so peaceful, so beautiful, and had almost changed his mind? That he had almost torn up the note and had wanted nothing more than to take his chances? Except that the chances he'd be taking didn't involve him, they'd involved her and he had no right to play Russian roulette with her life for the selfish reason that he couldn't live without her.

He'd learned how to.

Matt said nothing in response. Instead, he asked, "Do you still want to talk to Montgomery?"

"Yes."

He nodded. "Then let's go."

Chapter 7

The automatic smile that appeared on Luke Montgomery's lips as she entered his office, followed by Matt, faded instantly when Natalie confronted him with her first question.

It was obvious that Montgomery didn't like being questioned or put on the spot, especially not by an LVPD detective that also just happened to be the daughter of a man who had once scoffed at his efforts to get started in the casino business. Harold Rothchild's exact words had been that he would look forward to being a witness to his failure.

A man didn't forget words like that. They either crushed him or spurred him on. For Luke, it was the latter.

He absently wondered if the senior Rothchild knew that he was, at least in part, responsible for the influential man he had become. Nothing like wanting to prove someone wrong to make a man become driven.

"Am I under arrest, *detective?*" The casino mogul deliberately enunciated her title as if he were an adult humoring a child deeply entrenched in the world of make-believe.

Inwardly, Natalie bristled at his tone but kept it under wraps. She knew that a display of temper was what he was after.

"Would you be more inclined to answer my questions if you were?" she countered, a cool, polite smile on her lips. "Because if that's what it takes, we can do that dance and waste a lot of each other's time. You can call your lawyer, and he can come down and brief you as to what you can and can't say to me and I can hang around, waiting. *Or* we can act like mature adults and get on with it—" Her eyes pinned his. "I'm assuming, of course, that you have nothing to hide."

Luke fixed her with a look that would have made a person with less to lose nervously retreat. But Natalie was in this to win, to get answers about her sister, and she wasn't about to back down.

"You assume correctly. I have nothing to hide," he informed her in a voice that was completely devoid of any emotion.

We'll see about that, Natalie promised silently. "Great. So what was it that you and my sister argued about last night?"

"Who said we argued?" Montgomery wanted to know. The look he slanted toward Matt said that, as far as he was concerned, the question was rhetorical.

"A few of the people who attended the gala last night mentioned that you were less than pleased with

Candace and that you both raised your voices at one another," she told him.

Her response to Montgomery's question surprised Matt. He'd fully expected her to tell his boss that she'd gotten the information from him.

He smiled to himself. *Still full of surprises, aren't you, Natalie?*

For a moment, Luke said nothing, as if debating just how much he was willing to admit to. He might be flamboyant when out in public, but there was a part of him that was exceedingly private. The irony of wanting privacy and running a business in a town like this was not lost on him.

But, he decided, stubbornly refusing to answer Rothchild's question would be more trouble than it was worth.

"Your sister thought we could pick up where we left off. We couldn't," he ended simply. "That didn't make her very happy." It was an understatement, and they all knew it. Candace had been a drama queen from way back. "Neither did my telling her that she was taking the spotlight away from a very worthwhile charity, and I wasn't going to allow it."

Natalie nodded. Even though she hated to admit it, that sort of thing sounded exactly like something Candace would try to do—upstage a charity event. Sadly, her sister was that shallow.

"That sounds like Candace," she acknowledged with a sigh.

Montgomery rose from his desk, giving every indication that he intended to walk Natalie to the door. "So, are we done?" he demanded.

Natalie remained where she was. "Just one more question, Luke—you don't mind if I call you Luke, do you?" She didn't wait for an answer, but continued talking. "Where were you last night from the hours of eleven to three?"

The look in his eyes told her he really resented having to account for himself. When he answered, it was through clenched teeth. "The first part I was at the gala. Hundreds of people can vouch for that," he added crisply.

"And the second part of that time frame?" she prodded.

Luke's eyes darkened. "None of your business."

Oh, but it was, she thought. She felt Matt move closer to her. Was he going to back her up or draw her away? She didn't wait to find out. "This isn't for some blog, Luke. I'm asking as a homicide detective. Where did you go after you left the gala?"

Montgomery took offense at her line of questioning. "Then I *am* under suspicion?"

His voice had risen. She was determined to keep hers level. "*Everyone* is under suspicion until their alibi is checked out," she said.

And then, just like that, Montgomery relented. His voice became almost mild. "I was with a lady in her hotel room."

That was going to have to be verified, and they both knew it. "I'm assuming this 'lady' has a name." She waited for him to give it to her.

Montgomery shrugged. "Most likely. I don't happen to remember it."

Was he deliberately being vague—or was he lying? In either case, Natalie shook her head, her eyes never leaving his. "Not good enough."

"But I do remember the room number," Montgomery added after a beat.

It seemed to Natalie that he was intentionally playing some sort of a game, wording this so that she was led to assume that he might have had something to do with Candace's murder. The possibility had occurred to her. After all, it was no secret that Montgomery and her father were less than friendly rivals. She'd heard her father rant about the other man more than once, complaining bitterly that the latter was encroaching on territory that should have been his. It seemed as if the Rothchild fortunes were taking a downturn just as Montgomery's were on the upswing.

"Good," she ground out when he didn't immediately volunteer the number. "What was it?"

"Room 1312. Oh," he added innocently, "and she said something about having to get back to the East Coast by this evening so I'd hurry getting up there if you want to catch her to back up my 'alibi.'" Montgomery tossed the term at her with a smug satisfaction that told her he was either way overconfident—or he wasn't guilty of anything more than being arrogant.

"Thanks for the heads-up," she responded.

Natalie kept a poker face despite the wave of acute disappointment. It would have been gratifying to lay Candace's murder at Montgomery's doorstep. But that would have been far too easy, and she knew from experience that ninety-five percent of the time, the easy route never led to the right conclusion.

"Okay, I don't need you anymore," Natalie told Matt the moment they hit the lobby. She was striding toward the elevator banks. "You can go back to whatever it was you were doing."

He'd been a reluctant participant, but now that he was with her, Matt felt an even greater reluctance to pull away. "Thanks, but I think I'll stick around a little longer. You might find you need me."

"Not in a million years," she said a tad too vehemently.

Matt pretended not to hear. What he did hear, as they hurried past the front desk, was the tall, statuesque woman say that she was checking out of her room. 1312.

Catching hold of Natalie's arm, he pulled her back.

"What do you think you're—?" she demanded.

He merely pointed toward the front desk. "That's room 1312," he told her.

The woman who was Luke Montgomery's alibi looked vaguely familiar to Natalie. She made the connection when introductions were made. Her name was Erikka Hanson, and she was a model of some moderate fame, on her way back East for a swimsuit shoot.

A genuine redhead, Erikka was a full head taller than Natalie with a complexion that filled dermatologists with envy. Candace, Natalie judged, would have scratched her eyes out, had it come down to a tug of war for Montgomery. Her sister passionately resented any woman who was prettier than she was, and this model was in a class all by herself.

As she introduced herself, Natalie had her ID out to confirm her identity.

"I'm sorry to bother you Ms. Hanson, but I'm investigating a homicide. I need to ask you a couple of questions." She slipped her wallet back into her pocket. The model, she noticed, was busy checking out Matt.

Not exactly a one-man woman, are you? she mused.

"What kind of questions?" Erikka wanted to know.

"Was Luke Montgomery with you in your room last night after the gala?" Natalie asked bluntly.

If the model found the question invasive, she gave no indication. On the contrary, a wide smile curved her more than generous mouth.

"He most certainly was." Each word vibrated with enthusiasm. Montgomery, Natalie concluded, had to be good in bed. No wonder Candace had been put out when the casino mogul didn't want to rekindle their affair.

"What time was he there?" Natalie asked. She had deliberately refrained from mentioning which hours needed verifying.

"The *whole* time," Erikka answered with a heartfelt sigh.

The woman was obviously not a Rhodes scholar, Natalie thought dryly.

"Specifically?" she pressed. Then, in case this word, too, was beyond the model's grasp, she broke it down for the woman. "If you could remember what time he came into your room and what time he left, that would be very helpful."

Erikka paused to sign the credit slip the desk clerk submitted to her. Handing it back, she placed the pen on the counter and thought a moment.

"From the time the gala ended—whenever that was—until this morning." Her smile deepened. "If you think he did something wrong, he didn't." She sighed, clearly reliving a moment or two. "As a matter of fact, he did everything just right."

More than I wanted to know, Natalie thought, suddenly feeling like a voyeur. "Is there somewhere I can reach you in case I have more questions?"

The model looked somewhat impatient, but she foraged through her purse and came up with a card. "That's my agent's number," she pointed to it on the card. "He can usually find me."

Or cover for you. But Natalie forced a smile to her lips as she pocketed the card.

"Thank you for your time," she murmured, then moved away from the reservation desk. Erikka and her considerable luggage went in the opposite direction.

Matt found he had to lengthen his stride to keep up with Natalie. She always moved fast when she was agitated, he recalled. "You don't look very happy," he observed.

Natalie shot him a dirty look. "Why should I be happy? I've spent all day questioning people, and all I have is a dead end."

He'd gotten good at spinning information when it was necessary. "You could think of it as having ruled out several possibilities."

She stopped walking for a moment and gazed at him. He was looking at this in a far more positive light than she was.

"Since when did you become an optimist?"

Optimist was a lot better label than spin doctor, he mused. "Sometimes, in this line of business, you have to be."

They were in the lobby of the casino with its ever-present noise and crowds of people. This was where they should just come to a parting of ways. He knew that the right thing to do would be to let her go back to her home or the precinct or wherever it was she was going. But the frustrated disappointment in her eyes got to him.

He was never going to be over her, Matt thought, no matter what he told himself.

"Have you had lunch yet?" he asked.

An odd little smile came and went from her lips. "I haven't actually had breakfast yet." She'd heard the call about her sister's homicide come in just after hitting a fast-food restaurant. Three bites were all she'd had before her stomach rebelled. She'd thrown the rest away.

"We need to remedy that," Matt told her. "Come with me."

She began to follow, then stopped. Old habits died hard, but he had no right to take charge like that. "Why would I want to do that?" she challenged.

He took a couple of steps to cross back to her. "Because you've been working hard, and you haven't had anything to eat. You need to keep your strength up if you're going to play the part of a bulldog," he said matter-of-factly, then smiled. "Besides, The Janus just landed a first-class world-famous chef, and I'm told he makes a filet mignon that has you believing you've died and gone to heaven."

"I'm not interested in 'dying and going to heaven.' Or eating," she informed him. "What I'm interested in is—"

He finished the sentence for her. "Solving your sister's murder, yes I know. But you can't continue functioning indefinitely on an empty stomach," he insisted. Then he added, "Humor me."

It was the wrong thing to say. She didn't want to

humor him, she wanted to double up her fists and beat on him. She wanted this damn ache in her chest that came up each time she looked at him to go away. She wanted to have never laid eyes on him in the first place. Humoring him didn't even make the top one hundred on her list. "Why would I want to do that?"

"Because," he told her patiently, "if we're going to be working together, there's going to have to be some kind of give and take."

"There already was." The words spilled out, refusing to be dammed up any longer. "As I recall, I gave, you took—and then you threw it back at me."

Was that how she remembered it? "That wasn't the way it played out."

Her expression darkened, making him think of a thunderstorm over the desert. "Oh, wasn't it?"

He didn't want to go into it. Not here, not now. Not ever, actually. But she was forcing him to revisit his actions. "I did what I did for a reason, Natalie."

"Right. I believe the term is 'cold feet.' All the way up to the neck," she said sarcastically. "You suddenly realized that you were making a commitment, and it scared the hell out of you."

And why did it still hurt so much, all these years later? *Why aren't I over you, damn it?*

Someone jostled him. Matt hardly noticed. His entire attention was focused on the petite spitfire before him. The woman, if the gods had been kinder, who would have been his wife for several years now. Maybe even the mother of his children. "Is that what you think?"

"Yes," Natalie bit off. "That is *exactly* what I think."

He tried to take hold of her arms, but she shrugged him off. "You're wrong."

"Then what was your reason?" she challenged. "Why would you leave me that way without so much as a decent explanation?"

The answer was very simple. "Because if I gave you one, you would have tried to talk me out of it." He knew how she thought. In her place, he would have done the same thing. But he hadn't been in her place; he'd been in his and the action he took was necessary. "And what I did was for the best."

"Right. For the best," she mocked. "Whose best? Yours?"

"No." *Damn it, you little idiot, I did it because I loved you.* "Yours."

Lifting her chin, she tossed her head defiantly. Her short brown hair swayed from the movement. "I don't believe you. You're only saying that because you think it makes you out to be noble. Well, you're not. You're a coward," she spat out.

He took a firm hold of her shoulders. This time he didn't let her shrug him off. People were watching, and he didn't want this getting back to anyone.

"There's no point in arguing about it, Natalie. It's all in the past."

No, she thought. *Not all of it.* She only wished from the bottom of her heart that it was. But her feelings were very much alive and in the present. But that was her problem, not his.

"You're right," she replied in a monotone voice. "It is."

Touching her, even so slightly, had awakened so many feelings he was incapable of burying. He found himself not wanting her to leave. "About that lunch," he prodded.

Natalie stared at him. "How can you possibly think I'd want to break bread with you after—after—" Frustrated, she couldn't even find the words to finish her sentence.

"Because you need to keep up your strength," he repeated, "and you're going to have to eat sometime. Might as well be something good and on the house. C'mon." He nodded toward his right. "The restaurant is this way." Then, in case she was going to take offense at his leading again, he added, "I know you don't exactly know your way around The Janus."

There was no denying that. Still, she thought of turning on her heel and just walking away. Of letting Matt lead the way only to turn around at the restaurant to find that she had gone.

But in the end, she followed him.

This was business, strictly business, she told herself, and to act on her impulse would have been petulant. She did need Matt as long as her investigation took her into the heart of Montgomery's casino, and she had a feeling that somehow, some way, Candace's death was tied to her coming here last night.

The restaurant was only doing a moderate amount of business. It was the lull between lunch and dinner, and the pace was less hectic. The waitress came to take their order barely minutes after the hostess had shown them to a table.

Matt ordered the meal he'd mentioned earlier, then looked at Natalie who was perusing the oversized, velvet-covered menu. He didn't want to rush her. "Need more time?"

"No, let's get this over with." It was a cruel thing to say, but she felt herself sinking fast. Agreeing to eat with him had been a mistake. She could feel it in her bones. Natalie surrendered her menu to the waitress. "I'll have what he's having," she told the young woman.

"This isn't penance, you know," he told her, focusing on her first statement.

She looked at him pointedly. "Isn't it?" And then she raised her hand, as if to erase her words from an invisible chalkboard. "Sorry. I should be more professional than that. I usually *am* more professional than that. It's just that I never expected to see you again," she confessed. "And it's kind of thrown me."

That smile she'd always loved curved one half of his mouth. Unsettling her stomach. "Welcome to my world."

She shook her head. Ignoring him and the effect he had on her was getting to be impossible. But she was determined to go down fighting. "I'll pass, thanks," she said.

Several minutes passed. Despite the low level din around them, silence sat like an awkward, uninvited guest at their table, making them both feel uncomfortable.

It had never been like this, Matt thought. Not even from the very start. He took a stab at stereotypical conversation. "So what have you been doing with yourself, besides becoming a police detective?"

"That's about it," she said, her tone sealing the doorway that led into her life. "You? Where did life take you after you made your escape?"

"I didn't escape, Natalie," he pointed out patiently. "I did it for your own good."

Second verse, same as the first, she thought. "You

broke my heart for my own good," she mocked. "How do you figure that?"

There was no point in rehashing this. He couldn't go into specifics. "I don't want to get into it now."

"Of course not. Because you're making it up as you go along, and you're at a loss where to go next with this. News flash, I'm not buying. Any of it." Suddenly making up her mind, she stood up. "You know what? I'm not hungry."

He glanced to the side and saw the waitress approaching with their meals. "Why don't you stay a while?" he coaxed. "The waitress is coming with the food."

"You eat it. Or don't. Take it home in a doggie bag, or leave it here. I really don't care," she informed him. And with that, she stormed away.

All she wanted was to get out of the restaurant and the casino. And most of all, she wanted to get away from him.

Chapter 8

Natalie got as far as the other side of the Rainbow Room's entrance.

That was where Matt, after tossing down several bills on their table to cover the meal they weren't having, managed to catch up to her. Taking hold of her shoulders, he swung Natalie around to face him. Agitated, trying to deal with a host of jumbled emotions, he hadn't the faintest idea what he was going to say to her.

As it turned out, he didn't say anything.

Instead, he acted. Before he knew it, his instincts had taken over and completely overruled even a glimmer of common sense.

Matt brought his mouth down on hers before he could think better of it or try to stop himself.

He didn't want to stop himself.

Natalie struggled to pull back for less than half a

heartbeat. That's all the time it took for her longing and the hunger that was eating away at her to kick in. It surged through her veins like a runaway wildfire.

A bittersweet feeling of homecoming washed over her. Her mind, all but spinning out of control, just utterly shut down.

She was instantly propelled eight years into the past as a tidal wave of euphoria materialized out of nowhere, sweeping over her. Robbing her of her senses as she clung to him.

God she'd missed him. Missed the feeling that only he could create inside her.

Not that she let anyone else even try. She hadn't taken any relationship on a test drive since theirs had ended. Hadn't even allowed herself to become involved in one. It was far too much trouble. She'd become all work, no play. Relationships brought the specter of heartache with them, and her quota had been filled up for a lifetime.

Besides, Candace went out with enough men for both of them. There was no need for her to participate in this madness. So, for the last eight years, she'd been a virtual nun.

She wasn't acting like a nun now.

Deep down in her bones, Natalie knew she shouldn't be doing this, knew that this momentary aberration had just made her life a hundred percent harder. The amount of backpedaling that was going to be required to balance this out was going to be enormous.

But for this tiny island of time, it didn't matter to her.

All that mattered was riding this lightning bolt until it disintegrated beneath her feet.

Her arms tightened around his neck as her body sealed itself to his.

How had he managed to survive without this? Without her in his life? How had he managed to wake up each morning without finding her in his bed? Right at this moment, he hadn't a clue.

All his noble reasons for walking away from her turned to confetti and blew away in the wind like so many tiny squares of colored paper.

The feel of her body against his lit a fire in his veins. If they weren't out in the open like this, in a public place undoubtedly garnering attention, he would have swept Natalie up in his arms and taken her to his bed—or to any handy flat surface in a pinch. And succumbing to a moment of weakness, undo everything that had cost him so much to do in the first place. Leaving her hadn't even been the hardest part. Staying away was.

He still loved her.

If he'd harbored any doubts about that, they were gone now. Moreover, he was *still* in love with her, which was a completely different thing, and even he could understand the basic distinction now.

Lost in a fog, Matt was thinking more clearly than he had these last agonizing eight years. Passion filled him as he deepened the kiss.

Struggling to find the strength that she'd always prided herself on possessing, Natalie finally managed to wedge her hands against his chest and push Matt back.

"I had no idea you'd be that grateful for a doggie bag," she quipped hoarsely. Clearing her throat, she searched for her bearings as well as her voice. "I have to get going."

"Natalie—" he began, not really certain what it was that he wanted to say, only that he didn't want her to leave. Not yet. Not after he'd discovered that the passion between them was just as red-hot as ever. Maybe even more so.

She looked into his eyes and could see what he was thinking. Maybe because the same thoughts had raced across her mind.

"This doesn't change anything," she told him. "You still left me. Still hurt me. One kiss, no matter how hot, isn't going to erase that or mend any of the fences that you broke in your hurry to leave."

Reluctantly, Matt withdrew his hands from her waist. "I know."

But you could try, damn it. You could pretend to go through the motions. Tell me you were stupid and wrong. I'll listen.

Disappointment filled all the crevices that passion had just occupied. Matt had given up much too easily. Pulling herself together, Natalie glanced at her watch. She really did have to go. Her father had said something about wanting her present at the emergency family meeting he was calling. He'd mentioned four o'clock. Even if she drove with her siren on, she was going to be late.

But then, probably so were the others. No one in the Rothchild family was known for punctuality. She was the one who came the closest. Her stepsister, Silver, didn't even own a watch. But then, Silver was a rock star who moved to her own inner timepiece.

"I've got to go," she repeated, doing her best to sound cool and removed, even though her body temperature was still bordering on feverish, thanks to him. "Call me if you find out anything new that has to do with Candace," she instructed.

"Can I call you if I don't?" He hadn't meant to say that, but then, he hadn't meant to kiss her, either. An afternoon in her presence and all his control seemed to splinter into useless pieces.

"No."

The single word hung in the air as she turned on her heel and quickly walked away. Before she broke down and sealed her mouth to his again. He was an addiction. She'd only fooled herself into thinking she'd kicked it. It owned her.

To her surprise, half a beat later, Matt fell into place beside her. Annoyed, Natalie stopped walking. "Where do you think you're going?"

"With you," he replied simply. "You said you wanted me to work with you, remember?"

"I was referring to here, at The Janus." God knew she knew better than to have him around for any length of time beyond that. If she'd thought otherwise, her reaction to his kiss showed her just how weak she was when it came to him.

Matt shrugged in response to her answer. "Two heads are better than one."

A sarcastic remark hovered on her tongue, but never made it to her lips. In this case, the direct approach was better. "Not this time. I'm due at the house. My father is calling an emergency family meeting. Last I looked, you weren't family." *And whose fault is that?* she added silently.

"No," he agreed, "but maybe you could use the moral support."

She took it as a direct slam about her inner strength. Her eyes narrowed as she informed him, "I can handle my father."

His tone was nonconfrontational. He wasn't trying to get into a fight; he just wanted to help. When they'd been together, she was the one who'd wanted the kind of family that could only be found in human interest stories and carefully crafted feel-good movies.

"Never said you couldn't. But I hear that your new stepmother is a piece of work."

It was more than true but would have required some interaction on his part to learn for himself. "How long did you say you were back?"

"A couple of weeks." He guessed the reason behind her question. "Word gets around fast," Matt told her. *Especially when you ask questions*, he added silently.

"Thanks, but showing up with you would be like waving a red flag in my father's face. He doesn't really like you," she told him honestly.

Matt laughed shortly. "Yeah, I know. He made that pretty clear."

Her curiosity was instantly aroused. Just how full had those two weeks of his been? Had he come around the mansion without her knowing it?

"When?"

It was ancient history. Matt saw no reason to keep it secret any longer. "When he tried to buy me off."

That didn't make any sense. How could her father try to buy him off—and why would he?—if he had a cash flow problem? "I thought that your family supposedly lent my father money so he could get out of the financial hole he was in."

"That's now. I'm talking about before."

Natalie still wasn't following him. "How much before?"

He waved her question away. Maybe he shouldn't have said anything. "Doesn't matter."

"It does to me," she insisted. Her eyes pinned him in place. He wasn't going anywhere and neither was she until he answered her question. "*When* did my father offer you money?"

"Before." The expression on her face indicated that the single word did nothing to satisfy her curiosity, so he gave her more. "Eight years ago."

She felt her heart twist. She'd been better off not knowing. "That's why you left? Because he paid you off?" she asked incredulously. "Why you son of a bit—" Stunned, speechless, she raised her hand, ready to slap him across the face at the insult.

Matt caught her wrist, blocking contact. He knew that for simplicity's sake, he should hold his peace and let her believe the worst about him. But something wouldn't let him. He didn't want her believing that he had been bought off.

She could think he was a rotten human being, not worth her time and certainly not her love, but he didn't want her believing that she'd been cast aside for thirty pieces of silver.

"He *tried* to buy me off," he corrected. "Offered me a bit of money, actually. Back then, your father thought you were worth a quarter of a million dollars. Or maybe that was what getting rid of me was worth to him, I don't know. *But I didn't take it,*" he told her, emphasizing each word.

Confusion washed over her. "If you didn't leave because of the money—" A wave of jealousy struck. "Was there someone else?"

His eyes met hers. "You know better than that, Natalie."

"No, I don't." She sighed, weary of this uncertain feeling she'd been carrying around with her. It wouldn't matter if she didn't feel anything for him, but she did. She wanted answers. "I don't know better than that. *Why* did you leave me?"

There was nothing to be gained by this. "It's in the past, Natalie. Let it go."

If only she could. She'd tried hard enough, Lord knows, but she'd never gotten to that point. "I can't."

"Yes you can," he assured her firmly. This was an argument that was not about to be resolved. Not now, not ever. "If you don't want me coming with you, I won't," he agreed. "But you're going to be late if you don't get going."

He was giving her the bum's rush. Okay for now, she conceded reluctantly. But the gateway to the past had opened, if just a crack. She intended to wedge a crowbar into the tiny space and work it until she managed to open it up all the way.

But right now, she wasn't up to waging potentially futile battles, so she turned away without a word and just kept walking. Wishing with all her heart that she had never set eyes on Matt Schaffer. Or that, at the very least, he was still back in Los Angeles.

She didn't need this type of anguish on top of Candace's murder.

Candace.

She was her top priority. All that mattered was

finding out who killed her sister. Finding it out and bringing the bastard down. Whatever that took.

The wide, winding driveway before the mansion that she had once called home was packed with various expensive automobiles. Hers looked like a poor relation. Poor, but energy conscious, she thought wryly.

Recognizing the other vehicles, she realized that she was probably the last to arrive. Couldn't be helped, Natalie thought.

Couldn't it? a small, inner voice mocked. *You didn't need to kiss him back. Didn't need to stand there, talking to him, hanging on his every word the way you used to.*

Wow, now she was getting into an argument with herself. She was *really* losing it, Natalie thought.

Might as well go in and get this over with, she told herself.

When she rang the doorbell, Clive opened the door almost immediately. His expression appeared to be rigid until he saw it was her. And then he smiled, as if to say, "Ah, the normal one."

Natalie was about to ask the butler if he had stationed himself at the front door to get as far away from her family as possible when she was interrupted by a crash that sounded as if it was coming from the living room.

She raised her eyes quizzically up to Clive's face.

"That would be Master Ricky," he informed her, answering her unspoken question.

She frowned. Her half brother was a whirling dervish in search of an accident. A walking example of Attention Deficit Disorder, he constantly left chaos in his wake. Her father was at a loss how to handle him and his mother, Rebecca Lynn, refused to, believing the boy was better off if he was allowed to "express" himself.

This did not have the makings of a good outcome. "Dad called a family meeting, but I thought he meant adults only."

"Sadly, no," Clive told her. "Miss Rebecca Lynn wants Master Ricky present. She said something about Miss Candace being an object lesson for him."

On how not to live your life, apparently, Natalie thought. She couldn't help taking umbrage for Candace even though she felt that *no one* should attempt to emulate her late twin's lifestyle. But then everything connected with her stepmother seemed to irritate her to no end. The woman was like a rash for which there was no cure.

And her father seemed apparently blind to all of his wife's shortcomings.

Reluctant to walk into the lion's den, Natalie stalled for a moment. "How's the meeting coming along?" she asked the butler.

A whimsical half smile fleetingly played along the older man's lips. "No one has killed anyone yet."

"Always a good sign," Natalie agreed.

She unconsciously squared her shoulders, the way she always did when she was about to face Stepmother 2.0—which was the way she'd taken to referring to Rebecca Lynn. The thinly veiled animosity between the woman and the rest of the family had never really died down.

Too bad her father'd had that midlife crisis of his. Instead of buying a new sports car—he already had more than ten housed within his cavernous garage—he'd shed his second wife and married a woman young enough to be his daughter.

As far as she was concerned, Natalie had always preferred her father's last wife. Anne Worth Rothchild not only had pedigree but she had class. She was a lady in every sense of the word. In contrast, Rebecca Lynn was a grasping gold digger in every sense of *that* word.

Try as she might, she just couldn't get herself to like Rebecca Lynn, or her spoiled brat of a half brother. The only male heir in the family, Ricky, even at this tender age, radiated an aura of entitlement. Something, Natalie had no doubt, that had been taught to him by his mother. As someone who preferred to earn her own way, she found it absolutely repugnant.

Rebecca Lynn, Natalie was certain, was angling to be become the sole heir of the Rothchild fortune—once Harold Rothchild passed on.

Over her dead body, Natalie vowed. Not that she wanted *any* of the money. She just didn't want Rebecca Lynn getting her hands on it exclusively.

Natalie stopped just short of the living room. As a matter of fact, now that she thought about it, Candace's sudden death dovetailed nicely with their stepmother's plans. She'd bet her last dime that Rebecca Lynn would have liked nothing better than to have Candace's fate befall her and her two remaining siblings—her sister Jenna and stepsister Silver.

Can't tell the players apart without a scorecard, Natalie thought dryly.

Forcing herself to walk into the living room, Natalie saw her youngest sibling, Jenna, a self-assured twenty-five-year-old, currently heading up her own party planning business, crouching on the floor. She was busy picking up the pieces of what had been, until moments ago, a colorful vase from a trip to Hawaii.

The vase, for reasons unknown, had suffered Ricky's sudden displeasure. He would have gone on a rampage except that Harold had grabbed him.

Rebecca Lynn took immediate possession of their son, giving her husband a dark, censoring look. When that faded, it was replaced by a disdainful expression that took up residence on her perfectly made-up face.

Everything about the woman screamed "fake," Natalie couldn't help thinking. Rebecca Lynn's hair was currently a riotous cloud of red that could not be found anywhere in nature.

Silver, Anna's daughter, was sitting over in a corner, her expression barring anyone from attempting to approach her.

Ever the outsider. Although, from what she'd heard, in the last few years, Silver and Candace had actually gotten closer. However, the relationship had come about for all the wrong reasons, at least when it came to Candace, who had orchestrated the "friendship." Her twin had been extremely jealous of their stepsister. Silver, who was the same age as they were, had been born beautiful. With her mother's support, she had become a singing sensation by the time she turned sixteen. This after bringing the modeling world to its knees.

Silver, Natalie had always felt, could have become anything she wanted to be.

Looking around the room at the various members of her extended—or was that distended?—family, Natalie viewed them all with a disparaging eye and now just shook her head.

Talk about dysfunctional families. Hers would probably be up for some kind of prize—if there were prizes given for something like this.

His temper on edge because Rebecca Lynn had usurped his authority to discipline their son—again—Harold Rothchild looked at the latecomer with no attempt to hide his displeasure.

"So you've finally decided to grace us with your presence."

"Yup, finally," Natalie echoed in the same tone her father had just used.

So far, it'd been one hell of a day, and the rest of it wasn't shaping up to be any better. Making her way over to a chair that was near Silver, Natalie sat down. Her stepsister slanted a glance in her direction and nodded a silent greeting.

"All right," Natalie said, bracing herself for anything. "Let's get on with it."

Chapter 9

After Natalie took her seat, Harold didn't begin speaking immediately. Instead, he moved restlessly about the wide, cathedral-ceilinged living room like a caged man desperately searching for the way out and only coming up against dead ends.

Finally, his back to the baby grand piano his wife insisted on getting for their son, he said, "By now, you've all heard the news. Candace is dead."

"Is that why you called us here, to make sure we all knew?" Silver asked incredulously, raising her voice to be heard over her stepbrother's high-pitched whining. "There's been nothing else all over the news all morning," she pointed out.

"No, I called you together because we need to make funeral arrangements." His intense blue eyes shifted toward his wife.

Rebecca Lynn took immediate offense. "Hey, don't look at me. I've never handled things like that." A disdainful expression crossed her face. "Funerals give me the creeps."

Anything that required work gave the woman the creeps, Natalie thought. "Eloquently put," she murmured under her breath.

The general tone, since the words were not audible, earned her a dirty look from her stepmother. Bored and frustrated, Ricky's whining went up a notch. It was a little like walking into an insane asylum, Natalie realized.

Her father shifted his attention to her. "Natalie, exactly when can we expect to have your sister's body released?"

Her father was a reasonably intelligent man. He should have known the answer to that. And then it occurred to her that he expected her to have some kind of special pull at the coroner's office. The system didn't work like that.

"As soon as the ME finishes the autopsy and determines the cause of death," she replied patiently.

Horror registered on Silver's face. "You mean they're gutting her like some kind of fish?" she asked, not bothering to stifle a shiver.

"We know the cause of death," Jenna insisted. When Natalie looked at her, waiting, her younger sister declared, "Someone killed her."

Was everyone being deliberately obtuse, or had the fuse on her temper been shortened by Matt's sudden reappearance into her life?

"That's not the cause, that's the effect," Natalie explained, trying to at least sound patient. "If we know how, we might know who."

"What good is that going to do us?" Jenna asked sullenly. "She'll still be dead."

"No, Natalie's right," Harold cut in. "If we know who, then we'll know if killing Candace was personal—or personal." Was his daughter killed by a jealous lover, or someone who had it in for the family, for him, and this was their way of striking out?

A loud, exasperated sound escaped from Rebecca Lynn's lips. The other women in the room all looked in her direction. "Okay, you've officially gone off the deep end," she told her husband nastily.

"Don't go declaring him mentally incompetent just yet, Rebecca Lynn, although I'm sure that the thought is near and dear to your heart," Natalie said, a deliberately fake smile on her lips. Turning to her father, her "smile" vanished. "Just what do you mean by that?" she wanted to know.

Before Harold could say anything, Rebecca Lynn presented herself to him, her hands fisted at her waist. "Are you going to let her talk to me like that?" she demanded.

"Why not?" Silver interjected. "You talk to him like that all the time."

Whatever heated words Rebecca Lynn retorted to her stepdaughter were drowned out by Ricky's screams because no one was paying any attention to him. The next moment, he was scrambling up onto the piano bench and banging on the keys, adding yet another layer of dissonance to the cacophony.

Jenna's voice was almost shrill as she demanded, "Will someone *please* shut that kid up?"

Harold looked as if he was down to his very last

nerve as he implored his wife, "Rebecca, please, take him out of here."

Rebecca Lynn crossed her arms before her, a portrait of immovable stubbornness. Everyone in the room knew that there was nothing she hated more than to appear as if she was being ordered around. "Why don't you? He's your son, too."

Though she wanted nothing more than to just withdraw and go home, Natalie found herself coming to her father's rescue.

"In case you hadn't noticed, Dad's the one who called the meeting." Rebecca Lynn patently ignored her and picked up her all but empty second glass of gin and tonic. She'd raised it to her lips when Natalie added, "But I'll be happy to take my little brother out of here."

A look of alarm descended over Rebecca Lynn's face. Swallowing a curse, she set her glass down hard on the coffee table and quickly rose to her feet. Striding across the room, she grabbed her son by the hand and yanked him off the piano bench. The boy's screams only swelled in volume. Glaring at Natalie, Rebecca Lynn dragged her son from the room.

Ricky was heard kicking and screaming all the way up the stairs to his room.

If she knew Rebecca Lynn, Ricky was quickly going to become the housekeeper's problem, Natalie thought, feeling sorry for the older woman.

Harold took advantage of Rebecca Lynn's absence. His young wife had a way of intimidating him that neither Anna, nor June—the late, lamented love of his life—ever had. "Can't you put some pressure on this ME of yours?" he asked Natalie. "I want to get Candace buried and put this whole nasty business behind us as soon as possible."

"He's not my ME," Natalie pointed out, then realized something. "You're worried that this is just the beginning, aren't you?"

"What do you mean, just the beginning?" Confused, Jenna looked from her father to her sister. "Just the beginning of what?"

"Nothing," Harold dismissed Jenna's question much too quickly. The look he shot Natalie said that he'd told her what he had in confidence.

If she'd felt that this only involved Rebecca Lynn, she wouldn't have said a word in front of Silver and Jenna. But her father had given her the impression that this thing went beyond her grasping stepmother and her unruly half brother.

Natalie looked pointedly at her father, passionately wishing he had a backbone. "They have a right to know, Dad."

Jenna's eyes nervously shifted from her to their father. "Know what?"

Since her father still wasn't saying anything, Natalie took the matter into her own hands. "Dad thinks that the ring is cursed."

It still didn't make any sense. Jenna exchanged looks with Silver, who looked no more enlightened than she felt. "What ring?" Jenna wanted to know.

Again, Natalie waited for her father to say something. He didn't. So she did. "The Tears of the Quetzal."

The mention of the priceless diamond dissipated the fog Silver seemed to be encased in. They all knew that the gem was rumored to be theirs. Half the time, she thought it was all a myth, made up by her stepfather to court publicity.

"What does that have to do with Candace's—?" Silver stopped abruptly as the realization suddenly occurred to her. "Was Candace wearing the ring when she was killed last night?"

"Either the ring, or a damn good paste imitation," Natalie answered. But they all knew Candace. Her late twin couldn't abide fakes. She took great satisfaction in flaunting the real thing. The stone had certainly looked real enough on the casino tapes she'd viewed. "When they interviewed her on camera last night, just before she walked into The Janus, Candace was waving her hand around for all the world to see."

"Then anyone could have broken into her condo and killed her for it," Jenna speculated.

"Yes," Natalie agreed. "Except for one thing." The two women and her father looked at her, waiting. "Candace knew her killer."

"What makes you say that?" Jenna demanded, sounding almost hostile about the suggestion.

"There was no sign of forced entry," Natalie told them. "The room where they found her was a mess, as if she was trying to fight off whoever she'd chosen to bring home with her. But it was obvious that she was the one who had opened the door in the first place."

Harold sighed and sat down in the winged armchair that his wife had vacated. He closed his eyes wearily. "I always knew this was going to happen."

The nature of Natalie's job forced her to look beyond the obvious and delve deeper. She gave her father's words a different interpretation. He wasn't talking about her twin's lifestyle.

"You're talking about the curse, aren't you?" Harold seemed almost beaten down, and he made no answer. He merely lifted his shoulders in a half shrug before letting them fall again. The ring was part of family lore, but to her recollection, her father had never elaborated on it. "Just why is this ring supposed to be cursed?"

"There's no such thing as curses," Jenna snapped. She ran her hands up and down her arms even though the day had been unseasonably warm. "I wish you'd all just stop talking about it."

"It doesn't matter why," Harold told Natalie, his voice weary but firm. As far as he was concerned, the subject was closed. "It just is, Natalie. Let's leave it at that."

But she had no intention of tiptoeing around the subject because it seemed to upset her father and, for different reasons, Jenna. She didn't like unanswered questions.

Natalie tried to make him understand. "Sure it matters. Say, if it was originally stolen from someone, then we're looking at a revenge motive. If this is nothing more than some kind of 'curse' handed down through the ages, then we're looking for some kind of wraith or ghoul, and we're going to need to get ourselves a ghost buster."

It took Harold a moment to realize that she wasn't serious about the second half of her reasoning. He scowled at her. "This isn't funny, Natalie."

"No," she agreed. "Death never is." She studied his face. "Now, is there something more you want to tell us about this ring, Dad?"

There was no hesitation on his part as he barked, "No."

There was something else going on here, she could swear to it.

"Then why do you look like you've got something to hide?" she asked, trying her best to keep her voice neutral.

"Stop badgering my husband," Rebecca Lynn ordered as she walked back into the room. Ricky, mercifully, was nowhere in sight.

Natalie really hated the woman's high-handed manner. "He was our father before he was your husband, Rebecca Lynn," she informed her stepmother. Glancing at her father, she felt sorry for him. He suddenly looked a great deal older than his sixty years. "But, for now, I'll back off."

Harold attempted to flash a smile of thanks toward her, but the corners of his mouth hardly rose.

"We still haven't talked about Candace's funeral arrangements," he pointed out heavily, uttering each word as if it weighed a ton.

"Oh God," Rebecca Lynn moaned, rolling her brown eyes heavenward. "Just put her into the ground and be done with it."

Natalie instantly took offense for her late twin. Granted Candace had a myriad of faults, but she was dead and deserved respect. She threw up her hands in exasperation. "I'll take care of it, Dad," she told him.

Harold looked as if a huge boulder had been lifted off his shoulders. "You really will?"

"Yes, I really will." What choice did she have? She could see this "family meeting" degenerating into name-calling and buck passing. She didn't need to be part of that. "As soon as her body is released, I'll have Candace cremated and place her urn in the family crypt—beside Grandpa."

Silver suddenly spoke up. "What about a service?" she wanted to know.

That was easy enough to address. "We'll have a memorial service," Natalie told her. "Just for the family."

But even that drew an objection from Rebecca Lynn. Hostility entered her voice. "You're not planning to include that woman, are you?"

They all knew that "that woman" was Rebecca Lynn's way of referring to Anna Worth Rothchild, the ex-wife Harold had unceremoniously dumped in order to wed his current trophy wife.

"I most certainly am," Natalie informed her. She would have invited her former stepmother even if it hadn't irritated her present one. That it did was just icing on the cake. "Anna was like a mother to Candace."

Fuming, Rebecca Lynn spun around on her heel and looked at her husband, expecting him to back up her position. "Harold!"

She was unpleasantly surprised. "She's right," Harold replied. He looked like a mongoose that had accidentally fallen into a snake pit.

Rebecca Lynn refused to accept defeat. "But she wasn't her mother, was she?"

Her stepmother's high-handed tone finally managed to arouse Silver's ire. "If my mother wants to come, she can come," the child-star-turned-pop-diva spat out.

Rebecca Lynn glared at her stepdaughter, barely refraining from a bevy of ripe words. She knew she was outnumbered, but refused to admit she was outmaneuvered. Turning to Harold, she delivered her ultimatum with a dramatic toss of her head. Flaming red hair undulated all around her.

"If that woman comes to the service, Harold, then I won't."

"And miss a chance to be photographed by the paparazzi?" Natalie asked, feigned surprise. The look on her face told her stepmother that she was as transparent as a glass of water. "I sincerely doubt that, but the choice," she said pleasantly, "is yours."

Furious, Rebecca Lynn stormed out of the room, cursing them all to several levels of hell, each hotter than the last.

Harold merely shook his head. Though he was still under her thumb, his new wife had lost much of her charm for him. "You really shouldn't antagonize her like that, Natalie."

In response, Natalie smiled at him. "Rebecca Lynn makes it much too easy, and I have such few simple pleasures."

Harold didn't bother commenting. Instead, he asked, "How's the investigation going?"

As she started to answer, Natalie noticed Jenna edging closer, as if afraid she might miss something. That was a surprise, she thought. She would have expected that from Silver, who, thanks to Candace's deceptive machinations, thought of Candace as her friend.

With five years between them, Jenna and Candace had never known a close moment—again, thanks mainly to Candace. But then, Natalie reflected, maybe she'd misjudged her younger sister.

It wouldn't have been the first time her judgment had failed her, Natalie reminded herself.

Her father was looking at her expectantly. Did he

think she was some kind of a magician? "It's only been a day, Dad. I'm still following leads."

An impatient sound escaped his lips. "And you'll tell me when you find out who?"

When, not *if.* He either had a lot of faith in her or was playing the guilt card. Most likely the latter, Natalie decided.

A spasmodic smile came and went from her lips. "You'll be the first to know."

"Do you have any, you know, suspects?" Jenna asked.

The immediate male population. Out loud, Natalie said, "Someone the camera caught Candace smiling at."

Jenna's eyes widened. Natalie thought she heard her stop breathing. "Who?"

"Unfortunately, the person was *off* camera, so we don't know. But I'm doing my best to try to piece it all together."

"If anyone can do it, my money's on you, Nat," Jenna said.

Natalie said nothing. She only wished she had half the confidence that Jenna had.

Natalie remained at the mansion another hour or so after her sister's departure. Her father detained her with his incessant questions about the murder investigation, while stressing how crucial it was to locate the mystical ring that was all but a third party in all this. Finally disentangling herself from him, she went home to see if she could make any more headway with the copies of the tapes that Matt had given her.

It took a little doing before she could pull them up on her own computer. The computer, she had long ago decided, was not her friend.

But she did what she could and made progress using baby steps.

Engrossed, Natalie didn't hear the doorbell at first. And then, when the repeated noise finally penetrated her consciousness, she decided to ignore it.

But whoever was ringing the doorbell patently refused to be ignored. It went on pealing, setting her teeth on edge.

With a sigh, Natalie rose from her desk and crossed to the front door.

She paused only long enough to get her service revolver.

In her experience, it was never a given who was on the other side of the door, and she had to admit that her father had looked spooked enough about this curse business to at least make her take a small measure of precaution. And even if she didn't believe in curses, as a police detective she knew that she was a living, breathing target for some wacko looking to even some imaginary score.

"Who is it?" she called out as she approached the door.

"Delivery boy."

Was that—?

No, it couldn't be. It couldn't be Matt. He didn't know where she lived. She'd sold the condo where they'd been together, bought this place and took strict care to remain unlisted and off everyone's radar. This was just her imagination, working overtime.

Reaching the door, she said, "I didn't order anything."

"Look, lady, all I know is that your name's on this bill."

Definitely Matt. She'd know his voice anywhere. But what was he doing here?

Still holding her weapon, its safety off, Natalie opened the door.

The gun was the first thing Matt noticed. "You can put that away," he told her. Opening his jacket with one hand, he held the side out for her inspection. "I'm unarmed."

After a long pause, she finally put up her weapon. But she still held the door ajar and made no move to get out of the way. "What are you doing here, Matt?" she wanted to know.

"Bringing you the dinner you abandoned earlier." He held up the pristine white bag. The Janus's logo was on the side. "Knowing you, I figured you didn't take the time to stop and eat."

Her eyes narrowed. *I'm not the person I used to be. The one whose heart you stomped on.* "You *don't* know me," she informed him tersely.

He looked as if he was willing to give her the benefit of the doubt. "Did you stop to eat?"

She realized she could lie and be done with it, sending him on his way. Why she didn't was beyond her. "No, I didn't."

His mouth curved. "I rest my case. And I'd like to rest this—" he indicated the large bag he was holding "—because it's getting hot."

She frowned, then stepped back, opening the door wider. "I can't help feeling like I've just opened my door to the Trojan horse."

Walking in, Matt grinned at her. Her stomach tightened instantly. "Don't worry, there're no tiny men wearing armor in the bag."

It wasn't tiny men in armor she was worried about. It was the very large, very real one who was walking into her house that concerned her.

Chapter 10

Natalie pointed Matt toward her kitchen.

He crossed to it quickly, setting the bag down on the table. Then he went to the sink and ran cold water over his hands to take the sting out.

"So how did the family meeting go?" he asked in a conversational tone. When she didn't answer, he looked at her over his shoulder. Natalie returned her weapon to its holster, putting the safety back on. "I figured you might want to vent a little."

She handed Matt a dish towel to dry his hands. "Why are you being so nice?" she inquired.

Taking the towel, he dried his hands, then left the towel on the counter. "Why do you always have to question everything? Just accept what's happening."

Natalie folded the towel and put it back in its place.

"I did that once and had my heart ripped out of my chest. I'm a little more cautious these days."

His eyes were drawn to her hands. "You're not married." It was a rhetorical statement. He already knew that.

Her first instinct was to hide her hands behind her back, but she didn't. Instead, she took out a handful of napkins from a supply she kept in the pantry.

"No."

"Were you?" he pressed, watching her move about the kitchen. "Ever?"

She shot him an impatient look. "Did you bring dinner or a questionnaire?" And then she sighed as she took out two tall glasses from the cupboard. "No," she answered stiffly. "I've never been married. I decided that the male species was just too unstable to build a relationship with or to trust."

He had the good grace to wince. "Ouch."

Moving Matt aside, she opened the bag he had brought and saw that there were two large covered containers inside it instead of just one. Natalie raised her eyes to his face.

"There're two portions here."

His expression was the soul of innocence. "I didn't eat, either."

Removing first one container, then the other, she placed them both on the table.

"And they're still warm."

He nodded interceptively. "They do some pretty magical things in that Rainbow kitchen."

"The waitress was bringing these out eight hours ago—when I left," she reminded him. Natalie opened the containers one at a time, and a small cloud of steam emerged from each.

He spread his hands wide, adding a little shrug at the end. "Like I said, magical."

Yeah, right. "You ordered fresh portions, didn't you?"

Why was he going through all this trouble for someone he'd walked out on? Someone he made no effort to contact in the last eight years? Why was he messing with her like this?

Matt held his hands up in front of her, his wrists touching as if he expected to be led off in handcuffs. "I always loved that steel-trap mind of yours. Take me away, Officer Rothchild."

She had a very real urge to double up her fist and punch him in the arm.

"That's Detective Rothchild," she corrected, then shook her head and blew out a loud sigh, hoping that it would sufficiently distract him from seeing the involuntary smile on her lips. But Natalie could see by his grin that he hadn't missed it. "Idiot," she pronounced.

There was no arguing with that. "In more ways than one," he assured her.

This time, her sigh was weary. "Why are you talking in riddles?"

The serious lapse was gone. "I thought women liked men of mystery."

Oh no, he wasn't going to suck her into an exchange of banter. She wanted some kind of answers.

"We were way past the 'liking' stage once, Schaffer." Taking out two forks and steak knives, she deposited them on the table, then took down two dinner plates to join them. "You were the one who left, not me."

He watched her move around, taking in every fluid motion. A deep-seated longing took root. "We can still be friends."

"No," she replied emphatically, "we can't. I'm not one of those broad-minded women who thinks that turning her exes into 'pals' is the adult thing to do."

He looked confused. "Then why did you ask me to help you?"

Natalie deposited the contents of one container onto a plate, then followed suit with the other. She flung the empty containers into the lined garbage pail beneath her sink before answering.

"Because, whether I liked it or not, I needed your help. You got me the tapes—thank you," she tagged on as an afterthought, the two words all but burning her tongue as she uttered them.

He knew that cost her, and he couldn't help being amused. "You're welcome."

"And having you there got me an 'audience' with your boss." She needed to rule her father's chief rival out. "I can bluff my way through this, but the fact of the matter is, I'm a pariah as far as investigating my sister's murder goes."

"You *are* too close," he pointed out.

So much for his taking her side in this, she thought bitterly.

"No one else is close enough," she countered. "It's a high-profile case, but let's face it, we're not exactly without dead bodies in this town. This isn't Parker and Davidson's only homicide."

"And it is yours?" Matt questioned. He was well aware of the fact that the LVPD's homicide division was understaffed.

There were open cases on her desk but none that mattered to her as much as this one. Besides, she couldn't work on them off the job.

"I'm on bereavement leave," she reminded him, "so, yes, right now it is." Moving from the table, she crossed to the refrigerator to get a diet cola for herself. "You want a soda? Or something a little stronger?" she added, recalling that he didn't much care for diet drinks and that was all she stocked in the way of soda.

He opted for the latter. "A little stronger."

She waited for him to follow up his choice with something more specific. "What?"

You.

Matt wondered how she'd respond if he'd said that out loud. Probably tell him to go to hell. But he was there already, because seeing Natalie and not having her was much harder on him than he'd ever thought it would be.

"Vodka, if you have it. Or beer," he amended. From where he sat, he could see into the refrigerator. There were a couple of bottles in the door. "Anything, really. I'm easy."

She turned around, holding two bottles of beer in her hands.

"No," she replied. "You're not." Taking a bottle opener out of the drawer, she flipped the cap off one bottle and then the other. Natalie handed him the first one and rather than sit down, she remained standing over him. "What are you doing here, Matt?"

He avoided her eyes. He'd gotten good at lying, but he never could to her. Which was why he'd left a note in his wake rather than stay to talk to her.

"I told you, I wanted to bring you dinner."

Liar. "Is that the only reason you're here?" she pressed. "To make sure I eat?"

This time he did raise his eyes to hers. "That, and because I still like looking at you, Natalie. You are still one of the most beautiful creatures God ever created."

Wow…he sure did know how to press her buttons. How to torture her.

"I can't do this," she told him suddenly. "I can't do this."

He didn't follow her. "Do what?"

"I can't sit here opposite you and pretend I don't feel anything, that I don't still—"

She didn't get to finish.

Pushing his chair back, Matt was on his feet, sinking his hands into her hair, tilting her face up to his. Immobilizing her lips by feverishly pressing his own against them.

The explosion that occurred within her came just as suddenly. The bottle slipped from her fingers, hitting the floor. It didn't break, but sent up an amber wave that managed to christen both her bare legs and the legs of his slacks.

The splash barely registered on the perimeter of her mind. She was otherwise occupied.

The heat that flared between them swiftly mushroomed in depth and intensity.

Eight years.

Eight years she'd gone without making love. Without feeling like a woman. Everything within her rallied forward to rekindle that old, familiar feeling of sheer ecstasy.

Logically, Natalie knew she should be pushing him away. Knew she should be calling him names and accusing him of all sorts of things, of using her vulnerability to satisfy some inner selfish need of his to see that she still wanted him. Right now, he had all the proof he could want—and didn't that go a long way toward feeding his ego?

But even so, she couldn't make herself stop, couldn't pull back. Couldn't even get her hands to stop their frantic movements as she yanked away at his clothing, stripping him of his shirt, his slacks, his underwear, anything and everything that could get in the way of what she so desperately needed.

And she was thrilled to feel his hands on her, doing the exact same thing. Making her clothes vanish and her body sizzle.

Within seconds, Matt had her on the kitchen floor, his hands and mouth making love to every inch of her with the enthusiasm and zeal of a dying man in the desert who had stumbled onto an oasis filled with water and fig trees.

His mouth was everywhere, setting her skin on fire.

Natalie moaned and twisted beneath his lips, eagerly scrambling toward the light, toward that supreme burst of incredible sensation that she hadn't experienced for so long.

For forever.

It was weak of her and she knew it, but she didn't care. All she wanted in this moment in time was to stop feeling like a member of the living dead. And only Matt could do that for her. Could make her feel, however briefly, alive again. He was the only man she had ever wanted. The only man she had ever loved.

How had he managed? Noble intentions or not, how had he been able to stay away from her for so long when she was life itself to him? Not to mention that kissing Natalie's lips was the single biggest turn-on he'd ever experienced.

The more he kissed her, the more he wanted her.

He'd known it would come to this. The second he had agreed to return to Vegas to oversee the overhauling of the security system at The Janus, he'd known that somehow, some way, he would end up here, making passionate love with Natalie.

And feeling whole again.

He hadn't fully realized the extent of just how diminished he'd felt all these years without her until just now.

He didn't want this to ever end.

He didn't want to live another day without having her in it. Nothing had changed, but he so fervently wanted it to.

Unable to hold back, pivoting on his elbows, Matt slid into her. He caught his breath, feeling her quicken around him as he entered.

Matt groaned, struggling to hold back for just a few more moments. He was determined to bring Natalie up with him, determined to have her share the moment. Because it had never been about self-satisfaction, not even the first time. It had always been about her, about them, about the magic they created together.

Feeling Natalie begin to frantically move beneath him, Matt locked into a rhythm, going faster and faster as the ever evolving sensation urged him on to race to the top of the mountain, then seized him in its grip.

He heard Natalie cry out his name, felt her arching beneath him to absorb every nuance of the climax he'd brought to her.

His heart surged.

With every fiber in his being, Matt struggled to prolong the feeling, to postpone, as long as humanly possible, the dizzying descent back to earth. And to reality.

But even as the euphoria began to softly loosen its hold on him and slip away, Matt held her tightly to him. Just glorying in the feel of her beside him.

"You tip every delivery boy this way?" he murmured the question against her temple, his lips brushing against her hair. "Because if you do, you might be onto something."

Her heart still hammering the last stanza of the "Anvil Chorus," Natalie turned her body into his. His playful mood was infectious. "I was a born-again virgin until just now."

One eyebrow arched as he looked at her quizzically. "Born-again virgin?"

That was the way she'd come to think of herself. "I haven't been with anyone in eight years. So I figured that pretty much qualifies me as a beginner if not born-again virgin altogether. So I figured..." She let her voice trail off as she shrugged.

The sound of Matt's laughter echoed around the room and brought a burst of sunshine into her soul. The way it always had in the past. There was something about the sound that lifted her spirits and coaxed a smile from her lips. Even on those occasions when she didn't think there was anything to smile about.

Matt laced his hands together around her shoulders, holding her close to him. Content to remain like that all night long. He didn't have to be anywhere until nine the next morning, and there was nowhere else he wanted to be than here.

"So where does this put us, other than the floor?"

She drew in a breath. This was where she could reclaim her dignity. But the only thing she resorted to was the truth.

"Nowhere," she answered. "I'm assuming that whatever made you leave is still there, still a reality that you're dealing with."

He thought of the phone call from his brother, the frantic one that demanded he "do something. Make it right." Those were always Scott's words when he asked—demanded really—that he come to his rescue. Pointing out that if Scott had behaved, if he'd kept his pants on to begin with, there'd be no need for his brother to put him on the spot and "make it right."

He'd resigned himself to the fact that Scott would always be Scott. A leopard whose spots didn't change with time.

But, like it or not, Scott was family. *His* family and he couldn't just stand by and let something happen to Scott, no matter how tempted he was to hit his older brother upside the head in hopes of knocking some kind of sense into him.

Not likely, Matt thought.

Scott's world revolved around Scott and no one else—until he feared retaliation because of some stupid transgression on his part. Like the time his brother bedded Candace.

"Yes," he told her quietly, "nothing changed."

She really was an idiot, wasn't she? And now Matt knew it as well as she did. Doing her damndest to keep her tears in check, Natalie began to rise.

She was surprised when he wouldn't let her. Matt

tightened his hold on her, making her stay put. She raised her arm to push him away when he stopped her cold with his words.

It was time to tell her. He didn't want her imagination conjuring up false, negative theories, didn't want her believing something that wasn't true. Believing that he didn't love her. Natalie deserved to know the truth.

"You want to know why I left that morning?"

She stopped struggling. "Considering that I've asked you several times since yesterday, I'd say you just made a very clever leap to a conclusion."

Her sarcasm didn't affect him. He knew it was her shield, her way of keeping the pain at bay. Hopefully what he had to tell her would minimize the pain. "I left for you."

So he kept trying to tell her. "Oh, please." She rolled her eyes. He was more clever than that. "You're going to have to do better than that. That's right up there with that old saw, 'it's not you, it's me.'"

"It *was* me," he insisted, then amended. "Or more accurately, it was my family. And it still is my family. The morning I left, I'd gotten a call from Scott. He was in some kind of trouble—"

"What kind?" she asked.

"It doesn't matter. What mattered was I realized that he and the rest of them would always keep pulling me back in. I've tried to separate myself from my family, to go my own way and just pretend they didn't exist, but—"

"They're still your family," Natalie supplied with a sigh. How well she knew that feeling. There'd been a time when she'd considered changing her last name. But that still wouldn't change who she was, or that they were her family. "Welcome to *my* world." She propped herself up on her elbow and looked down at him. Was it as simple as that? He'd pulled away from her because of his family? "Look, if you can put up with mine, I can put up with yours."

There was one basic flaw with that philosophy. "Yours doesn't kill people. Doesn't have people after them because they want to 'even' some score. I left you because I couldn't put you in that kind of danger just because I couldn't live without you."

"Too late," she declared. "Candace's murder just changed the rules of the game. There might be a very good chance that my sister was killed because someone was looking to get even—" Natalie abruptly stopped, her eyes widening as she just now recalled the end of his statement. "Did you just say you couldn't live without me?"

Maybe he shouldn't have told her. But now that he had, he wasn't about to say that he hadn't meant what he'd said. "Yes."

Feeling her heart beginning to accelerate, Natalie struggled to sound calm. "And how long has this been going on?"

He told her the simple truth. "Since the first moment I laid eyes on you."

If she was smart, she wouldn't believe him. But she'd already proven she wasn't smart. Because she was lying on her kitchen floor, naked—and wanting more.

Natalie laughed softly and shook her head as she moved closer to him. "You know, for a monk—" which was what he'd alluded his life was like "—you have a very smooth tongue." Each word was separated by a small, flittering kiss as her lips lightly grazed different parts of his anatomy. She felt him stiffening against her and smiled. "Encore?"

"I thought you'd never ask," he told her just before he brought her up to his level and sealed his mouth to hers.

Chapter 11

She was getting nowhere.

And the worst part about it, she was getting there in slow motion.

Natalie could feel her frustration mounting, governing her every waking moment—and keeping her from finding sleep for more than a few fitful minutes at a time.

Thanks to Matt's connections, over the last week she had been able to question anyone at the party who might have seen her twin interact with people at the gala. The upshot of that had been that, other than posing for the cameras and exchanging a few words with reporters, Candace hadn't really talked to anyone besides Luke Montgomery and Matt himself.

Matt, at least, didn't seem to have anything to hide. She wasn't all that sure about Luke yet.

Not only had Matt covertly gotten her a copy of the

tapes that her own department had commandeered but he had also given her Montgomery's guest list under the guise that it was public knowledge who had attended. For her part over this last week, Natalie had judiciously gone down that list, calling or going to see as many people on it as she physically could.

All she had managed to garner over and over again was not information but condolences. For the most part, once she identified herself as Candace's twin, the people she spoke with focused on the words "so sorry for your loss." When it came to saying something kind or flattering about Candace, there was far less enthusiasm. The kindest thing that anyone could offer was that her sister was "a woman who knew how to have a good time."

Natalie sincerely doubted that. What Candace had actually done was try desperately to numb herself, to party to the point of exhaustion. She'd gone at an almost frenzied pace from man to man in hopes of finding *the* man, never realizing that relationships did not spring out of the ground fully formed but actually took work. Constant work. With luck, that work made the relationship better. Made it golden.

Candace wasn't the only one to be disappointed, she thought now, sitting at her desk in the semidarkness in the room she used as her office.

That was the kind of relationship, eight years ago, she would have sworn she had with Matt. And yet, look how wrong she'd been about that. The first perceived bump in the road and he had vanished without a trace. Never mind that the bump originated with him and not her…and that he'd done it supposedly for selfless reasons. What it came down to in her mind was that he hadn't thought enough of her to ask how she felt about this sacrifice he was making. He hadn't even bothered to ask if she agreed with his reasoning.

If he had, she would have talked him out of it. Then. But now, there was no point in going over old ground. Too much time had passed, too many years of hurt that hadn't been remedied. Despite the lovemaking that first night—and the second and the third and all the rest that followed—the path they were on had been set. Try as she might, she didn't see them going off into the sunset together.

Besides, he hadn't said anything about getting together, not in any sort of permanent way. For the last week they *had* gotten together every evening to discuss their combined lack of headway in this investigation. Somehow these discussions always culminated with them going to bed together. Natalie mused that their insatiable desire for one another was most likely the result of an attraction that should have come with its own asbestos container because, left out in the open, it was as combustible as nitroglycerin.

So here she was, slipping out of her bed, padding in bare feet into the next room, dressed in a longer-than-usual-peasant blouse she'd pulled on and nothing more. Restless, her mind going in three different directions at once, Natalie wanted to look over her notes in order to see if there was something she'd somehow missed. Anything, no matter how tiny, that might finally send her off in the right direction.

She'd been at it less than twenty minutes when she became aware that she was no longer alone in the room. Matt had come up behind her.

The next moment, he lifted her hair away and pressed

a kiss to the back of her neck. "Bed's cold without you," he murmured.

His breath was warm on her skin, sending shivers down her spine.

"This is April in Vegas. Nothing is cold in Vegas in April." She struggled to sound coherent. She would've thought that after the torrid session they'd had together, she couldn't be aroused again so soon.

But she could and she was.

"Relatively cold compared to before," Matt amended. As he spoke, he placed his hands on her bare shoulders.

It was a possessive gesture she found oddly comforting. She never did think clearly around him, Natalie mused.

"Have a sudden inspiration?" he asked, looking over her shoulder at her notes.

With effort, she focused on what had drawn her out of bed.

"I wish." Natalie sighed. "I don't even know if Candace was killed and the ring was stolen to make it look like a robbery, or the ring was the object of the crime and she was killed when she wouldn't give it up."

"Does it matter?" There was an ironic tone to his voice and she knew what he meant. That either way, the outcome was that Candace was dead.

"It might help me figure out who did it," she explained. "If Candace picked up someone and brought them home, then that explains why the door wasn't jimmied and points to the killer being a stranger. If it was someone she knew, she opened the door because of that—and whoever killed her did it for personal reasons."

Matt took her argument a step further. "Maybe the 'personal' reasons was that he—or she," he inserted although it was obvious to Natalie that he really didn't think that a woman was responsible for Candace's death, "felt the ring actually should belong to them and not Candace."

That was an odd thing to say. "I thought the ring was always in our family."

"I heard a rumor to the contrary the other day."

Natalie was immediately intrigued. Swinging around to look up at him, her mouth dropped open. She hadn't realized that Matt hadn't put anything on when he'd come looking for her. Her present position put her at a definite disadvantage as far as clear thinking went. Clearing her throat, she rose from the chair, doing her best to keep her eyes on his.

"Why didn't you say anything earlier?" she wanted to know, her voice quavering just a little.

They'd gotten into it pretty hot and heavy almost from the moment he'd walked in the door. She'd been on his mind the entire day. By the time he'd come over, all he'd wanted to do was make love with her until he dropped from exhaustion.

"Earlier I was occupied," he told her.

No, she wasn't going to allow herself to get side-tracked. Not this time.

"This is important," she insisted, hitting his shoulder with the flat of her hand.

He merely grinned. "So was what I was doing earlier," he answered, before returning to the subject at hand. "Besides, it *was* only a rumor, and I hadn't heard anything to back it up."

Still, it was a new idea, a possible new direction to go in. "We need to follow that up."

She remembered the note her father had told her he'd gotten. A note that seemed to threaten all of them. She'd kept that little tidbit from Matt on the pretext that she didn't want him to worry. Now her father's fear had gotten legs.

"If someone thought the ring belonged to him, or was stolen from his family, well, that could be motive enough to kill Candace when she wouldn't surrender the ring—" She caught her breath as she felt Matt slip his hand up along her thigh. "What are you doing?"

"Sliding my fingers along the softest, most tempting piece of flesh I've ever had the good fortune to touch," he told her seductively.

Her pulse began to scramble. "I can't think when you do that."

"That's the whole idea," he admitted. Taking her hand, he began to draw her from the room. "Come back to bed, Natalie. It's three in the morning. The only people who are up at this hour are the gambling addicts and the pit crews who make their living off the addicts. We'll pursue this angle in the morning," he promised her. He pressed another kiss to her temple. "Right now, all I want to pursue is you."

Damn but he could reduce her to a quivering mound of jelly in an instant. "That would be assuming that I was on the run."

The grin on his lips grew wider—and all the sexier for it. He was already making love to her with his eyes. "Yeah."

She could feel the heat radiating from his body. Encompassing her. Making her yearn for contact. "I'm not running."

"Even better," he murmured, closing his arms around her and pulling her to him.

Damn it, she was supposed to be concentrating on finding Candace's killer, not surrendering to a man with whom she had one hell of a past and no obvious future.

What was she thinking?

That was just it, she wasn't thinking. She was feeling. Feeling an entire cauldron of emotions that were swirling madly through her.

And then, while her mouth was still sealed to his, she felt herself being lifted up in the air. Lifted and carried back to her bed.

The journey, punctuated with a myriad of hot, passionate, open-mouth kisses, was slow going. But half the fun, she knew, was in getting there.

By the time they did, he had her so worked up that she was all but ready to attack him.

The passion escalated to heights she didn't think could be achieved, especially with someone who knew her the way Matt did.

She knew that in the not-too-far distance, the inevitable waited. Matt would leave again, and she would let him go. Because he felt that ultimately they didn't belong together, and she had too much pride to beg him to reconsider.

But for now, they had this little piece of paradise together, and she was going to make the very most of it for as long as she possibly could. She knew she was living on borrowed time, and it made every moment that much sweeter, that much more precious.

Matt sat on the bed, watching Natalie get dressed, silently marveling that such a simple act could exude such poetry at the same time. "I could come with you, you know."

Natalie slipped on a pair of black pumps. Her entire outfit was as tasteful and subdued as Candace's had always been flamboyant and scintillating.

Her eyes met Matt's in the mirror above the bureau as she put in a pair of diamond studs.

"I know. But it's better all around if you don't." She was aware that the answer she'd given him wasn't the one Matt wanted to hear, even though he didn't challenge her on it. Feeling guilty because he was being so nice about it, she tried to explain. "Seeing you is going to remind my father that he owes your family money and—"

Natalie abruptly stopped talking. What she was saying was making Matt's point for him, or at least part of it. He'd told her that he felt they couldn't make a go of it because of their families. That his would always keep reeling him in. That, no matter what he did on his own, he would always be thought of as part of the Schaffer family, a family who had underworld ties and who poisoned everything it touched.

He hadn't wanted their reputation to touch her.

She'd stopped talking so suddenly, he thought something was wrong. Matt got up off the bed and crossed to her.

"What's the matter?"

"Nothing." She forced a smile to her lips in an effort

to convince him that everything was fine. "If you want to come to the memorial service, then come," she said, inviting him. And then she added, "I'd like that." Her eyes swept over him. He was dressed in the suit he'd worn last night. It was light gray with a dark blue shirt to set off his eyes. He looked much too vibrant for a memorial service. "Do you have a dark suit?" He gave her a look that all but said, *You have to be kidding.* "Okay, then," she decided out loud. "If you're serious about wanting to be with me, then yes, I'd love to have you at Candace's memorial service." She tried not to think about her father's reaction to seeing Matt there.

"Not that I'm trying to jinx this, but what just changed your mind?"

She gave him an innocent look as she spread her hands wide. "I'm female."

He laughed then and brushed a quick kiss against her lips. "Yeah, I noticed."

It took Matt less than a half hour to get ready, a fact that left her in more than a little awe, especially since part of that time included driving over to his place in order to change into a navy-blue suit.

"Approve?" he asked her as he got back into her vehicle.

"Approve," she replied with a nod and a smile. And so, she added silently, would every woman over the age of five and under the age of one hundred. If they had a pulse, they would definitely approve of the handsome man sitting beside her.

Her father, however, would be a different story. Driving to the small chapel on the cemetery grounds where the service was to be held, Natalie braced herself.

It had been years since she had sought or needed parental approval, but she still hated confrontations.

They weren't the first ones in the chapel. Her father and his wife, her stepsister and younger sister were already there.

She was aware of the looks she was getting from her family the moment she walked through the chapel doors with Matt walking beside her. Jenna's face registered first surprise, then looked pleased. Silver just looked stunned. Natalie was well aware that her famous stepsister was sizing up the man who was with her. Silver wasn't Candace, she didn't see every man as a possible key to happiness, but she made no secret of the fact that she did like a good, decent specimen of manhood when she saw one.

Daggers and hostile glares came her way courtesy of her father and his trophy wife. Most likely for different reasons, Natalie surmised, pretending not to notice either of them.

The minister she'd engaged for the service was at the podium. Their eyes met and Natalie nodded, giving him the signal to begin even though the chapel was only half full. She was well aware of the fact that Candace had so-called friends who thought that watches were a conspiracy by the government to entrap them in small, confining boxes that were dictated by the sweeping hands of a clock.

The upshot was that half of the "friends" she'd invited weren't here. She figured it was either because they'd forgotten the day, because they didn't want to acknowledge the fact that a life force like Candace was actually gone—or because they simply didn't care.

All Natalie knew for sure was that the bottom line was they weren't here and somewhere, wherever Candace was, she was disappointed at the relatively small showing.

Had she made this service public, Natalie was certain the paparazzi would have come out in force. That might have been enough to lure out the so-called friends who weren't here now.

Part of her almost felt that she should have done that. Because this was for Candace, not her. But in the end, she decided that her twin's life had been a three-ring circus for years and not in a good way. Her death shouldn't be allowed to follow that same path.

It was a short service.

When Natalie delivered the eulogy, she tried very hard to concentrate on only the good moments and spoke, for the most part, about Candace's generous heart when they were growing up together. It was a life, she concluded, cut short much too soon because she wanted to believe that the best was yet to come for Candace.

Afterward, a few of her friends spoke, saying they would miss her at parties and that she left very big shoes to fill. There was not much to say after that. Natalie was painfully aware that her father said nothing. At one point, he looked as if he was about to stand up, but Rebecca Lynn had linked her arm through his, even while they were seated, and she restrained him from rising. With a shrug, he remained where he was.

As the participants filed by the minister on their way out of the small church, Natalie realized that her father had brought his housekeeper with him. It was she who was in charge of Candace's two children. With a boy tethered to each hand, the woman managed to keep the boys in check. Mick and David looked oddly subdued, as if they understood what was happening.

In her heart, she sincerely hoped not. Funerals and memorial services were no place for children. Natalie noticed that her half brother was mercifully missing from the service.

Bending down, Natalie looked from one boy to the other. She smiled at them. "You guys okay?" she asked, doing her best to sound upbeat.

Two mop-heads bobbed up and down as they mumbled, "Uh-huh."

What was going to become of them? she wondered. She doubted that her father was going to allow the boys to move in with him and that would mainly be the fault of the empty-headed witch of the west. Rebecca Lynn would not welcome children who were not her own.

She was tempted to claim the boys herself, but she was realistic. Because of the nature of her work, she knew she wouldn't be allowed to take them in or adopt them. The job called her away at odd times of the night and day. It was certainly not the most stable environment for two little boys.

But there was time enough to worry about that later, she told herself. Rising to her feet again, she slanted a glance toward Matt. For now, she had more than enough on her plate.

"May I see you for a moment, Natalie?" her father requested, his voice taking on that formal tone that, as a child, used to tell her that she was in trouble.

She turned to Matt. "I'll only be a minute," she

promised. He nodded and stepped back, after saying, "Sorry for your loss, Mr. Rothchild."

Harold made no acknowledgment that he even heard him speak. "What were you thinking?" her father demanded the moment Matt stepped away.

She was still angry at him for not getting up to say something, however small, in tribute to Candace. For God's sake, his daughter was dead. Didn't he care?

"You're going to have to be more specific than that, Dad."

"You know perfectly well what I'm referring to," Harold insisted peevishly. He looked at Matt. "How could you bring Schaffer here with you?"

It was on the tip of her tongue to say, "My arrangements, my choice," but that would put her in the same low class as Rebecca Lynn, so she focused only on addressing his question. "Because he said he wanted to pay his respects to Candace."

"Respects, huh." Harold blew out an angry breath. "The bastard just wants to keep tabs on me."

"I'm sure if that's what he has in mind, Dad, he would see a reason to have to do it at a memorial service," she mocked. Turning serious, she added, "Come on, now. I really doubt that this would be the place he'd plan on a confrontation. Besides," she reminded her father, "you said you owe money to his family, not to him."

A harsh laugh escaped his lips. "Same thing."

"No," she said firmly, thinking of how she related to her own family and their actions; they might share the same last name, but they were *not* one and the same. "They're not."

Chapter 12

When the memorial service was finally over and Candace's ashes had been placed inside the family mausoleum at the cemetery, Natalie was more than ready to put the whole ordeal behind her. Being around her family for any length of time always managed to exhaust her emotionally if not physically.

Not to mention the fact that the sadness had finally really hit her.

Candace was dead.

All of her life, she had always been accustomed to being one half of a whole. That was just the way things were. She and Candace hadn't been identical, but there was no denying that there was still an indelible bond. Even when she didn't see Candace for months at a stretch—other than the usual tabloid in-your-face stories that periodically featured her twin—she knew Candace was out there somewhere. Breathing. Doing. Being her other half.

Now that was gone, and she was no longer part of a set. She had to rethink her existence. Become accustomed to thinking of herself in the singular.

It was an odd, odd feeling. She sincerely doubted that anyone who had never lost a twin would understand, but there was this acute feeling of being lost, of something missing.

Almost, she thought ruefully, slanting a covert look toward Matt, like the feeling she'd had when she'd woken up that fateful morning and realized that he had left her for good.

She supposed that maybe that was her fate in life. To be left behind. Granted that Candace, as self-centered as her twin could sometimes be, hadn't any control over severing their tie.

But Matt had.

As for now, there was no doubt in Natalie's mind that, as fantastic as the lovemaking was, Matt was only here temporarily. He'd told her about being based in Los Angeles, and she knew that whenever whatever it was he was attending to for Montgomery was over, Matt would be on the next plane bound for L.A. and out of her life.

Again.

She couldn't dwell on that now, Natalie told herself, couldn't fixate on what was to be. She could only live in the moment.

That, and find Candace's killer, no matter what it took.

"You're awfully quiet," Matt commented as he escorted her out of the mausoleum. Outside, the sun seemed particularly bright and the weather oppressively hot for that time of year.

Natalie stripped off her suit jacket. The sleeveless black-and-white silk blouse felt as if it was sticking to her spine. "Just thinking."

It wasn't a stretch to guess who she was thinking about. He couldn't remember Natalie ever looking this sad before.

"About Candace?"

And you. But there was no point in mentioning that, so she merely nodded. "Yes."

Compassion filled him. "I know what it's like to lose somebody." He didn't seem aware of the quiet sigh he uttered before continuing. "It's the kind of grief that sticks with you. Eventually, you make peace with it and go on, but it's always there, somewhere in the shadows, no matter how small and manageable you think it's ultimately become."

Natalie stopped walking and looked at him. He sounded as if he was talking about someone he'd loved. Had Matt found someone else after he'd left her after all?

Of course he had, you idiot, she mocked herself. Eight years was a long time for a virile man like Matt to do without female companionship. He hadn't been that self-contained monk she'd imagined.

A tiny sprig of jealousy sprang up inside her chest. With concentrated effort, she yanked it out by the roots. What was the matter with her? She was an independent woman. Her *own* person, not some moonstruck young girl—the way she had once been.

Her voice gave none of her feelings away as she asked, "Who did you lose?"

To be honest, she half expected Matt to shrug off her question, or at the very least, to change the subject. But instead he answered her.

"The only one I was ever close to in my family, my mother, Amy. The most selfless woman to ever walk the face of the earth. Even on her deathbed, she wasn't thinking about herself, but of the family." He sighed heavily. "She asked me to watch out for my older brother. Scott always had a tendency to get himself into situations that he couldn't get out of."

She heard the sadness in his voice. He was serious. "Your mother?" she repeated.

"Yes." He noted the surprised look on her face. "What did you think I was going to say?"

She lifted her shoulders in a half shrug. "Some unforgettable love of your life."

He looked at her for a long moment. "There's only been one." His tone of voice left no room for doubt. "There's only one chance at the brass ring in this life," he told her solemnly, taking her arm and continuing to walk. "If you're lucky, you get it. If you're not…" His voice trailed off, leaving it to her to fill in the blank.

They had almost left the cemetery grounds and Rothchild mausoleum, where her paternal grandparents and her mother were said to be buried, when she noticed him. Had he been there all the time? At the chapel and then at the cemetery? How had she missed him?

"Conner?"

When Matt looked over toward the person she had called out to, Natalie felt him stiffening at her side. "If you want to have a word with him, I'll wait for you by the car," Matt offered, his tone almost formal.

The suggestion caught her off guard. "You don't have to go, Matt," she told him even as Conner was approaching them.

Matt shook his head. "Better this way," was all he said as he retreated, then turned on his heel and walked away.

There was obviously no love lost between the two men, she thought. A lot of that going around, she mused.

Her cousin, Conner Rothchild, was a defense attorney for the family's large, prestigious legal firm: Rothchild, Rothchild & Bennigan. Tall, with hazel eyes and dark brown hair, the thirty-three-year-old lawyer was the older son of her father's younger brother, Michael. Though Michael Rothchild was a brilliant attorney in his own right, it was obvious to the family that he resented Harold and felt as if he could never crawl out from beneath his older brother's shadow.

Lots of discord in this family, she thought sadly just as Conner reached her side.

"Hello, Conner," she greeted him politely, deliberately dispensing with the obligatory air kiss that was so popular among the rich and famous. "I didn't see you in the church," she confessed.

"You had a lot to deal with," he countered. "And I was in the back. I came late. I wasn't really sure how Uncle Harold would react to my attending the service. You either," he added with a smile that always had her guessing as to its genuineness.

But that was mainly because they had grown up as adversaries, thanks to the efforts of both their fathers. Until Ricky's birth five years ago, Uncle Michael enjoyed rubbing her father's nose in the fact that he had only females in his family while he, Michael, had fathered two strong, strapping sons: Conner and Michael Jr. The implication was not lost on her. To Uncle Michael, women were second-class citizens.

She remembered always feeling as if the family gatherings they had were merely excuses for some sort of competitive comparison. Birthdays, Christmas, Thanksgiving, it didn't matter. The agenda was always the same. Each brother tried to top the other, and neither was above using their offspring and pitting them against one another like some human form of cockfighting.

Time and again, she could remember being played against Conner and his brother. The competition turned more serious as they grew up. Then it was accomplishment against accomplishment, career against career. More than once, the criminals she had arrested wound up being put back on the street, thanks to the efforts of Conner and her uncle.

"You're welcome here," she replied tersely. "It's a memorial service, not one of those family competitions we were all forced to endure."

He made no comment about that, or the use of the word *forced.* He'd been born competitive and loved nothing better than winning. Competitions, to his way of thinking, kept you sharp and on your toes. And the world belonged to the winners, not the losers.

He put on his best somber face. Was he acting? Natalie wondered. "I was sorry to hear about Candace. Do the police know who did it?"

He was pumping her, wasn't he? She wasn't about to give him the satisfaction of sharing any information. "It's too soon to tell."

"How about Schaffer?" Conner nodded toward Matt in the distance. The latter stood waiting beside his car at the curb. "Anyone look into where he was the night in question?" he asked. Then, before she could respond, he commented, "Pretty brazen of Schaffer coming here like this."

There was that protective feeling again, she thought. "And why is that?"

Hazel eyes shifted to her face. "Don't play dumb, Natalie. It doesn't become you. Everyone knows your father and Schaffer's people are connected, but it wasn't a match made in heaven. More like something that the devil had a hand in orchestrating." He laughed shortly. "I figure that Matt's just like the rest of them." He grew more sober as he added, "Don't turn your back on him, Natalie."

Since when did Conner care what she or any of her side of the family did or didn't do? "Your concern is touching."

If he was aware of the sarcasm, he didn't show it. "You are my cousin," Conner pointed out. "Little amusing rivalries aside, I wouldn't want to see anything happening to you." And then he shrugged, as if he knew that his words were being deflected and that she didn't believe him. "But you'll do what you want. You were always headstrong that way." He paused, as if debating adding anything. And then he did. "Just be careful," he warned again.

"I'm a cop," she told him. "I'm always careful. I have to be," she added. "Especially since you managed to put so many of the people with grudges against me back on the street."

"The cases were weak," he pointed out. "And remember, innocent until proven guilty."

Others might buy into her cousin's charm, but she didn't. She was immune to it. "Or their money runs out, whichever happens first."

Conner didn't bother contradicting her. He actually looked as if he was amused by her rejoinder. And then he took his leave. "Hope the next time I see you, it'll be under happier circumstances."

She nodded, then, just as he was turning to go, she decided to ask Conner one question.

"Where's Uncle Michael?" She knew her other cousin, Michael Jr., was out of town on business, but Candace had been her uncle's niece. She would have thought that he would have put aside any differences, petty or otherwise, that he had with her father and attend the service. Natalie knew she'd sent him an invitation.

"Home," Conner confessed, and she saw that he wasn't entirely comfortable with what he was telling her. "Funerals depress him. He likes to avoid them whenever he can."

"Obviously, he thought he could," she concluded with a sigh. Maybe it was better this way after all. Maybe the sight of his younger brother would only further upset her father. "I'd like to say it's nice seeing you again, Conner, but, well, you know…"

For a moment, they were on the same wavelength and her cousin seemed compassionate. She knew better than to think it might continue.

"Yeah, I know," he answered. "Well, take care of

yourself, Nat." And with that, Conner turned away and walked off in the opposite direction, where he'd parked his car.

Matt came to attention and dropped his arms to his sides as he saw Natalie part ways with Conner and begin to head toward him. He waited until she was only a few feet away before he asked, "So what did your cousin have to say?"

She couldn't help wondering if Conner had come out of a sense of obligation, because no one else from his side of the family had attended—or if there was another reason for his presence. Her suspicious mind was due in part to her job description and in part because of her family background. Hardly anyone did something for no reason at all.

"Why?" she asked, stopping at the curb. "Were your ears burning?"

Matt looked mildly surprised. "Your cousin didn't have anything better to do than talk about me?" He held the passenger-side door open for her.

Independent or not, she had to admit she liked encountering touches of chivalry. And if nothing else, Matt knew how to treat a woman like a lady. Surrendering a smile, Natalie got into the car.

"Not talk about you so much as warn me about you," she corrected.

He'd just rounded the hood and was getting in himself. He stopped mid-motion, then slid in behind the wheel. "Warn you?" What the hell was Rothchild warning her about?

"Uh-huh." Pulling on the shoulder strap, she fastened

her seat belt securely. "Seems that he thinks you might have an ulterior motive for being here. Or at least that you have some kind of an agenda."

His first comment was drowned out by the sound of the engine turning over. She had a hunch that maybe it was better that way.

"We all have agendas," Matt told her as he pulled away from the curb and wove his way into the flow of traffic. "Mine is keeping you safe."

It had been a very long time since anyone had even pretended to take care of her. "Excuse me?"

"Just in case this does involve some kind of a vendetta." He couldn't tell if his answer offended her sense of independence. To be honest, he didn't much care. What he did care about was making sure nothing happened to her. But, to keep the peace, he explained himself. "You'll have to forgive me, but that's the kind of culture that I grew up in. Vendettas and paybacks. If that is the case, you're going to need someone watching your back."

"I'm a police detective," she once again reminded him. "I can watch my own back. Besides," she reasoned, "I'm practically estranged from my family and I am *so* not like a Rothchild. Why in heaven's name would I be in any kind of 'danger'—assuming there's a shred of truth in this theory of yours?"

He didn't bother telling her that he had a gut feeling about this. That there was more to this ring business than Harold was telling her and that, for some reason, it had cost Candace her life. What he did was try to spell it out in neutral terms.

"Because, if it does involve revenge, whoever is responsible most likely is not your garden-variety rocket scientist who has carefully thought this all out. Most people who seek revenge are driven by emotions, not logic." And that Matt knew for a fact. If growing up a Schaffer had taught him nothing else, it had taught him that.

Her suspicions were aroused. Natalie studied his face closely as she asked, "Do you know something I don't?"

Actually, there was one piece of information he did have that she didn't, but he wanted to look into it a little more before sharing, so when he answered her, it was in the negative.

"No," he confessed. "I'm just spinning theories and trying to take everything under consideration."

She was quiet for a moment as she digested what he was saying. Something didn't quite fit.

"Not that I don't appreciate the help. After all, I was the one who initially dragged you into this." As with a suspect she was questioning, Natalie moved in for the so-called kill. In this case, it was his motives she was after. "But when did you suddenly become so dedicated to finding Candace's killer?"

"The first time I made love with you." He saw her brow furrow in confusion and realized his mistake. "The second first time," he corrected. "Meaning this time around, not eight years ago."

"I know what that means," she interrupted, then asked, "And that's the only reason?"

"Yeah." Taking a right turn, he glanced at his watch. It was getting late. "Mind if I drop you off at your place? I only took a few hours off, and Luke's expecting me at the casino for a meeting at one." It was close to that now.

"I don't mind you dropping me off," she told him

agreeably, then added, "but make it The Janus instead of my place."

Matt was immediately suspicious. She'd already put in a great deal of time there. "Why?"

"Why don't you leave that up to me?" *Because if I tell you, you'll give me an argument, and I don't feel up to arguing.*

He looked at her incredulously just as he squeaked through a yellow light that was about to turn red. "You still don't trust me? What is it that Conner said to you?" It couldn't have been just an ambiguous warning. There had to be something more to it, he reasoned.

But Natalie waved her hand at his question. "Conner doesn't matter. I'm never sure about anything he says," she admitted. Her cousin was very capable of lying to put her on the wrong trail for his own reasons. She didn't have time or the inclination to try to unravel why he was warning her about Matt. "We weren't exactly encouraged to have a close, honest relationship as kids. We were always being pitted against one another, and he liked winning far too much for my taste. As a matter of fact, he still does."

"You still haven't answered my first question," Matt persisted. This time, when the light flashed yellow, he stepped on the brake so he could look at her. People had trouble lying if they were looked at head-on. Decent people, at any rate. "You don't trust me?"

"It's not a matter of trust," she insisted. He wasn't going to give up, she could see that. Natalie decided to give him just a little and hoped that would satisfy him. "If I told you why, then I'd be involving you and you might have to pick sides. I don't want to put you in that position."

When had this happened? "It didn't seem to matter to you a week ago."

"That was a week ago." Why couldn't he just let things be? She waved her hand at the road before them. "Stop acting like some two-bit private investigator and just drive, okay?"

"Okay. I'll take you to The Janus," he conceded. "And I won't ask any questions." *For now,* he added silently. Sparing her a glance, he told her, "You're going to look out of place in that outfit."

Unlike Candace, who had always been very particular about her clothes, insisting on only the latest fashions and the most expensive designers, Natalie could care less about her so-called image. She merely shrugged at his observation.

"Won't be the first time. Won't be the last."

"Suit yourself," he told her. But if she thought that he wasn't going to try to find out what she was up to, she really didn't know him anymore.

Her answer was self-assured. "Thanks, but I usually do."

He smiled to himself as he pressed his foot down on the accelerator. That she didn't have to tell him. "Yeah, I remember."

Chapter 13

With the gala tapes she'd viewed all but burned into her brain, Natalie's main reason for returning to The Janus was to retrace her sister's steps that night as closely as possible. By trying to see things from Candace's line of vision, she was really hoping that something might strike her that hadn't previously.

Nothing did.

The case was getting colder, and though some crimes were solved months, even years after they'd taken place—often by accident after an incredible amount of man-hours had been put into the endeavor—most cases were either solved in the first seventy-two hours or forever remained open.

Natalie was aware that it had already been longer than that, but she absolutely refused to have her sister's murder fall into that black hole known as cold cases. If she had to take a leave of absence, she would, but she planned to devote herself to solving this crime if it was the last thing she did.

Matt hadn't lied to her when he told Natalie that he needed to get back to The Janus for a meeting, one that hinged not only on his attendance but on his delivering a report to his employer. It concerned the overall present state of security not just in the casino itself but in the hotel and the surrounding grounds as well. However, the moment his meeting with Montgomery was over, Matt quickly returned to his office.

He not only closed the door but he locked it and shut the blinds as well. He didn't want to take a chance on anyone walking in on him while he was on his private line.

Something regarding the missing ring had come to his attention late last night, and he wanted to verify the information before mentioning it to Natalie. The fastest way he knew how to get started was calling in one of the many favors that he was owed. Even so, part of him loathed doing it.

Because even if it was calling in a favor that was owed him, it theoretically placed him in debt to the person who was reciprocating the favor. And that person belonged to the Schaffer family network.

To say he disliked dealing with any of them was an understatement—he spent most of his time trying to disentangle himself from their vast tentacles. But in this case, it was the only way to proceed.

Besides, he told himself, he was doing this for Natalie.

And maybe, he thought as he listened to the phone on the other end ring, he was also doing it for

Candace. He and Natalie's twin had never gotten intimate the way Natalie had suggested, but, if he was being honest, he felt sorry for the dead woman. In a lot of ways, Candace had reminded him of a female version of his brother: a perpetual screwup unconsciously hunting for approval. And always hunting in all the wrong places.

Was that what had happened the last night of her life? Was the person Candace had hoped would light up her world responsible for bringing an end to it instead?

The ringing stopped. A husky voice, laced with the ragged remnants of sleep, came on the other end of the line. Matt glanced at his watch. It was close to two o'clock. But then, his cousin Vinnie was a player, and players in Vegas rarely ever got up until the sun went down.

"Whoever this is, you'd better have a damn good reason for waking me up," Vinnie growled, a snarling bear prematurely dragged out of hibernation.

"Vinnie, it's Matt," he began, then paused to let the name sink in.

True to form, his cousin wasn't processing information yet. "Matt?"

"Matt Schaffer. Your cousin. Scott's brother." Pausing between each sentence, Matt went down the line of several more filial connections they shared before finally saying, "The guy who saved your butt when the police were ready to haul you off to jail for that burglary they thought you'd committed."

The incident had turned out to be a case of mistaken identity and, at his aunt's tearful behest, he'd flown into Vegas to see what he could do to help her son. He'd stayed in Vegas less than three days that time. But even so, he'd been ever aware of the possibility that his path would cross Natalie's. That time, it hadn't.

He remembered smothering a kernel of disappointment as he flew back to L.A.

"Oh, *Matt,*" Vinnie cried as if his brain had suddenly kicked in. "How the hell are you? Still in L.A.?"

Matt leaned back in his chair. This might be slow going. "No, I'm here in Vegas."

"Vegas? Hell, you gotta let me have a chance to pay you back for what you did for me, man. Where're you staying?" Matt heard rustling on the other end, as if his cousin was hunting for his clothes. "I can swing by and pick—"

He stopped him before Vinnie could work up a full head of steam. "That's not necessary, Vinnie. But if you really want to pay me back, I do need a little information."

"Hey, you got it. My brain's your brain. Ask me," Vinnie invited, sounding eager to get out from under the weight of owing a debt.

Matt decided that he was going to have to give Vinnie a little background. Otherwise there were going to be endless questions.

"You know about that Rothchild woman who was found dead in her condo the other week?" With Vinnie, he took nothing for granted. Vinnie was generally oblivious to the outside world. He'd once gone an entire year before realizing that the price of postage had gone up.

This time, however, Vinnie was on top of things. "Yeah. Candace. A real party girl. We're really going to miss her around here." He almost sounded sad. "Damn waste if you ask me."

Matt paused, wanting to phrase his question just

right. He didn't want his cousin thinking that what he was asking would get back to the police. Any hint of the police would have Vinnie clamming up as if he'd swallowed a mouthful of crazy glue.

"According to the paper, they think she was wearing that big diamond ring." He played dumb. "Tears of the Quetzal I think the thing is called."

He heard his cousin's high-pitched laugh and remembered how grating a sound that could be. "Hell of a name, isn't it? I can't even pronounce it. Neither could Aunt Lydia."

Aunt Lydia. If he remembered his family dynamics, Aunt Lydia belonged to his mother's side of the family, once removed.

Matt smiled to himself. Maybe this was going to be easier than he'd initially thought. Just before he'd gotten together with Natalie last night, he'd become aware there was a rumor that had once made the rounds that the ring in question had fallen into the hands of his family for a while. If that was the case, then maybe someone in the family thought it should be returned. The members of his far-flung clan and their associates were capable of anything.

"Why would Aunt Lydia need to pronounce it?" Matt asked his cousin, trying to come across as only mildly curious.

Fully awake now, Vinnie cackled. "'Cause the crazy old lady claimed that the ring was hers. Said she 'found' it next to her dinner plate one evening when she was on this cruise down to Mexico. The same so-called cruise that Harold Rothchild supposedly whisked her off to when he was in-between wives," Vinnie added for good measure. It was obvious that he believed none of what Aunt Lydia had said.

This probably wasn't going to lead to anything, but since he had Vinnie on the phone, he wanted to hear whatever details his cousin had.

"Which wives?"

He'd obviously amused Vinnie. This time when his cousin laughed, Matt held the phone away from his ear until the noise stopped.

"Good question. Some guys never learn, do they?" Vinnie marveled, going off on a tangent. "His first wife croaks, and instead of being glad he was free, the damn fool starts looking around for another wife." Matt cleared his throat, and Vinnie got back on track. "But to answer your question, it was after his first one died and before he married the second one. Anna something-or-other I think. Anyway, that's the story Aunt Lydia tells."

Well, at least it was a starting point, Matt thought. Better than nothing. Everyone knew that Lydia Silecchia was several sandwiches short of a picnic basket. Maybe she had seen Candace flashing her ring on TV on one of those entertainment programs that made a point of recording every breath a celebrity took and decided to confront Natalie's sister.

Matt frowned. He knew this was a damn long shot, but right now, it was the only lead he had to go on so he might as well pursue it. With luck, it might actually lead him to something that made more sense.

Since there didn't seem to be any more information forthcoming, Matt decided to end the conversation before Vinnie got off track again. "Thanks, Vinnie, you've been a big help."

"Hey, what about us two studs getting together and having our way with the Vegas female population? You can be my wingman."

Aunt Lydia wasn't the only one who was delusional, Matt thought. "I'll get back to you on that," he promised, breaking the connection before Vinnie could say anything else. He replaced the receiver just as he heard a knock on his door. Now what? He was hoping to be able to go find Natalie, but that obviously was going to have to wait.

"Come in," he called out. When whoever was on the other side rattled the doorknob, Matt remembered that he'd locked the door. Not something he normally did. "Be right there."

Flipping the lock, he opened the door and found himself looking down at a very frustrated-looking Natalie. Her afternoon hadn't gone very well, he surmised.

"I just wanted to let you know I was leaving," she told him.

"I take it that whatever you were trying to do didn't pan out?"

She didn't feel like going into detail. "Something like that."

Matt glanced back at his desk. There was nothing going on that needed his immediate attention. He made a quick decision. "Want to go for a ride?"

There were times when she actually enjoyed cruising the more colorful streets of the strip, but she really wasn't in the mood this afternoon.

She shook her head. "Maybe some other—" And then Natalie stopped. The look on Matt's face told her that this was more than just a careless invitation to go for a drive. Did he find something out? She didn't bother containing the surge of excitement that entered her voice. "What's up?"

He didn't want her getting her hopes up too much. "Maybe nothing," he cautioned.

She knew Matt. He wouldn't have mentioned anything unless he was at least partially sure there was something to it. "And maybe something?" she countered.

He allowed a smile to curve the corners of his mouth. "Maybe."

She realized that they were walking out of his office and he had taken her arm. "Damn it, Matt, tell me. Why am I going on a ride with you?"

"Because you'll enjoy it?" He couldn't resist teasing.

That would have worked eight years ago. A lot of things would have worked eight years ago. But she'd done a lot of growing in that time. And a lot of hardening as well.

"What I don't enjoy is being in the dark."

"Oh, I don't know." His warm smile wove its way into her gut despite her efforts to block it. "Being in the dark has its advantages. As long as it's with the right person."

She studied his face. He wasn't just teasing her. There was something to all this. "You're on to something, aren't you?"

He looked at her for a long moment, his mind going places it had no business going. Because nothing had changed from last night, or the nights that had come before that. Nights they had spent making love and keeping the world at bay. He was still a different man than he had been when he had originally left Vegas—and her. A different man who, for better or worse, was set in his ways.

And she still deserved better.

"Yeah, I might be," he admitted, then cautioned, "But this still might be nothing."

She had never liked riddles, never enjoyed searching for puzzle pieces. She always wanted all the pieces out in the open, where she could see them.

"I swear, if you don't start giving me some tangible details I'm not going to be responsible for what I do to you, Matt."

"I heard that that ring of yours—"

She immediately interrupted him. He needed to get this straight. She had absolutely no interest in finding the ring. Her only interest in it was how it figured into her sister's death.

"My father's ring," Natalie corrected with feeling. "It's not my ring. It's my father's. And I don't care what he does with it."

And if Candace had felt the same way, she would probably still be alive, Natalie thought sadly.

"Sorry, your father's ring. Anyway, I came across a rumor that my family might have had possession of it for a while. If so, knowing my family, maybe someone decided that they should get it back."

They were crossing the casino floor, approaching the slot machines by the entrance, and Natalie stopped walking. "Your family?" she echoed, stunned. "That's a new one on me." She laughed dryly, shaking her head. It amazed her how much she still didn't know about what went on in her family. "But then, my father has never been exactly forthcoming about the diamond." *Or anything else,* she added silently.

"I'm not even sure just how he got hold of it. Supposedly my grandfather found it in his mines in Mexico, but that's never been verified. For all I know, Grandpa might have stolen it from someone." Even as she said it out loud, it made sense to her. "Joseph Rothchild wasn't exactly a man whose background could stand close investigation."

She resumed walking. The electronic doors opened wide for them. "So where is it exactly that we're going?" she wanted to know.

He nodded toward the closest valet. No words needed to be exchanged. The young man immediately went to retrieve Matt's sports car. "To see my Aunt Lydia."

More surprises, she thought, turning to look at Matt. "You have an Aunt Lydia?" He nodded in response. "You never mentioned her," she pointed out.

But then, when they'd been together all those years ago, they'd been wildly in love and very much into one another. Family history hardly mattered. In fact, she'd naively thought of them as being one another's families. Showed how much she knew.

"I never mentioned a lot of people in my family," he told her. And there was good reason for that. "I figured that the less you knew, the better off you were. Besides," he sighed, "it's not as if I was exactly thrilled about them."

Some were harmless and some even he was better off not knowing. When he was in his late teens and early twenties, it had been exciting, being part of an underground world. But then he grew up and the allure of that way of life quickly faded.

A lot of his relatives who were older than he was never grew up.

"Does your Aunt Lydia know who might have actually had the ring?" Natalie asked.

The valet arrived with his vehicle. Getting out, the valet—Skip according to his name tag—surrendered the keys to Matt and raced around to the other side to hold the passenger door open for Natalie.

"Aunt Lydia's the one who claims to have had the ring," Matt told her as he got in behind the steering wheel.

His sports car purred to life as Natalie's mouth dropped open. "Oh." And then she smiled as they sped away. It would have taken her a while to unearth this piece of information. "You know, sometimes you're a handy man to have around."

"Sometimes," he agreed.

When Lydia Silecchia had been a young girl, she dreamed of being a glamorous movie star. But several forays into little theater groups and a handful of some rather nasty reviews had her abandoning that world after a couple of years. Instead, she became a Vegas showgirl, ever on the lookout for a high roller who could give her the kind of life she longed for.

When she married Carlo Silecchia, he'd promised—and placed—the world at her feet. She hadn't known at the time that the world was on loan and that he was but a struggling underling in a long, winding chain that made up the Schaffer family structure. The American sounding name "Schaffer" having been adopted by Giovanni Scarpetta when he originally stepped off the boat at Ellis Island several generations ago.

Life for Lydia became a series of disappointments. So much so that she felt it necessary for her vivid imagination to fill in a few blanks in order for her to survive these shortfalls that life—and her husband—kept serving up. Her fantasies included building up her husband's importance in the world he labored in until, eventually, Lydia envisioned herself as the wife of a Don much like the celebrated one she'd seen in *The Godfather*. Whenever her own life lacked the drama she craved, she improvised.

How much she improvised became apparent to Natalie within the first ten minutes of their visit. Now a widow, living in a small, cluttered apartment on the good graces of "the family," which prided itself on taking care of its own, Lydia came to greet them wearing a floor-length electric-blue caftan that allowed her to sweep about the room like an anorexic Joan Crawford.

"Yes, the Tears of the Quetzal was mine. Beautiful, beautiful," she declared, her eyes getting a faraway look. "Never saw anything as beautiful as that ring," Lydia swore wistfully.

"What happened to it, Aunt Lydia?" Matt asked politely.

She lifted her bony shoulders, then let them fall again, and it was unclear if she was indicating that she didn't know or that what had happened to the ring was no longer of overwhelming consequence.

It turned out to be neither as she began to explain. "Strange things started happening soon after Harold gave me the ring."

"He gave it to you?" Natalie questioned. There wasn't the remotest chance that this was true. She knew that Rebecca Lynn had tried to wrest the ring away from him so she could show it off, and he had refused.

"I found it by my dinner plate one evening, during our Mediterranean cruise, but I knew it was from him," she said, a smug little smile on her face. "But, as I said, strange things started happening soon after I got the ring."

"Strange things?" Natalie coaxed when the woman's voice had trailed off along with her gaze.

"Yes. Horrible things. My son was shot. I lost money in investments. That ring *was* cursed, just like they said it was." She lifted her chin dramatically. "So I threw it away."

Matt looked at her, stunned that she would say something so absurd. "You did what?"

"I threw it away," Lydia repeated with a toss of her head, sending thin strands of impossibly blond hair flying over her shoulder. "I waited until everyone was asleep, then walked out onto the deck, stood right at the bow of the ship and threw the damn thing right into the ocean."

Natalie exchanged looks with Matt. His aunt was describing a scene from the end of *Titanic*.

"You went on another cruise to throw the ring away?" Matt asked.

Lydia looked a little confused for a moment, as if she hadn't realized that the ring had to have been in her possession for a little while in order for the "horrible things" to have happened.

"Yes. Yes, I did," Lydia said emphatically.

"I see." Matt stood up. Natalie was quick to join him. "Well, thank you for your time, Aunt Lydia."

"Don't mention it." She regally led the way to the front door of her small, memorabilia-crowded apartment. "I must say you took that a lot better than Anthony did."

"Anthony?" Natalie questioned. She looked to Matt for an explanation.

"Another cousin. Aunt Lydia's nephew," Matt filled in.

"I'm going to have to start keeping a scorecard to keep all the names straight," Natalie murmured under her breath. She caught the flash of a quick grin on Matt's face.

But Lydia hadn't heard the comment. She was too busy spinning her story and enjoying being the center of attention for a change. No one came to visit her anymore. "Anthony got real nasty. He said I had no right to do that. That the ring belonged to us. That we could have been rich if I hadn't lost it."

"Lost it?" Matt repeated innocently. "I thought you said you threw it away."

Lydia looked annoyed that he seemed to be trying to trip her up. "I lost it by throwing it away. Aren't you listening? I lost it and then she found it."

"She?" Natalie repeated, even as she wondered if anything this woman was saying was actually true. Was there someone else involved? Someone who might actually have once had the ring and for some reason, lost it to her father? Someone who'd gone to great lengths to get it back? "Who are you talking about?" she pressed, trying not to sound too eager.

Lydia's face puckered into a deep frown. "That blond tart. The one who likes to wiggle her body all the time. I saw her waving her hand at the camera. *She had on my ring,*" Lydia insisted. "Just ask Anthony. He saw it, too."

Chapter 14

That blond tart.

Natalie's heart quickened. Matt's aunt was talking about Candace. Had this delusional woman actually been instrumental in Candace's death by pointing out the ring to Anthony Silecchia?

Matt asked Lydia the question before she could. "You pointed the ring out to Anthony and said that it was yours?"

Lydia's expression became impatient. When she answered, it was as if she was talking to someone who was slow. "Yeah, well, he was in the room when that show that talks about celebrities was on." Impatience melted into annoyance, but it was aimed at Anthony. "He came by to ask to borrow some money. Like I had any," she sneered. "I told him all the money I coulda had was on that snooty broad's finger."

Her eyes narrowed as the thought seemed to strike

her for the first time. Matt could almost see the rusty wheels turning. "He seemed pretty interested in that ring. Got real quiet, then left right after the show was over." She ended her story in a whisper, as if she was telling the details to herself.

Maybe they finally *were* on to something. "Where is Anthony staying these days?" Matt asked.

Lydia waved her thin, veined hand around vaguely. She avoided his eyes as she said, "Who knows? He can't hold on to a steady job, so he moves around, stiffing landlords."

Matt had the impression that Lydia knew, but was deliberately being evasive. Knowing her, she probably wanted to be paid for the information. Didn't matter, he thought. It would be a simple enough thing for him to find out where his cousin was holed up these days. Scott would know. His older brother and Anthony had been fairly close all their lives. He knew for a fact that Scott's wife hated Anthony and thought of him as a bad influence, but that didn't stop Scott from getting together with his cousin.

It was time to get going. "Thanks for your time, Aunt Lydia."

"Sure." Standing in his way, she made no attempt to move. Instead, she looked at him expectantly. "Got a little sugar for your Aunt Lydia?"

Instead of kissing the old woman's cheek, the way Natalie assumed he was going to given the expression, she was surprised to see Matt digging into his pocket. Taking out his wallet, he handed the older woman several hundred dollar bills.

Lydia Silecchia beamed. Her satisfied, wide smile

seemed to create tiny fissures in the thick, caked-on foundation she wore, accenting her flaws rather than hiding them.

"You were always a good boy," Lydia said, quickly stuffing the bills into the folds of the flowing electric-blue caftan.

Natalie took in a deep, cleansing breath the moment they walked out of the stuffy apartment with its aging dust.

"As I remember it," she said to Matt as they went down the stairwell, "you were a bad boy, not a good one."

At the time, it seemed expedient to cultivate that kind of rebel persona. Beneath it all, he was always the same honorable guy. Even though that brought consequences with it.

"You do what you have to do in order to survive," he told her, then allowed himself a momentary smile. "Was that what attracted you to me? Because you had a thing for 'bad boys?'"

What had attracted her, she thought, was that she believed she saw the good heart beneath the rebel act. But she knew he'd deny it if she mentioned that.

"It had a certain appeal back then," she told him vaguely. He held the outer door for her. They didn't have far to go to reach his vehicle. She noticed that a couple of teens were wistfully eyeing the sports car.

Matt hit the security locks and they popped up in harmony. "And now?"

He knew the answer to that without her saying anything. She'd already given too much away by making love to him. She got in on her side of the car.

"Now we're on the trail of a killer," she said, her tone all business. The click of her seat belt as the metal met the groove underscored her words. "Do you think your cousin is capable of killing someone?"

He gave her question minimal thought. "Anthony has a short fuse and flies off the handle a lot, but as far as killing someone, no I don't think so. Anthony's always been just a lot of noise, no substance."

But everyone had their breaking point, she thought as they pulled away from the curb.

"Candace could drive people crazy. She rubbed more than a few people the wrong way," she recalled. "If he tried to steal the ring from her and she started to fight him off—"

Natalie didn't finish her sentence. Instead, she looked at Matt, waiting for either his firm denial or tacit agreement.

"Could have happened that way," he agreed with a thoughtful nod. "But she would have had to *really* tick him off. I want to talk to Anthony before I make up my mind one way or another."

That sounded reasonable. "Sure, let's go." Everything about her alert body language said she was ready to confront this cousin of his.

"Not this second," Matt informed her. "Aside from not knowing where he is at the moment, I've got to get back to The Janus and take care of a few more things before I go hunting for my cousin. Want me to drop you off at your house?"

What she wanted was to start hunting for Anthony immediately. But she knew that tone Matt was using. He would get to it when he could. There was no point in trying to argue him out of it.

So she shrugged her shoulders in a careless manner

and straightened in her seat to stare straight ahead. "Sure, my house is good."

Natalie had agreed a little too quickly, he thought. That wasn't good. "Promise me you're not going to go off on your own to see Anthony."

"How can I?" Natalie countered innocently. "I don't have his address, remember?"

He knew her too well. That wasn't enough to deter Natalie when she made up her mind about something. He wanted her word.

"Promise me," Matt insisted. "Or so help me, Nat, I'll tie you up and leave you in the trunk of my car until I can go with you."

He was probably perverse enough to make good on that, she thought. "Okay, okay, I promise." She saw Matt slant a skeptical glance at her as he drove through the green light. "What's the matter, Matt? Don't you trust me?"

No further than I can throw that great little butt of yours. "No," he said flatly, "not when it comes to things like this."

"I'll wait," she told him, making an *X* across her heart and holding up her hand in a solemn pledge. "As long as you promise that we'll go find him today."

"The minute I finish up at The Janus," he said. He saw her frustrated frown. "I do work for a living," he reminded her. "Okay, so it's settled? I'm taking you to your place?"

She changed her mind and shook her head. "No, drop me off at the police station. I want to see if I can get either Parker or Davidson to tell me if they've made any headway."

He remembered the disapproving look on the beefier detective's face when Parker saw that she was trying to view The Janus's security tapes. "I thought that you people aren't supposed to talk about a current investigation."

"Today was Candace's memorial service. I think that's enough for one of them to cut me a little slack in the territorial department."

Her answer made him laugh. "You know, Natalie, you're devious enough to be a Schaffer."

"Or a Rothchild." Natalie wasn't smiling as she said it.

"Touché," he replied.

Natalie stood in front of the police station steps and waved as Matt drove off. Turning, she walked slowly inside. But once within the building, she didn't go upstairs to the homicide division to touch base with either of the two detectives handling her sister's murder. Instead, she took the stairs down to the basement where the forensic lab was housed and the computer techs all did their work.

Her specific target was Silas Hunter, a highly skilled computer tech who had a crush on her. Barely twenty, the blond-haired Silas was far too young for her—even if she were inclined to date, which she wasn't—and she had gently told him so more than once.

However, she knew he still wanted to curry favor with her, and just this one time, because it was so important, she was going to let him ride to her rescue. The best part about Silas was that he was long on abilities and short on questions.

He brightened up the moment he saw her walking into his small section of the room. After exchanging a few pleasantries with him and accepting his condolences regarding her twin, Natalie took a blank piece of paper from his desk and wrote down Anthony Silecchia's name. She slid the paper in front of Silas.

"I need an address for this person," she told him.

Silas looked at the name, then raised his eyes to hers. "Fugitive or suspect?"

She didn't want to brand Silecchia yet. "Just someone who likes to stay one step ahead of the bill collectors," she said, plucking the first answer out of the air she could think of.

Silas laid the paper back down on his desk. "What was his last known address?"

"Don't know," she admitted.

Silas nodded his head as if that was a perfectly acceptable answer. His fingers began to race over the keyboard. Within seconds, he had Anthony Silecchia's likeness on the screen. He'd pulled up the man's driver's license.

"According to his Nevada license," Silas read, "he lives, or lived, on Galaxy Street." He tagged on the house number. "1589."

"Okay, that's a start," she said. He probably wasn't there any longer. Lydia had said he moved around. "Thanks."

"Hold it," Silas called after her, halting her retreat.

More furious typing and within seconds, Silas had pulled up an entire credit history complete with several more known residences, including a motel that wasn't too far away from the casino that her father owned.

And very close to the condo where Candace was killed, she realized. Natalie's fingertips turned icy.

Before she could ask him to, Silas had hit the print

button, and the printer beside his computer spit out two pages in rapid fire. He held them out to her. "Anything else?" he wanted to know.

Taking the pages, Natalie skimmed over them, and she shook her head. She couldn't have asked for more. The man had to be at one of these places. If he wasn't, then maybe someone there knew where he had gone.

"Nope. This'll do fine. You're a doll, Silas. I owe you." As she walked away, she heard the young tech sigh, as if he knew that the one thing he would have wanted, he couldn't have.

Walking toward the stairwell, Natalie went down the list of past addresses more slowly. From the looks of it, Anthony's residences had been taken up in progressively worse areas.

With the proceeds from the ring—if he *had* the ring—he could move back up in the world.

She could feel her scalp tingling as she studied the last address. Was he there? For how long? Maybe he was preparing to leave, even now.

A restlessness pervaded her.

Natalie knew that she'd promised Matt she wouldn't do anything or go looking for Anthony on her own. She knew she'd said she'd wait until he was free, but what if waiting cost her the opportunity to corner Silecchia?

She couldn't just stand around, killing time until Matt was free.

Besides, if this turned out to be a wild goose chase, she didn't want Matt wasting his time. He might grow impatient with the whole thing and tell her to leave it to the police.

At which point, she'd be on her own. Something she

normally was, but this one time, she had to admit she liked being partnered with him. Besides, it wasn't going to be for that long. He'd be gone soon enough.

At least that was the excuse she gave herself, the one that she decided would be acceptable to Matt if he called her out for going back on her word. She *wasn't* going back on it, she insisted silently. She was just bending it a little.

Besides, Matt knew her. He hadn't really expected her to do nothing, had he?

Natalie posed the rhetorical question to herself as she took a card out of her wallet. On it was the number of a local cab company. She needed to get to that motel quickly.

Twenty very long minutes later, the cab arrived. Another minute after that, she was on her way over to Anthony Silecchia's last known address, struggling to subdue her growing agitation.

The ride there took less time than waiting for the cab had.

"Want me to wait?" the cabbie asked as he brought his green-and-white vehicle to a stop at the curb. Beyond it was the motel. It appeared to be somewhat rundown, even from a distance.

"No, thanks." Getting out, she paid her fare. Natalie included a healthy tip because the cabbie hadn't droned endlessly on and on during the ride but had let her have her solitude.

Glancing at the money, the cabbie's thin lips parted in a smile.

"You sure?" he asked, sounding genuinely concerned as he glanced once more at the surrounding area. "This ain't the nicest neighborhood, Miss."

"I'll be all right," she assured him, stepping away from the cab.

She didn't have her usual second weapon strapped to the inside of her thigh because, after all, she'd attended a family funeral. But that didn't keep her from bringing along her personal small handgun, housing it in her clutch purse.

Natalie fervently hoped that she wouldn't have to use it.

Verifying Silecchia's room number with the bored-looking clerk behind the desk in the rental office, Natalie hurried up the outer stairs.

Room number 221 was in the middle of the second floor. It looked out onto the front parking lot.

She knocked on the door. There was no response, no sound of someone moving around inside. Waiting a moment, Natalie knocked again. Still nothing.

Dust-laden curtains hung at the window, drawn, but not meeting completely. She shifted so that she could see into the motel room. Squinting, she could make out the form of a man, his back to the window, sitting in a chair. His head looked as if it was dropped forward.

She realized that the man's hands were pulled back behind him. They were tied. Something was very definitely up.

"Time to make an entrance," she murmured, reaching into her purse for her weapon. She tried knocking one last time. This time, there was a frantic noise from within the room. As she peered in, she realized that Anthony Silecchia had twisted around and was looking straight at her. There was desperation in his eyes as he frantically tugged on the ties on his wrists.

Natalie quickly studied the door. She judged that it wasn't that sturdy. Backing up, she raised her leg and kicked the door as hard as she could. The wood groaned but ultimately stayed where it was.

She tried again. It took Natalie three very strong kicks before the door surrendered, separating itself from the doorjamb.

One forceful shove from her shoulder was all that was necessary. Natalie quickly let herself in.

"Anthony Silecchia I presume?" she quipped, crossing to the man in the chair.

Tucking the handgun she'd had out just a moment before into her waistband, she started to loosen the man's ties. Or attempted to.

That was when she heard it. The very distinctive click of a gun being cocked.

At the same time she heard a husky, whiskey-lubricated voice order, "Drop it."

She knew that voice.

Stunned, Natalie turned around.

"I said drop it!" Lydia shouted at her. She appeared to be less than half a step away from being enraged. "And while you're at it, raise your hands up over your head." When Natalie didn't obey, Lydia gestured with the gun she was holding. "Now," she growled.

For the time being, Natalie played along and did as she was told. "I thought you said you didn't know where he was."

"I got lucky," Lydia snapped impatiently. "And this is none of your damn business. I know who you are," she shouted angrily. "You're that blond tart's sister. Thought you fooled me, didn't you?" she accused.

There'd been no attempt at any deception. "Matt told you my name when we first came over," Natalie reminded the woman.

Lydia didn't appear to remember, or if she did, she gave no indication. Instead, the bloodshot hazel eyes shifted over to the nephew she'd caught off guard and tied up.

"I want that ring back, Anthony. Do you hear me?" She cocked the trigger. "I want it back. It belongs to me!"

Anthony looked at his aunt as if she was insane. "I don't have any damn ring, you crazy old hag."

"Not any damn ring," Lydia shouted into his face. "*The* damn ring. The Tears of the Quetzal. It's mine," she screamed at him. "I *earned* it. I was nice to that horrible bastard with the cold hands. *Real* nice," she emphasized.

Natalie felt nauseous. The thought of Lydia and her father together made her stomach turn and threatened to bring up her hastily consumed lunch.

"The ring doesn't belong to you," Natalie told Lydia as calmly as possible. The calmer she sounded, the more agitated Lydia became.

"The hell it doesn't. What doesn't belong in this picture is you. You stumbled into the wrong damn place this time, girlie. I'm going to get rid of you as soon as Anthony tells me where the ring is." A nasty, cold smile curved her thin, cracked lips. "Maybe even before. That'll teach you not to stick your nose where it doesn't belong."

As she spoke, she shifted the small gun barrel so that it could deliver a nice sized hole to whatever area she chose.

Chapter 15

Natalie raised her hands as she was told and kept a watchful eye on the gun in Lydia's hand.

"You don't want to do this," she said to the woman.

Something almost maniacal flashed in Lydia's eyes. "Oh, yes I do."

She meant it, Natalie thought. The woman really was crazy. "Did you kill Candace?" she asked Lydia bluntly.

Lydia cocked her head as if that could make her think better. She reminded Natalie of an aging bird.

"If I had, I'd have the ring, wouldn't I? No, *he* killed her. Anthony," Lydia declared, momentarily shifting both her line of vision and her weapon, pointing both at her nephew.

Taking advantage of the woman's momentary distraction, Natalie moved to grab her.

But Lydia was surprisingly agile for a woman in her deranged state.

"Uh-uh-uh," she cautioned in a singsong voice. "I wouldn't do that if I were you." The red lips parted in a cold smile. "Not unless you want to die a few minutes earlier."

Natalie was aware that the disheveled, bedraggled Anthony was frantically tugging on the ropes around his wrists—and getting nowhere.

"Aunt Lydia, get these damn ropes off me and stop talking crazy. I don't have the freakin' ring, and I didn't kill that woman. When I got there, she was already dead. And the ring was gone," he insisted.

Natalie could just picture Matt's cousin ready to eagerly pull the diamond off her sister's dead hand. She stifled her rage. That wouldn't help her get out of this situation.

"I got the hell out of there," he swore, pleading with his aunt.

"Do you drive a navy-blue sedan?" Natalie asked suddenly. Just yesterday, a woman had called in on the tip line. She'd said that she was walking her dog in the vicinity of Candace's condo around midnight the night she died and had seen a navy-blue sedan peeling away.

Confusion mingled with fear in his eyes. "Yeah, what about it?" Anthony whined.

"She's looking for her sister's killer, that's 'what about it,'" Lydia taunted, talking to him as if she were the one with superior intelligence. "She doesn't care who she pins it on, as long as somebody pays. Your cousin Matt brought her sniffing around." When Lydia frowned, her mouth pointed downward. "Never did like him."

The woman was incredible, Natalie thought in disgust.

She remembered what Lydia had said when Matt handed her the hundred-dollar bills. "But you took his money."

Lydia tossed her head proudly. "I *always* take the money." And then her expression changed, her eyes narrowing into slits. "Okay, I'm getting bored. This is where you check out. And don't worry, I won't miss. The only thing my worthless husband taught me was how to shoot and get what I aimed for."

Just as Lydia was about to squeeze the trigger, the door banged open for a second time in less than fifteen minutes. It crashed against the opposite wall. Startled, Lydia jerked her head around to see who was behind her.

It was all that Natalie needed.

She lunged at Lydia, tucking her head down and aiming for the woman's hips. They both fell to the stained, tattered carpet. With a death grip on her weapon, Lydia's finger jerked, firing the gun. Behind her, Natalie heard Anthony scream. She didn't get a chance to look up to see who had come in until, straddling Lydia, she pinned down the woman's toothpick-thin arms.

"Matt," she cried, relief flooding through her. "And you brought reinforcements." Natalie's smile went from ear to ear. "Nice to see you."

"You, too," he wisecracked, in order to hide the swell of emotion he was feeling. If he'd been half a minute later, she might not have even been alive. He felt like strangling Lydia with his bare hands. But instead, he stepped aside and let the two policemen he'd brought with him take over.

"I'm bleeding to death!" Anthony all but shrieked. "Help me, Matt!

Matt took Natalie's hand and helped her up to her feet. He glanced toward his cousin. It looked as if the bullet had hardly grazed him. There was a bullet hole in the wall right behind him.

"It's a flesh wound, Tony. Suck it up." One of the policemen untied Anthony while the other led Lydia away. She was cursing at everything in sight, most venomously at him. Matt completely ignored the woman. His attention was focused on Natalie. "And as for you—" He didn't know whether to hug her because she was alive or shake her because she could have been killed. So he just held onto her shoulders for a moment, exhaling a rather loud breath. "I knew I couldn't trust you."

He had to understand. "It's not a matter of trust. I just wanted to spare you some unnecessary work. In case you haven't noticed, your Aunt Lydia is a loon," she said, looking as the woman was being led out the door, "and she could have made the whole thing up. I just wanted to make sure she hadn't."

And then the circumstances suddenly dawned on her. How had he managed to come in the nick of time? "I thought you said you didn't know where Anthony was staying."

"I didn't," he confirmed. "But I figured my brother Scott would, so I gave him a call." He looked at her, his eyes saying volumes. "Lucky for you I did." *And lucky for me*, he added silently.

Natalie saw no reason to dispute that. "Lucky," she echoed, walking out. Both Anthony and Lydia were being placed in the backseat of the police car. Within seconds, they would be on their way to the police precinct.

"Find out anything?" Matt asked her, bringing her attention back to him.

Turning her head, she realized that they were less than a couple of inches apart—and she had this overwhelming desire just to lay her head on his shoulder. "Anthony admits to being at my sister's condo. According to him, she was already dead."

"You believe him?" Matt asked. He was inclined to. His cousin was a lot of things, most of them unsavory, but he sincerely doubted that the man was a killer. He was too much of a coward for that.

Natalie shrugged, not sure what to believe. "We had a tip from a dog walker who saw someone driving a car like Anthony's away from the scene about midnight. The ME thinks Candace was killed before then." She looked at the departing police vehicle. "Frankly, right now, my money's on your aunt. She's crazy enough to have done it and spacey enough not to remember doing it." She looked back at Matt. "I want to be there when they question her."

He had no doubt that she would get her way, even though this still wasn't supposed to be her case. "I'm sure you'll pull it off."

Natalie nodded. Suddenly, she felt as if her facade was crumbling. She looked up at the man beside her. "Thanks for not trusting me and coming to the rescue."

He grinned, for the moment forgetting the agitation he'd experienced when he couldn't reach her on her cell phone.

"Anytime." And then he grew serious. His eyes swept over her as if to reassure himself. "Did she hurt you?"

Natalie shrugged. "I'll probably have some bruises.

She's a very bony old lady, but no, she didn't." She took a deep breath, as if to fortify herself. "Could have been a lot worse if you hadn't shown up."

He laughed shortly, draping one arm protectively around her shoulders. Grateful that he'd acted on impulse.

"It was the funniest thing. Right in the middle of going over the revised expense report for the new surveillance equipment, I had the oddest feeling suddenly come over me. A premonition I guess. I had this very clear image of you—and you were in trouble. I just 'sensed' it." His voice had a mocking quality to it because he was the type who usually didn't believe in those kinds of things.

"Maybe you're taking Candace's place," Natalie theorized. "When Candace and I were younger, I swear each of us knew when the other was in trouble or even needed the other. When we grew up, that didn't happen so much. I think we were both just blocking that sixth sense out." Her expression grew very serious. "But the night Candace was killed, I had this horrible, icy sensation slice right through me. I was just falling asleep, and I bolted upright."

She shrugged. "But I thought I was just having a nightmare, so I let it go. Maybe it wasn't a nightmare. Maybe it was Candace, trying to reach out to me one last time for help."

Matt didn't try to argue her out of it. Neither did he agree outright. There were things in this world, he had come to know, that just defied logic and straightforward explanations. Like his suddenly feeling that she'd needed him.

"Maybe," he finally echoed. He looked around the motel parking lot. "Where's your car?"

"I took a cab from the police station. I didn't want to waste time going home to get my car," she explained. "I was afraid that maybe, if he *had* killed Candace, your cousin would bolt."

Matt nodded. In her place, he would have thought the same thing. "Worked a little magic on the computer to get the address?"

Her smile struck him as almost shy. Something stirred within him, and he recognized it for what it was. Not just yearning, but deep affection. "More like worked a little magic on the computer tech."

"Poor guy probably couldn't say no to you." A fond smile curved his mouth. "I know the feeling."

She thought of the letter she found beneath his pillow that awful morning. "As I recall, you said no in your own way."

He made no comment. Instead, he asked her, "Need a ride?"

She was feeling suddenly very vulnerable around Matt, but it would take time to get a cab to come and pick her up. "Yeah."

Matt opened the passenger door for her and waited until she got in.

They went to the police station where Natalie filled in an annoyed Detective Parker on the latest details regarding her sister's case. In exchange for this information, Parker grudgingly allowed her to sit in on the interviews. Anthony held fast to his story that he had nothing to do with Candace's murder, that she was already dead when he got there.

Lydia, however, rambled on and on. Finding holes in

her story and discovering that she believed the ring really belonged to her, the detectives began to believe that she had been the one to end Candace's life. When Parker finally confronted her and asked if she shoved Candace, causing the heiress to fall backward and hit her head on the marble coffee table, Lydia merely shrugged and said "Maybe."

Lydia was booked for Candace's murder within the hour.

"But then where's the ring?" Matt voiced the question out loud that was on both their minds.

Upon leaving the precinct, he'd brought Natalie back with him to The Janus. He needed to pick up his wallet, he told her, explaining that when he couldn't reach her on her cell phone, he'd left in a hurry, inadvertently leaving his wallet in his desk. He wanted to get it before he filled her in on his agenda.

Following Matt to his office, Natalie shrugged. "Who knows? She might have it, or she could have lost it, along with her mind. As far as I'm concerned, if the ring is lost, well, good riddance. It's brought my family nothing but bad luck."

Opening the middle drawer of his desk, Matt took out his wallet and tucked it into his pocket.

"Maybe not." He took her arm and gently guided her back out again. "In an odd sort of way, it brought you and me together."

She was very aware that he was touching her and drew away. She might as well start getting used to the separation. "But for how long?"

They were out on the casino floor now and perforce,

he had to get closer in order for her to hear him above the din. "That depends."

She felt his breath along her neck and throat. Not a good thing when she was trying to harden herself. "On what?"

"On how long you'll have me."

Those were the last words she expected to hear. Natalie came to a dead stop and looked at him. "Have you for what?"

"For anything you want." He took her hands in his. "I can't begin to tell you what it did to me when I thought something had happened to you." It was time to stop playing it safe, he told himself. Time for admission because life could be very short and what he had with Natalie was rare. He'd been a fool to walk away from it, even for the best of reasons. "I never stopped loving you, Natalie."

"Then why did you disappear like that?" she wanted to know. "An occasional card on Christmas would have been nice."

The only defense he had was the truth. "I left for your own good. It wasn't for mine." However, that was in the past, and he was going to find a way to make this work, no matter what. "But I realized that I really can't make it without you."

He watched her face, afraid of what her answer might be. Matt was incredibly relieved to see her smile. "Took you long enough."

Thank you, God. I owe you one, he thought. "Some of us are slow learners."

She bit her tongue to keep from making a comment. Instead, she asked, "Now what?"

This was where his agenda came in. He'd already

made plans. "Now I'm going to take a few weeks off and show you a good time. And then, after we get back, you can decide if you want to marry me."

It took everything she had not to let her mouth drop open. But she managed. "I already made that decision," she told him. "Eight years ago."

Oh damn, how did one man get to be so lucky, he wondered. There was another side to the legend of the ring, he recalled. That in the right hands, it brought true love almost immediately. Neither one of them had laid their hands on the ring, but it was as if it was still working its magic.

"And you haven't changed your mind?" he asked her.

She shook her head. "Not even when I wanted to fillet you. Idiot," she declared, lacing her arms around his neck. "I gave my heart away once—and it never came back." She sighed, as if resigned. "You still have it."

His arms closed around her. "Nice to know," he told her.

He was watching the Rothchild woman from across the casino floor. She had a lot more class than her twin'd had, but that wasn't going to save her. Class or breeding, or whatever the hell they wanted to call it, wasn't going to save any of them.

They were all living on borrowed time.

He was going to bide his time and take them out, one by one, the way he'd promised he would in his note to the old man.

Sins of the fathers, he thought, feeling righteous. They couldn't avoid their fate.

But for now, Patrick Moore was going to enjoy himself by getting under her skin like the media reporter he was pretending to be. Unlike Candace, he knew that Natalie Rothchild hated publicity and shunned it. She just wanted to live her life like an ordinary woman.

But she wasn't an ordinary woman. She was a Rothchild, and all the Rothchilds had to pay for what they'd done to his father. To his mother. And thus, to him.

Coming to life just as he saw the Rothchild woman kiss her companion, Patrick elbowed and pushed his way through the crowd. As he did, he raised his voice, calling out her name, doing his best to ruin her moment and get people to look in her direction.

"Hey, Natalie! Detective Rothchild! Word's out that they caught your sister's killer. What do you have to say about that? Think they've got the right person, or is he or she still out there, waiting to get another one of you?"

He got a kick out of asking, out of taunting her. It was doubly delicious because he knew the deranged old woman hadn't killed Candace.

He had.

Not on purpose, but by accident. But hell, that accident felt damn good when he realized she was dead. One look at her face had told him Candace Rothchild had posed for her last picture.

As he drew closer to his target, Patrick held a press card over his head to identify himself. It was like a brazen shield that indicated he had every right to bombard her with invasive questions. He knew it infuriated her.

Shoving people out of the way, he was intent on getting right up into Natalie's face, and the crowd was making that almost impossible. Getting into her face was part of his plan. He'd already done it twice to her father. He intended to do it to all of them, to make all their lives as miserable as possible—just before he ended them.

"Damn it, get out of my way," he cursed, punching the heavyset man in front of him in the kidneys.

Rather than doubling up, the man swung around and punched him in the face. Ten feet short of Natalie, Patrick Moore found himself entangled in a fistfight with a beefy stranger who was growling curses at him.

Patrick had always had a short fuse, and it had only gotten shorter with time. It took very little to unleash his maniacal side. He swung back, trading blows with the stranger. The man clearly outweighed him, but Patrick had been raised on the street. As a street fighter, he knew every dirty move there was.

Blessed with antennae when it came to his own survival, above the stranger's cursing and the crowd cheering them on, Patrick heard the man with Rothchild calling for security. The next second, the guy came running over to break up the fight himself.

Security would call the police!

The thought telegraphed itself through his brain, ushering in a sense of panic. He wasn't afraid of the police, or being in jail. Hell, he could do time standing on his head. But he couldn't afford to have the police frisk him. They'd find the ring in his pocket.

Damn it, what was he going to do now?

Out of the corner of his eye, as Patrick ducked out of the way of another punch and gauged that his opponent's arms were getting too heavy for him to keep swinging them like that, he saw a tall, willowy blonde in a body-clinging red minidress. She was almost tottering from side to side in her stiletto heels. The blonde looked a little spooked and definitely out of her element.

An out-of-towner, he thought. Even so, there was something about her that set her apart. Patrick was confident that he'd be able to pick her out of a crowd if he had to.

Besides, he didn't have much of a choice.

Swinging around, he deliberately brought the fight into her area, knocking the other guy into her. The oversized purse she was hanging on to as if her very life depended on it went crashing to the ground. Its contents came flying out.

In the middle of the fight, Patrick flung an apology her way, grabbing up the purse and holding it out to her before the other man hit him again. What neither she, his flagging opponent nor the crowd that had gathered around them seemed to notice was that Patrick Moore swiftly transferred the Tears of the Quetzal from his pocket into the depths of the cavernous purse.

"Break it up!" Matt shouted, ramming his shoulder between the two men. "You boys want to go down to the precinct to cool off?"

"Hell, he started it," the offended stranger complained, gasping for breath. "I was just trying to get back to the slot machines."

"Sorry, man. Lost my head," Patrick mumbled, nursing his cut lip. "If I don't get in a good story by the end of the day, my editor's going to fire me. I got a family to feed."

The other man looked instantly sympathetic. But Matt didn't.

"Well, you're not getting a story here," Matt informed

him, moving so that his body actually blocked the man's access to Natalie.

Patrick held up his hands, as if surrendering. Right now, it was important to just be able to slip away. There was time enough to get back to the Rothchild bitch. She wasn't going anywhere.

"Okay, okay, sorry. Won't happen again," he promised, backpedaling.

"See that it doesn't." Matt turned back to Natalie, already forgetting the incident. Having the pair arrested would mean more paperwork, and he had something better to do. He had a date with a beautiful lady and a lot of lost time to make up for.

Seeming to rub his cut lip, Patrick hid his smile behind his hand and then looked around.

The smile vanished.

As had the woman with the oversized purse.

* * * * *

HIS 7-DAY FIANCÉE

BY
GAIL BARRETT

Gail Barrett always dreamed of becoming a writer. After living everywhere from Spain to the Bahamas, raising two children and teaching high school Spanish for years, she finally fulfilled that lifelong goal. Her writing has won numerous awards, including Romance Writers of America's prestigious Golden Heart. Gail currently lives in western Maryland with her two sons, a quirky Chinook dog and her own Montana rancher turned retired coast guard officer hero. Write to her at PO Box 65, Funkstown, Maryland 21734-0065, USA, or visit her website, www.gailbarrett.com.

To my wonderful editor, Susan Litman,
with appreciation for all that you've done.
Thank you so much!

Acknowledgments

I'd like to thank the following people for their help: Destry Labo for answering my questions about Las Vegas; John K. Barrett, for his information about guns; Mary Jo Archer for her usual super help; and as always, Judith Sandbrook, critique partner extraordinaire. Thank you all!

Chapter 1

He was watching her again.

Fear razored through her belly like the slash of a switchblade—swift, hot, deep. It rippled through her awareness, stripped away her composure, shattering the illusion of safety she'd so desperately built.

Leaving her weak, defenseless, exposed.

No. Amanda Patterson wheezed air past her strangled throat, pressed her palm to her rioting heart. She wasn't weak, not anymore. And she refused to be vulnerable again.

She jerked her gaze past the line of stretch limos, inhaled deeply to steady her nerves. Cars idled by the casino on the gridlocked Strip, their horns blaring, stereos booming. Neon lights beckoned and flashed. And people streamed past, an endless parade of humanity—laughing, fearless people out to have fun on a warm April night.

She let out her breath, eased the death grip she had on her wrist, forced her shoulders to relax. She was imagining things. Wayne wasn't watching her. He wasn't even in Las Vegas. Her ex-husband was in Maryland, in prison, exactly where he belonged.

She was safe. *Safe.* She was thousands of miles away from Wayne, rid of him forever. She was in a new house, getting a new job, starting a new life.

Her sister, Kendall, finished paying the taxi driver and flashed her a smile. "Ready to rock?"

She dragged in another breath, tugged up the corners of her mouth. "You bet."

Kendall tilted her head. Her thick, honey-brown hair slid over her sculpted dancer's arms. "What's wrong? You're not worrying about Claire already are you?"

Her sister knew her too well. "No, of course not. Mrs. Schmidt seems great."

"She is great. And you warned her about Claire's allergies a dozen times. So stop worrying. Claire will have a great time. Mrs. Schmidt will spoil her to death."

To death. Amanda's heart squeezed. Dread shivered through her veins, but she shook off the gloomy thought. This was ridiculous. She was safe. Her three-year-old daughter was safe.

And she wasn't going to let her old fears ruin her new life.

"Then what is it?" Kendall probed. "It better not be Wayne because if you're going to let that creep—"

"It's not him. And I'm fine, really," she lied, embarrassed to let her sister know how rattled she was, how hard it was to quell that horrible feeling that he was spying on her, controlling her, even after all these months.

Kendall studied her with those perceptive hazel eyes.

Then her mouth softened. "Nothing's going to happen. You know that, right?"

"Right." She wouldn't let it. No matter how badly she'd mucked up the past, she owed her daughter a safe and stable life. Heck, she owed it to herself. She'd endured a hellish marriage, the terror of being stalked.

Now she was done with the past, done with the paranoia and fear—and on to a much better life.

She straightened her shoulders, tugged the hem of the tight red minidress Kendall had insisted she wear and tried for a lighter tone. "But getting arrested for indecent exposure isn't exactly what I need right now. Are you sure this dress is legal?"

Kendall tossed back her head and laughed, her trademark exuberance drawing the gazes of passing men. "Mandy, this is Vegas. The place where anything goes."

"Yes, I know, but—"

"But nothing. That dress is fabulous—although I still say you should have lost that ugly purse. Now, come on," she continued when Amanda opened her mouth to defend the huge, battered bag. "Lighten up. This is your lucky night out, remember?"

"Luck. Right." She latched on to Kendall's arm, turned toward the arched entrance to the famed Janus casino. "But walk slowly. I'm not used to these skyscraper heels."

"You're not used to having fun. Which is exactly why we're here. You're going to let loose for once—gamble, meet some hot men, have a ball."

Amanda grimaced. She had no intention of meeting men, hot or otherwise. She knew her limits too well. But Kendall was determined to light up the town, and the least she could do was try.

"Wait until you see this lobby," Kendall added as they

walked by a gleaming Bentley, then climbed the marble steps. "You're going to love it. It's right up your alley."

"My alley? Since when is gambling my thing?" She'd never placed a bet in her life.

"You'll see." The uniformed doorman swung the door open, and Kendall shot Amanda a knowing smile.

Amanda dutifully followed her inside. She gave herself a mental pep talk, tried to resist that constant urge to scan the crowds and monitor her surroundings for Wayne—a habit born of the need to survive. But she didn't need to worry about Wayne anymore. And she was *not* going to let him ruin this night.

She stepped past the doorway into the lobby, looked up and abruptly stopped. A huge, vaulted ceiling soared above her. Beneath it towered an enormous stone aqueduct, its tri-level arcades a marvel of ancient times.

"Oh, my," she murmured, and every thought of Wayne fled her mind. Captivated, she twirled in a circle, ignoring the people streaming around her, intent on absorbing every detail—the statues of Roman emperors, the decorative medallions and columns, the chariot perched on a marble dais.

"I told you," Kendall said while Amanda still gaped, trying to take it all in.

"You were right." This place was amazing. Fabulous. She felt as if she'd been dropped into ancient Rome.

Her gaze lingered on the colorful murals, the display of early black-glazed pottery, and the closet archaeologist in her thrilled. Whoever designed this place deserved an award. She couldn't believe how authentic it looked.

A woman brushed past, jostling her, and Amanda staggered to stay on her feet. She knew that she needed to move, that she was blocking the entrance, but she couldn't seem to budge. She wanted to absorb everything—the gurgling fountains, the flickering torches on the walls, the lions pacing restlessly behind glass. *Lions.* She shook her head, incredulous. This place was unreal.

Then her eyes settled on a plaster relief of Janus, and the tight ball knotting her belly began to slide loose. Janus, the Roman god of doorways and gates, endings and beginnings—the perfect symbol for her new life.

And for the first time in ages a sliver of optimism surged inside her, a long-buried glimmer of hope. She really was going to be all right here. She'd find a new job. Her daughter would thrive. She'd finally find the peace she deserved.

She smiled then, inhaling the soothing scent of moisture from the splashing fountains, the heavenly aroma of roses and gladioli brimming from urns. Still smiling, she turned to join her sister. The tang of a man's aftershave teased her nose.

Wayne's aftershave.

Her heart tripped. She stumbled, anxiety drumming through her. She glanced around, frantic to find the source of the scent, but a crowd formed around her, blocking her view.

Calm. Stay calm, she urged herself sternly. Wayne wasn't here. This had nothing to do with him.

She hauled in air, struggled to swallow around the tension gripping her throat, determined not to overreact. She stepped to the side, tried to work her way through the noisy throng to find where her sister had gone. But the people shifted and trapped her in.

"Get out of my way," a man in a white shirt shouted beside her, and his rough, raised voice agitated her nerves.

"The hell I will," another man answered.

Amanda glanced up, caught the first man's glowering face and took another step back. They were too close. Too close. Trying to beat back the onrush of panic, she cleared her throat. "Excuse me."

They ignored her. Her anxiety building, she prodded the nearest man with her elbow, intent on getting past. But another whiff of aftershave curled through her senses, and her heart made a frenzied throb.

Stop it, she lectured herself. She had no reason to be afraid. This man had nothing to do with Wayne.

And these people were not going to hurt her. She had to get over the irrational fear, this wrenching need to escape.

She pivoted, wobbled on her too-high heels, determined to get free of this mess. But then a fistfight broke out. Someone shoved. The white-shirted man pushed back, sending the beefy man into her side. Thrown off balance, she gasped, dropped her purse, and nearly fell. The contents of her handbag spilled over the floor.

Great.

Her hands trembling, urgency making her head light, she knelt, scooped up her cell phone and keys. The man in the white shirt squatted beside her. "Sorry," he muttered, his voice gruff. His aftershave assailed her, setting off a spurt of panic, unleashing a bone-deep reaction she couldn't control.

"Just leave it. Please. It doesn't matter," she pleaded, needing him to move far away. But he snatched up her wallet and tissues with his thick, stubby fingers, and stuffed them into her bag. Desperate now, unable to meet his eyes, she grabbed her purse, clutched it to her chest and rose.

"Break it up!" someone shouted as she turned and stumbled away from the arguing men. She searched through the crowd for her sister, found her waiting a few yards away.

"There you are," her sister said. "What are you doing?"

"Nothing." Her voice came out high and rushed, and she sucked in a calming breath. "I just got bumped and my purse spilled."

"I told you not to bring that bag."

"I know." She reopened the drawstring top, pawed through the jumbled contents, double-checked that her wallet was there. Relief flooded through her, and she blew out her pent-up breath.

"Well, try to keep up this time," Kendall said, and shook her head.

Feeling foolish, berating her loss of control, she trailed her sister across the room. So she'd smelled Wayne's aftershave. Big deal. He'd worn a popular brand. She'd let her imagination run away from her.

And she had to stop it. She couldn't keep letting him do this to her. Every time she thought of him, he won.

But as they crossed the enormous lobby—past the restless lions, past the Roman arches leading to intriguing gardens and baths—that feeling of trepidation crept through her again, as if eyes were boring into her back. She straightened her shoulders, determined not to assume that submissive hunch, and tried to shrug the sensation off. But it only intensified, crawling up her spine, her neck, growing stronger with every step.

Her temper flared. This was ridiculous. She didn't deserve this constant fear. She had to put an end to the lunacy now.

"Wait a minute," she said to Kendall. Defiant, she stopped, whipped around.

And met the dark, searing eyes of a man.

But not the one who'd bumped her. This man stood apart from the rest, his feet planted wide, his hands braced low on his hips, like an ancient conqueror surveying his realm.

His thick black hair gleamed in the lights. Heavy beard stubble shadowed his jaw. He had black, slashing brows, taut, masculine cheeks and a mouth so sensual it made her breath catch. A black suit gloved his tall frame.

He was handsome, riveting—shockingly so. But more than his dark looks commanded attention. He had a stillness about him, a feral intensity that exuded intelligence, authority, power.

Her heart thumped, made a funny zigzag in her chest. The word *predator* flashed through her mind.

The edge of his mouth kicked up at her blatant inspection. His eyes smoldered even more. Then his own gaze dropped, making a long, slow slide over the length of her, trailing a firestorm of heat in its wake.

Her knees trembled. A zap of awareness sizzled her blood. And a completely different type of tension arose in her nerves.

Her face burning, she whirled back toward her sister.

"Whoa, when I said hot men, I didn't mean that hot," Kendall said.

"What?" Breathless, mortified that she'd responded so outrageously, she grabbed her sister's arm and hauled her away.

"You know who that was, don't you? That was Luke Montgomery. *The* Luke Montgomery. Oh, for goodness sakes," Kendall said when she shot her a blank look.

"Don't you know anything? He's the billionaire who owns this place."

"You're kidding." She'd been ogling a billionaire? How ridiculous could she get?

"No, I'm not kidding. And I can't believe you haven't heard of him. He's been in the news for weeks. You know, because of that woman who was murdered, that casino heiress, Candace Rothchild?"

"No." Amanda slowed to navigate the steps into the gaming pit. She'd been too worried about her own precarious situation to follow the news.

Her sister paused at the bottom of the stairs and huffed out her breath. "You're hopeless. It's a good thing you're in my hands now. I'll get you caught up on tabloid gossip and have you living in sin in no time."

"Great." A wry smile nudged the corner of her mouth. "Just what I need. My own personal guide to corruption."

Kendall grinned back. "Hey, don't knock it."

"I'm not." Her sister might not lead a conventional life, but she did know how to have fun. And at least she hadn't screwed everything up like Amanda had.

Determined to forget all that, she glanced around at the flashing lights and jangling machines, the kaleidoscope of colors and noise. "All right, what's first?"

"Slots. Once you win a little, gain some confidence, we'll graduate to blackjack."

Amanda sighed. She was pathetic. Even her sister knew she couldn't just plunge in and enjoy herself. She had to be coaxed in slowly, teased into having fun.

Her sister took her arm, led her down the aisle to a couple of empty stools. "Here. These machines are loose. They pay out more often."

"How do you know that?"

Kendall propped one slim hip on the stool, squirmed to keep her own short dress from creeping up. "They do it on purpose. They figure if you win here, they can lure you back to the tables and steal your shirt. Now sit down and listen up."

Amanda slid onto the next stool over. She placed her purse on her lap, her amusement growing as her sister gave her a crash course on gambling with slots.

Not that her sister's expertise surprised her. Growing up, Kendall had been everything Amanda was not—confident, popular, outgoing. She'd been the star of every party, the diva on every stage. And she hadn't been afraid to pursue her goals. The day after high school ended she'd hopped on the first bus to Vegas and landed her dream job dancing in a show.

Whereas the far-too-cautious, ever-responsible Amanda had become a teacher and married Wayne.

"Got it?" Kendall asked.

Amanda pulled her thoughts from the past. "I think so." She tugged a twenty dollar bill from her wallet and fed it into the machine, saw the credits appear.

"Here goes." She inhaled, selected the maximum number of coins, and pushed the button to spin the machine. Bars whirred, then stopped. More credits appeared, and she widened her eyes. "Hey, I won."

"I knew you would." Kendall's smile was smug. "I told you your luck was going to change tonight."

"Maybe so." Buoyed by that small success, she pushed the button again. Three lemons. Getting the hang of it now, she threw herself into the game. Cherries combined with sevens. Lemons were followed by bars. Bells dinged. Colored lights flashed. Credits accumulated, then disappeared. Beside her, Kendall cheered, groaned and clapped at her own progress. And a half hour and a free margarita later, Amanda felt like a seasoned pro.

"Ready for the blackjack table?" Kendall called over the noise.

Amanda glanced up. "Go ahead. I'll be there in a minute. I've just got a few pulls left."

"Okay. It's in the back." Kendall drained her drink, hopped off her stool and then jiggled her legs to straighten her dress. "Don't forget to take your ticket. We'll cash out before we leave."

Amanda waved her off and returned her attention to her machine. In the periphery of her vision, she saw Kendall collect her ticket and leave.

She pulled the lever. Lemon-bar-seven. *Drats.* She pushed the button again and won. She grinned, pleased with her take so far. Not too shabby for her first attempt at gambling. She was ahead by fifteen bucks.

And she had to hand it to her sister. It was fun to do something mindless for once, to forget her problems and relax. Kendall had been right to insist that they come.

She gave the button a final press, then waited for the tumbler to stop. "Come on, jackpot," she murmured. A seven stuck. Then another. She held her breath, her hopes rising, her eyes glued on the machine.

The scent of Wayne's aftershave drifted past.

Her heart went still. Every cell in her body tensed.

The machine stopped. She stared at it blindly, her palms suddenly sweating, her pulse pounding so hard she could barely hear.

Wayne wasn't here. He couldn't be here.

Then why was this happening to her?

She gripped her purse like a lifeline, fought the urge to glance over her shoulder and check. She couldn't keep doing this. She couldn't keep panicking and falling apart. Dear God, it had to stop.

But the need to look back grew even stronger—the instinct to protect herself, take cover. *Survive.* Unable to stand it, she leaped from the stool and whipped around.

No one was there.

She didn't move.

Lights flashed on another machine. A woman squealed and laughed down the aisle. Amanda hitched out her breath, ran her gaze up and down the rows, but there was no sign of the man who'd bumped her, no sign of Wayne.

Thoroughly rattled, she turned back to her machine and printed out her credits with trembling hands. Had she imagined that scent? Was that even possible? Her mentally ill mother had hallucinated before she'd—

No. She was not losing her mind.

Maybe it was a flashback, a delayed reaction to stress. The past few years had worn her down completely—Wayne's abuse, the constant fear for her daughter's safety, the painful divorce and move. No wonder she was suffering now.

And she would conquer this fear. *She would.*

Her heart still racing, she inhaled to calm her nerves. Then she walked deliberately toward the back of the casino, refusing to let herself rush. There was nothing to be afraid of. Nothing.

She paused at the end of the aisle, unsure which way to go. Taking a guess, she turned right.

The scent of aftershave hit her again.

Her stomach balled tight. Her heart sped into her

throat. She picked up the pace, walking faster now, even though she knew there was nothing wrong. She was safe, *safe.*

She hurried past a group of noisy gamblers. A bell dinged, and someone cheered. Knowing she was acting foolish but unable to stifle the fear, she walked as fast as she could on the spindly heels. *Run, run, run* bludgeoned her nerves.

She reached the end of the aisle, turned again, then reached some swinging doors. Oh, no. She'd gone the wrong way. The blackjack tables had to be across the pit.

She stopped, started to turn, but Wayne's scent swarmed her again. A hard, narrow object bit into her back, and she froze.

"That's right," the man said. "Stay quiet, and you won't get hurt."

Her knees buckled. A dull roar invaded her skull. The obscene smell of aftershave permeated the air.

"Walk over to the doors. Slow now." He rammed the gun deeper into her back, and she stepped forward, trying to battle through the hysteria and think. It wasn't Wayne. He had the wrong voice. But then what on earth did he want?

"Stop," he demanded when she reached the double doors. "Now give me the ring. And no fast moves."

"R…ring?" He wanted her jewelry? But she didn't wear any. She wheezed in the too-thick air. "But—"

"Now." His voice turned harsher. He prodded her again with the gun.

"But I don't…"

The double doors swung open. A waitress stepped out, balancing a tray.

Now or never.

She lunged, slammed into the waitress. The woman shrieked, staggered back and dropped the tray.

Amanda didn't hesitate. She ran.

Chapter 2

The soft buzz of his private telephone line cut through the silence—muted, deceptively quiet, like the rattle of a Mojave Desert Sidewinder preparing to strike. Luke Montgomery stared out his penthouse window at the Las Vegas skyline shimmering against the dark velvet sky. He'd left instructions not to be disturbed. A call now could only mean one thing.

Trouble. Just what he didn't need.

He exhaled, knowing he couldn't postpone the inevitable, and padded across the carpet to his desk. He punched the button to answer the phone. "Yeah."

"Mr. Montgomery. Frank Ruiz in security. I'm sorry to bother you, but there was an armed robbery attempt in the gaming pit. I thought you'd want to know."

"I'll be right there."

Luke disconnected the phone and frowned. An armed robbery attempt. Interesting timing with the investment consortium scheduled to vote in just two weeks. A coincidence or something more?

Thoughtful, he pulled his suit jacket from the chair where he'd tossed it, slipped it on as he strode to the door. Coincidence or not, he couldn't afford the bad publicity. Candace Rothchild's murder had caused enough problems.

Not that being suspected of murder had hurt his business. He exited his penthouse, the edge of his mouth ticked up in a cynical smile. Crowds flocked to his casino, whipped up by lurid rumors in the tabloids, hoping to glimpse the man who'd supposedly clubbed the heiress to death.

But his consortium investors weren't nearly as intrigued. The murder—combined with the downturn in the economy—had made them nervous. Too nervous. More problems now would cause them to bolt.

And no way could he let that happen.

His gaze hardening, he crossed to his private elevator, then leaned back against the mahogany panels as it started down. He had everything riding on this project. He'd spent twenty years meticulously constructing his empire, amassing money, power.

Twenty years plotting revenge.

The elevator doors slid open, and he headed toward the security office, ignoring the employees scurrying out of his way. Nothing could jeopardize this project. Nothing. If this robbery attempt was legit, he'd hush it up, keep it out of the papers until the deal went through. And if it wasn't…

He mentally shrugged. Whoever had planned this escapade had made a mistake, a big one. No one played Luke Montgomery for a fool.

A lesson the Rothchilds should have learned long ago.

He entered the office, met the eyes of the guard on duty behind the desk. The balding man leaped to his feet. "Mr. Montgomery." He tugged at the tie dangling from his beefy neck.

Luke nodded, got straight to the point. "What's going on?"

"A woman said she was held up at gunpoint near the slot machines. I've pulled up the surveillance tapes. She's in the next room."

"Let's see the tapes." He rounded the desk as Ruiz lowered himself into his chair and keyed the bank of monitors to the proper time.

The screens flickered, and suddenly a woman strolled into view from a dozen angles. Her full hips swiveled with a seductive swing. Her high breasts shifted and swayed.

Luke's gaze cut to her face, and his heart made a sudden swerve. Well, hell. It was the blonde he'd admired earlier in the lobby.

He studied her now with frank appreciation. She was on the tall side, slender, but the tight dress revealed her ample curves. She had long, shiny hair, sweetly rounded hips, the kind of killer legs that could fuel his fantasies for years.

He slanted his head. She wasn't the usual overblown Vegas type, despite the skimpy dress. She seemed more natural, unstudied—a rarity in Sin City, a place where illusions ruled.

She stumbled on the mile-high heels, regained her balance and glanced around. The cameras caught her darting gaze, and his gut went still.

She looked furtive. Guilty.

Bad move, babe. Better to look nervous *after* the guy with the gun shows up.

As if on cue, a man appeared on scene. The newcomer kept his head bent low, his face carefully hidden from the camera's view. His long, stringy hair swung past his jaw, hiding his features even more.

Luke's gaze narrowed on the man's pleated blue shirt and black bow tie—the uniform his dealers wore. "Is he one of ours?"

"We don't know yet. We're checking the records now."

He rubbed his stubble-roughened jaw, watched the episode play out. The galley doors swung open. A waitress stepped out, carrying a tray. The blonde crashed into her, then bolted off, while the man ran the other way.

He raised a brow. The blonde thought fast on her feet, he'd give her that much. "Who is she?"

The guard consulted his notes. "Amanda Patterson. Said she arrived in Las Vegas last week. She's staying with her sister, Kendall Patterson, a dancer in your ten-o'clock show."

Luke thought back to the brunette he'd seen with her in the lobby. A dealer and a dancer. An inside job, then? Probably a scam to sue the casino.

The spurt of disappointment took him by surprise. He knew better than to expect the blonde to be innocent. This was Vegas. Everyone was on the make. Even the prettiest face masked a conniving heart.

The guard switched to another screen, and Luke watched the man exit the casino, still hiding his face. He checked the time on the tape. Twenty minutes ago. No point looking for him now.

"Let me know what the employee search brings up. Contact legal, call the police. Get Martinez over here if you can." He and Martinez went way back to their childhood in Naked City, the slums beyond the Strip. He could count on him to keep the story hushed until the Phoenix deal went through.

He turned, headed down the hall to interview the blonde. Chances were that this was an inside job, but he couldn't rule out the Rothchilds. Harold Rothchild was buried in debt, his empire on the verge of collapse. Luke's project would seal his doom.

Which was exactly what Luke planned.

Of course, if the Phoenix project failed, he would suffer instead. He set his jaw. Good thing he didn't intend to fail.

He pushed open the office door, spotted the blonde standing by the desk. She turned toward him as he entered the room.

His gaze met hers. A sudden awareness shivered between them, and he hesitated in midstride.

She was even more attractive close up. Her eyes were a deep, startling blue, as vibrant as the desert sky. She had pale, creamy skin, a smattering of freckles on her feminine nose. Her lips looked soft and lush.

She was pretty, damned pretty—stunning if he factored in those world-class legs.

But this close he could also sense an aura of vulnerability about her. She stood with her shoulders hunched, her arms crossed tightly across her chest. Dark circles shadowed her eyes.

The sudden urge to protect her caught him off guard.

He frowned, shook himself out of his daze. This woman didn't need his protection. For all he knew, she was here to swindle him. "Amanda Patterson?"

"Yes." Her low, smoky voice slid through him, doing strange things to his insides.

He crossed the room. "I'm Luke Montgomery."

"Yes, I know, I…" A blush crept up her cheeks. "My sister pointed you out earlier."

He'd bet. He reached out his hand. She hesitated, then gripped his palm. The smooth, silky feel of her skin arrowed through him, deleting his thoughts. He was held immobile by those amazing blue eyes. His heart beat hard in his chest.

After several long moments, he realized he was still holding her hand. He scowled, pried his fingers loose, annoyed by the effort it took. What the hell was that about? He hadn't been that affected by a woman in years.

And this one could be trying to deceive him.

"Have a seat." Anxious to put some distance between them, he retreated to the desk, then leaned back against it and folded his arms.

She perched on the leather chair in front of the desk and crossed her legs. His gaze fell to her lean, bare thighs, traced the elegant curve of her calves. Realizing his thoughts were derailing again, he lifted his eyes.

"So what happened?" His tone was more brusque than he'd intended, and she blinked.

She sat up straighter, flexed her wrist as if it ached. Her chest rose as she drew in a breath. "I was going to the blackjack tables to find my sister, but I got lost. I've never been here before. I started to turn around but then a…a man came up behind me."

Her voice trembled convincingly, but he was determined to stay objective. "He was armed?"

"I think so. He jabbed something into my back. I thought…it felt like a gun."

"Then what?"

"He said…he wanted my jewelry, my ring."

His gaze cut to her unadorned ears, to the cleavage bared by the plunging dress, and his mind flashed back to the tapes. He hadn't noticed any jewelry before the attack. A slipup there.

"So you handed it over?" he asked, knowing damned well she hadn't.

But she surprised him by shaking her head. "No, I…I don't have any jewelry, not anymore." She lifted one slender shoulder and lowered her eyes. "I sold everything a while back when I needed the money."

So she was short on cash. Good motive to run a scam.

He pinched the bridge of his nose and sighed. No matter how attractive she was, he didn't have time for this farce. He'd make sure the Rothchilds weren't involved, keep this damned thing out of the news, then let the police handle the rest.

"So you're saying a man held you up with a gun you didn't see, and demanded jewelry that you don't have."

A small frown creased her brow. "You don't believe me? You think I made this up?"

"We have cameras all over the casino. I saw the tapes." He raised his brows. "You looked nervous even before the man showed up."

Her smooth lips parted. The color drained from her face. "But that's because I thought…I thought…" She pressed her fingers to her lips and closed her eyes.

"You thought what? That you'd pretend to be attacked and sue the casino?"

Her eyes flew open, and she gasped. "You think I'd pretend about something like that? Are you joking?"

She let out a high-pitched laugh. "Oh, God. This figures. I thought…" She shook her head, gathered her bulky purse and rose. "Forget it."

"The hell I will." He pushed himself away from the desk and blocked her path. "You thought what?"

"Nothing. It doesn't matter." She tried to step around him, but he reached out and grabbed her upper arm. She flinched, jerked back. "Let me go."

He dropped her arm, stunned by the urgency in her voice, the flash of fear in her eyes. She quickly scuttled away.

He studied her, taken aback. She couldn't be this good of an actress. She was actually afraid of him.

He eased apart his hands, made his expression neutral, his voice nonthreatening so she wouldn't bolt. "Look, I'm not trying to hurt you. I just need to know what happened."

"I…" She nodded, sucked in her breath, as if to pull herself together. "I didn't really… It was just…my ex-husband. Wayne Wheeler. I thought he was here."

He eyed the distance she'd put between them, the wary way she watched him—defensive, alert, like a cornered animal ready to run. And anger stirred in his gut. He had no patience for abusive men. And unless he was wildly off base, this woman had been attacked.

He struggled to keep the emotion from his voice. "Your ex lives around here?"

She shook her head, sending her silky hair sliding over her arms. "He's in Maryland, in jail. It wasn't him. It wasn't even his voice. But I thought, earlier… I was just nervous. I overreacted. I'm sorry." She rubbed her forehead with a trembling hand, sank back into her chair.

He frowned. He didn't doubt her story. Her fear looked real… And the facts would be easy to check.

So what should he do about it? Assuming she was telling the truth, this still didn't eliminate the Rothchilds' involvement. Or her sister's. It wouldn't be the first time an unsuspecting family member had been an accomplice to a crime.

Which led him back to his original problem. He paced across the room, pivoted, then returned to lean against the desk. He had to contain this, keep it out of the news. He couldn't let that consortium implode.

Which meant making sure Amanda Patterson didn't talk.

But somehow the thought that anyone would hurt this gentle woman made it hard to stay detached.

"I need to go." Her eyes pleaded with his. "My sister will be wondering where I am. I left her a voice mail that I'd meet her in the lobby."

"You can leave as soon as you talk to the police." A knock sounded on the door, and he rose. "That's probably the detective now. I'll walk you out to the lobby when you're done."

"All right." Their gazes held. The vulnerable look in her eyes tugged at something inside him, urging him to shelter her, to keep her safe.

He shook it off. Her life, her problems were none of his concern. The only thing he needed to do was convince her not to talk. But she had been attacked in his casino. He could at least alleviate some of her fear. He turned, strode out the door.

Ramón Martinez from the Las Vegas Metropolitan Police Department was waiting for him in the hall. "Martinez." Luke shook his hand, briefed him on the situation, and the need to keep it quiet for now. "Could you check on the ex and make sure he's still in jail?" he added. "The name's Wheeler. Wayne Wheeler."

"No problem." The detective flipped open his cell phone, called in the information. "It'll take a few minutes to run him through the system. I'll get a statement from the Patterson woman and get back to you on that."

"Thanks." Luke returned to the main office, had his security guard run the tapes again as he waited for the detective to finish up. Now that he'd heard Amanda's version of events, the anxiety in her eyes made sense.

His gaze lingered on the seductive flare of her hips, those endless legs. It was too bad she wasn't his type. She was a damned attractive woman. But he only dated celebrities, supermodels, women willing to hang on his arm for an evening in exchange for a fancy meal.

He didn't have relationships, and he didn't mix dating with business. And that's all Amanda Patterson could ever be—a business concern. One he needed to wrap up now.

She emerged from the office a few minutes later. "I heard back about Wheeler," Martinez said from behind her. "He's still in jail."

"Good." He caught Amanda's gaze, and that disturbing attraction rocked through him again. His eyes dipped from her face to those killer legs, and he had to struggle to remember his plan. "I'll walk you out."

He nodded to the detective, held the door open for Amanda, then accompanied her down the carpeted hall. He liked how her long strides kept pace with his, how her height made it easy to meet her eyes.

"Thanks for checking on Wayne for me," she said, her voice subdued. "It helps to know he's far away." Her eyes held his, and the worry lurking in those vivid eyes bothered him more than he cared to admit.

"No problem. I have a favor to ask, though." They reached the door to the lobby, and he paused. "I'd like to keep this incident out of the news—at least for a couple of weeks. I'm in the middle of some negotiations right now, and I don't want the publicity. So if anyone calls you—any reporters, the tabloids—I'd appreciate it if you didn't talk."

"Okay."

"The paparazzi can be persistent," he warned her. "I doubt they'll get wind of this, but if they do they'll call, show up at your door, follow you around."

"But that's ridiculous." Her forehead wrinkled. "Why would they care what happened to me?"

"They won't. But I'm big news these days."

"I see." She bit her lip, made that flexing motion with her wrist again.

He frowned. "Did you get hurt back there?"

"What?" She looked at her wrist. "Oh. No, it's an old injury. It aches sometimes."

He nodded, tugged his business card from his inside pocket and held it out, determined to make sure she complied. "Here's my number. Call me if they show up. I'll top whatever they're willing to pay."

She blinked, shot him a look of disbelief. "You're offering to pay me not to talk?"

"I told you that I don't want the publicity right now."

"Well, neither do I." Stunned outrage tinged her voice. "I have a daughter to protect. I don't want to be in the news."

But money had a way of changing minds. And the tabloids' pockets were deep. "Take the card, Amanda." He pressed it into her hand. "Just call me if they contact you."

She glanced at the card and shook her head. "There's really no need. I told you that I won't talk."

He let out a cynical laugh. "Promises don't mean much when money's involved."

"Well, mine does."

Her eyes simmered with indignation.

He tilted his head, impressed. Despite her air of fragility, the woman had courage. He liked how she held her ground.

Hell, he liked a lot of things about her. His gaze lowered, traced the sultry swell of her lips, then flicked back to her brilliant blue eyes. And hunger pulsed inside him, the slow, drugging beat of desire.

But this woman had no place in his plans. He stepped away, crushing back the urge to touch her, giving them some much-needed space.

She cleared her throat. "I'd say good-night, but it hasn't really been good, has it?"

"No, not good." Especially with this disturbing attraction between them.

"Farewell, then." She turned, pushed open the door.

He followed her into the lobby, then stopped, inhaling deeply to clear his mind. His eyes tracked the alluring swivel of her hips as she continued across the marble floor. She joined her sister, and the two women walked to the door.

But suddenly she paused, glanced back. Her eyes met his, and another bolt of electricity zapped his nerves. Then she pivoted on her high heels and went out the door.

For a long moment, he just stood there, the image of

those lush lips and long legs scorched in his brain. Then he slowly eased out his breath.

So that was done. She was gone. He had no reason to see her again. His security chief and the police could handle the investigation from here.

He hoped her ex-husband left her alone, though. He hated to think of her afraid, cowering before some brute.

And he hoped that he could trust her. Amanda Patterson was a wild card, an unknown, someone beyond his control.

Someone, he had a feeling, it would take a very long time to forget.

Chapter 3

The telephone was ringing again.

Amanda sat motionless on her sister's patio, her muscles tensing, the teaching application she'd filled out forgotten in her hand.

"Phone, Mommy," Claire announced from her turtle-shaped sandbox in the yard.

"I know." Amanda tried not to let fear seep into her voice. "But Aunt Kendall's at rehearsal. We'll let the answering machine pick it up." And hope to God it wasn't another hang-up call.

The answering machine kicked on, and her sister's perky voice floated through the open sliding glass door. The machine beeped. The abrupt silence of the disconnected line made her stomach churn.

She set down her papers and rubbed her arms—chilled now, despite the heat. It was just another wrong number or a junk phone call. There was nothing sinister about people calling and hanging up. Annoying, yes. Dangerous, no.

Even if the hang-up calls had only begun three days ago, after the casino attack. Even if they now got a dozen such calls a day. Even if whenever she answered the phone, there was only heavy, ominous breathing—nothing more.

It couldn't be reporters. They would talk to her, ask questions, not just breathe and hang up.

This was something Wayne would do—something he had done to unsettle her nerves. But Wayne was in jail. That detective had checked.

She set her pen on the table and rose, placed a rock over the job application so it wouldn't flutter away. Regardless of who was calling, she wasn't going to let this get to her. And she wasn't going to let Claire sense her fear. She'd moved here to give her daughter a safer, more peaceful life, and she would succeed.

"It's time to get the mail and have our snack." She struggled to make her voice cheerful, but Claire still looked at her and frowned. "How about some apple juice and animal crackers today?"

"Okay." Claire trotted over, and Amanda brushed the sand off her daughter's bottom and hands, adjusted the sun hat flopping around her sweet face.

"Wait. Brownie." Claire grabbed the bear she'd propped on the patio chair and hugged it close. Too close. Had Claire picked up on her fear?

She forced a smile to lighten the mood. "Is Brownie going to help us get the mail?" She knew the answer, of course. Claire didn't go anywhere without her bear. Brownie ate with her, slept with her, played with her.

She'd hugged off most of its fur, kissed the color from its once-black eyes. Amanda prayed that bear never got lost, or Claire would be destroyed.

"You two can lead the way," she added, and followed her along the walkway to the gate. Her sister lived in one of the new developments that had sprung up during the recent building boom. It was a modest, family-oriented neighborhood with two-story stucco homes, a far cry from Wayne's luxury condo at the Ritz Carlton in DC. And thank goodness for that. Wayne had been all about status, appearances. He didn't care that there'd been no place for Claire to ride a bike or play.

She unlatched the gate, waited for Claire to toddle through. She couldn't even begin to imagine how Luke Montgomery lived. She'd read up on him during the past few days, learned that he was a notorious playboy, a megabillionaire developer who owned casinos and resorts throughout the world. That suit he'd worn had probably cost more than her car.

An image of his broad, muscled shoulders, the dark, sexy planes of his face flashed into her mind. She didn't doubt the playboy part. The man was lethally attractive with his deeply graveled voice and intense eyes. And that moment in the hallway when she'd thought he was going to kiss her…

She shut the gate behind her with a forceful click. Surely she'd imagined his interest in her. Luke Montgomery operated completely outside her orbit—which was fine with her. She had all she wanted in life right here. Maybe she didn't hobnob with billionaires, and maybe she'd once dreamed of a more exciting life, but she had a great sister, a daughter she adored. And soon she'd have a job and her own house, too.

She just needed to lose this constant fear.

"Wait for me," she warned Claire. She grabbed her daughter's hand to make sure she didn't dart off, then walked with her toward the mailbox. The warm sun shimmered off the neighbors' red-tiled roofs. Palm fronds rustled in the breeze. Laughter and the thump of a bouncing basketball came from some teens shooting hoops down the street.

She let Claire open the mailbox and pull out the advertisements and bills. She lunged forward to catch a sheath of junk mail tumbling loose.

"Mine," Claire cried and clutched the mail.

"I'm just getting the stuff that fell." She scooped up the ads and stray letters and then closed the box. A plain white envelope in her hand caught her eye.

She paused, turned it over. No name. No address.

A sliver of foreboding snaked up her back.

She shook it off, exasperated by her overreaction. She was getting ridiculous, imagining danger at every turn. It was probably an advertisement. She tore open the back flap, pulled out the contents—a piece of white paper, some photos.

Photos of Claire.

Her heart stopped.

She flipped through the photos. Claire riding her pink tricycle. Claire eating at the kitchen table. Claire sleeping next to Brownie in her bed.

The air turned thick. Her hands shook as she unfolded the note. *"Put the diamond in the mailbox or else."*

Her lungs seized up. Sheer panic roared through her veins. She fought to maintain her composure, but every instinct screeched at her to snatch Claire up and flee.

Calm down, she ordered herself fiercely. Don't let Claire see your fear.

Forcing her feet to move slowly, normally, she followed her daughter back to the house. She looked casually to the neighbor's windows—no movement there. She opened the gate and let Claire through, then snuck a glance at the street. Empty.

But someone was spying on them, taking photos of Claire.

Her panic intensified, threatening to overwhelm her, but she ruthlessly crushed it down. She ushered Claire calmly into the house and locked the sliding glass door. She lifted Claire to the sink and washed her hands. Still working on autopilot, she took out the juice, helped Claire into her chair, opened the animal crackers and propped up the bear.

"What's wrong, Mommy?" Claire asked, her voice tight.

"Nothing. Nothing at all." Her falsely cheerful voice sounded too far away. "It's just a little hot in here. I'm going to close the drapes to keep it cool. I'll be right back."

She forced her lips into a brittle smile, closed the blinds on the sliding glass door and strolled sedately into the hall. Then she raced around the house like a maniac, locking the windows, yanking the drapes closed, scrambling up and down the stairs, rushing from room to room to room, throwing the deadbolts on every door.

She returned to the kitchen, sank into a seat across the table from Claire and covered her face with her hands. What on earth was going on here? What diamond? She'd sold her wedding ring as soon as she'd left Wayne.

Besides, Wayne was in jail. It couldn't be him.

Unless he'd hired someone else to harass her.

Trying to compose herself, she scrubbed her face with her quivering hands. God, she was sick of this. So bloody tired. All she wanted was a life without fear. Was that too much to ask?

The phone rang.

She jerked up her head, stared at the phone. Her palms started to sweat.

The ringing stopped. The answering machine turned on. Her sister's message ended, and the machine made its high-pitched beep.

And then there was heavy breathing.

"Tonight." The single word cleaved the silence, detonating her nerves. The machine clicked off. The tape whirred softly as it rewound.

Her adrenaline surged. Panic wiped out her thoughts. She had to run. Flee. Go somewhere, anywhere, and keep her daughter safe.

She looked at Claire, saw her daughter's lower lip quiver, the anxiety pinching her face. And she knew with dead certainty that she couldn't run. If this was Wayne, he'd only find them again. For Claire's sake, she had to end this terror now.

And if there was one thing she'd learned about her ex-husband, it was that he thrived on power and control. He wanted to see her run, plead, whimper with fear. And she'd be damned if she'd play his sick games.

She rose, her knees knocking so hard she could barely stand, and crossed the kitchen to the answering machine. She ejected the tape, slipped it into her pocket and disconnected the phone.

Then she grabbed her purse from the counter and

fumbled through her wallet for Detective Martinez's card. She found Luke Montgomery's number instead.

She hesitated. Should she call him? If the letter and phone calls were related to the casino attack, he would want to know.

But her priority was Claire, keeping her safe. Which meant reporting this to the police—no matter what Luke Montgomery might want.

Still, the memory of the skepticism in his eyes made her pause. He hadn't trusted her; that had been clear. He thought she'd sell her story to the highest bidder, even though she'd given him her word.

And maybe she was a fool to care, but there was something sad about a man that cynical, who thought that money always talked. And if she didn't call him now, she'd only confirm his jaded beliefs.

So maybe she should warn him. Maybe she should update him on this latest threat first and then inform the police.

And pray that whoever was watching them didn't see them go.

She met her daughter's frightened eyes, and a frigid pit formed in her gut. Claire was right to be afraid. Because if their watcher learned what she was up to, her daughter would pay the price.

The Las Vegas police were certainly thorough. Three hours later, Amanda still hunched on a folding metal chair in the Las Vegas Metropolitan Police station while Claire dozed on her lap. She'd turned over the evidence, given multiple statements, submitted fingerprints so they could exclude her prints from the note. Now several people crowded around her in the air-conditioned room—the detective she'd met in the casino, a petite police officer named Natalie Rothchild, several others whose names she couldn't recall.

And Luke Montgomery. He'd arrived shortly after she had, to her surprise. Now he sat in the chair beside her, the sleeves of his crisp white shirt rolled up, his dark forearms braced on his knees, listening intently while Natalie Rothchild summed up the case.

The police officer tucked her short brown hair behind her ears, then cleared her throat. "All right, then. In light of these developments, I think we have to consider the possibility that the ring isn't lost after all."

"Damn," Luke muttered.

Amanda glanced around at the circle of grim faces, confused. "What ring?"

Detective Martinez shifted his bulky frame in his seat. "We had a murder case recently—a woman named Candace Rothchild. You might have read about it in the news."

"Yes." She'd read up on the sensational case after she'd met Luke.

"She was Natalie's sister," he added.

"Oh." Amanda shifted her gaze to the other woman. "I'm sorry."

Natalie nodded. A pained look shadowed her eyes. "The night she was killed, Candace was wearing a diamond ring, a family heirloom we called the Tears of the Quetzal. We never found it, so we assumed it was lost. But we'll have to rethink that now."

Amanda frowned. "You think my note is related to that ring?"

"I think we have to consider that possibility, yes."

"But I just moved here. How could I possibly be involved?"

"That's what we need to find out. And it might not be related. But we can't rule it out, especially since the man who held you up demanded a ring. And that note is similar to the one my father received." She turned her head, spoke to one of the men. "Get that note to Lex Duncan at the FBI, will you?"

Amanda's head whirled. She gaped at the nodding men. Surely they were joking. She was tangled up in a diamond theft? It didn't make any sense.

She gave her head a sharp shake, tried to recall the facts of the case. From what she'd read, Luke had hosted a jewelry convention in his casino a few weeks back. Celebrities from around the globe had attended the glitzy event—including the casino heiress Candace Rothchild. Later that night she'd been murdered, her ring stolen. The priceless diamond ring—rumored to be under a bizarre curse promising the wearer love at first sight—had never been found.

Luke had originally been a suspect, although he'd later been cleared of the crime. She cut her gaze to his harsh profile, noted the rigid line of his jaw. No wonder he'd come here. He was as involved in this case as she was.

She pressed her hand to her throat, still unable to process it all. It was bad enough to think Wayne could be watching her. But a vicious murderer…

"There's something else I need to tell you," Natalie said gently.

Dazed, Amanda jerked her attention from Luke. The other police officers rose and began filing out. "I'm sorry. What?"

"Your ex-husband was released from jail last week."

Shock rippled through her. She tightened her hold on Claire. "But…Detective Martinez said he was in jail."

Natalie made a face. "I'm sorry. There was a computer glitch, and some of the data didn't get entered on time. Wheeler reported to his parole officer in Maryland yesterday, though, so you shouldn't have to worry about him."

"You don't know Wayne." He was clever. Cunning. And he knew her habits, her fears. She closed her eyes, felt her skin go cold. Her worst nightmare had just returned.

Natalie stood. "We've increased our patrols in your neighborhood, and we'll have someone monitor the house tonight in case anyone goes near that mailbox. We've also told Maryland to alert us if Wheeler breaks his parole."

It wouldn't do any good. Wayne had gotten around those measures before. A tight ball of terror knotted her gut.

Natalie shook her hand. "We'll be in touch."

"Thank you," she whispered, knowing there wasn't much else the police could do. She'd learned that fact back East.

"Claire, honey." She nudged her daughter gently to wake her. "It's time to go."

She roused her daughter, helped her to her feet, then left the room on quivering legs. Behind her, Luke and Natalie began to talk.

So Wayne was out of jail. He would come after her, if he hadn't already. He'd promised her he would. And if that weren't enough, she had a killer on her heels, demanding a ring she didn't have. Hysteria gurgled inside her. Could her life get any worse?

And what on earth should she do? Clutching Claire's small hand, she exited the building, then squinted in the blinding sun. She had to go home, warn Kendall. But then what? Should she leave town?

Would it do any good? Running from Wayne was hard enough. How could she flee an enemy she didn't know?

"Mommy," Claire said, her voice anxious.

Realizing she'd been squeezing Claire's hand, she relaxed her grip. "Don't worry. Everything's okay," she lied. She knelt, ignored the pavement sizzling her bare knees, and gave her daughter a hug. She buried her face in her hair, inhaled her little-girl scent, held her small, warm body tight against hers.

But a terrible dread lodged inside her, a wild, desperate fear that seeped like ice through her bones. How could she protect her daughter from a killer? She'd never felt more terrified in her life.

But she had to succeed. Claire's life was in her hands. She opened her eyes, smoothed the silky strands of hair from her daughter's cheeks, then eased her grip and rose.

"How about macaroni and cheese for dinner?" she suggested. This was definitely a comfort food night. "And then we'll watch a movie, maybe *Mary Poppins.* Would Brownie like that?"

Claire whispered to her bear, then held it up to her ear. Her big blue eyes met hers. "*The Little Mermaid,* too."

"Sure, we can do that." They might as well watch movies all night. No way would she fall asleep knowing a killer was lurking outside. She grabbed Claire's hand and stepped off the curb.

"Amanda, wait." She glanced back, surprised to see Luke Montgomery hurrying toward her, his black hair glinting in the sun.

He caught up to her and stopped. He glanced at Claire, then leveled his whiskey-brown eyes at hers. "We need to talk."

"Sure." Although she couldn't imagine what he'd have to say. She motioned to her green Honda Accord across the lot. "I parked in the shade. Why don't we talk over there?"

"All right." She started across the lot with Claire, and he slowed his pace to theirs. Without her high heels on, she was more aware of his height, the power in his fluid stride.

She slid a glance at the hard male planes of his face, that sexy, carnal mouth. His eyes captured hers, and a sudden tension sparked between them, igniting a flurry of nerves. She quickly turned away.

They stopped in the patch of shade beside her car. He leaned back against it, folded his muscled arms across his chest. His gaze caught hers again, touching off another rush of adrenaline, and she forced herself to breathe.

"What kind of security system do you have?" he asked.

"On the house?" She frowned, led Claire around the car to the rear passenger door, hoping the distance would quiet her nerves. "We don't have one, just locks on the windows and doors."

"That's what I figured." He turned to face her, propped his forearm on the roof, drawing her gaze to the black hair marching across his tanned arm. "If that killer's out there, you need better protection than that."

Her stomach clenched. "I know." But it would take time to get a security system installed—time she didn't have.

"I have a place you can stay," he said, and she raised

her brows. "A house. It's in a gated community on the north side of town. It has an alarm system, round-the-clock security guards. You'll be safe there."

She stared at him over the roof. He was offering her the use of his house? "That's nice of you, but—"

"I'm not doing it to be nice. Not entirely." The edge of his mouth quirked up. "You and your daughter need protection. I don't want any bad publicity right now. If you're in a safe place, the attacks will stop. It solves both our problems.

"The house is comfortable enough," he continued. "It has a pool, tennis courts, a home theater. If there's anything else you need, you can let me know."

Comfortable enough? He had to be joking. She'd seen pictures of the mansion in the tabloids. It put a sheikh's desert palace to shame. "Comfort isn't the issue."

"Then what is?"

She made an exasperated sound. "Well, for starters, I don't even know you."

He lifted one broad shoulder in a shrug. "You'd hardly see me. I spend most of my time in my penthouse. And it's only until they find this guy."

"Even so..." She shook her head, opened the car door for Claire. It was impossible, crazy. "What if the tabloids find out? Won't that make things worse?"

"I doubt they'll find out. They won't expect it, and I pay my staff not to talk. Although..." He drummed his fingers on the car roof, and a calculating look entered his eyes. "That's not a bad idea. We could spin it, play that angle up. Hell, the consortium might even approve."

"I'm afraid you've lost me."

"If the media thinks we're engaged, it would give

them something to speculate about besides the murder. I'd need you to attend a few events with me, though."

"Engaged?" Her jaw dropped. He wanted her to pose as his fiancée? "But...that's ridiculous. No one would believe it. I'm not even your type."

Amusement crinkled his eyes. "They'll believe whatever story we feed them. Besides..." His gaze dipped, making a long, heated slide over her breasts, and her heart fluttered hard. "I think I know my own type."

"Right." Her voice came out breathless, and her face turned warm. This was nuts. She had to get a grip and control herself before she totally embarrassed herself. "Except that if I'm in the news, Wayne and that murderer will know where I am for sure."

"But at least you'll have better security."

She couldn't argue that. She and Claire were vulnerable right now. She'd even dragged her sister into this mess. But moving into Luke's mansion...

"I appreciate the offer," she said carefully. "I really do. But I'll have to think about it."

His expression turned sharp. "You think I murdered Candace Rothchild? Is that the problem?"

"What? No, of course not." She ducked, helped Claire into her car seat to avoid his scrutiny. Truthfully, she didn't know what to think. According to the tabloids, Luke had argued with the murdered woman that night, and they'd had a tumultuous, romantic past. But the police had cleared him of the crime. And she couldn't imagine him killing anyone, considering how gentle he'd been with her.

But she was a lousy judge of men.

She straightened, flexed her wrist—a stark reminder of just how flawed her judgment was.

Luke's gaze stayed on hers. "I didn't do it. I despised the woman, but I didn't kill her. That's part of the problem, though. If they reopen the case, I'll be back in the news. The police might investigate me again."

"I'm sorry. It's just…this is pretty sudden. I need to think." She closed Claire's door, walked around the car to the driver's side. Luke straightened and stepped out of her way.

"You'd like the house. You both would," he said as she climbed inside. She nodded, closed the door, then rolled down the windows to let in air.

He bent down, putting his face just inches from hers. She tried to ignore the virile beard stubble coating his jaw, the disturbing effect of his riveting gaze. "It's a safe place, Amanda." His deep voice caressed her nerves. "No one will bother you there."

Except him. "Thank you. I really will think about it."

Of course she couldn't accept the offer. It was beyond ludicrous. She'd already moved in once with a man she'd barely known, and that had been a disaster. She couldn't compound her mistakes.

She backed out of her parking space and drove to the nearest exit. While she waited for a break in traffic, she glanced in the rearview mirror. Luke stood by a gleaming black Jaguar convertible, watching her with those arresting eyes.

She shivered. No wonder the women flocked to him. Just being near him had a devastating effect on her nerves.

And he was wrong about the media. Even if she agreed to the fake engagement, they would never buy it. She spotted a break in the traffic and gunned the car, anxious to leave Luke behind. She'd seen photos of his dates in the tabloids—gorgeous, voluptuous women, the kind who wore designer clothes, shoes that cost more than most people's mortgage payment. A-list women who vacationed on exotic beaches and sunbathed on yachts.

Whereas she was a high school history teacher. A single mother with a three-year-old child. And she couldn't forget that fact.

She sighed, changed lanes, then worked her way through the city streets toward home. That was the mistake she'd made with Wayne. She'd been flattered when he'd asked her out, impressed that a rich, charming man had showered attention on her. She hadn't cared about his money, but it had been so darned nice to have someone pamper her for once. All her life she'd worked to put food on the table, to keep sanity in their unstable lives. Wayne had made her feel sheltered, cared for. She'd even admired his self-control.

Big mistake. One she couldn't afford to repeat.

She turned into her sister's street, pushed thoughts of the past from her mind. She neared the house and slowed the car, and every cell in her body tensed. She inhaled, blew out a long, slow breath, trying to stay calm. But what if Wayne was nearby? What if the killer was here? Her knuckles turned white on the wheel.

She pulled into her driveway and idled the car, hardly able to breathe. She scanned the neighbors' bushes and yards, watched for movement around her house. Nothing. She pried her hand from the wheel, hit the button on the remote to open the garage door, checked the street in the rearview mirror.

Everything was fine. No one was there.

The garage door swung open, and she drove inside,

her pulse flaying her skull. God, she hated this fear, this constant anxiety, the need to listen, watch, run. She cut the engine and set the brake. Still scanning the garage, she unlatched her seat belt and opened her door.

The side door burst open. A masked man lunged toward her, a crowbar in hand.

She shrieked, slammed her door shut and hit the locks. Her heart rioting, her hands fumbling, she jammed the key back into the ignition. But the man leaped around the car and smashed Claire's window.

Claire wailed. Amanda's heart went berserk.

She cranked the engine, rammed the gearshift into Reverse, shaking so hard she couldn't think. She yanked off the brake, slammed the accelerator to the floor. The car rocketed out of the garage backward, shot down the driveway into the street—and crashed.

Amanda screamed, her voice merging with the din of twisting metal and shattering glass. The car jumped forward from the impact, hurling her against the steering wheel, and she gasped at the sharp jab of pain.

The car rocked backward again, then stopped. The sudden silence rang in her ears. Stunned, she looked up. The man in the garage ran off.

She swiveled around in panic. Claire still sat in her car seat, sobbing, clutching her bear, her face streaked with tears. But she was all right. She was all right. They'd both survived.

But who had she hit? She looked out the rear window. A cop emerged from his crumpled car.

She closed her eyes, rested her throbbing forehead against the steering wheel, ignored the blood trickling down her cheek. The cop banged on her door. She gestured for him to wait.

And the horror of it all washed through her. She'd nearly lost Claire. That man had tried to abduct her. She'd nearly failed to protect her child.

She sucked in her breath and knew she no longer had a choice. Whether she knew Luke or not didn't matter. They were moving into his mansion tonight.

Chapter 4

Luke had a reputation for being ruthless in business—a reputation he deserved. He crushed all opposition, never let emotions interfere with a decision and never lost sight of his goals.

Which didn't at all explain the turmoil now roiling through him, this odd hesitation to involve Amanda in his plans.

He prowled across his sunny patio toward the pool, the Italian tiles warming his bare feet. He watched Amanda steer her daughter through the sparkling blue water, the kid's arms buoyed by inflatable wings.

Bringing Amanda here made sense. She needed security, which he could provide. In exchange, she would lend him an air of stability, help pacify the consortium until they voted on the project next week. It was a logical arrangement, mutually beneficial—vital now that he'd read the morning news.

He scowled, skirted one of the twenty-foot Canary Island palm trees ringing the pool, tossed the offending newspaper onto a chair. He needed her help, all right. His project's success hinged on this plan.

Hell of a time for a crisis of conscience.

She glanced up from the pool just then and shielded her eyes from the sun. "Luke."

"Mind if I join you?"

"Of course not. Come on in." She steered her daughter to the side of the pool.

He dropped his towel on the chair and dove in, then swam underwater to where she stood in the shallow end. He surfaced near the others, shook the water from his eyes. The kid giggled and ducked behind her mother's back.

"Say hello to Mr. Montgomery," Amanda told her.

"Luke," he corrected.

Amanda smiled, her blue eyes warming, and his heart made a sudden lurch. "Say hello to Luke then."

The kid peeked out. "Luke then," she whispered and giggled again.

Luke grinned back and gently splashed her, and she squealed with delight. Claire was a miniature version of her mother with that angel-white hair and big blue eyes. A little shy, cute as hell.

Her mother wasn't cute. She was a knockout. Thick, dark lashes framed her dazzling eyes. Her hair was wet from the swim, slicked back, emphasizing the feminine lines of her face. Water glistened on her lips and shimmered in the hollow of her throat.

He looked at her shoulders, over the tantalizing cleavage bared by the scoop-necked suit. Water lapped over her breasts, bringing them in and out of focus like a desert mirage, tempting him to peel down that conservative suit, lick the sparkling drops from her skin.

Aware that he was staring, he jerked his mind to why he was here. "I've got news."

Her full lips pursed, and she glanced at Claire. "Let me get Claire settled down for a nap. It won't take long."

"Take your time. I'll swim some laps." He watched her maneuver her daughter to the steps. Water streamed from her shoulders and back as she climbed from the pool. His eyes followed in the water's wake, skimming her naked back, her perfect butt, the taut, creamy skin of her thighs.

She picked up a towel and quickly wrapped it around her waist. The modest gesture amused him, piquing his interest even more.

But it was an interest he couldn't indulge in right now. He plunged back into the water and began counting laps, relying on the exertion to settle his mind. A mile and a half later, his arms and shoulders tired, and the tension pounding in his temples eased. Feeling more controlled now, he touched bottom and waded to the side of the pool.

Amanda waited in a nearby lounge chair. She'd changed, and her snug, sleeveless T-shirt hugged her round breasts. Her hair had dried, and wispy blond tendrils fluttered around her face. Her shorts bared her elegant legs.

So much for regaining his focus.

He sighed, braced his hands on the edge of the pool and heaved himself out. He caught her eyes wandering over his shoulders and arms, down to his abdomen, and below. She bit her lip, looked away.

So she felt the attraction, too. Good to know, even if the timing sucked. He grabbed his towel, shook the water from his hair, then pulled up the chair next to hers.

Her blue eyes met his, and that unnerving sizzle jolted through him again. "I want to thank you again for letting us stay here," she said. "The house is beautiful. And this view…" She waved at the mountains beyond the golf course. "It's fabulous."

"You're comfortable then?"

She shot him a look of disbelief. "This place is amazing. It's like a palace. I've never stayed anywhere so nice."

He nodded absently, blotted the water still trickling down his jaw. "I talked to my security chief this morning, Matt Schaffer. He's engaged to Natalie Rothchild, the police officer you met yesterday."

"What did he say?"

"No one showed up at the mailbox last night."

Her forehead creased. "So they didn't catch the guy who attacked us."

"No, but the FBI thinks the note matches the one Natalie's father got. They won't know for sure until they run tests, but on the surface it looks the same."

Her face paled, making the freckles stand out on her nose. "So the man who tried to kidnap Claire… You're saying he might have been the killer?"

"Maybe."

Her eyes searched his. "You think he'll figure out where we are?"

He handed her the morning newspaper. She unfolded it, glanced at the headlines, and blanched even more. "Oh, God."

"Yeah." The lead story rehashed the missing ring

and murder, his possible role in the crime. Beneath that was a photo of Amanda with Claire.

"But how did they get this photo?" She sounded bewildered.

"Hell if I know."

She gnawed her lip. Stark fear shone in her eyes. "So he knows where we are now. He'll come after us for sure."

"He can't get in. Even a pro would have a hard time cracking this system. And I'm hiring extra guards, just to be safe.

"This was always a risk," he continued, wanting to reassure her. "I thought we'd have more time before the news broke, but it shouldn't affect our plan."

"Our plan?" She sounded numb.

"To pass you off as my fiancée. There's a charity event at the Rothchilds' tomorrow night. My investors will be there. If you're up to it, it's a good place to make your debut."

She passed her hand over her face, turned her gaze to his. "I'm sorry. I'm a little lost here. Investors in what?"

"A project I'm building—a casino and high-rise complex called the Phoenix. It was all set until the real estate market flatlined. Then Candace got murdered, and all hell broke loose." Every damned investor had threatened to bolt. "I've been making progress, getting the investors back on board, but they're still nervous. They're not going to sink money into this project if they think I'm going to jail."

She frowned. "What exactly do you want me to do?"

"Nothing hard. Just hang on my arm and smile, act unconcerned. If you're not worried about the rumors, it will calm them down. They vote on the project next week."

Her forehead furrowed, and for a moment she didn't speak. The warm breeze rustled the palm fronds overhead, dappling shadows over her face.

"Security's tight at these events," he added. "You'll be safe enough." But there was no guarantee. Unease wormed through his gut again, setting off that inconvenient feeling of guilt.

And he knew he had to be honest. No matter how important this project was, no matter how much he needed her help, he couldn't force her to risk her life.

"Look," he said. "You don't have to do this. I can send you somewhere else until this thing blows over—on an extended cruise or to some resort. You might feel safer that way."

Her troubled gaze met his. And then she rose, walked to the hedge along the patio wall. She stopped with her back to the pool and hugged her arms. She looked so lonely, so in need of protection that he had that damned urge to comfort her again.

He picked up his towel and joined her at the wall. For a long moment he just looked at the mountains beyond the golf course, their brown peaks shimmering in the rising heat. And the irony of his predicament made his lips curl. All his life, he'd stared at those mountains. When he was a kid in the slums, they'd seemed huge to him, formidable, like everything he wanted to become—powerful, bigger than the rest. And he'd vowed that someday he *would* be someone, that he'd have money, respect…revenge.

Now it was finally within his grasp. His plans would come to a head next week. But he couldn't put this woman's life at risk, no matter how important the goal.

Amanda turned to him then, and this close he could

see the fatigue tightening her eyes, the dark circles bruising her skin. She looked delicate, wounded, as if she hadn't slept in days.

"I'm serious," he told her. "I can have you and Claire out of here and halfway around the world by tonight."

She sighed. "Thanks, but it won't do any good."

"Sure it will."

"You don't understand." She looked toward the mountains again and flexed her wrist. "My ex-husband, Wayne… He was violent, volatile. I lived in fear of him for years. It was like living in a war zone. I was always on edge, afraid that something would set him off and make him explode. And I…I can't live like that anymore."

"But this isn't about your ex."

"Maybe not, but it doesn't matter. It's exactly the same thing. If this guy thinks I have the ring, he's not going to give up. No matter where I go, he'll follow me. I'll always be looking over my shoulder, wondering if this is the day he finds me, if this is the day he attacks. Wondering if he's watching, waiting."

She rubbed her arms, her eyes frightened, trying to be so brave it made Luke's chest hurt. And he couldn't resist the need building inside him, the need to defend her, protect her. Touch her.

He stepped close. He reached out slowly, giving her time to react, but she didn't flinch, didn't move away. He stroked the velvet skin of her jaw with his thumb, brushed the feminine line of her throat. She was so soft, so gentle. And yet, she was determined to stand her ground.

And something stirred inside him. Something beyond sympathy. Beyond the instinctive need to protect. The realization that this woman was different, special.

Her eyes turned dark. Her pulse raced against his thumb. He leaned closer, so close that his thighs brushed hers. Her warm breath feathered his face.

He knew he should let go, back away, put some space between them. He couldn't move.

His gaze dropped, traced the lush, sultry swell of her lips, then flicked back to her mesmerizing eyes. And a deep ache surged inside him, the need to pull her into his arms, fit that sweet, curving body to his, taste the provocative heat of her lips.

But this woman needed comfort, protection—not sex. He fisted his hand and stepped back.

"You're sure about this?" His voice rasped in the quiet air. "It's not too late to change your mind."

"I'm sure. I'll stay." Her voice was as throaty as his.

"Good." They were committed now, their bargain struck—until his deal went through and the killer was found. "Then I'll pick you up tomorrow at nine."

She hesitated. "I need to check with Kendall first and see if she can get the night off. Claire might not stay with anyone else, especially in a strange house."

"I'll clear it with her boss. She can go on paid vacation for the next few weeks."

"All right then."

He frowned, wishing he could reassure her, wanting to erase the concern from her face. But there were no guarantees. And he didn't trust himself to stay.

Before he could reconsider, he strode across the patio to the house, then paused at the door and looked back. She still stood by the hedge watching him, her eyes worried.

And he knew he had to be careful. There was something different about this woman. Something too compelling. If he didn't watch out, she'd slip under his guard, become far more than a means to clinch the Phoenix deal.

And that was a risk he couldn't afford.

Amanda stood beneath the chandelier in the private ballroom of the Rothchild Grand Casino, her sister's dire warnings about Luke still ringing in her ears. He was an incorrigible playboy, cutthroat in business, possibly even a murderer—a dangerous, worldly wolf to her naive and innocent lamb.

But dangerous or not, he'd been the epitome of charm tonight. He'd introduced her to his investors, hovered attentively at her side, acting the enamored fiancé to the hilt.

He leaned close, and the scent of his warm male skin, the sight of his white teeth flashing in his handsome face made her heart rate climb. "Champagne?" he asked, and his deep voice rumbled through her nerves.

"Sure." Now that she'd survived the first round of introductions without a major faux pas, she could relax.

Luke motioned to a passing waiter and scooped a drink from his tray. The motion tightened his black tuxedo jacket across his broad back. She admired his freshly shaven jaw, the strong lines of his corded neck. And images paraded through her mind like an erotic slideshow—his biceps flexing as he surged from the pool, the dark hair arrowing down his muscled chest. And that delirious moment when his eyes turned to molten gold and she thought that he might kiss her… She inhaled, pressed her hand to her belly to subdue the jitters rising inside.

He turned to her, held out the drink and their eyes locked. And tension ignited between them again, that electric spark of desire. She took the drink with trembling hands, struggled to act composed. They were only pretending, for goodness' sake. The worst thing she could do was start spinning fantasies about Luke. She'd end up mortifying them both.

But just one glance from those carnal eyes and everything inside her went wild.

"I see someone I need to talk to by the bar," he told her.

She cleared the thickness from her throat. "I'll wait here." She could use a moment to compose herself.

He nodded. "I'll only be a minute."

She sipped her drink, watched him work his way across the room. Women latched onto his arm like long-lost friends. Men greeted him with deference and shook his hand. These were the high rollers of Las Vegas, the elite. And they all kept their eyes on Luke.

She drained her glass, hummed to the piano music lilting in the background. A burst of laughter broke out nearby. Waiters in crisp white jackets wove past, scooping up discarded glasses and refreshing drinks.

How many events like this had she attended with Wayne? Not that he'd moved in quite these circles, but they'd been lofty enough. And at every party, he'd worked the crowd, charming clients with that smarmy smile, arranging illicit affairs with the wives. And she'd had to smile through her teeth, play the role of the devoted wife—until she'd finally squirreled away enough money to escape.

A waiter materialized at her elbow. "Another drink, ma'am?"

Goosebumps rose on her arms at the sound of his voice. She cut her gaze to his face, but he just stood there, his expression polite.

She pulled in a breath, forced herself to relax. She didn't know him. He was just a waiter doing his job, wanting to swap out her empty glass. Feeling foolish, she thanked him, exchanged her flute for the full one left on his tray. He bent, picked up a stray glass from a table and strolled away.

She sipped her champagne, determined not to revert to survival mode and start scanning the crowd. She had to stop jumping at shadows. Luke had promised she'd be safe here. She had to forget her fears and calm down.

She looked for Luke, spotted him talking to a gorgeous brunette. Jenna Rothchild. Amanda had met her earlier. The woman clung to his arm, her pose intimate, suggestive, and whispered into his ear. Luke flashed her a wicked smile, then turned to watch her walk away.

Amanda's head throbbed. So much for the enamored fiancé.

But she didn't care. She didn't. Her relationship with Luke was an act, a ploy. He could flirt as much as he liked.

She didn't plan to stand here and watch, though. She drank more champagne, lifted her wrist to check the time, but she'd left her watch at the house. No sporty watch, no bulky purse allowed tonight, her sister had decreed, only the small, sequined clutch that matched her borrowed dress.

Suddenly weary, she pasted a smile on her face, nodded to one of the investors—a balding man she'd met earlier—and wandered toward the corner where the pianist played. She glanced around for a chair, did a double take when she spotted the pianist's face. Silver Rothchild, the former teen pop star. Her career had fizzled as she'd aged, but Amanda had always loved her songs. And goodness, that music she was playing took her back—back to a time when she'd had dreams, her whole life still ahead.

Before she'd met Wayne.

She grimaced and pushed away that depressing thought. She hummed a few bars of the song, glanced at Silver again and noticed how exhausted she looked. Her face was pale. Dark smudges shadowed her eyes. Amanda could relate. She hadn't slept well in days.

A wave of dizziness hit her, and she pressed her hand to her pounding head. Talk about tired. And this headache was getting worse. She pushed back the fatigue, drank the last of her champagne, then glanced around for Luke, but he still chatted across the room.

A man stepped into her path, his dark eyes hard on hers, and her heart made a sudden swerve. But it was just the waiter, the same one she'd seen earlier. She was getting paranoid now.

And Lord, she was tired. Her head whirled. The entire room seemed to tilt. She set the empty glass on his tray, but it fell off and bounced on the rug.

"I've got it," he murmured.

"Thanks," she said, her voice slurred. Oh, God. Was she drunk? That was all Luke needed, for his fiancée to act like a fool. But how could she be drunk? She'd only had two tiny flutes of champagne.

Her face grew hot. Sweat trickled down her scalp and beaded her upper lip. The waiter still stood there, looking expectantly at her, and she used her purse to fan her face.

What did he want? Why was he staring at her like that? She lurched past him, searching for the ladies' room, desperate to find a place to sit down.

But her heart started to race. Her skin felt clammy,

then chilled. She staggered, bumped into the wall, narrowly missing a huge gilded frame. She paused, her face burning now. How could she be sweating when she felt so cold?

She fumbled with the clasp on her clutch purse, searched for one of the tissues she'd stuck inside. The purse was empty.

She frowned. She'd folded up three blue tissues and tucked them inside, next to her lipstick and blush. And she hadn't opened her purse since she'd left the house.

Confused, she veered to a nearby table, grabbed a cocktail napkin from the stack, knocking the rest to the floor. Too dizzy to pick them up, she dabbed her streaming face.

"Ma'am?" someone asked. She turned her head, and the waiter's face wove into view. "Do you need help?"

"Help?" Was that her voice coming from so far away? She stared at him, shocked when his face morphed into Luke's. She blinked, and the waiter's vaguely Hispanic face reappeared.

Someone grabbed her arm. "No," she whispered, and the waiter laughed. Luke's golden eyes seared into hers. The room faded, began to twirl.

And then everything went black.

Chapter 5

Her eyelids refused to open. A dull pounding buffeted her head. *Claire. Where was Claire?* She had to make sure she was safe.

Amanda wrenched open her eyelids, then squinted at the blast of bright sun. Her gaze landed on the copper-colored bedspread, the Navajo rug on the wall. Luke's mansion. She'd made it home. She slumped against the pillows in relief.

"You're awake." Luke's deep voice rumbled from the corner of the room.

She turned her head as he heaved himself from an armchair, then prowled across the room to her side. His thick hair was tousled, his eyes somber. He had on loose, faded jeans, a wrinkled shirt that he'd left undone, inviting glimpses of his muscled abs. Morning whiskers darkened his jaw, giving him a virile, gunslinger look.

She sank deeper into the pillows and closed her eyes. He looked sexy as sin, conjuring thoughts of torrid nights and sweaty sheets. Whereas she probably had raccoon eyes from her makeup and rat's nest hair.

"How do you feel?" he asked.

As if she'd been dragged through a garbage chute. "Not great." She turned her head to the side, winced at the pulsing pain. "What time is it?"

He perched on the edge of her bed near her hip, and she scooted over to give him more room. "Noon. You've been out since I brought you back last night."

She shut her eyes, massaged the ache between her brows. Her eyes felt gritty, and she desperately needed to bathe. "Where's Claire?"

"In the kitchen with your sister. We told her you were tired and needed to sleep. She left you something, though."

Amanda opened her eyes, saw Brownie propped on the pillow beside her head and a huge rush of love warmed her heart. She picked up the bear, pressed the threadbare fur to her cheek. "I hope she didn't see me come in."

"She was asleep."

"Thank goodness." The last thing she wanted to do was frighten Claire. But what must Luke think of her? She'd passed out at the reception, created a scene. "I'm so sorry," she said. "I didn't mean to embarrass you last night."

He lifted one massive shoulder, his expression inscrutable. "Don't worry about it."

"But people must be talking."

"It doesn't matter."

"Of course it does." He'd wanted to avoid bad publicity and give the impression of settling down. Instead, she'd made things worse. "The investors... They must have seen me." And who knew what they'd think?

"We'll adjust." His eyes wandered over her face, her lips. She felt the heat rising from his body, the tantalizing scent of his hair. She fiddled with the bear, her breathing suddenly labored, her heart fluttering in her chest. Lord, he was sexy. The sheer maleness of him made her body hum.

She peeked under the covers, relieved to see she had on her knee-length T-shirt. Kendall must have undressed her. At least she hoped it was Kendall and not Luke. Her face turned hot at the thought.

"So what happened?" he asked.

Good question. She set down the bear and frowned, trying hard to think back. "I'm not sure. I felt fine, a little tired. I saw you talking to Jenna Rothchild."

She eyed his chiseled mouth, the lean, masculine planes of his face. She couldn't blame Jenna for flirting. If he weren't so far out of her league she'd be tempted herself. "I had some champagne, and then I felt dizzy."

"How much did you drink?"

"Two glasses, hardly enough to make me drunk. Plus, I'd eaten a lot of hors d'oeuvres."

Brackets deepened around his mouth. "You think it was food poisoning?"

"I doubt it. That wouldn't make me black out. And I didn't feel sick, just dizzy and tired."

His eyes narrowed, and she could tell he was flipping through possibilities, calculating the odds. "Had you taken any pills? Anything that could have reacted with the alcohol?"

"Nothing. Not even an aspirin." He slanted his head, his eyes turning grimmer yet, and the sudden realization of what he was thinking took her aback. "You think it was drugs."

"They can knock you out fast."

"But that's ridiculous. Who would want to drug me at the gala? The gunman wasn't there."

He rose, paced to the window, then stood facing out, his hands braced low on his hips.

"Luke?" He didn't answer, and her voice rose. "Why would anyone there want to hurt me?" What kind of mess was she in?

He turned and met her gaze. "To get you out of the picture, cause the investors to balk. This project will hurt the Rothchilds' business. Harold's trying to stop it from going through."

"Even so… You really think he'd drug me? Isn't that extreme?"

"He's done worse. In fact, I should have expected a move like this. There's a lot at stake here. He's probably getting desperate by now."

Her mind reeled. This was all she needed. She had a murderer on her heels, an abusive ex-husband who'd vowed to hunt her down—and now a deranged businessman might be drugging her drinks.

She had to admit that the drug explanation made sense, though. That dizziness had come over her fast. And there'd been something about that waiter's voice… But he couldn't be the same man who'd attacked her in the casino. Why would he be at the Rothchilds' event?

For that matter, Luke could have drugged her. She eyed the tight set of his jaw, the intelligence in his amber eyes. She really knew nothing about him, except the little she'd gleaned from the news.

And what if the rumors were true? What if he had

murdered Candace Rothchild and was now after the ring? Just before she'd blacked out, she had seen his face.

But that was absurd. If Luke had wanted to harm her, he'd have done it here, in his house, not in a public place. And certainly not in front of the investors he hoped to impress.

She rubbed the ache pulsing between her brows, struggling to sort through the confusion. Luke wouldn't hurt her. He wasn't a brute, not like Wayne. He was cynical and tough in business, but he'd been nothing but gentle with her.

So had Wayne at the start.

She flexed her wrist, trying not to go off the deep end and imagine the worst. Besides, there was another explanation for her blackout, one that had nothing to do with drugs.

One she dreaded even more.

She glanced around, spotted the sequined clutch on a chair, and her heart struck an uneven beat. She didn't want to look, but she had to find out the truth.

She tossed off the covers and rose, tugged her long T-shirt over her hips. Then she slowly advanced on the purse.

Her pulse pounded as she picked it up. She undid the clasp, hardly able to breathe. She jerked the sides apart. Her heart faltered. The tissues were there, tucked next to her lipstick, exactly how she'd placed them last night. Her hand rose to her throat.

"What's wrong?" Luke asked.

Her purse had been empty. Those tissues had been gone. But then how had they reappeared? "Nothing. I thought I lost my lipstick, that's all."

She set down the purse, her hands shaking. Had she imagined that they'd disappeared? Her mother had hallucinated, suffered from dizzy spells and blackouts…

She thought of the waiter morphing into Luke and back and quickly blocked off the thought. No. This couldn't be happening. She wouldn't let it. If she had inherited her mother's mental illness, she might have to give up Claire.

But what else could have happened? Who had moved the tissues, and why? The only people who'd been near her purse were her sister, Claire and Luke.

She swallowed hard, battled the hysteria surging inside her. She didn't know which was worse—thinking someone had drugged her or losing her mind.

Luke stalked toward her from across the room. She looked up and met his eyes. "I think… I was just overly tired." She made her voice firm. "And then the champagne… I'm sure that's all it was."

He stopped. Deep lines wrinkled his brow. "Do you want me to call a doctor?"

"No." The last thing she wanted was a doctor documenting this.

"He could do a blood test, find out if you'd been drugged."

And what if the answer was no? "I just need to rest. Really. I'll be fine."

"You're sure?"

"Yes." He moved closer, tipped up her chin, and his rough fingers tingled her skin. He studied her with narrowed eyes, as if to discern the truth. She struggled to look convinced.

"You'd better be all right," he said. "You scared the hell out of me last night."

He'd worried about her? She blinked, touched. She couldn't remember the last time anyone had worried about her. She'd always been the responsible one, the dependable one, the one who'd had to take charge and cope.

"Thank you," she murmured. "For everything. For bringing me back here, for helping—"

"Shh. Forget it." He pressed his thumb to her lips. The slight touch set off a storm of sensations, turning her insides to liquid heat. His hand slid to her cheek, cradled her jaw. His eyes didn't move from hers.

The moment stretched. She couldn't think. She was lost in his hot, hot eyes. He slanted his head, tilted her jaw up and she dropped her gaze to his mouth.

Would he kiss her? Her pulse raced. Excitement hammered her nerves. She tried to swallow, but her throat refused to work.

And then his lips touched hers and her heart jackhammered to life.

His lips were warm, smooth. Pleasure sizzled and rushed through her veins. She gripped his steel-hard arms, slid her palms up his powerful neck, thrilled to the erotic rasp of his jaw.

He felt so strong, so rough, so male. She wanted him closer, wanted that tough, muscled body hard against hers.

As if reading her mind, he tugged her against him, then prodded her lips with his tongue. She shuddered at the sensual invasion, at the deep, pulsing hunger she could barely contain.

He tasted like sin, her darkest temptation, a lure to excitement that she'd never known. The warm, male scent of him ignited her senses. The taste of him shorted her brain. And a sudden urgency consumed her, a desperate need to pull him close. She wanted his hands on her breasts, her naked skin. She wanted to throw off caution and live.

He groaned, widened his stance. The thick, massive feel of him scorched through her blood. She tightened her grip on his neck, bringing her aching breasts tighter against his chest. And still it wasn't enough.

But he stopped, pushed himself away, and she swayed at the sudden loss. And for several long seconds he just stared at her, his eyes glittering with hunger, arousal. Regret?

She blinked, dazed, tried to think through the thick fog of lust. What had come over her? She never acted that impulsive. And the door was open. Claire could come in at any time. She glanced at the doorway, appalled.

"I, uh…" He grimaced, lifted his hands, as if to ward her off. "You'd better rest."

"Right." Her face flamed. Her behavior mortified her. What must he think of her now?

His frown deepened. He inched closer to the door. "About the investors. We'll figure something out." He strode to the door, glanced back. His hot eyes blazed into hers. "And Amanda… Don't worry. I'll keep you safe."

He fled the room, and she sank onto the bed, her whole world spinning apart. What had just happened? How could a kiss affect her like that? She'd never felt such brazen urgency, so frantically turned on in her life.

Sex with Wayne had been tepid at best, revolting later on. She'd assumed that the problem was her, that she wasn't the physical type. Wayne had told her as much.

But that kiss… Dear God. She closed her eyes, pressed her hand to her still-throbbing lips, unable to believe her response.

Luke said he'd keep her enemies at bay—but who would protect her from herself?

As mistakes went, that kiss ranked up with the big ones.

Luke paced across the kitchen two nights later, watching Amanda at the table with Claire. He'd had no business touching Amanda. He'd only intended to offer comfort and calm his raging fear. Because the thought that someone had drugged her… His blood still congealed at the thought.

But giving comfort was one thing. Surrendering to those soft, sweet lips had been totally out of line.

He pivoted at the sink, stalked back toward the table, listening to the lilt of her voice. Even worse, no matter how many numbers he'd crunched, no matter how hard he'd worked in the past two days, he couldn't get her out of his head. He kept veering back to those warm, moist lips, the erotic brush of her breasts. That kiss had left him so knotted up that he'd do anything to touch her again.

Which was crazy. She wasn't even his type. He dated fast, jaded women. Women out for a night of hot sex. Amanda was too innocent, too vulnerable. She even had a kid.

She glanced up as he passed her again and blushed. *Blushed.* He shoved his hand through his hair, appalled. He didn't get involved with women who blushed. He'd lost his friggin' mind.

"Time for bed," she told her daughter. She rose, bent to help Claire from her chair, and his gaze zeroed in on her hips. She wore those shorts again, the ones that hugged her lush behind, exposing the tempting skin of her thighs. And images flashed through his mind—Amanda naked, stretched seductively over his bed, dressed in nothing but a pair of high heels.

"Say good-night to Luke," she said, and he jerked his mind from that scene.

"'Night, Luke." Claire trotted over and lifted her bear. "Give Brownie a kiss."

"A kiss?" Caught off guard, he frowned at the scruffy bear. But the kid was watching him with those huge, blue eyes, and he hated to let her down. Feeling awkward, he took the bear, pressed it to his cheek, then flipped it into the air. It spun, started down headfirst, and Claire made a startled gasp. He caught it on his knee, juggled it several times like a soccer ball and launched it back in the air. He snagged it on the down curve and handed it to Claire.

Her eyes were wide, her mouth open. But then she giggled, clutched the bear and ran back to her mom.

Amanda's eyes crinkled. Her lips curved into a smile—a warm, easy smile that softened his heart. Not his type, he reminded himself firmly. He turned, tracked those killer legs as she sauntered away, mesmerized by the swing of her hips.

When she'd disappeared from view, he leaned against the counter and crossed his arms. Okay, this was getting out of hand. He prided himself on his self-control. Hell, he was famous for it. So why was she getting to him?

He frowned out the window at the darkening sky. If she were different, he'd indulge in a brief affair. That always got a woman out of his system and took the edge off his sexual needs.

But there was something special about Amanda,

something he'd felt from the start. She threatened his distance, kicked up feelings he'd long suppressed.

And that was dangerous.

He gave his head a hard shake. He only had one more week until the consortium voted. One more week to masquerade as her fiancé. He could control himself until then.

Determined to regain his focus, he crossed the room to his wine vault, selected a bottle of *Riserva* he'd picked up in Tuscany the previous spring. He popped the cork, set the bottle on the counter to breathe while he waited for her to come back.

She strolled into the kitchen a moment later, then started gathering her papers into a pile.

"What are you working on?" he asked to get his mind off the intriguing way her breasts swayed as she reached for a paper that fell.

"My teaching credential." She set the wayward paper on the stack. "I need to get it validated in Nevada. They have a reciprocal agreement with Maryland, so I don't need to retake the tests. I just have to file the forms."

He pulled two wine glasses from the cupboard and held them up. "Wine?"

"Thanks, that would be nice."

He set down the glasses, watched as she stuffed Claire's crayons into the box. The overhead lamp made her blond hair shine and highlighted the curve of her cheeks. "What do you teach?"

"High school history." Her gaze met his. "I love your casino, by the way. You did an amazing job on the lobby."

He shrugged. "I didn't do it. I told the interior designer to make it look like Rome, then left the rest to her."

"Well, it's wonderful…magical. Ancient Rome must have looked exactly like that."

A wistful smile softened her face, and another spurt of warmth curled through his chest. He realized that he liked pleasing her, liked basking in her approval.

He scowled, turned back to the wine. Since when did he care what anyone thought? He worked alone, rarely asked for opinions. The only approval that mattered was his.

"Speaking of casinos, we need to make another appearance together." He poured the wine, crossed to the table and handed her a glass. "I'd like to do it soon. The consortium meets again early next week to review the final plans."

"All right."

"We should probably include Claire this time. She'll help us look more settled." Especially with the rumors now swirling around. Half of Vegas thought Amanda had an addiction that made her black out at the gala. The rest believed he'd tried to do her in.

But there was no point worrying her with that.

"I'm not sure about Claire." She sat and sipped her wine, her expression doubtful. "She gets shy around strangers, especially if we go somewhere new. Could we invite them here instead?"

He lowered himself into the chair next to hers. "I don't see why not." In fact, it was a good idea. It would give them a more domestic look. He leaned back in the chair, sipped the rich, dark wine, tried to ignore the tempting scent of her skin. "There are six investors, their wives and us. Fifteen people. I'll contact the caterer first thing."

"I don't mind cooking. In fact, I'd like to." She glanced around, and her lips turned up. "You have a fabulous kitchen to work in. And I make pretty good Mexican food—unless you want something fancier."

"No, Mexican's great." And having her cook would add to the homey look. "You're sure you don't mind?"

"I need to do something. I can't just sit here and worry all day."

The anxiety in her voice caught his attention. "Has something else happened?"

"No." She shook her head, but her eyes didn't quite meet his. "It's just the stress, not knowing where the killer is. There hasn't been any word?"

"Last I heard they were still waiting for the lab report."

She nodded, looked away, but this close he could see the fatigue shadowing her eyes. He took a swallow of wine, still studying her face. She was worried, no doubt about it. "You're sure there's not a problem?"

"No, nothing. Everything's fine."

He didn't buy it. She looked as if she hadn't slept in days. But he'd couldn't force her to talk. He nodded toward the papers stacked near her glass, decided to lighten the mood. "So you've never been to Rome?"

"I've never been anywhere. I've never even left the country."

"Why not?"

She shrugged. "Money, life. When I was younger, my mother…wasn't well. She couldn't work, and the disability checks didn't go too far, so I worked to help pay the rent. Then Kendall left for Vegas, and I stayed to help my mom."

He raised a brow. "That doesn't seem fair."

"Kendall sent money, and she came home when she could. Later she offered to move back so I could leave. But it didn't seem right to make her give up her dream. I mean, you can only dance when you're young, right? And I could study any time."

He didn't agree, but nodded for her to go on.

"I didn't mind teaching," she added. "It wasn't as exciting as being an archaeologist, but I liked the kids, and I had enough time off to take care of my mom."

He frowned. Her childhood sounded a lot like his with a mother who couldn't work. And no matter what she said, he doubted her sister had helped much. Amanda had probably taken charge of her mother like she now did Claire.

Disturbed by that thought, he drained his wine, then rose and paced to the sink. It was better if he didn't get involved with her, didn't know her past. It made her too sympathetic, too real.

Too damn hard to resist.

But when she came up behind him, he had to ask. "So where did Wheeler come in?"

She didn't answer at first. She rinsed her glass, wiped her hands, then finally leaned against the counter and sighed. "I met him after my mother died. I was planning to go to graduate school so I could study archaeology and get a job in the field. But he kept pressuring me to move in with him.

"I didn't want to. I hardly knew him. But then…well, I got pregnant, and I didn't want Claire to grow up without a father like I did." She grimaced. "Obviously, he wasn't the man I thought."

"No." He knew Wheeler's type. He'd seen a few violent men when he was growing up—bullies who fed their egos by terrorizing the weak. They were all about power, control. In fact, Wheeler had probably knocked her up just to keep her in his control.

That thought needled him, and he clenched his jaw. He didn't like knowing she'd suffered abuse at the hands of a scumbag. He didn't like knowing she lived in fear of the man.

And he sure as hell didn't like how she stood watching him with those big blue eyes, looking too damn defenseless as she clutched her wrist. His hold on his temper slid. "What happened to your wrist?"

"Nothing."

Like hell it was. "And that's why you hold it all the time?"

She flattened her lips, as if reluctant to talk, but then she let out a heavy sigh. "It was Wayne. He flew into a rage and broke it." Her eyes filled with remembered fear. "I found drugs in the house and confronted him. It was dumb. I never should have challenged him like that."

His mouth thinned. He didn't want to picture it. He didn't want to think of her cowering before that thug. And if he ever got his hands on Wheeler… Anger blazed through his gut.

"That's when I knew I had to leave," she added. "I didn't want drugs or violence around Claire."

That fit. She'd cared for her mom, sacrificed for her sister. And now she protected her child. But who'd ever protected her?

He caught hold of her injured wrist. She tugged back, but he stroked the delicate skin of her wrist with his thumb, felt the frantic beat of her pulse. And emotions swirled inside him. Respect, admiration, desire.

He slowly lifted her wrist, pressed his mouth to the sensitive skin, heard the sudden catch in her breath. Her seductive scent wrapped through his mind.

"Luke…" she whispered.

"I know." His voice came out too deep. "It's a bad idea."

"Very bad." Her pulse sped under his thumb. Her gaze didn't budge from his.

Get out, he urged himself. *Don't let this happen.* He didn't want to get involved with her. He didn't want to know her worries, her pain.

And he sure as hell didn't want to hear her plead for his touch, watch her eyes turn blurry with need or sink into that warmth and make her his.

She tugged her arm. He let her go. "I can't," she said, sounding desperate. "It's too complicated. Claire… There's too much else going on."

"Right." *Distance.* That was what he'd wanted. That was what he'd come for—to forget this attraction, to regain control, to prove that he could resist.

To stay detached.

But as he stared into her eyes, his gut roiling with hunger, he had a feeling it was already too damned late.

Chapter 6

The cilantro had disappeared.

Amanda stared into the refrigerator, unwilling to believe her eyes. She'd put it on the top shelf, right next to the artichoke dip. So where on earth had it gone?

She pawed through the vegetable drawers, her anxiety rising, then checked behind the enchiladas and rice. But the cilantro was nowhere in sight.

She straightened, pushed the refrigerator door closed with her hip and tried to keep herself calm. Okay. She knew she'd bought it. She'd ticked it off her grocery list. She remembered putting it on that shelf. But then how had it disappeared?

A sliver of dread trickled through her, but she struggled not to overreact. So she was acting a little bizarre these days, getting absentminded. She'd left her wallet in the bathroom, her comb in the silverware drawer.

She'd turned off lights, only to later find them switched back on.

But that didn't mean she had a mental illness. Anyone would forget things under this kind of stress.

She barely ate. She hardly slept, thanks to that awful paranoia that nagged her again, the feeling that someone was watching…waiting. And when she did give into exhaustion and nod off, memories of Luke invaded her dreams, leaving her breathless and aching with need.

"Mom. Help me," Claire called from the table, where she was coloring clothes for her paper doll.

"Not right now. We need to run to the store. I forgot something, and the guests will be here soon." She glanced at her watch, then gasped. Yikes. It was later than she'd thought. She had to get that cilantro fast.

She grabbed her purse from the counter, hustled Claire from the table to the garage and set the alarm. Luke wouldn't approve of the errand. Neither would Kendall. They'd both urged her not to budge from the house. But there was a grocery store just outside the entrance to the gated community. She could get there and back in fifteen minutes tops.

She strapped Claire into her car seat, backed quickly out of the garage. It felt good to get out, she decided moments later as she followed a gardening truck down the street. Luke's house was gorgeous—like a luxury resort—but after nearly a week, the confinement was starting to chafe.

She kept the windows rolled down, and the warm desert breeze ruffled her hair. Despite her current danger, she had to admit that she liked Nevada. She liked the wide-open spaces, the mountains jutting against the brilliant blue sky. There was something adventurous about the west. Even the air seemed to pulse with excitement, as if anything were possible here. It was a great place to start a new life—or it would be, once she escaped her current mess.

The supermarket sat in a small, modern strip mall just outside the community's gates. She found a parking space close to the cart return and rushed Claire into the store. She just prayed that they had cilantro, or she'd have to drive across town.

"I'm cold," Claire said, shivering in the air-conditioned store.

"I know. So am I. We'll hurry." She hustled her through the produce section, giving wide berth to a bin of peanuts that would trigger an allergic reaction in Claire. To her relief, there was plenty of cilantro. She shoved a fresh bunch into a plastic bag, grabbed a *jicama* to slice up for the dip. Seconds later, she'd led Claire through the checkout line, then exited to a blast of dry heat.

She pulled out her keys and checked her watch. Oh, God. She had to rush. Taking a firm grip on Claire's hand, she hurried up the row toward her car.

It was gone.

She stopped, whirled around, glanced up and down the row. This had to be the right spot. She'd parked by the cart return, right where a blue Corvette now sat. Bewildered, she scanned the spaces again, then walked between the cars to the next row. But there was still no sign of the car.

Where could it have gone? Had someone stolen it? But who'd take her old Honda with all the BMWs around? The repair shop had done a great job fixing the damage from that accident, but it was still hardly a prize.

"Mom," Claire complained, and she realized she was squeezing her hand.

"I'm sorry, honey. I just can't find our car." She turned in another circle, frantically searching the lot. And then she spotted it two rows away—nowhere near the cart return.

Her heart fumbled a beat. Her breath grew shallow and fast. She didn't remember parking there, had no memory of it at all. But no one could have moved it. No one else had a key.

Still clutching Claire's hand, she warily walked toward the car, feeling as if she were approaching a bomb. Dread pounded her skull. Her palms moistened with sweat. The car had Maryland plates on the brand-new bumper, Claire's car seat in the back. It was hers, all right. And it was locked.

But how could she not remember parking it here?

Her head buzzing, she unlocked the doors, buckled Claire in her seat and started home. Sprinklers swished on the nearby golf course. Laughing children bicycled past. She drove down the road like a zombie, her eyes glued straight ahead, too numb to process it all.

Still dazed, she parked the car in the garage, carried the groceries into the house, trying to focus on the evening ahead. Luke was depending on her to make a good impression tonight, and she couldn't mess up again. She'd think about the lost car and missing cilantro later, after the guests had gone.

She rinsed the cilantro, put it in the colander to drain, went to get the jalapeños from the fridge. She swung the door open, then froze.

The cilantro was back. Right where she'd left it on the shelf.

Her head felt light. The air turned hot and thick. She whipped around, searched the kitchen for signs of intrusion. But the windows were closed. Claire's paper dolls and crayons sat undisturbed at her place. Everything was fine.

Except for her.

Dear God. She was losing her mind.

Something was bothering Amanda.

Luke studied her as she fidgeted with the napkins on the patio table and smiled at Fletcher Coddington, their last, lingering guest. He doubted anyone else had noticed how nervous she was. She'd been the perfect, gracious hostess all night—smiling, keeping the conversation going, making sure everyone stayed comfortable and involved.

And the investors had fallen for her hard. They'd devoured the food she'd made, listened avidly to her stories about local history. Even Claire had behaved like a model child, giving him a stable, domestic appearance.

A car door slammed in the distance, and Amanda's head jerked up. His eyes narrowed. That was it, right there—the way she jumped at routine noises, the way her eyes tightened with the same anxious look he'd seen on that surveillance tape. All evening long her voice had been a little too high, her smile too bright.

Something was wrong, all right, and he intended to find out what. But first he had to get Fletcher Coddington to leave.

He headed toward her, and she glanced up. She straightened, her eyes going wide.

"You must be tired," he said smoothly. He slid his

arm around her waist and pulled her soft, curving body against his.

She stiffened. "I…I'm fine."

"You're sure?" He leaned down and nuzzled her neck, and she didn't quite stifle her gasp.

The hug was for show, part of the charade they'd been playing all night. But the scent of her skin, the feel of her full, round breasts brushing his arm sent a jolt of heat through his blood.

"Luke," she whispered when he nibbled her jaw. "Fletcher will see."

"I hope so." He moved his mouth to her ear, inhaled the aroma of her perfume. "I'm trying to make him leave."

It worked. Coddington set down his whiskey tumbler and glanced at his watch. "Montgomery, it's been a pleasure."

Amanda extracted herself from his arms and rushed to their guest. "I'm so sorry your wife couldn't make it tonight."

Coddington offered her his arm, and Luke followed them through the house. Amanda kept up the chatter until they reached the door.

"You'll have to stop by and see my arrowhead collection," Coddington told her. "I used to dig around the *pishkuns* in Montana when I was young. They frown on that now—can't dig in historical places, you know. I'll probably donate them to a museum some day."

"I'd love to see them," she said, sounding sincere, and Luke frowned at a sudden thought. They'd never discussed their eventual breakup, or exactly how long they'd keep up this charade. But they'd have to continue at least until that killer was found, and Amanda was safe.

Coddington turned to him then. "I take it you heard about the protests?"

He turned his mind back to business. "It's not a problem."

"I don't want a lawsuit tripping us up."

"Don't worry. It won't get that far." He'd make sure of that.

The investor nodded and smiled again at Amanda. "Tomorrow, then." He stepped outside.

"Good night," Amanda called, and he closed the door.

For a minute, neither moved. Luke's eyes settled on hers. Ticks from the nearby grandfather clock rent the air. It seemed strangely intimate standing together like this, as if they really were a married couple, alone in their home at last.

His gaze swept her face. The hall light grazed the curves of her cheeks, showing the deep smudges under her eyes. "I meant what I said earlier. You look tired."

"I guess I am, a little." She turned and headed to the kitchen, and he trailed her there, admiring the way her dress molded her hips.

"You did a great job. The investors liked you."

"It was fun. I told you I like to cook." She picked up a stack of plates from the table and yawned.

"Give me those." He tugged the plates from her hands. "Go sit by the pool and rest. I'll bring you a glass of wine."

"It will only take a minute to clean up."

"Amanda, you're dead on your feet." Not to mention nervous as hell—and he intended to find out why. She opened her mouth to protest, but he held his ground. "Go."

"All right. I'll just check on Claire first."

He stacked the dishes by the sink and poured the wine, then went out the patio door. She sat on the low wall near the myrtle hedge, cocooned by the malibu lights. A cool breeze had sprung up, swishing the palm trees by the pool and tousling the ends of her hair.

He handed her the glass, then sat on the wall beside her, wondering where to begin. If he asked her outright what was bothering her, she'd either deny it or claim to be tired.

"So tell me more about your project," she said.

He sipped his drink, decided to bide his time. Talking about the project might relax her, get her to open up. "What do you want to know?"

"Where are you building it?"

"Naked City. It's not actually a city," he said, when she arched a brow. "It's just an area past Sahara Avenue, outside the Strip."

The corner of her mouth edged up. "Interesting name, though."

"Yeah." He took another swallow of wine. "But that's the only interesting thing about it. It's a slum, one of the worst in Vegas. It's where I grew up."

"Really?" She looked surprised, and he didn't blame her. He never talked about his childhood, couldn't imagine why he'd mentioned it now. But there was something soothing about Amanda, something that invited confidence, trust.

"I figured you always had money," she said.

"Hardly. But the Strip was only a few blocks away. I could see it from our apartment. It might as well have been on Mars, though. It was a world apart, all that luxury and wealth." Completely out of his reach.

"So what was your family like?"

He shrugged. "Small. Poor." He frowned down at his glass. "My father split before I was born. My mother was a cocktail waitress in Harold Rothchild's casino."

The old emotions roiled through him before he could block them—bitterness, helplessness, rage. Restless, he set down his glass and walked to the hedge. Then he stood with his arms crossed and stared out at the night.

Amanda joined him a moment later. Maybe it was the quiet way she stood beside him, her shoulder brushing his arm. And maybe it was the darkness, the intimacy of the night. But suddenly, he wanted to tell her, wanted her to know.

"Her back went out," he said. "She couldn't work. She needed surgery, but we couldn't afford it."

"You didn't have insurance?"

"No. The Rothchilds blocked the unions back then, so benefits were scarce. She tried to get another job but kept missing work because of her back. And then she got hooked on pain pills. She went downhill from there."

Amanda didn't answer, but he found her silence comforting, more soothing than anything she could have said. And he realized that she understood exactly what he'd gone through. She'd also cared for her mother at an early age.

"So what did you do?" she finally asked.

"Lived on welfare. But then the rent went up and we couldn't pay. We got evicted." By their ever-compassionate slumlord, Harold Rothchild.

That moment had changed his life. He'd been twelve years old, fighting off the street gangs, scouring the garbage for food. He'd gazed at the mind-boggling luxury of the nearby Strip, the towering casino that

Rothchild owned, and he'd vowed right then that he'd be rich and powerful someday.

And that he'd avenge his mother's death.

In one more week he'd finally do it. The Phoenix would rise from the ruins of that old apartment and crush Harold Rothchild for good.

"It's not easy being poor," Amanda said gently, and he switched his attention to her. He observed her soft, wide eyes, the sympathetic set to her lips.

"No," he agreed, his voice huskier now. "It's not easy." He reached out and brushed the curve of her cheek, traced the delicate bones of her jaw. And he wondered how she had coped. She'd had a mother to support, later a kid. But she was a lot like him, a survivor. Every time life knocked her down, she'd fought back.

He ran his thumb down the bridge of her nose, over the velvety skin of her cheek. His eyes roamed her face, her curving throat, down to the tempting vee of her dress.

She was amazing, all right. Determined, protective, arousing.

"You look good in this dress." His voice deepened. "Too damned good. If Coddington hadn't stopped ogling you, I was going to slam his face into the flan."

She blinked, then let out a laugh. "Don't be silly. He wasn't ogling me."

"The hell he wasn't."

"Oh, come on. He has to be seventy years old. I probably reminded him of his granddaughter."

"He's been married five times. His current wife is twenty-one."

Her jaw dropped. "You're joking, right?"

He shook his head.

"Oh, my. You do run with a fast crowd."

"Yeah. Fast. Bad." He brushed his hand down her arm, and her smile abruptly disappeared. Sudden tension vibrated the air.

He shouldn't touch her. He was pushing the limits, testing his already strained self-control. For hours he'd been watching her smile and talk, worry and frown. He'd memorized the provocative way her lips quirked and her forehead creased, how her hair shimmered over her back. And all night long he'd been holding her, stroking her, inhaling her feminine scent as he played the part of her fiancé.

It had been four hours of exquisite torture.

And if he didn't get away from her now, he was going to break. "It's late. You'd better go inside."

"I know." Her voice came out breathless. She stayed rooted in place.

He shifted closer, drawn to the heat in her eyes, the lure of her lush, sultry lips. He stroked his hands up her arms, his blood pumping hard. Hunger built in his veins.

Kissing her would be a mistake, a complication he couldn't afford. He needed to protect her, find out why she was worried, not muddy their relationship more.

Besides, they'd agreed to keep their distance. They'd agreed this idea was bad.

But her gaze stalled on his mouth. Her breath made a provocative hitch, and the small sound tore through his nerves.

To hell with control. Ignoring her gasp, he hauled her against him. He plunged his hand in her hair, slanted his mouth over hers. And then he devoured her with a hot, urgent kiss that demolished his self-control.

He was too rough, too urgent, he knew that, but he

couldn't be gentle or nice. The whole evening had been hours of tormenting foreplay, and he was already over the edge.

She wrapped her hands around his neck and sagged against him. He inhaled the erotic heat of her skin. He gathered her closer, giving vent to his unruly hunger, and his entire body turned hard.

She moaned and wriggled against him, sending a bolt of lust to his groin. He broke the kiss, blazed a path down her velvety neck with his tongue, and his desperation surged.

He had to see her, feel her. He caught the shoulder strap of her dress in his teeth, tugged on the bow. The fabric slid down, exposing one breast. She wasn't wearing a bra.

His mind went blank. Stark need roared through his blood. She was beautiful. So damned beautiful. All ripe, perfect curves and sultry skin.

And he wanted to take her, take all of her, make her writhe and quiver and scream. He wanted to hear her breath catch, feel her heart race, make her mindless and whimpering with need.

He cupped her breast with his hand and lowered his head, loved the smooth, creamy skin with his tongue.

"Luke." She moaned and clutched his hair. Then he kissed her again, knowing he was moving too far, too fast.

But she was kissing him back, running her hands over his shoulders, his back. And he needed to feel her right where he ached.

His hands went to her bottom, and he pulled her against him, and the sweet, hot feel of her made him groan.

"Mommy?" a small voice called.

Amanda instantly stiffened. He lifted his head, lust still hazing his brain, and tightened his grip on her hips.

They couldn't stop. Not now. He was too damned aroused.

"I'm coming," she called, and tried to wriggle from his grasp. He inhaled, reluctantly let go. She jerked up her dress and retied the strap.

Her eyes were dark, her lips swollen. Her hair was a tangle of silk. He wanted to sling her over his shoulder and drag her to bed.

"I have to go," she said, sounding breathless.

"I know." But this wasn't finished, not by a long shot. And he still needed to find out what had her on edge.

He shoved his hand through his hair, made a decision. "Get your sister to babysit tomorrow. We're going hiking."

"What? Where—"

"Not far from here. I've got something to show you. And a trip will do you good."

"But…you have a meeting. I heard you talking about it tonight."

"I'm rescheduling it."

She glanced at the house, looking torn. "All right," she finally said. "If you're sure." She turned and hurried into the house.

Sure? He scoffed at that. He wasn't sure of anything right now—least of all what he'd just done. He was canceling a meeting to go hiking? Was he completely out of his mind?

He didn't know. But keeping his distance from her wasn't working. It was time for a change of plans.

Chapter 7

She was a wreck.

Amanda trudged up the trail behind Luke the next morning, so exhausted she could hardly move. All night long, she'd tossed and turned, too wound up to sleep. She'd relived every second of the thrilling evening, from Luke's heated looks to his blistering kiss. And the feel of his mouth on her breast…

She flushed, dodged a twisting juniper pine tree, then hurried to pick up her pace. She'd lectured herself for hours during the restless night, trying desperately to regain her good sense. Their engagement was fake. They had no future together. He was a billionaire playboy, and she had a daughter to raise.

But none of that seemed to matter. All it took was the sound of his husky voice, one glance from those piercing golden eyes and she wanted to throw herself into his arms.

And if Claire hadn't interrupted them when she had…

She skidded on a patch of loose stones, and Luke whipped around and steadied her arm. "Are you all right?"

"I'm fine." Except that her heart was sprinting again. His eyes swept her body, her face, and her breath took an erratic turn. She tore her gaze away to calm her nerves.

"It's not much farther." He adjusted the pack he'd slung over his back and started walking again. She skirted a clump of cactus, knew she had to watch her step. But her eyes kept returning to the broad, strong ledge of his shoulders, his black hair gleaming in the sun. He wore loose, faded jeans—worn white in intriguing stress spots—and he looked so virile, so blatantly male that she ached to touch him again.

He stopped a moment later at a lookout point. She wiped her forehead on her sleeve, pulled her attention from his muscled biceps and looked out at the view. Directly beneath them was a small valley. A weathered wooden ranch house and derelict barn stood in the overgrown yard.

But the spot was spectacular, the views amazing. Blood-red sandstone lined the surrounding foothills. Smoky green sagebrush punctuated the rocks. The desert shimmered in the distance, topped by that startling, azure sky.

Luke glanced at her. "So what do you think?"

"It's beautiful." She inhaled the scent of juniper pines and sun-drenched earth. "How did you find this place?"

They'd driven for nearly two hours out of Vegas, most of it over teeth-jarring, washboarded roads. They'd eventually turned off the county roads onto private property and bumped along a tractor trail riddled with ruts. Then they'd hiked.

"I own it."

She blinked up at him. "This land is yours?"

He folded his muscled arms across his chest and looked out at the valley below. "I bought it about ten years ago. It's good land, a little isolated, but there's room for an airstrip near the house. There's a river and a small lake over that hill."

She glimpsed at where he was pointing, stunned. She never would have expected him to own a ranch. "What are you going to do with it?"

"Nothing, at the moment. I haven't really made any plans."

That was a relief. She'd hate to see him build a mega-resort or golf course here. She scanned the hills, absorbing the rugged, untamed beauty. The place had almost a spiritual feel.

"Did you buy it as an investment, then?"

"Not exactly." He frowned, shifted his attention back to the landscape.

Long seconds passed, so she tried again. "So why did you buy it?"

He shrugged. "It was a gift of sorts. I told you about my mother."

"Yes." She studied his profile, confused.

"She always talked about buying a ranch. You know, one of those 'when we win the jackpot' dreams. All the years I was growing up, that's all I heard about, how we were going to buy a ranch when we hit it big. So when this came on the market…"

He frowned. "It was dumb. She was already gone, and I sure as hell didn't need more land. But I don't know. It just seemed like the right thing to do."

He resumed hiking, and she followed more slowly,

her mind reeling from what he'd revealed. He'd bought this gorgeous ranch for his deceased mother. Oh, God. Emotions piled inside her, and a huge lump thickened her throat. Who would have guessed that this ruthless, powerful man had a tender side?

But she'd seen glimpses of it from the start. He'd checked on Wayne's whereabouts to ease her worries. He'd offered her the use of his house. He'd helped her when she'd blacked out, even canceled his meeting today so she could relax.

And this side of Luke scared her to death. The physical attraction was dangerous enough. But this softer side touched her heart and made her care.

And the last thing she needed now was to fall for Luke—he was a guaranteed broken heart.

But how was she going to stop?

"Be careful. This part is steep." He leaped down a small incline, then reached back and grabbed her hand. Awareness shimmered through her at the contact, and she sucked in a startled breath. Their eyes met, held. For a heartbeat, neither moved.

But then he dropped her hand and kept walking, and she struggled to regain her good sense. Maybe she was falling for Luke, but he probably just wanted sex.

And why was that so bad?

He stopped in front of a boulder. "Here it is."

Still unsettled, she glanced at the rock. An Indian petroglyph. "Oh, wow," she breathed, her turmoil abruptly forgotten. She rushed to the chunk of brown sandstone, captivated by the crudely drawn lizard etched into the rock. "I can't believe it. It's amazing."

"There are more."

"More?" She glanced around. "Where?"

He motioned ahead, and her heart skipped. Glyphs covered the surrounding boulders—etchings of deer and snakes, horses and human hands. She roamed through the rocks, entranced. "Luke, this is wonderful." To think that centuries ago, people had stood on this very spot, carving their messages into the rocks.

She studied a wavy design that might have meant water. "This probably marked a migration route or game trail." Especially since there was water nearby.

"Maybe, but there's another possibility."

Her face lifted to his. "What's that?"

"I'll show you, as long as you're not claustrophobic."

Her excitement built. "Are you saying there's a cave?"

A smile played at the edge of his mouth. "It's tight at the start, but it opens up. I'll go first with the flashlight. Just watch where you stick your hands. Rattlesnakes are active now."

Startled, she checked the ground, but not even the threat of a poisonous snake could deter her. Luke rolled aside some stones, pulled the pack off his shoulder, then squeezed through a cleft in the rocks.

She quickly followed. The opening wasn't too tight at the start, but Luke's shoulders were wider, and he had to angle them more. The air grew mustier as they entered the cave, the light dimmer. After a dozen yards, they both stooped over, then had to crawl. The walls squeezed in. There was no room to turn around. But Amanda couldn't remember when she'd enjoyed herself more.

"Almost there," Luke called back. Seconds later, the space opened up. He scrambled to his feet, still ducking, and helped her stand. "Watch your head," he cautioned. "It's low in spots." He raised the flashlight and shined it around the spacious room.

"Oh, my," she whispered, too overwhelmed to move. Primitive hunt scenes covered the walls. Hundreds of artifacts littered the ground. There were baskets, carved wooden implements, piles of arrowheads and shafts. It was incredible. She wanted to examine everything at once.

Thrilled, she twirled around.

"Easy." Luke caught her arm. She grabbed his shoulder and laughed.

"Luke, this is amazing."

"Yeah, amazing." He brushed a smudge from her cheek and angled his head. His gaze dropped to her mouth, holding her in place. And suddenly, the Indian artifacts faded away.

And then he kissed her. His mouth was warm and hard, sending waves of pleasure skidding along her nerves. And she melted into the kiss, overjoyed. This was what she'd dreamed of, longed for during that restless night.

His tongue swept her mouth. His big hand caressed her back. She moaned at the drugging sensations, the way her body pulsated with heat. She shifted closer, hoping he wouldn't stop.

But after a moment, he pulled away, then rested his forehead against hers. Her heart hammered fast. Her breath came in uneven rasps.

"Take a minute to look around, and then we'll go," he said, his voice rough.

She nodded, straightened, struggling to shift her attention back to the ruins. But she was far more interested in kissing Luke.

Still, this was the dream of a lifetime. He handed her the flashlight, and she roamed the cave, careful not to disturb anything. "Has this site been surveyed?" she asked as she examined an ancient atlatl.

"Not that I know. I've never seen it in any records. I don't think anyone knows it exists."

She skirted a stack of woven baskets, peered at a deer painted on the wall. The cave might have been a storage site, or maybe a ceremonial place, although she didn't see any remnants of fires. And it looked remarkably intact with no signs of digging or looting. The archaeologists would go berserk. "How did you find it?"

"The farmer had drawn a map. I found it with some old papers in the house."

She took another pass around the cavernous room, absorbing every detail. This was what had drawn her to archaeology—the thrill of discovery, wanting to see how ancient people had lived, wondering what they'd dreamed of, thought about and who they'd loved. The minutes passed by too fast.

"We'd better go," Luke finally said, and she reluctantly followed him from the cave. While she squinted in the blinding sunlight, he rolled the rocks into place and concealed the entrance with brush.

A short time later, they spread their picnic blanket in a patch of shade at the lookout point. Luke pulled out bottles of water and wraps.

Suddenly ravenous, she devoured her vegetable wrap, then dropped back on the blanket and sighed. She inhaled the soothing scent of sagebrush, watched a hawk ride the thermals in the sky. And for the first time in weeks, she felt relaxed, almost carefree.

"Thank you so much for showing me this, Luke. It's spectacular." To think she was one of the few people alive who'd seen it—and that Luke had realized what this would mean to her, how much she'd enjoy exploring the cave.

He stretched out beside her. "You looked tired last night, worried. I thought you could use a break." He lifted himself to one elbow, and leaned over her, kicking off a flurry of anticipation. She studied the hollows of his cheeks, the strong, masculine lines of his neck. A hint of emerging whiskers darkened his jaw.

"So what's been bothering you?" he asked. "And don't tell me it's nothing. You've been acting too jumpy for that excuse."

She sighed, knowing she could trust him, but reluctant to tell him the truth. She didn't want to reveal her mother's illness. If anyone suspected she'd inherited her mental problems, she could lose custody of Claire. And she'd die if she lost her child. Claire mattered more to her than the world.

But she also had to keep Claire safe. And if there was any chance she wasn't imagining things…

"I'm not really sure what's happening," she admitted. "It started the night I blacked out. I've been misplacing things, getting forgetful. But I really think it's just due to stress."

His eyes narrowed. "What kinds of things?"

"Small things mostly." She told him about the missing tissues and cilantro, the other bizarre events. His mouth turned hard as she talked, his eyes grim.

"And why didn't you mention this before?" His voice had a dangerous edge.

"There was no reason to. What could you do about it? You can't keep me from forgetting things."

"What if it's not you? What if someone's getting into the house? Have you thought of that?"

"Of course, I have. But you told me yourself that security system is good. And who would be getting in?

The cleaning crew hasn't been there all week. The gardeners don't come near the house. And Kendall doesn't know the code, so that just leaves me."

He leaned over her, looking predatory suddenly. "I can get in."

"And what would be your point?" She shook her head and scoffed. "You wouldn't hurt me."

His eyes bore into hers. "You're sure about that?"

The anger in his voice confused her, and she frowned. "Of course, I'm sure. You've helped me, let me stay in your house. I trust you."

His hand slid over her throat, and her heart beat fast. He looked powerful, angry…deadly. His voice dropped deeper yet. "A lot of people think I murdered Candace Rothchild."

He looked capable of murder. His eyes burned dark. His mouth was a lethal slash. Any hint of tenderness or vulnerability had disappeared.

But this was the man who'd made Claire giggle. This was the man who'd fulfilled his mother's dream, even when she wouldn't know. This was the man who made her heart race and her blood heat, who with just a kiss brought her more pleasure than she'd ever known.

This was the man she was falling for fast.

She tried to swallow. She lifted her hand to his face and traced the harsh lines framing his mouth. "You're a good man, Luke."

His eyes blazed. "The hell I am."

And then his mouth was on hers, and he was kissing her again—hot and hard and deep. She gasped at the delicious invasion, thrilled at the rough, sensual feel of his skin. The kiss was harsh, giving vent to his sudden temper, as if he wanted to prove she was wrong.

But the grinding kiss stirred her senses. She plunged her hands in his hair, roused by his delirious feel, abandoning herself to desire.

The kiss deepened, lengthened, spinning her further beyond control. She knew she should pull back, think things through, but he felt so darned good. And just once, she wanted to forget her worries, just once, she wanted to do something impulsive and surrender to the rampaging need.

He made a low, rough sound deep in his throat and shifted his weight over hers. He trailed his mouth down her neck, sending streams of pleasure rippling over her skin. She moaned.

He captured her lips again, making her head whirl. She clutched his shoulders and back. Urgency mounted inside her, and she made soft, mewling noises of need.

Then he slowed and softened the kiss, and excitement skidded through her veins. And she realized with a daze that he was an expert at this. He knew exactly when to charge and when to withdraw, how to tease and make her feel crazed. He was a connoisseur, a master of this sensual craft, and he was driving her out of her mind.

And she wanted to let him. She knew that this would change nothing. She couldn't spin this interlude into more than it was. This was sex, just sex, a brief respite from danger, a magical moment out of time.

But she needed this, wanted this. She wanted to submit to the mind-boggling pleasure, yield to the tempting bliss. All her life she'd been the responsible one, the hardworking one, the one who'd borne the weight of the world. Now, just for this moment, she wanted to forget all that—forget the fear, forget the threats, not think, not worry, just feel.

His kisses hypnotized her. The need to touch him grew frantic, overwhelming, urgent.

She gripped his shoulders and tried to pull him against her, but his mouth roamed to her throat. Then he slid his hand under her T-shirt, and his palm scorched her breast. She shuddered, growing insistent. He groaned against her throat.

He rose then and tugged off her shirt. His eyes stalled on her breasts.

Her face turned hot. She felt unprotected and exposed, even in the lacy bra. Embarrassment mingled with pleasure. His heated gaze incited her nerves.

"You're beautiful," he growled, and her breath caught. She knew it wasn't true. She wasn't gorgeous like the women he dated. And Wayne had dwelled on her shortfalls enough. But as Luke's gaze swept the length of her, she felt beautiful and desired.

Then suddenly, a gunshot shattered the silence. The sharp report thundered through the hills. Her heart froze, and she gaped at Luke. "What—"

He dove over her, mashing her into the blanket, covering her head with his chest. Her pulse scrambled. Panic seized her. Someone had shot at them, and they were out in the open, exposed.

"Behind the rocks. *Now.*" Luke rolled to his feet and yanked her upright. She scooped up her T-shirt and ran. A bullet whined past. Tension screamed through her nerves as they swerved through the scattered pines.

The edge of the cliff was littered with boulders. Luke ducked behind one, pulling her with him, and she huddled beside him and struggled to breathe. She jerked her T-shirt over her head, stuffed her arms through the sleeves, then searched for a way to escape.

The slope below them was steep and covered with sagebrush. Luke pointed to a distant cluster of pines. "Run to those trees. The trail's back there. Go straight to the car and wait. And don't stop, no matter what."

Her gaze flew to his. "But what—"

"I'm going to head him off. Now go!"

She bit her lip, reluctant to leave him. But they didn't have time to argue. The gunman could show up at any time. Luke gave her a nudge, and she leaped off the edge of the cliff.

She hit the ground and nearly fell but managed to stay on her feet. Fighting to keep her balance and control her momentum, she angled across the hill toward the trees.

She skidded in the loose dirt, plowed into some sagebrush and let out a muffled cry. But she couldn't slow, couldn't stop. She had to reach the safety of those trees.

But what was Luke doing? Had their attacker seen him? How could he stop a man with a gun?

Then another shot rang out. She zigzagged in alarm.

She reached the pine trees and whipped behind one, then whirled around to look. The hillside was empty. Luke was nowhere in sight. Where on earth had he gone?

And where was the gunman? *Who* was the gunman? Why had he been shooting at them?

She hauled in a ragged breath, forcing those thoughts from her mind. She'd worry about all that later. She had to get to the car and wait for Luke.

But the path wound below her across the open slope, visible from above. She hesitated, still struggling to catch her breath. What if the gunman had her in his sights?

She fought back a spurt of dread, trying to decide

what to do. Luke had told her not to stop. He was buying her time to reach the car. But then how was he going to get down?

Another shot barked out. Sheer panic bludgeoned her nerves. What if Luke had been hit?

She couldn't leave him. She had to go back and check. But both the hillside and trail were too exposed. She had to find another way up.

The only other route was over the rocks. She darted to the nearby boulders, scrambled through the silvery sage. A chuckwalla scurried past, and she bit back a startled shriek.

Calm down, she told herself firmly. The lizard wouldn't hurt her. She climbed over some rocks, eased around a yucca plant, then eyed the long stretch of sandstone above.

She had no choice. She had to climb it. At least it wasn't too steep, and there were bushes and ridges to grip. As long as she went slowly, she would be fine.

She clambered up, then crept across the rock face, the hot sun scorching her scalp. Her heart beat fast. Sweat beaded and trickled down her jaw. She grabbed a plant, boosted herself up, then reached for a nearby ledge.

An ominous rattle stopped her. Unable to move, she jerked her gaze to the side.

A rattlesnake hissed at her, preparing to strike.

Chapter 8

The wild scream shattered the silence, sending adrenaline streaming through Luke's blood. *Amanda.* She was in danger. He had to get to her fast. But he couldn't move yet, not with the shooter just a few yards away. Even the soft snap of a twig could tip him off.

He sucked air through his tightly clenched teeth and crushed back the mushrooming fear. He had to stay calm, think through the haze of panic, stay smart or he'd get them both killed.

Insects buzzed in the bushes around him. A turkey vulture soared overhead. Blood dripped down his left arm from where the bullet had grazed him, and his shoulder hammered with pain. He adjusted the handkerchief he'd knotted as a makeshift bandage, shifted his gaze to the bushes ahead.

Concentrate. Be patient. The man who stayed focused was the one who survived. He'd learned that lesson on Las Vegas's deadly streets.

He just wished he had a handgun or knife.

The bushes rustled, and his vision tunneled. His body shook with the need to attack.

His pursuer rose, crept into the open with his pistol drawn. Then he turned in the direction of Amanda's scream.

Big mistake.

Luke leaped out, slammed into his side. They hit the ground grunting and rolled.

Luke landed on top. The man twisted, thrust back his elbow. Luke took the jab to his chest. He groaned, shook off the pain and fought for an opening, landed a punch to the man's gut.

The man wheezed and quickly recovered, then raised his pistol to shoot. But Luke lunged, tackled him again, scrambling for an advantage in the thick cloud of dust. He grabbed the man's wrist and rammed it against the ground.

His muscles strained as he battled to hold him. Sweat burned into his eyes. He grappled for dominance, straining and shoving, until the man's hand finally went slack. The pistol skidded loose.

But the man butted his head into Luke's injured shoulder. Luke went dizzy with the fierce waves of pain. *Damn.*

He hauled back, slammed his fist into his attacker's head and the sickening thump vibrated through his arm. The man slumped against the ground and went still.

Luke wheezed in the dusty air, shook the stinging sweat from his eyes. He pushed himself up, his muscles trembling from the adrenaline dump. Then he staggered over and picked up the gun.

A 9mm Glock. He released the magazine to count the rounds, slammed it back home and racked the slide. Feeling less vulnerable now, he stuffed it into the waistband of his jeans.

But he couldn't go to Amanda yet. He strode back to his attacker and kicked him over, then lowered himself to one knee. He rifled through the man's pockets but came up empty. No identification, not even a damned set of keys. He took a long look at his face—Hispanic, swarthy complexion, high cheekbones. Late thirties, early forties, judging by the receding hair.

He scowled. Too bad he'd left his cell phone in the car. He could have photographed this thug.

Frustrated, he exhaled and glanced around. He didn't have a rope to restrain him, and he couldn't waste any more time. He'd have to leave him, hope the police picked him up later on.

His urgency mounting, he leaped up and ran down the trail, the memory of that scream echoing through his mind. He shouldn't have left her alone. What if she'd been captured or worse? He immediately pushed aside that awful thought, needing to focus on finding her fast.

At the top of a hill he paused and scanned the landscape, searching for movement, or anything out of place. The sun sizzled off the blood-red sandstone. A hawk passed by, dragging a shadow over the earth.

Then a speck of blue in the sagebrush snagged his attention, and his heart careened to a stop. She'd been wearing a blue T-shirt and jeans.

His gut balled tight now, he raced across the parched hillside, hurdling creosote bushes and rocks. Had she been shot? He hadn't heard another gun fire. But then why had she veered off the trail?

He reached her seconds later. She lay facedown in the dirt surrounded by yucca plants and sagebrush. He dropped to his knees, leaned close to check her pulse. "Amanda. Amanda."

"Luke." She groaned, lifted her head.

She was alive. Thank God. He sagged, closed his eyes and exhaled, his own pulse running amok. He snapped his eyes open again. "What happened?"

She propped herself on her elbows and hung her head. "There was a snake."

Oh, hell. "Where did he get you?" he demanded, running his hands over her back.

"He didn't. I fell down the rocks. I hit some cactus, and my ankle…"

She'd fallen? He scowled up at the wall of sandstone. "What were you doing up there?"

"I heard that gunshot. I thought you might have been hurt. I was trying to go back to see."

His jaw turned slack. He stared at her in disbelief. "So you tried to climb the cliff?"

She didn't answer, and he bit back a curse, his fear for her out of control. But he'd have it out with her later. He needed to get her to safety first.

With effort he held on to his temper and managed to gentle his voice. "Where did you hit the cactus?"

"The back of my leg." She groaned again. "My right thigh."

He scooted closer, wincing when he spotted a dozen thick spines embedded in her jeans. No way could she ride in the car like that. Taking off her pants might jar the spines loose—or twist them and torture her more.

"I'll have to pull them out," he told her. He rose,

quartered the area for sticks, finally found two the right size. "This is going to hurt like hell, though."

He knelt beside her again, caught hold of a spine with the sticks. "Brace yourself." He jerked it from her thigh, flicked it away. She bit off an anguished cry.

He grimaced, sorry to be causing her more pain, but he didn't have much choice. Working as fast as he could, he pulled out the spines and tossed them a safe distance away. Then he ran his hand carefully over her thigh. "I think that's it. We'll check you out better when we get back."

"Thanks."

He shook his head. She hardly owed him thanks. His big attempt to help her relax today had only made things worse.

"Here. Hold on to me," he said as she struggled to rise. He grabbed her waist, slung her arm over his shoulder and helped her to her feet.

She took a step, nearly collapsed. "My ankle." She tried again and gasped. "I think I sprained it."

"Lean on me more." He helped her adjust her grip, glanced at her dirt-streaked face. She looked a wreck—her long hair wild, one cheek bleeding, her blue eyes shimmering with tears. But despite the grime—despite her pain—her soft, natural beauty wound through him, touching his heart.

He'd never had anyone try to save him before. He lived in a high-stakes, cutthroat world—a world where money ruled, the strong survived and every man looked out for himself. It was a world he understood, a world he'd mastered. He'd clawed his way to the top, stopping for no one, and now he was the one with the power.

Or he would be, once that project went through.

But Amanda was different. She was loyal, gentle, protective—even of him.

And that thought disturbed him. It brought back memories of his childhood, the way he'd once been before reality had smacked him down, feelings he'd buried for years. Because gentleness weakened a man. It left him vulnerable, ripe for attack.

"Luke, you're bleeding."

Still unsettled, he shook his head. "It's just a graze. I'll take care of it when we get back to town."

She gnawed her lip, glanced around. "Where's the gunman?"

"Still up there. I knocked him out and took his gun." And hopefully, gained them some time.

But he couldn't afford to take chances. As they worked their way to the car, their breaths rasping in the quiet air, he focused again on the hills. They'd had a close call, too close, and he wouldn't be caught off guard again.

A few minutes later, they reached his Land Rover, only to find that the tires had been slashed.

"Oh, no." Amanda turned to him. "What are we going to do now?"

"We don't have much choice. We'll drive on the rims, at least until we can pick up a cell phone signal and call for a tow."

He helped her into her seat, climbed into the driver's side. Despite his denial, his left arm throbbed. It was going to be a long ride back for them both.

Ignoring the pain, he cranked the engine, relieved when it started up. He drove along the rutted tractor trail, jolted through a dried-out creek bed. The ruined tires slapped against the dirt.

The slashed tires bothered him. It felt personal, more

like an act of rage than an attempt to strand them—especially since the engine had been left alone.

He looked at Amanda. "What does your ex look like?"

"Wayne? He's about five ten, blond, a heavy build. Why? Was it him back there?"

"No. This guy looked Hispanic, maybe part Indian."

"Oh. I'd hoped..." She turned her gaze to the windshield and hugged her arms.

"What?"

"Nothing."

"Have you seen him before?"

She frowned, shook her head. "I don't think so. The guy who tried to kidnap Claire was wearing a ski mask, so I didn't see his face. I didn't see the man in your casino, either."

He swerved to avoid a hole. "I saw the surveillance tape. His hair was longer than this guy's, and lighter brown. It wasn't him."

She looked at him again. "The waiter the other night... He might have been Hispanic."

That didn't mean much. Half the western population had Hispanic roots. But if this was the same man, it meant Harold Rothchild had hired this guy. But then where did the casino gunman come in?

He scowled. Damn, this was complicated. And another thing bothered him—how had their attacker found them today? Few people knew he owned this land, and he hadn't announced his plans. Unless the gunman had been watching and then followed them here. He could have hung back, followed their dust trail. Without a breeze to disperse it, they'd probably raised dust for at least five miles.

He was still mulling that over when he reached the

barbed wire gate at the end of the tractor path. He idled the engine and hopped out. But as he dragged the gate open, he spotted a Jeep by the trees down the road.

His spirits rising, he jogged back and turned off the engine, then grabbed his cell phone and keys. "We found a replacement car. Come on."

"But how are you going to drive it without a key?" She opened her door, and he helped her out.

"Don't worry." He'd picked up more than just survival skills on the streets.

And this job turned out to be easy. The dashboard had already been torn apart, the wires exposed. "It looks like he stole it." No point searching the vehicle for clues about his identity, then.

He touched the wires and started the engine. "Ready?" She nodded, and he drove off. They hit a bump, and she moaned.

He kept his attention on the sun-baked road, trying to avoid the worst of the washboard and ruts. But as he drove toward the highway, a cloud of dust billowing in his wake, the memory of Amanda's scream shuddered through him, that god-awful moment when he'd feared that she could be dead.

This situation had grown more dangerous today. This wasn't just about the ring anymore, or even an ex-husband bent on revenge. Someone had tried to kill them. Someone had followed them into the hills and hunted them down. They'd only survived due to luck.

But Luke knew better than to trust in luck. He'd built his fortune on the harsh reality that luck didn't last, that every gambler eventually lost.

So how could he keep Amanda safe? She wouldn't leave town; he'd already tried that tack.

He glanced sideways, took in her dusty clothes and tousled hair, the way her full lips flattened with pain. And he realized he didn't have a choice. He had to stay close to protect her. This had gone beyond lust, beyond mutual favors, two people helping each other out. Amanda's life was at stake.

And from now on—whether she liked it or not—he wasn't letting her out of his sight.

Amanda stared out Luke's penthouse window later that night, watching the city lights glitter against the sky. She'd gone from extreme highs to terrible lows today, from the ecstasy of nearly making love to Luke to barely escaping death.

But at whose hands? Certainly not Wayne's—which was terrible news. Not that she wanted Wayne after her. But at least he was a known enemy, one who she could fight. And it would have explained the bizarre events in the house. Wayne was vindictive, controlling. It would be just like him to try to mess with her mind.

But that hadn't been Wayne on that hill.

Her stomach in turmoil, she adjusted her grip on her crutches and hobbled back to the couch. She sank into the soft, creamy leather, propped her bandaged ankle on the ottoman and closed her eyes.

What a disaster moving here had been. Her life had spun completely out of control. She'd escaped an abusive ex-husband only to land in an even worse mess.

And to top it off, she'd discovered that she might have inherited her mother's mental illness.

But she couldn't wallow in self-pity or dwell on her fears. She had Claire to keep safe. She exhaled again, trying to purge the anxiety from her voice, then punched in Kendall's number on her phone.

"It's about time," Kendall complained when she picked up. "Where are you?"

"Luke's penthouse."

"How's your ankle?"

"Just sprained." She'd phoned Kendall earlier from the urgent care clinic to update her on the news. "But I'm staying here tonight."

Silence greeted that statement. "It's not what you think," she added. Although it nearly had been back in the hills.

"Mandy..."

"You don't have to say it. I know."

"But you don't even know this guy." Amanda opened her mouth to argue, but her sister forged on. "I know he's rich, and I know he's letting you stay here, which is nice. But for God's sake, Mandy, get real. Luke Montgomery isn't your type."

Her temper stirred. The last thing she needed after her hellish day was a lecture from her sister about men. "So who is my type? Wayne?"

"Don't be ridiculous. You know I never liked that creep. But that's the problem. Luke might be just as bad."

"He's not—"

"It was all over the news today. He had a restraining order on Candace Rothchild."

Amanda's temper abruptly deflated. *A restraining order.* Her belly churned even more. She glanced over her shoulder at the hall to Luke's bedroom and lowered her voice. "That doesn't make him a killer."

"But you don't know what might have happened

that night. They argued in his casino—everyone saw it. And maybe she provoked him later on. Maybe he flew into a rage."

Amanda shuddered and rotated her wrist, remembering Wayne. But Luke wasn't like that. Yes, he was a hard man, a powerful one. But he'd saved her life today. He'd taken a bullet to keep her safe.

She shoved her hand through her freshly washed hair and sighed. "Listen, you don't have to worry about me. I know what I'm doing."

"Do you?" Kendall's voice went flat. "Look, I know I'm always after you to take more chances, but not this one."

"Don't worry. I'll be fine." She hoped. Gathering her courage, she fiddled with the tie on the thick, fluffy bathrobe from the spa downstairs. She dreaded asking but needed to know. "You're all right, aren't you? I mean, nothing strange has happened at the house today?"

"No, why?" Suspicion tinged Kendall's voice. "Is there something I need to know?"

"No." She closed her eyes, pressed her fingers to her temple. There went her last remaining long shot—that someone was targeting the house. "I just wanted to make sure you were both all right."

"We're fine. We've been swimming, coloring, reading books… Hold on." There was a muffled commotion in the background. "Here's Claire now."

"Hi, Mommy." Claire's voice chirped over the line. She babbled about Aunt Kendall and Brownie, the minutia of the day's events.

Amanda's throat turned thick as she listened. It would kill her to lose custody of Claire. But if she did have her mother's illness, she couldn't endanger her child. She had to do everything she could to keep her safe, even if it meant giving her up.

And she knew exactly how the illness would progress—the paranoia and delusions, the tormenting voices and suicidal thoughts. Not one medication on the market had helped her mother cope.

She beat back that frightening thought, then forced a peppy note into her voice so she wouldn't scare Claire. "Be good for Aunt Kendall tonight. And eat all your oatmeal in the morning."

Her chest aching, her throat so tight she could hardly speak, she told Claire she loved her and clicked off the phone. Then she closed her eyes, sagged back against the cushions and tried to think.

All right. So she might have inherited her mother's illness. The thought terrified her, but it was a possibility she had to face. She'd have to see a doctor for an evaluation, make contingency plans for Claire. But not yet. She still had time before her behavior got too erratic—assuming she really was ill. She'd take this day by day.

And she wouldn't just sit around pitying herself in the meantime. She was stronger than that.

Agitated, needing to do something, anything to take her mind off the fear, she grabbed her crutches and rose. She hobbled into the spotless kitchen and cleared away the remnants of the five-star dinner room service had brought.

Then, her emotions still all over the map, she dimmed the lights and started toward the guest suite to crash. Things always looked better in the morning, her mother had said. But nothing had improved for her mother. And somehow, she didn't see how a few more hours would remedy this mess.

Partway down the hall, she remembered Luke. She paused, wondering if she should check on him before she turned in. He might be having second thoughts about that pain medication he'd refused. Not that she blamed him for being leery given his mother's addiction. But at least she could ask.

She returned to the kitchen and grabbed the pills, then worked her way down his hall. Seconds later, she tapped on his bedroom door. "Luke?" He didn't answer, so she inched the door open and called again. "Luke?"

Still no answer. She went inside and scanned the enormous room. The overhead light was still on, and her gaze zeroed in on the bed. Luke lay face down on the oversized mattress, his arms stretched out, his face turned to the side. His upper body was naked, his lower half covered by sheets. Despite his claim that he'd had work to do, he'd apparently fallen asleep.

She put the pain pills on the bedside table with the antibiotics, poured water from a nearby carafe. Then she hesitated, debating whether to wake him. He needed another antibiotic soon.

Her pulse quickening, she set down her crutches and perched on the edge of the mattress. For a long moment, she indulged herself, letting her eyes travel over his back. His skin was tanned, smooth, the muscles of his broad back clearly defined. Her gaze lingered on his massive shoulders, the strong, rugged lines of his neck. His upper arm was bandaged where the bullet had grazed him, and the cloth gleamed white against his skin.

She touched his arm to check for infection, relieved that his skin wasn't hot. She knew she should wake him, then leave. She couldn't just sit here forever and stare.

But his face held her riveted—the dark, aggressive brows, the black whiskers coating his jaw. He had a strong, masculine nose, thick, ink-black hair, the most intriguing, sensual mouth. Her mind stalled on the memory of how he'd kissed her, and shivers rippled over her skin.

Even asleep he looked virile and dangerous. She'd never seen anyone so powerfully male.

No wonder women found him compelling. He had enormous wealth, the kind of good looks that drew women of every age. And that intensity in his eyes…

But how many women saw the caring part? How many knew about that land? How many glimpsed his complexity or sensed the pain that drove this man?

She snorted at that wild thought. She hardly knew him, either. Her sister was right about that. She'd only met Luke last week.

And as much as she hated to admit it, Kendall was right about something else. She probably shouldn't trust him. She'd made that mistake with Wayne. Marrying Wayne had been the one time she'd taken a chance, the one time she'd let impulse and wishful thinking override common sense. And that had been a disaster.

But if getting close to Luke was wrong, then why did he feel so right?

His eyes opened. He turned his head, and those golden eyes fastened on hers.

And suddenly the air turned too thick to breathe.

"I was dreaming about you," he said, his voice deep, husky.

Her throat went dry. She couldn't move. And she was suddenly, intensely aware of how close he lay, how naked she was beneath her robe.

And a torrent of erotic memories whipped through her—the heat of his mouth, the musk of his skin, the exciting caress of his hands.

His eyes darkened, holding her captive. Warmth pooled between her thighs. He'd dreamed of her, wanted her.

She hungered for him just as badly. She ached to relive that sensual pleasure, find out where it could lead. She wanted to abandon herself to this delirious attraction—forget the danger, forget her worries, forget the horrific time bomb ticking in her head.

He reached up, snagged the back of her neck with his hand and drew her close.

"Luke," she whispered, her voice raw. "Make me forget."

His eyes turned hotter yet. He tugged her closer until her mouth was inches from his.

He lowered his gaze to her lips, brushed the bottom curve with his thumb, making shivers dance over her skin.

"That's the hell of it." His voice came out rough, almost angry.

"What?" she whispered, too muddled with desire to think.

"I don't want you to forget. I want you to remember. *Remember me.*"

His mouth took hers. She would remember him, all right. How could she help it?

This was the man she was starting to love.

Chapter 9

She was heaven, absolute, erotic bliss.

Luke pulled Amanda against him, his mouth capturing hers in a hot, deep kiss that demolished his self-control. His tongue dueled with hers. Raw heat thickened his blood. He plunged his hand through her silky hair, felt her soft, full breasts pillow his chest, and the perfect, sensual feel of her shut down his mind.

He'd been fantasizing about her for days now—how she'd look naked, her moist heat pulsing around him, those endlessly riveting legs hooked over his back. Kissing her hadn't been nearly enough, had only fired his imagination more.

But even the most vivid dream couldn't match the reality of Amanda. The scent of her slick, creamy skin, the sweep of her satin hair over his chest drew a ragged groan from his throat. He dragged her further over his body, ran his hands up her legs beneath the robe, stroking the velvety sweep of her thighs.

She was so soft, so lush, so damned arousing. The way she yielded to him, melting around him, those provocative moans she made in the back of her throat.

But suddenly she flinched, gasped against his mouth. He broke the kiss, alarmed. "What's wrong?"

"My ankle." She winced, closed her eyes on a shudder of pain.

He silently swore. He'd forgotten her sprained ankle. "Let's change places." He tipped her gently onto her back, slipped a pillow under her foot so he wouldn't bump it again. Then, ignoring his own throbbing arm, he braced himself on his elbows above her.

Her gaze dropped to his bandaged bicep. "Your arm—"

"Doesn't hurt." Not nearly as much as another, painfully engorged part of him did.

But doubt clouded her eyes. She nibbled her bottom lip, her frown deepening, and he tried to beat back the lust.

"Having second thoughts?"

"No, not exactly, it's just…I have to tell you…" Her face turned pink, and her gaze flitted away. "You might not want… I'm not too good at this."

He would have laughed if she hadn't looked so distressed. Not good at this? He was so hot for her he was ready to explode. "What makes you think that?"

"My ex-husband. He said I wasn't…" Her blush deepened, and she fidgeted with the collar on her robe.

He went still. "He said you weren't what?"

"That I wasn't…exciting enough. That he needed to, you know…" Her face flaming, her eyes stayed on her robe. "Watch videos, or look at magazines to get..." Her voice trailed off.

He closed his eyes on a flash of anger, damning Wheeler for all the damage he'd done. Then he tilted up her delicate chin, let his gaze rove her sultry lips.

Her blue eyes were dark with lust. Her tousled hair cascaded around her face. He ached to fist his hands in that glorious hair, kiss the fragile sweep of her throat, explore every rapturous inch of her skin.

Keeping his eyes locked on hers, he trapped her hand and slowly, relentlessly pushed it over his chest and past his belly until she cupped him, cupped all of him, every rock-hard, throbbing inch.

Her eyes widened. Her lips parted on a soundless gasp. He pulsed against her, heavy, thick, ready to erupt.

"I think," he said gruffly, "we can safely say the problem wasn't you."

"No." Her voice sounded strangled. "Not me."

He nipped her lips, parting them with his tongue. And then he drove his tongue in deeply, letting her feel the violent need rocking his blood.

She whimpered in response, wrapped her arms around his neck, bringing her soft body tighter against his. Hunger rippled through him, the relentless beat bludgeoning him like shock waves from a nuclear blast. But he had to go slowly. He wanted to drive her to ecstasy, shatter every illusion she had about her lack of appeal, obliterate every single memory of Wheeler from her mind.

And make her remember *him.*

He forced himself to ease off, even as his body shuddered with need. He slowed and lengthened the kiss, caressed her with long, languid strokes. He slid his hands down her lush, smooth curves, seducing, teasing, arousing. She arched against him, her excitement growing, and he swallowed her moan with his lips.

Unable to resist, he grazed her jaw, her neck, then worked his way down her body, replacing his hand with his mouth. Her nipples pouted in invitation, then pebbled at his heated response. He smiled when she groaned and tugged his hair.

"You're so damned beautiful," he murmured. And her ex-husband was a fool.

He stroked her belly, her thighs, feathering kisses up her sensitive skin until she was shaking with need. He teased, circled, retreated, beating back his own burgeoning hunger, wanting to make this a night she would never forget.

But the restraint was taking its toll. His heart thundering now, his breath growing ragged and fast, he moved back up her body and took her mouth. He plundered deeply, moving over her, letting her feel his insistent need.

But he wanted to make her feel just as desperate, just as crazed. He raised himself up and looked at her—her parted lips, her sultry eyes, the silky tendrils of hair clinging to her flushed cheeks. She was open to him, her entire body exposed, looking like every dream he'd ever had.

He ran his palms down her breasts to her taut belly, back over her satiny thighs. His muscles bunched, and he struggled to keep his own raw needs in check. But she arched her back, and the movement sent a heavy jolt of hunger through his veins. She was torturing him, and he was fast veering out of control.

He poised his body over hers. "Open your eyes." His throat was thick, his voice hoarse. Her dazed gaze rose to his. He trembled, his control eroding, wanting desperately to plunge into that tempting heat.

"Luke," she whispered. "Do something." Her hands gripped his shoulders, his back, and she tried to tug him against her.

He framed her face with his hands, using every ounce of willpower he had to keep from taking her fast. He entered her as slowly as he could, giving her time to accommodate him, to adjust, but the hot, sensual feel of her incinerated his nerves.

When he'd sheathed himself completely, he closed his eyes and rested his forehead against hers, trying to breathe through the rampaging need. He throbbed insistently inside her, his body clamoring to move. But he had to slow down, make this right for her, erase the pain from her past.

He opened his eyes, ran his finger over her cheek. He looked into her eyes, wanting to reassure her, but those mesmerizing blue eyes held him enthralled.

Emotions poured through him, disturbing emotions. Emotions he didn't dare name.

This was sex. That's all this was—a night of sex, nothing more.

He kissed her again, his urgency soaring, his body lost to the need. She closed around him, warm and wet and tight. And his hunger intensified, riding him like a whip, a mandate he couldn't ignore.

He let his body find the primitive rhythm, fulfilling that most basic need. That's all this was, he assured himself through the blaze of heat. Just biology, a man and woman indulging in natural urges, nothing more.

It couldn't be more.

His heart thudded fast. The slow pace made him

crazed. Nothing had felt this urgent, this right in his entire life.

His desperation built. Desire clawed at him, threatening to pull him under. He slid his hand down her body between them, then stroked her most sensitive flesh.

She shuddered and bucked against him. "Luke," she cried. But she was holding back, fighting her release, her nails biting into his shoulders and arms.

But this was a war he intended to win. He gripped her chin, forcing her dazed eyes to his. Willing her to surrender to the pleasure. Submit. "Let go," he ordered.

Her eyes pleaded with his. "I can't. I—"

"Do it. Let go *now*."

She stiffened, came undone with a keening cry. His satisfaction soared. He felt like a conqueror for giving this woman what Wheeler never had.

He gripped her jaw and kissed her, a deep, wild kiss that showed her exactly how ravenous he was. And then he gave in to the need, let his instincts take charge. The pressure built, his body quickening beyond his control. And he exploded into her, his hoarse cry joining hers.

But as he drifted back to earth long moments later, he wondered what the hell he'd just done.

When Luke lifted his head from the pillow hours later, Amanda was gone. He blinked, his vision blurry from lack of sleep, and pondered the now-empty bed. But it was hard to hold on to a thought with pleasure still hazing his brain. It had been one hell of a night. They'd made love until dawn, then finally succumbed to exhaustion and dozed.

The sex had been phenomenal. Amanda had fascinated him with her surprising demands. She'd blasted past her inhibitions, demolishing her preconceptions, proving that her body was made for hot sex.

Made for him.

His own body was sated, depleted. He inhaled the scent of sex on the rumbled sheets, closed his eyes on a groan. Erotic images of the night flashed past, and his body predictably throbbed.

Maybe not so depleted.

And where was she, anyhow? He sat up, scrubbed his hand over his bristly jaw and rubbed his gritty eyes. And his mind danced around the other memories, the emotions that had surfaced during the night. But he pushed those confusing feelings aside. He'd analyze his reaction to her later.

He got out of bed, ignoring the burn in his injured arm, the insistent arousal her lingering scent caused. He pulled on a pair of loose sweatpants, padded barefoot down the carpeted hallway to the front room.

She stood in front of the floor-to-ceiling windows that comprised one wall, staring out at the early morning sky. Her arms were crossed, her shoulders hunched as if she was cold. The wave of possessiveness he felt caught him off guard.

But her eyes met his in the reflection, and something about her expression made him pause.

"Morning-after regrets?"

"I think you know better than that." Her voice turned soft, and he knew she was remembering exactly how much she'd enjoyed the night. "I just couldn't sleep."

It had been spectacular, all right. He walked to her, slid his arms around her waist from behind, and the feel of her warm, soft bottom stoked his desire. He savored the scent of her hair, slid his hands down her belly and thighs.

Her eyes locked on his in the glass. "Again?"

He grunted. He could spend days, months exploring every facet of this woman. But sex could wait. He didn't like that worried look in her eyes.

"So how come you're not sleeping?"

She sighed, and the soft sound twisted his heart. "I just had a bad dream, that's all."

"About your ex?"

"Wayne…the gunman. Everything that's been happening in the past couple weeks. I came out here to read so I wouldn't bother you."

Her lips wobbled, and even in the reflection he could see the fatigue darkening her skin beneath her eyes. He frowned. He hadn't helped much by keeping her up all night.

But maybe he could ease some of her cares. "I didn't have a chance to tell you, but I put in a phone call to Natalie Rothchild last night when we got back. They did a parole compliance check on your ex. He's still in Maryland."

"That's good." But she didn't look relieved. If anything, the fear in her eyes intensified. And he suspected that something else was bothering her, something more than the obvious danger. She'd had the same scared look back at the house.

And he still intended to discover the cause.

"Do you really think Harold Rothchild is behind all this?" she asked.

"It makes the most sense." He released her, walked to the window, braced his forearm on the glass and peered out. The darkness was fading, giving way to the dawn. It would soon be another scorching day under the desert sun.

"His business has been in trouble for years," he added. "He's taken out some high-interest loans that are coming due, and he won't make the payments." Loans from the mob-connected Schaffers. "I've timed it so the Phoenix will take away business at a critical time. He'll have to start selling assets soon. Once that happens, his entire empire will collapse." He couldn't keep the satisfaction from his voice.

"You're saying you planned this? You're doing this on purpose to make him fail?" She sounded appalled.

He swung back to her and met her gaze. "Don't pity him, Amanda. He's ruined enough lives in his time. He deserves far worse than this." The man's indifference had killed his mother, causing her addiction and early demise.

"I see." She let out a short laugh. "And you really think he'd try to kill us to stop this project?"

"He'll do anything to hold on to his power. This is a high-stakes game. No one plays nice, not even me."

Her voice turned low. "But you'd never kill anyone."

"No." But he'd done other things he wasn't proud of, things he'd had to do to win.

She hobbled to the window and looked out. For a long moment she didn't speak, just stared out at the pink sky streaking the horizon beyond the black peaks. "So where is Naked City?" she asked at last.

"Over there." He pointed out a darkened area just past the lighted Strip.

"So you can see your old neighborhood from here."

"Yeah. I can see it from here." It served as a reminder of where he'd come from, kept him focused on his goals. And before long he'd stand right here and watch bulldozers raze that slum.

She gave him a worried glance. "I hope canceling the meeting yesterday didn't cause any problems."

He shrugged. In truth, it had ticked off the investors. He'd spent hours the other night making phone calls, trying to make amends, which had been harder than he'd thought. Canceling that meeting had been a stupid move, foolhardy. This project was too damned important—everything he'd worked toward for twenty years. He couldn't afford to take risks now.

"Do you have a picture of it?" she asked.

"The project? Yeah, on the desk." He strode back to the sofa, got her crutches and handed them to her. Then he crossed the room to the desk.

He flicked on the desk lamp, spread out the rolled-up plans, and secured the corners with weights. She joined him a moment later.

She stood close enough beside him that their shoulders touched, and he inhaled her sensual scent. His eyes roamed her tousled hair, the tempting cleavage exposed by the gaping robe.

He wondered why he wasn't tired of her by now. Usually one night with a woman stifled his curiosity, leaving him bored. Hell, half the time he couldn't wait for the woman to leave.

But Amanda was different. Instead of wanting her out of his penthouse so he could get back to work, he couldn't draw his gaze from her lips.

"So what do you think?" he asked, oddly anxious to hear her opinion.

She pursed her lips, ran her finger over the architectural drawing, slanted her head to see the painted images along the sides. "It's fabulous." She shook her head, and her hair slid over her shoulders, glimmering as it caught the light. "It's a magnificent project, huge, like the ancient pyramids."

His mouth quirked up. "It's not that great." But her words sent warmth flowing through him. He was glad she liked it, that she approved.

He shifted his gaze to the painting of the mythical bird at the top of the plans. The Phoenix, the mighty, fabled bird, able to regenerate and recover from death. Crimson and gold, it would perch atop the casino—proud, regal, triumphant.

Just like him. Harold Rothchild had treated his mother like trash, like someone disposable, someone whose life didn't matter to him. He'd crushed her, assuming that an impoverished nobody could never battle his power and wealth. He'd been right.

But he hadn't reckoned on Luke.

Amanda's eyes returned to his. "I read an article about the project in the paper while you were sleeping." She hesitated, and another small line furrowed her brow. "It said people have been protesting this project, that they want affordable housing built there instead."

He shrugged, rolled up the plans and set them aside. "That's normal. There are always protests with a project this size."

Her troubled gaze stayed on his. "But what about the people who live in those apartments? Where are they going to go?"

"They'll find another place."

"Are you sure?"

"Yeah, I'm sure. It's not a problem." But his growing desire for her was. And suddenly, he didn't want to think about the project anymore, not with this warm, willing woman standing there naked beneath that robe.

He moved close, crowding her against the desk. The scent of her skin filled his nostrils and fired his blood. He slid his hand around her neck, studied the pale freckles sprinkling the bridge of her nose. "You worry too much."

Her mouth tightened. "I can't help it. There's a lot to worry about right now."

He couldn't deny that. She'd been shot at, held up at gunpoint, possibly drugged. Someone had even tried to steal her child. And she didn't deserve any of this. She was just an innocent victim, caught in the crossfire of his revenge.

"I'm going to keep you safe," he promised. From whatever threatened her. "I won't let anything happen to you."

"I know." She gave him a tremulous smile.

Her confidence floored him. And those emotions bubbled to the surface again, the desire to protect her, defend her, to claim her as his.

"I meant what I said yesterday," she whispered. "You're a good man, Luke."

"Not that good." Not much better than Rothchild in some respects. "Don't make me into something I'm not."

She slowly shook her head. "You're better than you think."

The hell he was. His anger flared—anger at himself for his ruthless past, anger at her for her misguided trust. He didn't want her looking at him as if he were a hero. He wanted her to see him, see who he really was.

He took the crutches from her hands and tossed them to the carpet, his gaze never wavering from hers. Then he lifted her onto the desk and stepped between her legs.

Right where he wanted to stay.

His hands went to the belt on her robe, and he made short work of the tie. He jerked the robe open and ripped it off. And then he let his gaze slowly rake every provocative, naked inch of her, from her sweetly curving breasts to the heaven at the juncture of her thighs.

His gaze lingered, traveled back up and her already-dazed eyes locked on his. Her lush lips parted. Her breath came in reedy gasps.

And that now-familiar hunger blazed through his blood.

"This isn't going to be nice or slow," he warned her. "I'm going to take you fast and hard."

Shock and excitement flared in her eyes. "I don't want nice or slow. I want you." She raised her hands to his shoulders. Her eyes stayed riveted on his.

Her trust made him even angrier. He slipped himself free of his sweatpants, lifted her bottom and in one, swift motion drove himself home.

They both groaned. But he'd told her the truth. And this time, he didn't play the cultured billionaire, didn't pretend to be nice. He took her hard and rough, treating her with brutal honesty, letting her feel the man he was.

A man raised in the gutter. The illegitimate son of a drifter. In a few hard thrusts, she convulsed.

He joined her barely a second later. Delirium deluged his blood. He was still pulsing inside her when a soft ring sounded across the room.

"That's my cell phone," she said, sounding distracted. "I'd better get it."

"Yeah." And suddenly, since the first time he'd touched her the night before, he needed distance. He didn't know what had just happened, but it scared the hell out of him.

Glad for the interruption, he quickly retreated. He adjusted his sweatpants, stalked across the room to get the phone. By the time he returned to the desk, she stood holding her crutches, safely enveloped in the robe.

Still shaken by what had just happened, he handed her the phone. She looked at the display and frowned, then clicked it on. "Hi. What's up?"

Her face paled. "Oh, God." She swayed, put out a hand to grasp the desk.

He tensed, kept his gaze on hers.

"I'll be right there." She snapped the phone closed, and her panic-stricken eyes met his. "It's Claire. I need to get to the hospital fast."

Chapter 10

Amanda despised hospitals. She hated the squeaky linoleum floors, the ubiquitous blue chairs, the too-soothing voices the nurses always used. And she especially hated that antiseptic smell that permeated the halls—as if it could somehow sanitize the truth and erase the harsh reality of illness, insanity, death.

And now Claire was here, in this despicable place—and it was all her fault. While she'd been indulging the most exhilarating time of her life, lost in the pleasure of Luke's arms, her child was suffering from anaphylactic shock, being rushed to the emergency room where she could die.

No. Claire couldn't die. She refused to even think it. She stuffed down the fear, passed a nurse in her flowered scrubs and sneakers and hobbled even faster toward the emergency-room desk.

"My daughter's here," she breathlessly told the woman in charge. "Claire Patterson. She's in the emergency room."

"Through the double doors." The woman shifted her gaze to a spot behind her.

Amanda turned, relieved to see Luke heading toward her. They'd raced here from his penthouse, only pausing to throw on clothes—and he looked it. His T-shirt was wrinkled, his hair unruly. Morning whiskers coated his jaw. And despite the guarded look in his eyes, she was glad that he'd come in with her, that she didn't have to be here alone.

She didn't know why he'd suddenly withdrawn back at the penthouse. He'd shut down just before she'd received Kendall's phone call. But she couldn't deal with that now. Her emotions were bouncing all over the place, from guilt and dread, to remorse and fear. She'd think about the incredible night and Luke's odd reaction later on.

Desperate to see Claire, she limped through the double doors, past strangers waiting in wheelchairs, people groaning and crying on cots. By the time they found Claire in a curtained-off section, she was so worked up she wanted to wretch.

"Mommy," Claire wheezed, and Amanda's heart plummeted, the dread blasting back full force. Claire looked like a burn victim. Her face was puffed, her lips huge and distorted. Splotchy red welts covered her skin. She clung to Brownie, her eyes nearly swollen shut, looking so small and lost against the starched white sheets that it was all Amanda could do not to cry.

She rushed to Claire's side, set aside her crutches, and perched on the edge of the cot. "Oh, honey. What happened?" She pulled her into her arms, rested her cheek on her head, inhaled her little-girl scent.

Kendall rose from the plastic chair on the opposite side of the bed. "She had a reaction to the oatmeal."

"The oatmeal?" She frowned. How could that be?

"She was fine until then. I used the EpiPen, then brought her here."

Amanda rocked, dabbed the tears from Claire's blotchy face, then shot Kendall a questioning look. "You gave her the stuff from the plastic container, right?"

"Absolutely." Kendall's worried eyes stayed on Claire. "I gave her exactly what you told me. But it happened right after she ate the oatmeal, so that had to be it."

"I believe you." She pulled her gaze back to Claire. Kendall knew all about Claire's allergy to peanuts and understood how serious it was. She wouldn't have made a mistake.

But then how could this have happened? She screened every morsel Claire ate, refusing to even take a chance on commercial cereals. She was so scrupulous, in fact, that she hand mixed a special breakfast blend for Claire using oatmeal, walnuts and flax.

"The doctor will be back in a minute," Kendall added. "She gave her a shot of epinephrine. She said Claire's going to be fine."

"Thank you," she whispered. She cradled Claire closer, grateful that her sister had been there. But it should have been her. She never should have neglected her child—especially for a night of sex.

Guilt tightened her throat, and she glanced at Luke. He stood at the open curtain with his strong arms crossed, his rugged face set in grim lines.

She flashed back to the first time she'd seen him in the casino. Her impression of him had been exactly right—he was ruthless, powerful…predatory.

But he was far more complex than that. He had a tender side, a good side, no matter what he might think. He'd sheltered her. He'd saved her life on that hill. And she could never repay him for last night, for all that he'd taught her about herself. He'd given her an amazing gift, freeing her from the doubts and insecurities Wayne had instilled.

Still, he'd retreated after the shattering intimacy they'd shared. But maybe it was just as well. Claire's accident was a sobering reminder that nothing had really changed since she'd met him. They lived in different worlds.

Maybe he'd punched holes in her protective walls. Maybe he'd made her dream for a while about a man she could never have. But that's all it was, a dream. She had Claire to think about, possibly an illness to confront. No matter how much Luke compelled her, she couldn't turn a brief sexual interlude into a fairy-tale romance. And she certainly couldn't go off the deep end and let herself fall in love with the man.

But as she pulled her gaze from those carnal eyes, she feared that her heart had already taken the plunge.

Three hours later, Amanda settled her exhausted, drowsy daughter down for a nap. The doctor had pumped Claire full of antihistamines and adrenaline, making the welts fade, the dangerous swelling in her throat subside.

Amanda smoothed back Claire's wispy hair, rubbed her back, smiling at the sight of the bear peeking over the sheet. They'd been lucky today. They'd had a bad scare, nothing more. It could have been far worse.

And she had to make sure it didn't happen again. Determined to root out the source of the problem, she pushed aside her own exhaustion and rose.

She limped through the quiet house into the kitchen. Her sister had gone home. Luke had closeted himself in his office to make some calls. Only the tick of the grandfather clock in the hallway and the muted buzzing of gardeners trimming hedges by the pool broke the hush.

She propped her crutches against the counter and opened the pantry, then pulled out the cereal she'd mixed. She popped the top off the plastic container, sniffed and peered inside. No sign of peanuts that she could tell.

Frowning, she closed the container and put it back, then grabbed the can of walnuts from the shelf. She turned the can, looked at the label. *Peanuts.*

She stared at the can in disbelief. *Impossible.* She couldn't have used peanuts by mistake. She never bought them, never even allowed them in the house.

Stunned, she pried off the plastic lid, but there were peanuts inside. And the can was still nearly full, recently opened, just like the one she had used.

Still unwilling to believe it, she frantically searched the shelf. But there wasn't another can. These had to be the nuts she'd used.

Her mind reeling, she stumbled to the table and sank into a chair. How could she have done this? She couldn't have bought the wrong nuts and added them to Claire's food—could she? Because if she had... This was so much worse than misplacing a comb or forgetting where she'd parked the car. *She could have killed Claire.*

Horrified, she dropped her face into her hands. She dragged in a breath, tried to wrap her mind around what she had done. If she'd made this mistake, it proved she had her mother's illness, and it was progressing faster than she'd thought. She would need to tell Kendall, make preparations for Claire's future before she endangered her even more.

But she still couldn't believe it. How could she have done anything so careless? She searched for a different conclusion, desperate for something—anything—that would explain it away. But who else could have done it? Wayne was in Maryland. The police had even said so. And she refused to believe Kendall or Luke could have done anything this vicious to Claire.

Which put the blame back on her.

She pressed her hand to her lips and closed her eyes. She didn't want to face it, but neither could she keep ignoring the proof. She really was losing her mind.

She inhaled, trying to calm herself down, to ease the panic surging inside. Somehow she had to get through this and cope.

But then the muscles along the back of her neck tensed. The fine hairs on her forearms rose.

And she felt it again—that creeping, crawling sensation slithering over her skin. It wormed through her nerves, beat into her skull—that whisper of menace, danger. The feeling that he was back again, watching her.

She gasped air to her strangled lungs, tried to shove the paranoia away. Wayne wasn't here. She couldn't overreact. She had to get a grip on her nerves.

But the fright only mounted, mingled with dread. And she could feel him now, getting closer, closer….

She leaped up and whipped around. The kitchen was empty. Nothing moved. Only the grandfather clock ticked down the hallway, its beats sounding out the relentless chant: He's here. He's here. He's here.

"Who's there?" she croaked.

Silence echoed back.

"Who's there?" she cried again, and her voice rose to a shriek. Her knees began to shake. Terror poured through her cells. She pressed her hand to her throat, struggling not to come undone, but the fear mushroomed inside her, threatening to explode.

This had to be Wayne. He had to be here. She couldn't be losing her mind.

Could she?

She hugged her arms and rocked, let out an anguished moan.

She'd never felt more terrified or alone in her life.

Luke had never felt more out of control. He entered the kitchen a short time later, his gut in turmoil, a headache beating at the base of his skull. His entire life was unraveling before his eyes.

Sex with Amanda had shaken him, affected him in ways he didn't want to examine. The sight of her poor daughter swollen and blistered from that allergic reaction had bothered him even more.

He didn't want to care about them. He didn't want to get involved with Amanda or her child. He needed to focus on his project, on getting revenge on Harold Rothchild and attaining his goal.

Especially now that he'd gotten more bad news. Now even his project was slipping from his grasp—and to save it, he needed Amanda's help.

He spotted her slumped at the kitchen table, her hands covering her face. He hated telling her this latest development and adding to her stress when she was worried about Claire. But he didn't have much choice.

She was as caught up in this mess as he was. The police might even call her in for questioning now.

He slid into the chair across from her, and she lifted her head. His heart skidded at the torment in her eyes. "What happened? Is it Claire?"

She pushed her hair back from her face with trembling hands. "No. She's better. She's napping, but she's going to be fine."

"Then what's wrong?" Her face had paled. Fatigue puffed the skin around her eyes.

"Nothing." Her gaze flitted away. "I'm just tired."

"And I'm Santa Claus."

Her brows snapped together, and he scowled back. "Come on, Amanda. Don't give me that crap. You look like hell. You've been jumping at noises for days. Something's wrong, and I want to know what it is."

Her lips tightened. "It has nothing to do with you. It's just...something I have to deal with alone."

Her answer should have relieved him. He wanted to back away. He'd been trying to distance himself from this woman since the moment they'd met. But he'd be damned if he could do it. The thought of her suffering some private torment tore his insides to shreds.

He reached out and trapped her hand, caressing the fragile bones with his thumb. "Tell me, Amanda. Whatever it is, I'll help."

"You can't help," she whispered. "There's nothing anyone can do."

"Try me."

Her stricken eyes searched his. And he saw her hope, her doubt. The fear.

"Trust me," he said, and after an endless moment, she sighed.

"All right." She squeezed his hand, then tugged her own away. "But there's really nothing you can do. I told you I've been misplacing things."

"Yeah."

"Well, this time I put peanuts in Claire's oatmeal instead of walnuts. I could have killed her."

"So you made a mistake."

She rubbed her arms, looking even more distraught. "It's worse than that. I told you my mother was ill. But I didn't tell you…she was mentally ill, schizophrenic. She suffered from hallucinations, blackouts. She forgot things, did bizarre things—like putting the wrong ingredients in food."

Oh, hell. He sat back and folded his arms. No wonder she was upset. "You think you have the same thing."

She clasped her hands, gnawed at her bottom lip. "It can be genetic. And sometimes it doesn't show up until later in life, until your twenties and thirties."

"You're not mentally ill," he said flatly.

"But—"

"But nothing." He didn't believe it for a minute. "You told me this started after you moved here."

"Right. The night of Rothchilds' party. But—"

"Did anything happen last night at my penthouse?"

"No." A blush rose up her cheeks. "At least nothing like that."

Their gazes locked. Hunger rose and vibrated the air. His blood pulsed hard, and he battled back the urge to haul her across the table into his arms. This wasn't the time for sex.

He cleared his throat. "Look at it logically. All these events have happened in the house."

"Not the time I forgot where I parked."

"But you were here right before that. Someone could have followed you there."

"Maybe." Misery deadened her voice. "But I didn't black out here. That happened at the Rothchilds' casino."

She was right. He shoved his hand through his hair. "So there are inconsistencies. Let's not worry about that right now. Let's just assume someone is doing this to you."

"But—"

"Just assume for a minute."

"All right." She watched him, her forehead creased. And he wanted to hold her, comfort her, erase that anxiety from her face. He got to his feet, paced a safe distance away so he could think. "So who knows about your mother's illness?"

"Kendall, of course. And you do now."

"How about your ex?"

"Yes, but Wayne's in Maryland. He made his parole check. You told me that yourself."

Another detail they'd worry about later. "Tell me more about him."

"Like what?"

"How he acted. Things he did."

She leaned back in her chair, blew out her breath. "Well, he was a pretty classic abuser. When we were dating, he was charming. Extremely attentive. He sent flowers, gifts, made me feel special…desired."

She gave him an embarrassed smile. "I was actually flattered when he started acting possessive. I had no idea… And once I married him, it got worse. He alienated me from my friends, pressured me to quit my job. Then the criticisms started, the violent mood swings…"

"How did you get away?"

She shuddered. "It wasn't easy. He controlled everything, the car, the money. I started substitute teaching when he was out of town and put the money in a special escape fund."

He locked his jaw against the sudden rush of anger. Some day, he was going to confront that brute. He was going to make him pay for hurting her.

And if Wheeler was behind these problems now, that day would come soon.

"It got worse after I left," she said, and her voice wobbled. "The stalking, the phone calls. When I got those hang-up calls at Kendall's, I thought at first it was him. But it couldn't have been him. He wasn't the one in the casino. It wasn't his voice. And he had nothing to do with that ring."

Luke paced to the patio window, mulling that over. He stuffed his hands in his pockets, stared out at the sprinklers forming rainbows in the sun. This situation was complicated. There were too many threads, and none of them seemed to connect.

He turned back to Amanda. "I take it Wheeler knew you were worried about inheriting your mother's illness?" She nodded, confirming his suspicions. "Does Wheeler get custody of Claire if you're ill?"

"No, I don't think so. Not with his criminal record and the abuse. Kendall would take her." She grabbed her crutches and rose. "Even if he could, I can't see that as a motive. He never cared about her. The last thing he'd want holding him down is a child."

"But losing Claire would hurt you." A fact that Wheeler would know. Anyone could see how much she loved and protected her child. "And he knows about Claire's allergy?"

She stopped beside him, and her wide blue eyes searched his. "Yes. He knows everything about us, even that I mix that oatmeal."

"So what's your gut feeling? Is this something Wheeler would do?"

"This is exactly like him. When I had him arrested, he vowed to come after me, to make me pay. And I wish it were him. I'd much rather deal with Wayne than lose my mind. But it can't be him. He's in Maryland."

"So it would seem." He frowned out the window at the golf course beyond the patio. A couple of carts glided past.

"We know he didn't hold me up in the casino," she added. "And he wasn't on that hilltop, either. Unless there really is more than one person involved..." Her face paled, and she looked so spooked suddenly that he dreaded telling her the rest.

But she needed to know the truth. "I just got a phone call from my security chief, Matt Schaffer. He told me the notes definitely matched. The one you got was written by the same person who wrote to Harold Rothchild."

Her face went whiter yet. "So the killer was the one who took photos of Claire."

"It looks that way. It gets worse," he added as she pressed her fingers to her lips. "They've reopened the investigation. They originally arrested Matt's aunt, but she just turned out to be a nutcase."

She frowned, and he knew she still didn't understand. "This isn't public knowledge, but in the note Harold got, the killer vowed to get revenge on the family. That means I'm their prime suspect again."

"I don't see how. We told them about the man who

attacked us yesterday. You even described him. And we showed them the note I got and the surveillance tape."

"But I have a motive. And I've been involved in this from the start. You even got attacked in my casino."

"What a mess."

"Yeah." He exhaled. "It's a mess. But let's solve your problem first. I'll get Matt Schaffer on it. He can set up surveillance, find out if someone's entering the house and bypassing the security system."

Her eyes stayed on his. "And if no one is?"

"Then we'll deal with it." Unable to resist, he fitted his hands to her waist, stroked the gentle sweep of her spine. No matter what else was wrong in his life, no matter how much she distracted him from his goals, holding her still felt right. "Don't worry. We'll get through this."

"Thank you," she whispered. "I thought…I thought you'd be so disgusted if you knew. Wayne—"

"Do me a favor." He tilted her chin up. "Don't confuse me with that bastard again."

Her eyes turned dark, her lips soft. "I could never, ever confuse you with him."

He pulled her close, slanted his mouth over hers, making sure to drive that point home. He didn't know what the future held. His life and emotions were in upheaval. But like it or not, last night had changed things. And for this moment at least, she was his.

He ended the kiss before it got out of hand, and pressed her head to his neck. And for a long moment he just stood there with her in his arms. Her warm, supple body curved against his. Her soft breath caressed his skin. He breathed in her womanly scent, feeling the inevitable lust build in his veins.

But then a thought intruded—the reason he'd sought her out. He had a party to attend that night. He needed to put on a good face, subdue the rumors Matt's crazy aunt's release would cause. And he needed Amanda by his side.

But Claire was sick, and he knew Amanda wouldn't leave her yet. He didn't have to ask. He'd seen the dismay in her eyes at the hospital, knew that she blamed herself.

And he couldn't leave them here alone. Candace's killer was on the loose. Wheeler could be lurking around, bypassing his security system and getting into the house. That thought made his blood run cold.

He could move her into his penthouse, but then Wheeler wouldn't show up. And they needed proof he was toying with her so they could trap him and end this mess.

He exhaled, knowing he didn't have a choice. He had to risk fueling the rumors and miss the event. He had to stay here and protect Amanda and Claire.

It could jeopardize his project, he knew that. The investors might see his absence as guilt.

But as his mouth devoured hers again, and he surrendered to the passion clouding his mind, his only concern was pleasuring her.

Chapter 11

Luke believed her. He didn't think she was losing her mind.

Amanda sank into the steamy kiss, her mind reeling, her heart flooded with gratitude to this man. He hadn't recoiled at the mention of her mother's illness, hadn't turned from her in disgust. If ever she'd needed proof that Luke was a thousand times better than Wayne, he'd just provided it in spades.

And she knew at that moment, that she was hopelessly, irrevocably in love with him.

His mouth covered hers, his tongue making deep, bold sweeps of her mouth, and she tightened her grip on his neck. She loved everything about him—his strength and self-assurance, his gruff tenderness. And the thrilling, arousing feel of him drove her wild.

She kissed him back, her heart overloaded with emotions, showing him how much his confidence meant. She ached for him, hungered for him, wanting to get closer yet. Feeling brazen, she rubbed her hips against his, and the long, rigid length of him made her moan. He laughed softly against her mouth.

He gentled the kiss, slid his lips to her jaw, her neck, sending pleasure streaming over her skin. "I'm addicted to you," he rasped.

"I can't stop, either," she confessed. She slid her hands over his hard, muscled shoulders to the short, silky hairs on the back of his neck. His whiskered jaw brushed her cheek, and excitement rushed through her veins.

He bent down slightly, wrapped his arms around her waist, then lifted her into his arms. She gasped at his strength, clutched his shoulders for balance as he turned with her and strode down the hall.

He carried her into her bedroom, kicked the door closed, then lowered her onto the bed. "Claire—" she began.

"I'll check on her. Don't move." He crossed the room and opened the adjoining door. He peeked into Claire's bedroom, then eased the door shut again. "She's asleep." He threw the bolt to lock them in.

Then he returned to the bed, looking predatory suddenly. He planted his feet wide, braced his hands low on his hips. The hungry look in his eyes made her tremble with need.

He stood there, watching her for a long, tense moment, as if debating how to proceed. "Since you can't stop," he said slowly. "Why don't you show me what you need?"

Her breath caught. Awareness rippled through her, and she realized what he wanted her to do. She nibbled her lip, suddenly uncertain, not sure if she had the courage. A week ago, she never would have dared.

But a week ago she'd been insecure about her sexuality, cowed by Wayne's cruel criticism, trapped in a cage of self-doubt.

Luke had unlocked that cage, set her free. And she refused to let her fears imprison her again.

She eyed the heat smoldering in his eyes, the hard set to his jaw, the definite bulge in his slacks. A delicious sense of abandon overtook her. The old Amanda was gone. Now she was going to shock him—shock herself—and take a risk. For once, she wasn't going to define herself by her doubts.

She scooted back on the bed, careful not to bump her injured ankle, then defiantly lifted her chin. And then she slowly dragged off her T-shirt and tossed it aside. She made much shorter work of her bra.

Luke didn't move. His gaze dropped to her breasts, the burn in them scalding her skin. Encouraged, she closed her eyes, let her head fall back, and cupped her breasts with her hands. And then she imagined Luke's hands instead of her own, how he'd touch and fondle and stroke, the feel of his rough, masculine palms, the scorching heat of his mouth. Her breathing grew fast, shivers sparked over her skin as her hands mimicked what she saw in her mind.

She arched back, opened her eyes. He stood frozen at the foot of the bed, his gaze riveted on her breasts. His body had gone rigid. A muscle flexed his jaw. His eyes were hot, dangerous, dark.

Good.

She sank back against the pillows. Keeping her eyes glued on his face, she inched off her shorts. Her underpants dropped to the floor next. His eyes tracked every move.

She paused, naked now, and battled a sudden flurry of nerves. She felt embarrassed, uncertain. But this was Luke, the man who believed in her.

"You're not stopping now." The rough tone of his voice made her shiver with need.

"No," she whispered back. "I'm not stopping now. I want you too much."

"Show me," he said.

She parted her thighs, showed him exactly what she wanted, responding to the slow sliding strokes of her hand. A heavy fullness rippled through her. The need grew into an ache, stripping away the last of her inhibitions.

He stood rooted in place, his hands clenched into fists, following every motion she made. Her skin grew tight. Her entire body tensed. She shuddered, lost in his eyes, willing him closer, needing his hands…his mouth.

"Luke," she whispered, the need unbearable now. And she couldn't stop. The hunger built and swelled, the need for him beyond her control. She breathed faster, harder, wanting him with a wildness she couldn't contain.

"Luke," she cried out again, and then she bucked hard, exploding with pleasure while he still stood immobile and watched.

Suddenly, he erupted into a flurry of action. He ripped off his shirt, kicked off his pants, tossing them to the floor. And then he knelt above her, plunging into her in one hard stroke, bringing her back to the brink. She gasped at the delicious invasion, thrilled to his hard, pulsating feel. He buried himself to the hilt, filling her, claiming her.

"That was the sexiest thing I've ever seen," he said, his voice hoarse.

He kissed her, plundering deeply with his tongue,

searing her with his blatant need. His muscles rippled under her palms. His wide shoulders bunched and strained. The kiss was fierce, provoking, and she kissed him back with everything she had.

Then her body grew taut, the ache unbearable. She moaned against his mouth. He thrust hard, and she combusted in an explosion of bliss. His deeper groans mingled with hers.

For several, long moments, neither moved. Breathing erratically, she trailed her fingertips over the stubble shadowing his jaw and traced the hollows of his cheeks.

He braced himself on his forearms, and she inhaled deeply, relishing his masculine scent. His gaze roamed her lips, her breasts. And then his eyes trapped hers, kicking off a riot of emotions in her chest.

"Do you have any idea how erotic that was?" he asked.

She trembled, shocked that she already wanted him again. She didn't think she could get enough. But it wasn't just the sex, she realized suddenly. His masculine virility compelled her, but it was his essence that captivated her heart.

Her throat closed on a sudden pang of longing, her love for him brimming in her chest. Not wanting him to see how vulnerable she felt, she averted her gaze, stroked the wide line of his shoulders, the firm muscles bulging beneath his sleek skin.

"You've done so much for me," she managed to say around the thickness in her throat. "I can never begin to repay you."

He tipped up her chin, but she kept her gaze lowered, afraid to expose the feelings she knew would show in her eyes. She traced the edge of his beard stubble, loving how sexy he looked with those straight, dark brows, those masculine lips.

"I know some ways you could try."

The seductive tone of his voice caught her attention, and she braved a glance at his face. His golden eyes gleamed with humor, and her heart warmed even more. "Is that a promise?" she asked.

"Count on it."

She loved this playful side of him, a side he rarely revealed. But she understood why he kept it hidden. She'd grown up just as he had, shouldering the weight of responsibility, facing the harsh realities of life at a too-young age.

She'd felt the same hopelessness, bitterness, the consuming need to survive. But she'd accepted her life, let go of the pain. She couldn't fight her mother's mental illness. There wasn't a concrete enemy to blame.

But Luke had a target—Harold Rothchild. That fury had sustained him, along with his all-consuming ambition and drive. And she understood his need for vengeance, for respect. She even understood why he feared letting people close.

She frowned, trailed her hand over the tendons running down his shoulder and arm. But waging a constant war took its toll. It hurt his enemies, and it hurt him. Even innocent people got trapped in the fight.

Like the people living in the slums he was going to destroy.

She nibbled her lip, knowing she would do anything this man asked. She just had. And she'd help him get that project approved if that's what he needed most. But maybe she could convince him not to go through with it, to let go of his need for revenge.

To let the pain heal.

He pulsed inside her, and her breath caught. His mouth went to her breast and ignited her hunger again. She closed her eyes, plunged her hands in his thick, silky hair, felt him move his body down hers. And then she didn't think at all.

Luke sprawled on the sofa the next morning, every inch of his body relaxed. He'd never felt so content in his life. Sex with Amanda just kept getting better. She continually surprised him, making him want to hole up with her somewhere and not emerge for months.

He passed a hand over his gritty eyes, pulled out his BlackBerry and yawned. She'd kept him so enthralled he hadn't thought about work for hours—the first time that had happened in years. He checked the phone log, saw that he'd missed a call from his security chief. He punched in Matt's number and waited for him to pick up.

He glanced at Claire playing on the carpet near his feet. The kid had made a full recovery and was busy chattering at her bear. It was just as well that she demanded attention. Without Claire to distract Amanda, he'd never get anything done.

"Schaffer here," Matt said.

Luke got right to the point. "Did you get anything?"

"Yeah. We struck pay dirt. One of the gardeners entered your house early this morning."

Luke went still. His eyes swerved to the window overlooking the pool. The thought of someone skulking around the hallways while he and Amanda slept made everything inside him cold. It was a good thing she'd been with him all night.

He lowered his voice so Amanda and Claire wouldn't hear. "Where is he now?"

"I don't know. He didn't stay inside long."

"How's he getting in?"

"He used the patio entrance this time. He bypassed the system, but he obviously didn't know about the new cameras we installed."

Luke went from the couch to the patio, examined the door. "There's no sign of forced entry."

"He's using the codes. We're checking on how he got them now. And he fits the description you provided—stocky, blond hair."

Wheeler. Satisfaction curled through him, merging with the deep, scorching rage. It was past time to confront that creep.

"Don't notify the police," he told Matt. He needed to think this through, set a trap. "And don't change the codes—we don't want to tip him off."

"All right."

"I'll talk to Amanda and clear it with her, but I want to catch him today." He scowled at a sudden thought. He had another meeting with the investors that afternoon. But he'd just have to postpone it again.

"Got it," Matt said. "By the way, Natalie decided to put me out of my misery and agreed to a wedding date. Mark your calendar for June fourteenth, here in Vegas."

Luke grinned. "I'll be there."

He disconnected the line and slipped his BlackBerry into the pocket of his slacks. So Matt and Natalie were going to tie the knot soon. He'd suspected as much. Their whirlwind romance had made the tabloids, lending credence to the rumors about that missing diamond ring's weird curse—that in the right hands, it brought true love. In the wrong hands, chaos ensued.

His gaze bee-lined to Amanda where she sat at the kitchen table. Her soft, shiny hair tumbled over her arms. Her snug T-shirt cupped her breasts. His gaze lingered, memories of how her skin had tasted stirring his blood. Just watching her filled him with a sense of rightness.

He'd never thought about getting married, never wanted to. But he suddenly understood Matt. The idea of having Amanda around for a while appealed to him—sleeping in her arms every night, waking up with her every day.

He frowned and angled his head, rolling that idea over in his mind. Maybe she wouldn't be in a hurry to leave when this was done. Maybe he could convince her to stay, at least for a while. This woman had a lot of facets he still wanted to explore.

His body stirring, he kept his gaze on her breasts. He had plans for her, all right.

But first they had to catch her ex-husband.

Amanda dragged her attention away from Luke at the patio door to the teaching application in her hands. She stared at the paper blindly, her brain still fried, unable to stop thinking about the rapturous night. She had to pull herself together, though. She was acting like a lovestruck teenager, mooning over him, reliving those delirious sensations he'd evoked.

She exhaled, blowing her loose hair back from her face. She loved Luke, but she had to be practical. He'd never mentioned any feelings for her, especially not love. All she knew for sure right now was that he wanted her sexually.

My, had he driven *that* point home. She closed her eyes, shivering at the erotic memories—his muscles flexing under her palms, his eyes blazing with need. The thrill of having all that power and intensity focused only on her. And the things he'd asked her to do. Her face warmed. She'd never known she had such a wanton streak.

But desiring her sexually didn't mean he loved her. He'd never proposed marriage, never mentioned a future together. Which meant she had to get herself back on track.

She looked at the front room, where Luke squatted down, talking to Claire. And Amanda knew she had to tread carefully. She'd made a big mistake with Wayne. Thanks to her faulty judgment, her daughter's life was at stake.

Luke wasn't Wayne. He wasn't even close. She would never believe the rumors about his supposed role in Candace's murder.

But he was definitely out of her league. And it wasn't just her own feelings she had to protect. Claire could end up attached to him, hurt when they had to leave.

Which meant she couldn't draw this out. She had to make plans, quickly find a job.

Luke rose in a fluid motion, then came toward her. Her gaze stalled on his powerful thighs, the way his shirt clung to his muscled abs. Her throat went dry at the sight.

She frowned at the application again. She had it bad, all right. She understood why that murdered woman had stalked him—especially now that she'd spent two nights in his bed. He was addictive, the perfect man. How could she settle for anyone else again?

"What are you doing?" he asked, sliding into the seat next to hers.

"Filling out a job application. There's an opening for a middle school history teacher."

"That doesn't sound exciting."

She shrugged, trying to keep her mind on the conversation instead of him. "It's a good job, and the school's not far from Kendall's house."

He leaned closer, and his nearness made it hard to breathe. "I thought you wanted to be an archaeologist."

She straightened the papers into a stack. "So?"

"So why don't you go for it?"

She shifted her gaze to Claire, watched her balance Brownie on the back of the couch. "It's not practical. I'd have to go back to school, do research. It would take years. And I have Claire to think about."

Besides, some dreams just weren't meant to be…like staying with him.

He looked as if he intended to argue, but then he shrugged. "I just spoke to Matt Schaffer."

Her pulse sped up. "What did he say?"

"The surveillance tape shows a gardener entering the house earlier today. He matches Wheeler's description."

She closed her eyes, clamped her hand over her lips. And the dread squeezing her chest began to ease.

"So it wasn't me," she whispered. "I really wasn't imagining things."

"No." He caught her hand in his, and gently squeezed. "You're as sane as I am, for what it's worth."

Tears misted her eyes, and her voice broke. "Luke… This is… I can't begin to thank you."

She inhaled, trying to hold back the emotions ricocheting inside. She didn't have her mother's illness. She wouldn't lose Claire. She was free.

And Luke had done this for her. He'd believed in her, helped her get proof.

She sniffed, grappling to stay in control, and wiped a tear from her eye. "How did he get by his parole officer?"

"I don't know. We'll find that out later. But you need to make a decision."

"What do you mean?"

"You have a couple of choices. We can contact the police right now and have him arrested."

He'd go to jail. But eventually he'd get released. And she'd be watching over her shoulder again, always waiting. The terror would never end. "What's the other choice?"

"We set a trap and confront him first, and then call the police."

Confront him. She'd have to see Wayne face-to-face? She tried not to panic at the thought. "What good would that do?"

He leaned back in his chair and folded his arms. "I'm going to put this baldly. He thinks he owns you. In his mind, you're his." His gaze held hers. "He's never going to stop trying to control you—especially since you defied him by getting away."

She shivered, his words chilling her. But Luke was right. Wayne had vowed to make her pay. "But then—"

"That's where I come in. I'll make it clear to him that you're mine now. That's how he thinks, Amanda. It's the only way he's going to let you go. You don't have to do anything," he added. "Just be the bait. You get him here, and then I'll make sure he understands."

She saw the anger simmering in Luke's eyes, the rage. He could do it. He could finally put an end to this perpetual fear.

But only if she had the courage to reel Wayne in.

She glanced at Claire. Her daughter stood clutching her bear now, watching her with anxious eyes.

Her anger flared. Claire didn't deserve this, and neither did she—the constant fear, the years of abuse. He'd even followed her here.

And he'd gone way too far when he'd poisoned Claire. That had been the final straw. It was time to bring this reign of terror to an end.

She locked eyes with Luke. "Let's set the trap."

Chapter 12

The waiting was killing her.

Amanda lay on one of the lounge chairs by the pool, feeling defenseless and exposed in her modest swimsuit, her stomach threatening to revolt. On the surface, the afternoon seemed perfectly peaceful. Insects droned from the nearby hedge. The soft breeze brushed her skin. Beyond the golf course, heat shimmered up from the desert floor, forming a wavering, watery mirage. But Wayne could show up any time now, and it was tearing her insides to shreds.

She focused her gaze on the distant mountains, forced herself to calm down. Nothing would go wrong. They'd gone over this a dozen times. She was not to provoke Wayne into an argument, was not to go anywhere with him—not even into the house. She'd just speed dial the cell phone the second she saw him and let Luke take it from there.

She patted the corner of the towel where she'd tucked the cell phone, squinted at the sparkling pool. Kendall had spirited Claire to the safety of Luke's penthouse. Luke waited just outside the compound, expecting her call. She glanced at her watch, her anxiety mounting as the minutes wore on. What if Wayne didn't show up?

He'd better come. She needed to end this today. She refused to spend day after endless day waiting, not knowing what he would do.

Her skin clammy despite the heat. She sipped her glass of lemonade, trying to soothe her parched throat. Then she flipped the page on the magazine she had in her lap in an attempt to look relaxed.

And then she smelled it—Wayne's scent. It wisped through the air and crept into her nostrils like smoke from a smoldering fire. She kept her eyes glued to the magazine, her heart accelerating into overdrive, her senses hyperalert.

Was that him? Was he behind her? Or had she imagined that scent? She inhaled but only smelled the chlorine from the pool. She didn't dare turn around to check.

Instead she reached for the lemonade again, brought the glass to her lips with a trembling hand. *Stop shaking,* she ordered herself fiercely. *Don't let him see your fear.*

The smell grew stronger. He was definitely behind her. Her breath wheezed out.

She had to call Luke fast.

She set the glass carefully on the table, reached for the phone under the towel. But a gun barrel was pressed against her temple, and she went dead still.

"That's right," Wayne said from behind her, and the sound of his voice made her nausea rise. "Now stand up, nice and slow, or you'll be dead."

She heard the rage in his voice the awful excitement. He actually wanted to kill her. He thought he had the right.

And she only had a second to act. She flicked her gaze to the towel, trying not to move her head. Then she stretched her fingers toward the cell phone, reaching… reaching.

The gun bit into her skin. "Pick up that phone and I shoot. Now get up."

Panic mingling with disbelief, she rose on quivering legs. This couldn't be happening. She couldn't let it. She had to follow the plan…

The gun eased away, and her hopes spiked. But Wayne circled into view, his weapon still aimed at her head. The stench of aftershave assaulted her senses, and she went rigid with fear.

Think, she urged herself fiercely. *Think.* She couldn't let him do this to her.

His face leered close and she forced herself to look. His skin was flushed. A bead of sweat crawled down his jaw. Hatred gleamed in his mean blue eyes.

How had she ever thought him handsome? How had she ever believed she could care for this man?

"I told you I'd make you pay," he said, and the violence in his voice congealed her blood. He moved closer, and his hot breath sickened her gut.

Without warning, he slammed the gun against her head. She cried out, slumped to her knees.

Stunned, blinded by pain, she gasped for air. Oh, God. This was worse than she'd expected. He was vicious, out of control. And she knew with a bone deep certainty that he wasn't going to let her live.

She staggered back to her feet. She battled the spasms in her injured ankle, the violent ache in her head. Blood trickled into her eye. Wayne circled her again, preparing to strike.

And suddenly, anger sparked inside her, outrage that this creep thought he could terrorize her. So what if she got hurt when she defied him? She refused to feed his ego again.

She stepped back, pretending to cower, moving close to the lemonade glass. "Don't," she whimpered, knowing it was what he expected from her.

He flashed that sadistic grin. She took another step back, pressed her too-slick palms to her thighs. "Please don't hurt me," she whispered again. He stepped toward her, and she knew that she'd run out of time.

She switched her gaze to a spot behind him. He fell for the trick and glanced back. She grabbed the glass of lemonade, flung the stinging liquid into his eyes.

He blinked, growled with anger. She hurled the heavy tumbler at his head. The glass bounced off his skull, but it momentarily stunned him, then shattered on the tiles at his feet. Her pulse frantic, she lunged for the phone on the chair.

It didn't matter. Luke vaulted the hedge, slammed into Wayne. The two men crashed to the ground.

Wayne didn't have a chance. Luke rammed Wayne's head against the tiles, punched his face and gut in a flurry of fists. Wayne groaned, cried out. The sickening thuds made her cringe.

But Luke was relentless, fighting with a fury she'd never seen. Within seconds, Wayne lay motionless and was bleeding on the ground, the gun a safe distance away.

Luke rammed his knee into Wayne's throat. "Leave her alone," he ordered. He shoved down harder, and

Wayne let out a helpless wheeze. "She's mine now. Amanda and Claire are mine. Do you hear me?" Wayne's face turned purple, and he gasped for air. "You come near them again and you're dead."

Wayne croaked out his agreement. Luke pressed down for a few more seconds, then finally released him and stood.

Her heart still thundering, Amanda dragged in a shaky breath. Then she walked to where her ex-husband lay. And for a long moment she just stared at him, this man who'd caused her such terror, such pain. He'd seemed so powerful once, so cunning and brutally strong. Now he was just bloody, pathetic, cowed.

And she realized it was over. It was finally over. She was free of Wayne at last.

Luke stood in his casino's ballroom that evening, his words still echoing in his head. *She's mine,* he'd told Wheeler. *Amanda and Claire are mine.* He'd meant the words only for show, to keep Wheeler from bothering them again. But the hell of it was, those words sounded right. Amanda did feel like his.

He glanced at her across the crowded ballroom, watched her fill her small plate with hors d'oeuvres. She wore a thigh-high black dress that molded her curves, showcasing those killer legs. The front was modest, but tight, the fabric cupping her breasts like a lover's hands. But in the back... The dress plunged dramatically to her hips, riveting every man's gaze to her tempting, naked skin.

His throat suddenly dry, he took a swallow of whiskey. He'd touched that skin, made love to every inch of that sensual body. He knew her scent, her taste.

He knew what made her moan, what made her sigh, how her flesh felt hot and moist. He'd made her swollen and aching with need.

She was beautiful, erotic.

And she was his.

She could have died today. Every time he closed his eyes, he flashed back to the image of her bloody scalp, the deranged look in Wheeler's eyes, and the frantic need to protect her consumed him all over again.

"Is the meeting still on for tomorrow?" a man standing beside him asked.

Luke tossed back his last swallow of whiskey, pulled his attention to Fletcher Coddington. The elderly investor's wife was with him tonight, and the voluptuous young woman smiled up at Luke, the invitation clear in her eyes. Luke scanned her collagen-plumped lips, her silicone breasts, the fake, come-hither smile. Maybe the giant rock on her finger was phony, too. It would serve her right.

He looked back at Amanda. She turned his way, smiling at something someone said, and his heart made a swerve in his chest. She was the exact opposite of Coddington's gold-digging wife—authentic, interesting, sincere.

"Montgomery?" Coddington said, sounding annoyed.

He jerked his eyes back to the investor, scrambling to remember what he'd said. The meeting. Right. "It's all set. Ten o'clock tomorrow." It was their final meeting, the day they'd sign the contracts on the Phoenix project and decide if it was a go. The day he'd toll the death knell for Harold Rothchild.

At last.

And he had Amanda to thank for it. Once again, she'd

soothed the investors with her warm smile and gentle voice. She'd diffused questions about the murder, showed everyone her confidence in him. And he knew damn well she'd kept several worried men from backing out.

She looked up then, and her eyes met his from across the room. That familiar heat jolted through him, that feeling of rightness.

"Excuse me," he said and headed toward her, leaving Coddington sputtering behind.

He worked his way through the chattering crowd, ignoring bids for his attention, anxious to get to her side. And that deep sense of possessiveness settled inside him again. He didn't know when it had started, only that it was there—and was growing stronger each day.

The scare today had clinched it. He realized he didn't want Amanda to leave, didn't want her moving back to her sister's house, even when the danger was gone. She belonged with him now.

And it was time to make that clear.

Amanda's pulse quickened as Luke strode toward her across the glittering ballroom, those bourbon-colored eyes locked on hers. Lord, he looked sexy. His broad shoulders filled out his tuxedo. Light from the enormous chandeliers glinted off his ebony hair. His stark-white shirt set off his tanned skin, and he looked so unapologetically masculine, so utterly sensual that thrills of excitement skipped through her nerves.

Breathless, she dropped her gaze to her plate. She had to get a grip. It was bad enough that she was in love with him. She couldn't embarrass them both by ogling him in a public place.

Not that every other woman in the room wasn't doing the same.

A waiter materialized at her side. "Wine?" he asked.

Startled, she studied the waiter's face. But he was too short, too dark to be the man who'd drugged her the other night.

"No, thanks," she said, and he moved on. She doubted anyone would try to attack her tonight, but she wasn't drinking, just to be safe—especially with Candace's killer still on the loose.

At least Wayne was no longer a problem. She nibbled on a crab-stuffed mushroom, relieved that he was locked up. He'd been arrested and charged with a litany of crimes—breaking and entering, stalking, committing numerous parole violations, including possessing a firearm and crossing state lines. He'd stay in prison for years. And when he did get out, he would leave her alone…thanks to Luke.

Luke joined her just then. Adrenaline raced through her veins. She wondered if she'd ever feel normal around him. Every time she looked at him, her pulse went amok.

"Join me on the balcony?" he asked.

"Sure." Her appetite gone, she set down the plate and took his arm. They strolled from the noisy ballroom, moving slowly because of her still-tender ankle.

And suddenly, a thought came out of nowhere, catching her off guard. Maybe he was going to end their arrangement now. Wayne had been arrested. Tomorrow his project would be approved and he no longer needed her help. Candace's killer was still at large, but surely the police would catch him soon.

Which meant Luke might want their masquerade to end.

Her breath fled in a surge of panic. It was too soon for her. Way too soon and not only because of the danger. She needed time to show Luke how much she loved him. Time to heal him from his past pain. Time to convince him to change his mind about the project, to let go of the bitterness and his need for revenge.

"Down here." He led her across the spacious balcony, away from prying ears. And with every step, her anxiety mounted. If he wanted to end it now, what could she say?

They reached the far corner of the balcony, and he stopped. She braced her hands on the railing to collect herself, looking out at the dazzling array of lights. Neon signs glittered and flashed. Honking horns and the muted roar of traffic drifted up.

And a terrible emptiness lodged inside her, threatening to destroy what little composure she had left. But she had only herself to blame for this mess. She'd known better than to fall in love with Luke. He'd been a fantasy from the start, completely unattainable. She'd known that it would end.

Which was poor comfort to her breaking heart.

"I've been thinking," he began, and she closed her eyes, determined to accept her fate with dignity.

"Now that Wheeler's out of the picture, you could stay with me. Move in for real."

Shock rippled through her. She opened her eyes and searched his face, not sure that she'd heard him right. She'd expected him to end their affair, not invite her to stay. "You want me to live with you?"

"There's no reason you have to go back to your sister's house, is there?"

Her lips parted. Confusion still muddled her mind.

"No, but..." This didn't sound very romantic. It was hardly the declaration of love she yearned for. "I...I don't know."

"What don't you know? It makes sense for you to stay. You need a place to live. And we're good together, Amanda." He crowded against her, tugged up her chin. The heat from his body seeped through her skin. "Very good."

He smoothed her hair away from her neck, lowered his mouth to the sensitive skin. She shivered at the sensual touch and closed her eyes, the familiar desire whipping through her like a blast of sand in a desert storm. They were more than good together. They burned.

Her head fell back. Her knees turned weak. He leaned into her, and she shuddered at the hard bulge pressing the juncture of her thighs.

She longed to obey her body's mandate. She ached to take him inside her and tell him yes. She wanted to feel that shocking pleasure every night, the exhilaration of his kiss every day. And she loved him madly. Staying with him was the answer to her dreams.

Almost. He hadn't mentioned marriage or love.

Trying to think through the hunger muddling her brain, she wrenched herself away. She pressed her fingers to her forehead, gazed out at the colorful display of lights.

His offer was tempting. Too tempting. She loved him and owed him so much. He'd awakened her sexually, freed her from Wayne. He'd even risked his life to save hers.

But he didn't love her.

Maybe with time she could make him love her, though. Maybe she could heal him and pay him back.

Maybe if she lived with him, she could convince him to let go of the bitterness, move on from the painful past.

Or maybe she was deluding herself again.

She drew in a breath of air, tried to think this through. She'd made a terrible mistake with Wayne. When she'd found herself pregnant, she'd taken a risk. Even though she hadn't known him well, she'd decided that love and compassion would come with time.

She'd been wrong. Horribly wrong.

She couldn't afford to make another mistake. She didn't only have her own heart at risk this time but Claire's. Her daughter already adored Luke. And before she would let Claire become even more attached, she needed a sign he was willing to change. She couldn't act only on faith, no matter how tempted she was.

"Luke…" She turned to face him again. He watched her with narrowed eyes. "Do you think your project will be approved?"

He planted his hands on his hips and frowned, the abrupt change of subject obviously taking him aback. "We're signing the contracts tomorrow. The investors are all on board."

She hugged her arms, looked out at the area just past the Strip where Naked City was. Not many lights twinkled there.

"Thanks for your help, by the way."

She nodded, then glanced at him again. "The thing is…I'm not sure I did the right thing by helping you. With your project, I mean."

His brow furrowed. "What are you talking about?"

"It's just… It bothers me that those people are going to lose their homes."

"They'll find another place to live."

"But where? What place? Prices are sky high here in Vegas. You know that. They'll end up on the streets."

He crossed his arms, falling into stony silence, and she tried again. "We got kicked out of our apartment when I was growing up. You said you did, too. Don't you remember what it was like? That awful fear?"

"I remember." His eyes turned cold. "Harold Rothchild was our landlord. He took away my mother's job, her house. He killed her with his indifference. And now he's going to pay."

Her heart chilled at the vengeance in his voice. He didn't understand. "But you're doing the same thing he did. There are children in those slums, Luke. Innocent children."

"Forget it," he warned her.

"But—"

"Stay out of this, Amanda." His tone turned hard. "I'm not shelving this project. Not for you, not anyone."

"But that's just it," she whispered. "This revenge… It's not good for you. Not healthy. It's eating you up inside. You have to let go of it, move on from the past."

"Right." He made a sound of disgust. "You mean like you have?"

She flinched at the sarcasm in his voice. "Yes, I—"

"You what? You think you've moved on?" His eyes turned so angry that her throat closed up. "Hell, you're so stuck in the past you're afraid to live your life. Why don't you forget that damn teaching job? Go back to school and become what you want. Start living for yourself for a change."

"But it's not the same thing. I can't just do what I

want. I have responsibilities—Claire. She needs stability, security. I don't have a choice."

He slowly shook his head. "There's always a choice. And you're choosing to stay in the past. You're too scared to take a chance."

The accusation stung. A dull ache pounded her skull. This wasn't about her. It was about him. How had this conversation gone so wrong? "Won't you at least think about it? Delay the project a bit?"

"No. It's all set. I'm not changing my mind."

Her heart plummeted. "Then I…I can't live with you, Luke."

"Because of the project." His voice sounded dead.

"No, it's not just that." Oh, God. She'd made a total hash of this thing. And she couldn't let it end like this. She had to take a risk, make sure he understood.

She dredged up her courage, laid her soul bare. "I don't want to just live together, Luke. I want it all—marriage, a ring, love. I want to have your children someday. And I want you to forget revenge."

His eyes turned even colder. "I'm not proposing marriage."

And she couldn't delude herself into thinking he would change. "Then there's nothing more to say."

He stared at her for a long moment. She thought she was going to be sick. What on earth had just happened? How could he not understand?

"You can stay in the house until the end of the week," he said. "I'll hire you a bodyguard and get a security system installed in Kendall's house to keep you safe."

He turned from her, strode back toward the balcony door. And then he stopped and glanced back. His glacial expression shattered her heart. "I'll call you a cab."

She swayed, clung to the balcony railing, desolation clutching her throat.

And watched the man she loved walk away.

Chapter 13

At one o'clock on a Saturday morning, Las Vegas Boulevard throbbed with life. Flashing lights lured gamblers into casinos. Thrill rides shot riders a hundred stories above the ground. Inebriated tourists milled in and out of strip clubs, spending their hard-earned dollars on shows.

Naked City teemed, too, but the action here was edgier, seedier, far more deadly.

Luke pulled his Jaguar up to the curb in front of his old apartment and cut the engine, then pushed open the door and climbed out. He paused, inhaled the stench of rotting garbage, stepped over the broken glass and trash. Chain link fences locked off the aging, one-story buildings. Graffiti covered the peeling stucco walls. In front of a motel sign missing half its letters stood an overflowing Dumpster, gang tags spray painted on its side.

Not sure what the hell he was doing here, Luke

scowled at the rundown apartments, the ripped-up sofa someone had dumped on the curb. He'd tried to bury himself in work after he'd left the party, tried to fine tune the contracts for the meeting later that day, but Amanda's rejection ate at him, destroying his focus. He'd finally given up and gone for a drive.

He'd ended up here.

And it ticked him off. He didn't want to look at his old neighborhood, didn't want to keep remembering what Amanda had said. She'd been out of line. The Phoenix project had nothing to do with the two of them. She had no idea what this meant to him, how many years he'd worked for this revenge.

He leaned back against the Jaguar and folded his arms, studied the trio of teens strolling toward him from down the street. The faces had changed over time, but Naked City still reeked of the same poverty and violence, the same desperate need to survive.

The teens stopped several yards away and eyed him. Their leader, a kid in pants with its crotch hanging down to his knees, swaggered over. He looked young, maybe all of thirteen with his baseball cap on backward and that peach fuzz gracing his lip.

But the kid sized him up with a worldly expression Luke knew well. He'd been just like that kid once—scared, hungry, too street savvy at an early age. And that's when he'd decided to leave this place. He'd stood right here, gazing at the high-rise casinos glittering on the nearby Strip, vowing to be someone, to never be hungry or powerless again.

And he'd worked his butt off to do it. He'd studied hard, landed a scholarship to a private high school, walked miles every morning to get himself there. He'd made connections at that school, learned how to work the system, taught himself to fit in with a better crowd. And then he'd started making money—lots of it—until he was wealthier than he'd ever dreamed.

But he'd never lost sight of his plan to take down Harold Rothchild.

And in a few more hours, he would succeed.

The kid stuffed his hands in his back pockets, glanced around. "You looking to score?"

Luke eyed the kid's scrawny frame, his hollowed-out cheeks, the desperation in his eyes. "No."

The kid moved closer, his gaze flitting to the Jaguar and back. "I can get good stuff."

"I'm not here for drugs."

The kid nodded. "You want some action. Gina's real hot. I'll go find her for twenty bucks."

The edge of Luke's mouth kicked up. The kid hadn't missed a beat. But then, kids learned early how to wheel and deal on the streets. They bartered for everything—drugs, sex, food, even their lives.

And suddenly, it struck him that he hadn't changed much. He was still cutting deals like this kid was, only with more money and higher stakes.

That thought knocked him off balance. Maybe he hadn't left this life behind. Maybe he was the same punk he'd been back then, just with a more sophisticated veneer.

A low-riding car rumbled up the street then, its shiny chrome flashing, its booming stereo vibrating the soles of his feet.

"Later," the kid said. He hurried back to his friends, and the teens melted into the night.

So the neighborhood's top dog had arrived. Probably the local pusher, the man with power.

And Luke suffered another jolt. He wasn't much different from that pusher, either. All his life he'd been consumed by a need for power, respect.

And Amanda had understood that. She'd seen what drove him, and had challenged him to stop—to stop being that punk from Naked City, to stop trying to prove himself and let the past go.

To give up his plan for revenge.

Scowling at that thought, he climbed back into his car and started the engine. Harold Rothchild deserved to be taken down. He didn't have to question that goal. Rothchild had plenty of sins to account for in his life, including his mother's death.

But if Luke went through with his plan, if he evicted those people from their apartments, he'd be no better than Rothchild was. Or Amanda's ex-husband, for that matter—a man bent on revenge.

He'd lose Amanda's respect.

He'd lose her.

He was going to have to choose.

He gunned the Jaguar's engine, burning rubber as he screamed past the drug dealer's car. He sped to the corner, leaving Naked City behind in a cloud of exhaust.

But as he downshifted for an upcoming stop light, another insight jarred him. And he finally realized what had been plaguing him all night, the real source of his discontent. If he did what Amanda wanted and let go of the need for revenge, what would he have left?

It unnerved him that he didn't know.

"So you want to tell me what really happened the other night?" Kendall asked.

Amanda sat beside her sister on the steps in the

shallow end of the pool, water lapping over her hips. Sunshine sparkled off the rippling water. Birds chirped from the nearby hedge. Claire played on the tiles behind them, giggling and talking to her dolls.

And the last thing Amanda wanted to do was rehash her argument with Luke. She'd spent the past two days struggling to forget about it, trying to erase his words from her mind. But her thoughts kept veering back to that argument like a missile zeroing in on a target, replaying every word, every gesture, analyzing every awful second of that fight.

"Mandy?" Kendall pressed.

She sighed, knowing the futility of trying to elude her sister's questions. Kendall always wormed the truth out of her eventually, so she might as well confess all now. She pulled her knees to her chest, exhaled again. "Luke asked me to live with him, to stay here for a while."

Kendall's mouth dropped open. "Are you serious? Luke Montgomery asked you to move in with him?"

"Yes." She propped her chin on her knees. "I turned him down."

"He asked you to live here and you turned him down." Incredulity laced Kendall's voice.

"I didn't want to just live together. I wanted more." Her mouth twisted. "I wanted marriage, love, the whole deal."

"Oh, God. You're in love with him."

"Dumb, huh?" She managed a wobbly smile.

"No, you're not dumb. He's totally hot. But Luke Montgomery…" She shook her head.

"I know. Completely out of my league." And she only had herself to blame. Kendall had warned her. She'd known a billionaire would never fall in love with her. She'd known straight off that she wasn't his type.

"But he's not like you think he is," she added. "He's a good man, Kendall. Really good." Gentle, caring, protective. Lethal in a fight. Dominant in an extremely exciting way.

She shivered, remembering the hours of unending pleasure, the ecstasy she'd found in his arms. "I've never met anyone like him." And she knew she wouldn't again. Luke was unique. The man she loved. It had been the real deal for her.

Her chest aching, her eyes heavy with unshed tears, she watched a hawk soar silently overhead. And she struggled not to wonder what Luke was doing, what he was wearing, if he was thinking about her at all.

She scoffed at that thought. No doubt he was busy with his project—meeting with the investors, reviewing the plans, attending another glitzy party. He wasn't obsessing over their argument like she was. If he was, he would have called. She had to move on, forget it, stop torturing herself this way.

"Okay, let's break this down," Kendall said, pulling Amanda's attention back to her. "First off, he's obviously attracted to you. Even I could see that much."

"But that's not love."

Kendall pursed her lips, splashed water over her arms. "No, but he watches you. He's always aware of where you are. It's pretty intense, actually. Sexy."

Intense was right. She kept reliving those delirious sensations, his kiss, his touch, the way he'd driven her wild with desire. She'd spent hour after sleepless hour aching to be back in his arms.

"Sex isn't love, though. Not for a guy." She lowered her voice so Claire wouldn't hear. "And he wasn't proposing marriage. He was clear about that."

"That's still a pretty big thing, though, asking you to move in with him."

"Not big enough."

Her brow knitted, Kendall leaned back, propped herself on her elbows and stretched out her sculpted legs. "Are you sure it wasn't more? I mean, I know he's a billionaire and off the charts, but the way he looked at you..."

"I'm sure." The pressure on her chest increased. "And anyway, it's over now. We argued. He was furious."

"You argued about moving in?"

"Sort of." She blew out a heavy breath, turned her gaze to the palm fronds swishing overhead, the cloudless expanse of blue sky. "Mostly about our goals, though. He said I should go back to school, become an archaeologist like I wanted. He claimed I was too afraid to take a risk."

"He's right about that."

Amanda glared at her.

"Well, you are." Kendall's tone gentled. "Listen, you know I love you. And I'll take your side no matter what. But he's right. You've always been too cautious."

"And that's bad? If I hadn't been cautious and practical we would have starved."

"I know. And I owe you big-time for that. If you hadn't taken care of everything, held it all together... You even stayed with Mom after high school so I could dance. But that's the point. You need to do something fun for once. Something you want, just for yourself. You deserve it."

"But I can't just run off to school. Claire—"

"Claire will be fine. You know she will. And I'll help out. I'll do anything you want. I owe you that much after the way you took care of Mom."

"I don't know."

"Life's short, Mandy. You need to go for it before it's too late."

Amanda sighed, watched the sparkling water swirl past. Kendall made it sound easy. But she'd have to take courses, do fieldwork, get an advanced degree. It would take years. But she'd love to examine ancient artifacts, to explore caves like the one Luke owned. Excitement surged through her at the thought.

"Well, think about it." Kendall glanced at her watch. "Listen, I need to go. I don't want to miss rehearsal. But call me if you need me tonight."

Amanda rose with her and grabbed her towel. "No, I'm fine. I don't have anywhere to go now." Not since Luke's project had been approved. "If you could watch her tomorrow, though, that would be great. I need to move our stuff back to your house."

She didn't want to think about moving. It was the final step, the end of her hopes with Luke. But she couldn't put it off. "I'll drop her off early," she added. "Don't forget Luke's security people are coming by to install that system." And a bodyguard would arrive after that. Luke had made good on his promise to protect her, even if he didn't want her around.

She was still trying not to dwell on the thought of moving as she settled Claire down for a nap. She hadn't brought many things to Luke's house—some clothes, Claire's favorite toys, a few books—so she could move out in a couple of trips. At least she wouldn't prolong the agony. Still, just thinking of leaving made her want to weep.

"Mommy, nap with me," Claire pleaded as she tucked her in.

She perched on the edge of the bed, smoothed the hair from Claire's face. "I can't, honey. I need to finish filling out some papers and pack up our things."

Claire clutched her bear, whispered something against the fur.

"What?" Amanda bent down to hear.

"Bad man's coming. Brownie's scared."

Her heart tripped. Her daughter was afraid. "No one's going to hurt us. We're safe now. The bad man's in jail." At least, Wayne was. Candace Rothchild's killer still hadn't been caught.

She gnawed her lip, not wanting to think about that. But the bodyguard and security system would keep them safe.

"But I'll sit here with you for a while, okay?"

She rubbed Claire's back, tucked the blankets tighter around her, waiting for her to drift off. But Claire's anxiety bothered her—bothered her badly.

Ever since Claire had been born, she'd tried to keep her daughter safe, to give her the stable life she'd never had. She'd wanted Claire's childhood to be the opposite of hers—comforting, secure, with a mother she could depend on.

But she'd failed. First Wayne had threatened them, and then the danger had followed them here—terrible danger. And despite her precautions, Claire had sensed it. She'd picked up on the fear. And now she was turning into an anxious, insecure child, exactly what Amanda had hoped to avoid.

Claire's breathing deepened into sleep, and Amanda stood. Still nursing her injured ankle, she left the bedroom door ajar and walked back into the kitchen, her mind a jumble of thoughts. She couldn't blame herself for all their problems. The casino gunman had singled her out for some unknown reason. That certainly wasn't her fault.

She'd made a mistake with Wayne, though. She never should have married him.

She sank into the chair at the kitchen table, stared at the teaching application she still had to complete. She picked up her pen, then set it back down. She didn't feel like teaching again. But she did need a job.

She picked up the pen again, tapped it on the table, tried to drum up some enthusiasm. But it occurred to her that she'd been teaching Claire the wrong lesson. Maybe she shouldn't have emphasized safety all these years. Maybe she shouldn't have tried so hard to avoid risks.

Maybe she should have been teaching Claire to stop being afraid, to go after what she wanted in life and pursue her dreams.

She stared at the application, unable to avoid the truth. Luke was right. She was afraid to change. Change was scary, painful. It took courage and nerve. It was easier to cling to the known, to not risk failure, to find excuses not to try.

She'd asked him to change, though. She'd asked him to give up his lifelong goal, to abandon his need to avenge his mother's death.

And yet she wouldn't even change her career.

She'd been unfair.

Her forehead pounded; her stomach swirled with guilt. That argument *had* been about her. She was more mired in the past than he was.

She shoved the job application aside, pulled her laptop over and booted it up. She clicked on the University of Nevada Web site, searched their listing of graduate programs until she found the right one. Anthropology. She could study right here in Las Vegas. She could do everything she'd always dreamed.

If she was strong enough to try.

She sat back, her mind spinning with all she would have to do. She'd have to retake the Graduate Record Exam, submit an application. Money would be tight. She'd have to live with Kendall longer, find a babysitter for Claire.

But she could do this. She was stronger than she'd once thought. If she could face down Wayne, surely she could make this change. She reached for the teaching application and ripped it up.

She stood, headed for the wastepaper basket, her chest lighter now. Maybe this wouldn't solve all her problems, but it was a start.

But then the telephone rang. She stopped, swiveled to face it, her senses suddenly alert. The only person who had her number here was Luke.

Her pulse pounding, she crossed the room and answered the phone. "Hello?"

"Amanda." Luke's voice rumbled across the line, and she closed her eyes. And suddenly, all the emotion she'd been trying to hold at bay for the past two days broke loose, like a flash flood ravaging a desert gorge.

"Luke…" Her voice broke. Oh, God. Was he calling for another chance? Was he going to admit he was wrong?

"Can you stop by here tomorrow at noon to drop off the keys?" he asked.

"What?" She blinked, her emotions in turmoil, trying to recoup.

"The house keys. I'd like them back."

"Oh, right." She pressed her hand to her chest, struggled to breathe. He only wanted to finish this business, make sure she left on time and returned the keys. Their relationship was over. *Over.* She beat back the rising despair. "I'll be there."

"Good. My penthouse at noon." He cut the connection.

She sagged against the counter and closed her eyes. Tears clogged her throat. Anguish welled up inside, and she shuddered, consumed with regret. He didn't love her. He *really* didn't love her.

And she had to face the stark truth. She couldn't fantasize anymore, couldn't delude herself with false hopes. Her life would go on. She'd move back in with Kendall. She'd raise Claire and pursue her dreams.

But those dreams wouldn't include the man she loved.

Chapter 14

Her stomach jittering, Amanda clutched the handrail in Luke's private elevator as it rocketed to the forty-fifth floor. She trembled at the thought of seeing Luke again—for what could be the last time.

She'd barely slept all night, could hardly hold a thought in her mind. Her emotions careened from hope to dread, joy to despair like a dried leaf buffeted by a storm.

But she knew one thing. She had to maintain her dignity. She couldn't break down, couldn't embarrass Luke by making a scene. She'd simply drop off the keys, thank him for his help and then leave.

The elevator dinged and came to a stop, and the agitation in her belly grew. The door slid open, and she stepped out, her throat suddenly parched. Struggling for composure, she wiped her sweaty palms on her jeans, hoisted her battered purse over her shoulder, forced her feet to walk to his door.

She stopped, glanced back at the elevator, fought down the urge to bolt. This was ridiculous. She wasn't a coward. She could certainly hand him his keys. She inhaled and rapped on the door.

A second later he pulled it open, and her gaze shot to his. And for an eternity she couldn't breathe. She drank in his amber eyes, his somber brows, the sexy grooves framing his mouth. He'd shaved recently, and only the barest hint of whiskers darkened his jaw. Her gaze traveled over the wide ledge of his muscled shoulders, back to his sensual mouth.

And he stared back at her, his eyes roaming her face, her breasts. The hall turned stuffy and hot. Her lungs barely squeezed in air. She wanted desperately to hurl herself into his arms.

But he stepped back. "Come on in."

She nodded, pressed her lips together to suppress the words she shouldn't say. He led the way through the marbled entrance, past the elegant living room, to the windows at the opposite wall.

He turned then, and she abruptly stopped. She tightened her grip on her purse, suddenly tongue-tied, all thoughts wiped from her mind.

And he didn't make it easy for her. He just watched her, his expression unreadable, as if expecting her to speak.

The keys. Her face burned. "Oh, I, um..." She reached into her purse, fished around for the keys and pulled them out. "Here."

"Just set them on the table."

"Right." She placed them on the end table. Her gaze boomeranged back to his.

Seconds passed. She couldn't move. She could only stare at him, soaking in the sight of his face while emotions tumbled inside her—there was so much she wanted to say.

But he didn't want to hear her explanations. If he'd changed his mind about their relationship, he would have told her by now. Instead, he'd only phoned once in the past two days to tell her to drop off the keys.

"You want something to drink?" he asked.

She should refuse. He was being polite. He had work to do, people to see. He might even have a date.

That thought made her want to wretch. She pressed her hand to her belly to quiet her nerves. "No thanks, I—"

"A glass of wine." He strode to the mahogany sideboard, and she struggled to compose herself.

"All right." One glass. She could handle that.

His back muscles flexed as he pulled out a bottle. He worked the corkscrew, extracted the cork with a muffled pop. Her gaze traced the riveting bulge of his biceps, the tendons that ran down his strong arms.

And she wondered how many women had pined for him, how many hearts he'd broken over the years. Wasn't that what they'd said about Candace Rothchild—that she'd been obsessed with Luke? He'd even had a restraining order issued in an attempt to keep her away.

Amanda could hardly blame her. She'd certainly never forget this man. Too choked up to speak, she dragged her gaze to the window and stared unseeing at the city below.

"Here you go." His breath brushed her ear, and she jumped. She hadn't even seen him approach. She inhaled his arousing scent, took the wine glass with quivering hands. She wanted to touch him so badly that she had to take a step back.

She sipped her wine. The silence stretched. He stared at her, his dark brows knitted together, and she had no idea what to say.

And she realized she'd made a mistake. She never should have come here and tortured herself this way. Kendall could have dropped off the keys.

"How's Claire?" he suddenly asked.

"Good. Great." She gulped her wine, and he fell silent again.

"Thank you for letting us stay at your house," she added. "And for what you did with Wayne… For everything."

Oh, God. She was dying here. Why didn't he say anything? She needed to end this ordeal before she completely broke down.

He frowned, looking uncertain suddenly, and a fierce pang of longing lanced her heart. What she wouldn't give to run her hands down his back, feel his muscles flex under her palms. Feel his raw urgency fueling hers.

"More wine?" he asked. She jerked her gaze to her glass, realized with a start that she'd drained it without even being aware.

"No. No, thanks." Breathless, she set the glass on the table next to the keys. How pathetic could she get? She was standing here fantasizing about him, ogling him, her desire clear in her eyes, while he waited for her to leave.

"Well, I'd better go." Before she broke down and begged.

"Amanda." His eyes met hers. He shoved his hand through his hair. "About the project—"

"It was none of my business, really." She twisted her hands, and the words broke loose. "I'm sorry. I shouldn't have said anything. It wasn't my place. Just forget it, okay? And you were right. About me, I mean. I—"

"Amanda—"

"I'm not going to teach. I threw the application away. I'm going to go back to school."

"You are?"

She nodded, her face flaming. So much for dignity and restraint.

The doorbell buzzed. Luke glanced at the door, then back at her.

"Anyhow," she added. "There's your key…and I need to go now. You're busy, and I—"

"No. Wait." He held up a hand. "Stay there. I have something to say."

He strode to the door, and she crossed her arms, wishing again that she'd never come. Luke didn't want to hear her news.

She glanced around the penthouse knowing it would be for the final time. Her gaze landed on the desk where they'd made love, and the images came tumbling back before she could stop them—Luke's eyes glittering with hunger, his mouth hot against hers. That electrifying way he'd watched her, his stark need driving him hard.

She swallowed, her breathing suddenly ragged. She looked at Luke at the door. This wasn't going to work. She had to get out of here now.

She headed toward him just as he shut the door and turned back. He glanced at the envelope in his hand, tore it open, pulled out the letter inside. His frown deepened, and he grew suddenly still.

Something was wrong. "What is it?"

His gaze rose to hers. The fierce intensity of his expression made her breath halt.

"It's another note, like the one you got."

Shock billowed through her. She pressed her hand to her throat. "You mean from the killer?"

"Yeah. He says to meet him in the blackjack pit."

"Now? He's here? In the casino?"

"So it seems." He crossed to the phone, picked up the receiver, then swore. "The line's dead."

"Dead?" Her blood drained from her face. How had he cut the phone lines? Any why? What did that killer have planned?

Luke tossed the note onto the table, tugged his cell phone from the pocket of his slacks. He punched in a number, waited, and his eyes turned even grimmer. "The lines must all be down. No one's picking up in security."

He tapped in another number, waited, then shook his head. "Voice mail. Something big must be happening if Matt's not answering his phone."

She bit her lip. "What are you going to do?"

"Alert security." He snapped his phone closed, slipped it into his pocket again. "Stay here. I'll be right back. You have your cell phone?"

"Yes, but—"

"Good. Call me if anything happens. And whatever you do, don't leave."

"I won't." She watched him head for the door. But that killer would be armed. "Luke," she said, her fear for him making her voice shake. "Be careful."

He paused, turned back, and his eyes held hers. "I will." And for several heartbeats, he just gazed at her, and beyond the urgency, beyond the determination, lay something deeper, something more intimate. Something that looked a lot like love.

"When I get back, we're going to talk," he promised, his voice gruff. "Now lock the door and stay put." He pivoted and strode out the door.

The door clicked shut. She raced to lock it, then sagged against the wall. Had that really been love she'd seen in his eyes? Was it possible that they'd have another chance?

She couldn't get up her hopes. She could be imagining things. Because if he loved her, then why hadn't he called? And why make her return the house keys? He was even having a security system installed in Kendall's house—a clear sign he wanted her gone.

But she couldn't think about that now, not with the killer so close. She had to stay calm, stay alert. Luke might call for her help.

She dug in her purse for her cell phone, then saw that the battery was dead. She hissed out her breath. Now what was she going to do?

Calm down, she decided. Becoming hysterical wouldn't do Luke any good. She'd just sit tight and wait for him to return.

The doorbell buzzed. Her heart jerked into her throat. She whipped around and faced the door.

Was that security? The killer? Luke couldn't be returning so soon.

She pressed her hand to her rioting chest, willing her pulse to slow. She was acting paranoid. It was probably just Luke. She couldn't let her imagination run wild.

"Who is it?" she called.

No one answered.

Her heart raced even more.

She eyed the phone—no help there. Her gaze landed on the hutch nearby and she saw the room key. He must have forgotten it. And now he'd come back to get it.

But then why didn't he answer? And returning for his room key hardly seemed like a priority with a killer running loose.

Unless he needed it to gain access to private areas of the hotel.

"Luke?" Her nerves twisting even tighter, she pressed her ear to the door. Silence. "Who's there?" she called again.

Nothing. Maybe he couldn't hear her through the door.

Her hands trembling, she scooped up the room key. But then she hesitated again. She couldn't open the door without knowing who was there. What if it wasn't Luke?

The door lock clicked. She watched in horror as the handle began to dip. Someone was coming inside.

And Luke didn't have his key.

Her heart raced wildly. She had to run, escape. *Move.*

She whipped around, searching frantically for a place to hide. She raced down Luke's hallway, ducked behind his bedroom door. She heard the door to the penthouse open and bang against the wall.

She stayed as still as she could and hugged her arms, struggling not to make any noise. It could be the killer. She couldn't let him know she was back here. But he already knew that. Like an idiot, she'd called out, giving herself away.

She listened hard, but her blood pressure roared in her ears. Terrified, needing to find out where he was, she inched back to the edge of the door.

She peeked out. A waiter stood in the entrance next to a room service cart.

Room service. She frowned, suddenly confused.

Maybe she'd overreacted. Maybe Luke had ordered lunch before she'd arrived. But then the waiter turned toward her, and she spotted the gun.

For a second, she stood petrified. The intruder's cold gaze slammed into hers. Then she gasped, jerked back behind the door.

It was the man from the Rothchild's casino, the same man who'd drugged her. And he'd just seen her. She had to run.

But where?

Frantic, she tried to think. The balcony was out. She was forty-five floors up. And all the phone lines were dead.

She dithered, then rushed through Luke's bedroom, raw terror fueling her steps. She should have gone into the kitchen. Back here there was only the bathroom—no way out.

A bullet whined past, splintering the wall beside her head, and the sharp bang deafened her ears. She shrieked, dove into the bathroom, searching for a way to defend herself.

But there was nothing. Not even a can of shaving cream. Her entire body shook.

And then she smelled it. That aftershave. The stench slithered through the air and assaulted her nose.

Her knees quivered hard. She turned and met the killer's eyes.

"All right," he said, and the sound of his voice made her heart quake. "I want that ring. And I want it now."

What the hell was happening? Why hadn't the gunman shown up?

Scowling, Luke hurried back through the hallway

from the security office, his apprehension mounting with each long stride. No one had reported any problems. The phones were still out, but the telephone company had it in hand. He'd alerted the police, posted guards throughout the casino, sent another to check on Amanda while he waited in the blackjack pit for the killer to show.

No one had come.

But why send a note and not show up?

Unless the killer had lost his nerve. Or the extra security guards had scared him off.

But then why did this fear keep gnawing at him, the feeling that something was wrong? The feeling that he'd missed something—something urgent. That danger lurked close.

And why didn't Matt Schaffer answer his cell phone? No one knew where he'd gone—which was too damned strange. His security chief never took time off on the job.

He reached the service elevators, spotted the housekeeping manager checking a maid's cleaning cart. "Has anyone gone up to my suite?" he asked.

She shook her head. "No, sir. Would you like something sent up?"

"No. So no one's used the elevator?"

She frowned. "No one from housekeeping."

"Room service just went up," the young maid beside her said. "He said he had your lunch."

Room service? He hadn't ordered food.

Dread slithered into his gut.

Amanda was there. He'd left her in his penthouse. *Alone.* Swearing, he ran to the elevator, swiped his spare key card in, then punched in the access code.

What had he been thinking? What if the security

guard had arrived too late? The gunman had been after her from the start.

And that note had been nothing but a decoy, a ploy to get her alone.

The elevator started up.

And Luke began to sweat.

Amanda stared down the barrel of the pistol. She was trapped in her worst nightmare, facing a killer. And now she was going to die.

This man had murdered Candace Rothchild. He'd bludgeoned the woman to death. And now he was going to kill her, too. She could see it in his cold, dead eyes.

Terror fought its way up her throat, building, swelling, threatening to explode in a primal shriek. She choked it back, wheezed a breath past her paralyzed lungs. She had to stay in control.

"Give me the ring," he repeated, his fury clear in his voice.

"I don't have it," she said, hating how badly her voice shook. "I told you that the other night."

His eyes hardened. The stench of his aftershave reeked in the air. "You have it. It's in your purse. Hand it over now."

In her purse? Her lips quivered, and she shook her head. "You're wrong. You have me confused with someone else. I don't have it. Really I don't."

"Like hell you don't. I put it there. In the lobby," he added at her blank look. "When your purse spilled on the floor."

She gaped at him. That had been planned? He'd bumped her, planted the ring in her purse. But then he'd changed clothes, accosted her with the gun. But why? It didn't make any sense.

She jerked her purse off her shoulder, held it out. "Here. Take it. Look for yourself." And as soon as he was distracted, she'd bolt past him out the door.

But he was too smart. He shook his head. "Dump it out. Right there."

Her throat convulsed. She wasn't going to get away. Her hands trembling, she pulled open the purse's drawstring, then inverted the contents onto the floor. Tissues tumbled out, then her nail clippers, her car keys, a couple of pens. She shook the bag, and her wallet followed, along with a comb and a travel-sized mirror.

"That's it," she whispered, her eyes on his. She flapped the bag again, but nothing else came out. "I told you, it isn't here."

"It has to be." His face turned red, his voice vibrating with rage.

And images flashed before her eyes—Claire holding her bear…her tiny arms reaching for a hug…Claire's sweet, flushed face as she slept. Luke risking his life to protect her…the hunger burning in his sexy eyes…the incredible bliss he brought to her life.

And suddenly she snapped. She didn't deserve this fear. She didn't deserve to die. And she was fed up with being the victim, fed up with being pushed around and attacked.

Wayne had been bad enough. She'd made a mistake, suffered a lapse in judgment and had paid the price.

But this creep—who the hell was he to threaten her?

"I don't have your ring," she gritted out, walking toward him. She gripped the straps of her empty purse. "I told you that from the start. Now leave me alone."

Furious, she whipped the purse forward, slapping the leather across his face.

The gun fired.

Heat tore through her shoulder, and she screamed.

Chapter 15

Amanda had been shot. *Shot.*

Her scream still echoing in his skull, Luke glanced around the hallway outside his penthouse, took in the dead guard slumped by the door. He slammed his key card into the lock, kicked the door open, and it crashed back against the wall.

He burst inside, desperate to find her, then frantically scanned the room. Empty. *Damn.* Where had that bastard taken her?

A soft cry drifted from down the hall.

Adrenaline stormed through his veins, but he fought to contain it, knowing he'd endanger her if he rushed. Forcing himself to walk softly—to not alert the gunman—he inched his way down the hall.

He'd never forgive himself if Amanda died. He'd been a fool to leave her alone. He pushed the panic to the back of his mind, refusing to think about that now. He had to focus, concentrate to keep her alive.

When he reached his bedroom door, he paused. He listened intently, but silence thundered back. Where the hell had they gone?

He flattened himself against the wall, then peeked inside. Nothing. The bedroom was empty. Only the bathroom was left.

He raced across the bedroom, pressed himself to the wall by the bathroom door, and listened again. And then suddenly he heard Amanda. She let out an agonized moan.

She was injured. She had to be bleeding. He felt wild at the thought. He clenched his hands into fists, trying not to let his mind go there…trying not to think about her suffering, dying.

He loved her.

The realization bolted out of nowhere, but he instantly knew it was true. He loved her. Amanda was his destiny. And he wasn't going to let her die.

His mind shut down. His vision hazed. The primitive need to avenge her raged.

And he couldn't control it anymore. He burst through the doorway into the bathroom. In a glance, he took in Amanda lying in a pool of blood, the gunman kneeling a short distance away.

Crazed now, insane with the need to protect her, Luke flew at the killer with a guttural cry. He slammed into his side, flattened him to the marble floor. And then he rammed his fist into his face, grunting, pounding, hitting him again and again, punching his jaw, his gut, his head.

The gunman stopped struggling and went slack.

"Luke," Amanda called. "Luke, stop." Her weak voice penetrated the haze.

He sat back on his heels, hauled in air to his heaving lungs, studied the unconscious man sprawled on the floor—the same man who'd attacked them in the hills. He confiscated the gun, whipped out his cell phone and called 911, then rushed to Amanda's side.

Oh, hell. Her face was too white. Blood seeped from her shoulder onto the tiles. Alarmed, he leaped up and grabbed a towel, then pressed it to her shoulder to staunch the flow. "Hold on," he urged her.

She peered up at him. Her pale lips tightened with pain. "Luke," she whispered.

"I love you," he told her, and pressed the wadded towel down hard.

She whimpered. Her eyes rolled back, and she went slack.

Frantic, terrified that she would die, he felt her wrist and checked her pulse. It was weak, but she was alive. He sagged back on his heels in relief.

But then he leaned toward her again, cradling her as best he could, keeping the towel pressed over her wound. She was so pale, so blasted weak. His throat wedged tight with dread. And he just held her, soothing her—this amazing woman he loved.

An eternity later, voices shouted down the hall. And then people swirled around him, police, paramedics. Radios squawked. Gurneys rolled in. People barked out orders and unloaded supplies. In his peripheral vision, he saw the police handcuff the gunman and haul him away.

"Mr. Montgomery," someone said. Luke ignored him, his entire attention focused on Amanda's face, willing her to survive. Her lips were tinged blue, her face so pale that her freckles stood out on her nose.

"Mr. Montgomery, you'll have to let go so we can help her. Please let go, sir. She needs our help."

The paramedics. "Right." He had to let her go.

The hell he did. He pried his hand from the towel, forced himself to rise and step back. The paramedics swarmed her, checking her vital signs, giving her oxygen, strapping her pale, fragile body into a gurney and rushing away.

And he knew right then that he couldn't do it. No matter what else happened in his life, no matter what anyone wanted, he could never let this woman go.

He loved her. And she was forever his.

Amanda surfaced from a deep, dark haze hours later. She blinked her eyes open, then zeroed in on Luke. He sat slumped in an armchair across the hospital room, his gaze trained on her.

He instantly leaped to his feet. "You're awake."

He rushed to her side, perched on the edge of her cot, and she couldn't take her eyes from his face. His hair wasn't combed. Black bristles coated his jaw. And he looked so dear, so much like everything she'd ever wanted, that tears sprang to her eyes.

He grabbed a glass from the metal table beside the cot. "Your throat's raw from the surgery. You've been out for a couple of hours."

He adjusted the straw, brought the glass to her face and she took a cooling sip. Her right hand was hooked to an IV. Heavy bandages encased her left shoulder, making it impossible to move. She thought back, tried to sort through the morass of memories—the gunman's chilling eyes, his rage when he didn't find the ring, the huge satisfaction she'd felt at whipping his face with her purse. Then excruciating pain. Luke bursting in.

Had he really told her he loved her?

Or had she hallucinated that part?

"They removed the bullet from your shoulder," he told her, not budging from the bed. She closed her eyes, enjoying the warm, solid feel of him, the way his thigh wedged securely against her hip.

"The doctor said it all went well," he added. He picked up her left hand and stroked it, and she sighed at how comforting that felt. "No complications. The bullet missed the critical parts. He's stopping by later to explain the operation and rehab."

"Gunman," she said around the dryness in her throat.

Luke helped her take another sip of water and made a sound of disgust. "The guy's a Houdini. He escaped. It was the damnedest thing. They had him handcuffed and were waiting downstairs for another ambulance to arrive. Somehow he got out of the cuffs, overpowered another guard and used his clothes as a disguise. No one knows how he did it. But he's smart. He even knocked out Matt Schaffer earlier to steal his key."

Her heart dove. So the killer was on the loose again. The danger wasn't gone.

"Don't worry," he added, as if reading her mind. "I've hired more bodyguards for you and Claire. And I've added even more security to my house. Claire's coming by later, by the way. Kendall thought it was better to wait."

Amanda frowned, wondering if the painkillers had muddled her mind. Why was he talking about his house?

He leaned closer, and his face was inches from hers.

She traced the crinkles at the corner of his eyes with her gaze, the faint lines creasing his brow. But his somber expression made her heart lurch.

"I'm sorry, Amanda. I never should have left you alone."

"Not your fault," she rasped out.

"Yeah, it was. It was my fault you were even there. If it hadn't been for the plans I wanted to show you... And then when I heard you scream...

"It almost killed me," he confessed, his voice so anguished it brought a lump to her throat. "Seeing you bleeding on the floor..."

He shook his head, and his voice turned fierce. "I won't make that mistake again. I'm keeping you safe for the rest of your life."

Her heart beat fast. She stared at him, not sure she understood.

"I know this isn't romantic," he said. "You deserve better. And I'll ask you again later, somewhere with flowers, music..." He shoved his hand through his hair. "Hell, I don't even have the ring. I left it in my safe. But I can't wait. I need to know."

His eyes pleaded with hers. "I love you, Amanda. Marry me."

Her lips parted in shock. He loved her? She hadn't imagined that part? "You bought me a ring?"

"I was miserable without you. You were right about the project, about the revenge. I didn't call you because I was having the plans redrawn. That's what I've been doing for the past two days, overseeing the drawings. I wanted to wait until they were done."

Her breath hitched. "You changed the project?"

"You'll like it." He traced the veins on her hand with

his thumb, sending shivers racing over her skin. "The investors are happy. It's still basically the same, but we modified it so it's more like a village. There's a training center attached, a place for career counseling, some affordable housing, too."

She squeezed his hand, her heart filled with love for this man. "It sounds perfect. You're perfect. I love you, Luke."

He reached out and touched her cheek. He gazed at her with so much love in his eyes that her own eyes flooded with tears. "Then you'll marry me?" he asked.

"I'll marry you. As long as you don't mind being married to a student. I'm going to be in school for the next few years."

His lips curved up. A sexy gleam lit his eyes. "I've got a cave you could survey—for the right price."

She smiled back. "A price, hmm? And just how much will this cave cost?"

His eyes heated. "You. Every day for the rest of my life."

"It's a deal," she whispered. And then his mouth captured hers, and she didn't speak again for a long, long while.

Two weeks later, Amanda put on her final touch of lipstick, then appraised herself in the bathroom mirror. Her skin color had rebounded since the shooting. Her dark circles had faded, thanks to Luke's constant pampering and insistence that she rest.

This was her first night out without the shoulder harness, and she was making the most of it with her slinky red dress—the same one she'd worn the night she met Luke.

Of course, she wore a few new accessories with the

outfit now—a brilliant gold choker necklace and matching earrings. A fabulous antique diamond engagement ring. She stretched out her fingers and smiled at the gorgeous stone.

"Ring, Mommy," Claire called from the other room.

"Just give me a minute." Her lips curved in amusement. Claire loved to look at her ring and admire how the diamond caught the light. Luke joked that they had a future gemologist in their midst.

"My ring," Claire said again.

Amanda misted herself with a bold new scent, then dragged in her breath. That was the best she could do. She just hoped it was good enough to catch Luke's attention tonight. Now that her shoulder was mending, she had a list of very sensual demands she was going to insist he fulfill.

She turned off the bathroom light, walked into her bedroom. Claire sat in the middle of the bed, surrounded by the contents of her purse.

"Oh, Claire. I have to leave soon, and I need my purse." She slipped on her high heels, then crossed to the bed. "Let's put everything back, okay?"

"My ring, Mommy." Claire held up her fist, and Amanda frowned.

"What have you got there?"

"My ring." Claire opened her small hand, and Amanda's jaw dropped. An enormous diamond ring sat in her palm.

She propped her hip on the bed, so stunned she could hardly breathe. "Let me see." Claire handed it over, and she held it up to the light.

"Oh, my God." It was incredible. Six or seven carats minimum, the diamond unlike anything she'd ever seen.

At least she thought it was a diamond. Colors sparkled and swirled in the center of the stone, changing from blue to violet to green.

"What are you doing?" Luke asked from the doorway.

She couldn't take her eyes off the stone. "Luke, look at this. You won't believe it." She held up the ring, and he frowned.

He strode to the bed and she rose, handing it to him. He studied it for a second, then let out a long, admiring whistle. "Well, I'll be damned. It's the missing ring. The Tears of the Quetzal. The one Candace Rothchild had."

"But where did it come from?" She jerked her gaze to Claire. "Where on earth did you find this?"

"Your purse," Claire said, and her bottom lip trembled. "My ring."

Amanda picked up her purse, staring at it in disbelief. "But it wasn't in here. I know it wasn't. I dumped everything out."

"In the hole, Mommy."

"The hole?"

She opened the empty bag and checked inside. She pulled the lining up, and sure enough, a hole had ripped along the seam, fraying the silky fabric. Her gaze flew to Luke's. "She's right. There is a hole. The ring must have worked its way through. It's been there all along."

His forehead furrowed. "We'd better get it to the police right away. We can drop it off on our way out."

"Good idea."

"We can't keep this ring," Luke said to Claire, his voice gentle. "Someone lost it, and we need to take it back. But how about if we buy you a special ring tomorrow? Will that be all right?"

"You could ask Aunt Kendall if she'd like to shop with us," Amanda added, and Claire consulted her bear.

"Okay. Aunt Kendall," Claire called, and scrambled off the bed. She raced from the bedroom, and Amanda smiled.

"I still can't believe we found the ring. It's gorgeous."

"Yeah, gorgeous." His gaze burned into hers, then dipped lazily over her lips, her throat…her breasts.

"They say it has a legend," she said, suddenly breathless. "That whoever has it falls instantly in love."

He moved closer, and his eyes turned hotter yet. "You think the legend came true?" His voice came out graveled and deep.

Her heart pounded fast. And she remembered the first time she'd seen him, right after her purse had spilled, just seconds after that gunman had slipped the ring inside. She'd definitely found true love at first sight.

"So what do you think?" he repeated, moving closer. And then his hands were on her back, her hips, pulling her firmly against him. Her body softened, anticipating his touch, and she dropped her head back with a sigh.

"Is the legend true?" he asked again.

"I think," she whispered back, "that at the rate we're going, we're worthy of a legend of our own."

He grunted in agreement. And then his mouth took hers, and she showed him her deep abiding love.

Epilogue

The man hunched behind the wheel of his car under the cover of darkness. He waited, his gut seething, his gaze trained on the police station door.

Damn them all. Damn the woman for hiding the ring. Damn Luke Montgomery for holing her up in his house. And damn the Las Vegas traffic that had kept him from overtaking Montgomery's car tonight. He'd been watching their house for the past two weeks, waiting for a chance at that ring.

But Montgomery had foiled him—again. He fingered the bruise discoloring his jaw, the ribs still aching from Montgomery's fists. He'd underestimated that billionaire.

His mistake.

The police station doors swung open just then. Montgomery and his woman strolled out, then paused in a circle of light. Montgomery pulled her close, and they started kissing, getting so hot and heavy he nearly blew the horn to force them apart. But they finally stopped and strolled away.

So the police had the ring now. It didn't matter. This was a blip, just a minor bump in the road. He'd lost the ring, but he would recoup. He would change his strategy, turn this to his advantage, let this lull them into thinking the matter was done.

And then he would strike.

One by one, he'd vowed. He let out a high-pitched laugh. If anyone thought this was over, they were dead wrong.

* * * * *

THE 9-MONTH BODYGUARD

BY
CINDY DEES

Cindy Dees started flying airplanes while sitting in her dad's lap at the age of three and got a pilot's license before she got a driver's license. At age fifteen, she dropped out of high school and left the horse farm in Michigan where she grew up to attend the University of Michigan.

After earning a degree in Russian and Eastern European studies, she joined the US Air Force and became the youngest female pilot in its history. She flew supersonic jets, VIP airlift and the C-5 Galaxy, the world's largest airplane. She also worked part-time gathering intelligence. During her military career, she traveled to forty countries on five continents, was detained by the KGB and East German secret police, got shot at, flew in the first Gulf War, met her husband and amassed a lifetime's worth of war stories.

Her hobbies include professional Middle Eastern dancing, Japanese gardening and medieval reenacting. She started writing on a one-dollar bet with her mother and was thrilled to win that bet with the publication of her first book in 2001. She loves to hear from readers and can be contacted at www.cindydees.com.

Chapter 1

If one more person told her that her thirties were going to be the best years of her life, she was going to spend that decade in prison, doing hard time for murder.

Silver Rothchild realized her pasted-on smile was slipping and reinforced it quickly.

Thirty years old. Gamblers all over Las Vegas must be losing their shirts tonight betting over whether or not she'd live to see this birthday. A few years ago, no one would have bet a plugged nickel on her chances of making it this long.

She had to admit that her twenties had been one heck of a wild ride. The holier-than-thou crowd was offended at any hint that she'd actually had fun jet-setting around the world, rocking out in front of huge audiences as a pop singer, partying till dawn and pulling dozens of crazy stunts, any one of which should have killed her. But the fact was, a lot of it had been a blast. Self-destructive in the end and rendering her jaded and cynical far beyond her years, but a blast, nonetheless.

Of course, she'd done a lot of growing up since then. She'd buried enough of her friends by now to know the dangers of the lifestyle, too. Since those days she'd sworn off harmful substances, and she'd made a concerted effort to drop completely off the celebrity radar. Heck, she'd made an appearance in a celebrity magazine a few months back in a "where are they now?" article. How pathetic was that? Thirty years old and she was a has-been.

"You okay, snookums? You look like roadkill."

"I hate it when you call me that," Silver muttered to Mark Sampson, her bodyguard and ostensible boyfriend of the past several months.

"It's cute. Like you and your perky little—"

She stepped away from his hand as he made a clumsy grab at her rear end and hissed through her fake smile, "Stop acting like white trash."

"Now, snookums. Be nice. Wouldn't want me to get all mad and accidentally say something to them reporters over there about our arrangement."

She sighed. He was right. She was the one who'd made the offer to him in the first place—she had no business getting bitchy with him over it. She looped an arm through his and guided him out to the dance floor. Dance nasty in front of Mark and he'd forget all about his threat. Men were such incredibly simple creatures.

Not particularly enjoying either the song or gyrating around in as slutty a fashion as she could muster, she was vastly relieved when a sharp vibration tickled her right hip. Her heart leaped in anticipation. *Could this be the call?*

Shouting over the blaring music, she yelled at Mark, "Phone! I've got to take this call."

He nodded, turned to the nearest half-naked bimbo without interrupting his own hip-thrusting Elvis impersonation, and kept on dancing.

Some bodyguard.

She found a secluded corner behind a potted palm in the hall outside and pulled out her brand-new crystal-encrusted cell phone, a birthday present from her stepsister, Natalie. She hit redial quickly.

"Hello, this is Silver Rothchild—"

"Silver! Hi, this is Debbie, from Dr. Harris's office."

Her blood pressure jumped twenty points right then and there. Oh, God. It was the call. Her test results were back. She let out a long, steadying breath and steeled herself to hear the news either way. "Thanks for getting back to me so quickly. I'm sorry I couldn't stick around the office to wait for the results, but I couldn't be late for my own birthday party."

The nurse at the other end of the phone laughed. "Well, I've got a birthday present for you, Silver. Your results are positive. You're going to have a baby."

A *baby*.

The word washed over her and through her like a warm and gentle blessing, calming all the way down to her soul. Her most cherished dream had finally come true.

"Silver? Are you there?"

"Uh, yes. I'm still here. That's…that's fabulous!"

Jubilation erupted in her heart all of a sudden, an elation that wouldn't be contained. She let out a whoop of joy that startled a couple walking past.

"You'll need to set up an appointment for next week. We need to do a sonogram and get you started on prenatal vitamins. And of course, the doctor's going to want to talk to you about managing your blood pressure. As you know, this pregnancy poses a certain risk, given your tendency to high blood pressure. Write down any questions you have as they occur to you or you'll forget them during your appointment."

"Right. I'll call back first thing in the morning."

Silver floated out from behind the palm tree, her feet several inches above the floor. Her hand stole to her flat belly. A tiny human being was growing in there! It was miraculous.

"There you are, Silver!" a female voice called out with a hint of irritation from down the hall. "Your father wants to give you his birthday present. You'd better hurry before he changes his mind."

Silver spied her perfectly groomed stepmother, only four years her senior, coming her way in a pair of high heels that mere mortals wouldn't dare attempt. But Rebecca, in true trophy-wife fashion, was a former model and wore the four-inch stilettos like they were an extension of her magnificent legs.

Okay, so sue her. She was jealous of her glamorous stepmother's height. It sucked being five foot two in a town full of six-foot-tall show girls. She looked like a twelve-year-old compared to them.

"I'm coming, Rebecca," Silver called.

A spark of curiosity grew within her. What had her father cooked up for her birthday? He'd been so mysterious about it. Usually, she could coax any secret out of him. But this time, despite her very best cajolery, he hadn't given so much as a hint of what her birthday present was...other than the fact that it was going to blow her mind.

It took a lot to blow her mind. Like right now. She was pretty blown away by the idea of a baby of her own. She loved kids. Always had. Born into another life, she'd have been a schoolteacher in a heartbeat.

As it was, her life had gone in a radically different direction. She'd always been a good singer, and with Daddy's money and the resources of a show town like Vegas behind her, she'd been trained into a polished performer. A few Rothchild connections in the music biz, and voilà, she'd become a recording artist and pop star. Whether or not she'd deserved it was open to debate. At twenty-two, she hadn't cared if she'd stolen the dream of someone more talented and less connected. But now...now she wondered about it sometimes.

Given a do-over of her life, it might be interesting to see if she could've made it in the music business without any help at all from her father. Of course that was easy to say with a wall full of gold records and the fame and fortune to go with them.

Not having to fake a smile this time, she joined her party once more.

"There's our birthday girl!" her father boomed.

She made her way to him through the crowd of well-wishers. She hugged several of her longtime partners-in-crime who'd managed to survive their youths and grow up to one degree or another. There was no sign of Mark, for which she was abjectly grateful. Had he actually been her boyfriend, she'd have been furious that he'd vanished to who-knew-where with who-knew-whom. But now that she was pregnant, it was a good thing she'd taken the precaution of setting up their arrangement.

Her father gave her a hand up onto the raised dais along the back side of the room. *Wait till he found out he was going to be a grandpa.* Once he got over the initial shock and got done lecturing her about not being married, he'd be tickled to death. At least, that was the plan. Harold was fiercely loyal to his family, but could be…mercurial. Which was to say, he could be a died-in-the-wool son of a bitch. It made him a great casino mogul, but at times, it made him a difficult father to deal with.

Silver acted appropriately amused as a giant, black-frosted cake was wheeled in. The Rothchild Grand's pastry chef had outdone himself, decorating the beastly thing with miniature fondant coffins, plastic wheelchairs, and tiny blue marzipan bottles of Geritol. It really was ghoulish. As if she needed the reminder that she was no longer twentysomething and in the bloom of her youth.

Then the toasts began. Oh, they were meant in good fun—the references to slowing down, growing up, and getting old. But the underlying message of it all was much, much worse. She'd become safe. Bland. *Boring.* To her, that was a thousand times worse than turning thirty. Where had the adventurous Silver gone? The one who dared to take the music business by storm? The one who didn't give a damn what anyone else thought? Who chased all her dreams, no matter how far-fetched?

The only thing that kept her from waxing suicidal at the black balloons, funeral dirge in lieu of "Happy Birthday," and nonstop old age jokes was her delirious secret. They could say whatever they wanted. She was finally going to have a baby.

When the birthday roast was finally over, her father raised his champagne glass. "A toast to my lovely daughter. May her next ten years be as successful as her last ten, and a lot less hard on this old man's heart."

The crowd laughed, and on cue, she looked appropriately abashed. For all his ranting and raving over the years to get her act together and grow up, he could really get over her twenties any day now. She had. She hadn't done anything to frighten or embarrass him in nearly seven years, but he still took every opportunity to remind her what a screwup she was.

That was Harold personified. Never missed a chance to sink a barb into someone if he could. Some people said it was impossible to love and hate a person at the same time. Obviously, they'd never had him for a stepfather.

Of course, now that she was turning thirty, she probably could get away with distancing herself from him and his overbearing ways. Maybe she should consider moving out of Las Vegas. Out of Nevada, even. Heck, out of the country! It was a shocking thought. Daring. But it took root in her head as surely as a baby had taken root in her womb. A new start. No ties to her past. No Rothchilds. No Harold.

Her father was speaking again. "…better thirtieth birthday present than to give my beautiful and talented daughter a special engagement at the Grand Casino…."

Whoa. Rewind.

Engagement? At the Grand? Her…*perform again?*

Silver's mind went blank. She wanted to resurrect her career almost as bad as she wanted this baby. And he was going to give her a shot? In total shock, she looked up at her father.

She whispered, "Are you serious?"

He laughed heartily. "As a heart attack, kiddo."

"My own show?"

"Yup. Seven nights. On the big stage. Orchestra, backup dancers, pyrotechnics, the works."

She flung herself into his arms and did something she hadn't done since she'd been a little girl. She burst into tears. Even he was startled by that.

"Hey now, what's this, kiddo? You're not unhappy, are you? I can cancel it—"

Oh, Lord. Was pregnancy weepiness kicking in already? Or maybe she was just overwhelmed by being broadsided with two such enormous pieces of news in quick succession. "No! I'm overjoyed, Daddy. It's incredible. I've dreamed of restarting my career for years…I don't know how to thank you…you're the best…"

Who'd have guessed he was capable of such a thoughtful and generous gesture? Maybe Candace's death had affected him more than she realized. Her stepsister's recent murder had hit everyone in the family hard.

Damn. Just when she'd resolved to cut the apron strings for good, he went and did something amazing. Something that would keep her firmly in Las Vegas for some months to come, preparing and rehearsing for her show. The guy's timing was uncanny, as always. Just let the thought of leaving cross her mind, and boom, he roped her back in.

He patted her back awkwardly. "No more tears."

She sniffed and smiled up at him damply. Regardless of his motives, it really was an incredibly generous gift.

Quietly, so the audience wouldn't hear, he said, "One condition, though. You stay out of trouble. Out of the bars and nightclubs. No wild partying, no more stunts, no more of your pop-star shenanigans. And stay out of the freaking tabloids." A hard edge entered his voice. "You go back to your old ways, and I'll yank this rug out from under you so fast your head spins. Understood? Keep it clean, and I'll give you another shot at singing. Screw this up, and I'll see to it nobody ever hires you again."

Ahh. That was more like the Harold she knew and loathed.

Careful to keep her voice even, she said, "That seems fair enough."

Oh, God. The baby. He'd just ordered her not to go off and

do anything impulsive or wild or that would land her in the tabloids…like, oh, getting pregnant out of wedlock. And if he—or the tabloids—found out the real circumstances of this baby's conception, the media would have a field day with it.

A baby or her career? How was she supposed to choose between those?

She took a deep breath. If she played her cards right and Mark didn't go and do anything stupid, maybe she could have them both.

Or maybe she could lose everything.

Chapter 2

Army Captain and Delta Force Team Commander, Austin Dearing, stepped out of the taxicab into the blast furnace heat of Las Vegas. Jeez. And it was only May. He'd hate to see this place in August. Of course, after living in full body armor in parts of the world where daily highs frequently topped one hundred twenty, Vegas wasn't so bad. But he was still grateful to step into the air-conditioned cool of the Rothchild Grand Hotel and Casino.

He looked around the gaudy lobby curiously. He liked his creature comforts well enough, but the job he'd been sent here to do overshadowed his appreciation of the beautiful, leggy women cruising the joint, sharklike, in search of fresh meat. In his world, this was what was known as a target-rich environment.

A silicone-enhanced bleach-blonde purred at him, "May I help you, sir?" She was almost tall enough that at six foot four, he didn't have to look down at her.

"I'm looking for Harold Rothchild."

A startled look flickered across her face, but she replied smoothly enough, "Is Mr. Rothchild expecting you?"

"Yes, he is."

"One moment, sir."

She pulled out a cell phone and made a discreet phone call. "He's at his daughter's birthday party at the moment. Would you care to wait in his office?"

"I'm under orders to report to him as soon as I get here, no matter what he's doing." The actual phrase Rothchild had used was more obscene and involved interrupting him even if he was having intimate relations with his wife. Austin snorted. Even an Army grunt like him was couth enough not to repeat such a thing to a lady, though.

Another discreet phone conversation.

"Mr. Rothchild's assistant says you're to go to the party. Would you like to check into your room first? Maybe freshen up a bit?"

He clamped down on his impatience. His orders were to see Rothchild immediately. Not after he took a nap and got pretty. Fingering the beard stubble of his past twenty-four hours' worth of travel, he said firmly in his commanding officer voice, "No. I'll see him now."

The blonde twittered, signaling how turned on she was by his display of manly resolve. *Groupie alert.* Women were forever hanging out at the places Special Forces soldiers frequented, trying to land guys like him. Usually, he could spot 'em at a hundred paces. But this one had snuck up on him. He'd lost his touch. Been out in the field too damned long. Two years since he'd taken a minute off. Only reason he was on leave now was because of his busted left eardrum. He'd blown it when an explosion had gone off too close to him a few weeks back. The doc said it would take several months to heal. Which meant he was left cooling his jets for a while.

Thankfully, his commanding officer, General Sarkin, knew him well enough to know that sitting on his butt for months would drive him completely crazy. With his entire unit deployed overseas, it wasn't like there was anything on a stateside Army post to keep him busy. So, Sarkin had arranged for this special assignment.

Austin had never heard of Harry Rothchild, but he damned well knew who Silver Rothchild was. Her father, eh? Austin sympathized. His daughter was possibly the most notorious wild child of the past decade. The dossier Sarkin had given him said that Rothchild was worth hundreds of millions and the Grand Casino was the crown jewel of his hotel empire. He had a big family, which he kept close by, including several daughters. One of them, Candace, had been murdered a few months back, which was why Austin supposed he'd been hired to play nursemaid to Rothchild's third daughter—the troubled Silver.

He'd fought the cream puff assignment, but Sarkin had been adamant. Ultimately, he'd been a good soldier and sucked it up. It wasn't an official job, of course. The military didn't make a practice of babysitting spoiled little rich girls, thank you very much. But when a man with the stature of General Sarkin, who held the future of a guy's career in his hands, asked him to do something off the books, the guy did it, like it or not.

And it was only for three months. Just until his ear healed and he was cleared to go back into the field. He could put up with pretty much anything for three months.

The busty blonde opened a door marked Private, and the sounds of a party in full swing slammed into him. The shock of it was a physical blow. He couldn't remember the last time he'd been in a gathering of people this large and boisterous. Claustrophobia closed in around him. So accustomed was he to the desolate, wide open mountains of Afghanistan that he'd been patrolling for the past two years, he could barely force himself into the crush.

Three months. He could do this.

He waded into the crowd. Using his height to look over the partiers, Austin searched for the florid face of Harold Rothchild from the dossier. There he was. On the far side of the room on some sort of raised platform.

A hand groped Austin's rear end, and he pivoted sharply, prepared to take out the assailant. A brunette leered up at him. He stood down, relaxing his hands from their knife-blade rigidness. *You're back in the real world, Dearing. Cool it.*

Easier said than done. Those lightning fast reflexes, the total lack of hesitation to kill, were the reason he was still alive and kicking. Lecturing himself about the rules of engagement for this particular type of jungle, he managed to cross the dance floor without causing anyone bodily harm.

Austin touched Harold Rothchild lightly on the shoulder. The older man spun around, startled. *Hmm. The Rothchild patriarch was plenty edgy.* Not to mention he was hiring ridiculously overqualified bodyguards for his kids. What was going on? The dossier hadn't said anything about why the mogul suddenly wanted someone like Dearing—who specialized in guarding heads of State—watching out for his daughter.

"You must be Captain Dearing. Your commander described you to a tee, I must say."

At least Rothchild sounded relaxed enough. "Call me Austin, sir. I'm not on the Army's clock at the moment."

Rothchild snorted. "You don't have to tell me. I'm the guy who wrote your first paycheck. It has already been wired into the Singapore bank account you gave my secretary."

Austin nodded, annoyed. Why did men like this think that men like him gave a damn about money? Just because Rothchild worshipped at the altar of the almighty dollar didn't mean everyone did.

He schooled himself to patience. Growing up poor had probably made him more cynical than most. But his family had gotten by. And he and his brothers had all turned out fine. They were all hardworking, law-abiding citizens who enjoyed their work. Sure, he could make more money as a civilian bodyguard—a lot more than his Army pay—but that wasn't remotely why he did his job. He loved his work.

Rothchild bellowed, "Silver, come over here. There's someone I want you to meet,"

A fist in his gut couldn't have knocked the wind out of Austin more thoroughly than his first glimpse of Silver Rothchild. Wow. He couldn't help it; he stared as the pop star made her way to them. Her face, familiar to him from newsstands around the world, wasn't the most beautiful he'd ever seen, although she was genuinely pretty. She didn't have the best body he'd ever seen—she was too petite to achieve beauty queen stature—but she was in great shape and shaped great, not to mention he didn't spot a hint of silicone or surgery. She was one of those rare women with innate sexual charisma, a woman whom men couldn't peel their gaze away from and didn't want to. A genuine blond bombshell.

It was, of course, the reason she'd been such a sensation on the pop music scene. Belatedly, it occurred to him that she was actually wearing a perfectly modest dress, not showing a hint of cleavage, nor an inch of extra thigh. Her signature platinum blond hair was twisted up in a clip of some kind behind her head, and her makeup was understated.

Those silver-blue bedroom eyes of hers penetrated right through him as she looked up at him politely. She held out a perfectly manicured hand. "Hi, I'm Silver. It's nice to meet you." Her voice was honey sweet, hinting at the million-dollar sound that had made her famous.

Suppressing an urge to stammer, he replied, "Austin Dearing, Miss Rothchild."

One graceful brow arched at his shift of her name into the formal. She glanced over at her father questioningly.

"This, my dear, is your other birthday present."

Silver's startled gaze shot back to his. Chagrin abruptly warmed his cheeks. He was a *birthday present?* An elite-trained, highly-decorated war hero who led men into the jaws of death on a routine basis? Harold made him sound like a damned trained monkey!

His brows slammed together. Favor or not, General Sarkin could take this job and shove it. He wasn't *anybody's* pet.

Silver murmured in an appalled undertone, "What are you up to, Daddy?"

"Austin is a bodyguard."

The rosy blush in Silver's porcelain face drained away, lending a faintly gray cast to her complexion. Austin frowned, his internal alarm system exploding to life. He was missing something, here. Silver Rothchild was deathly afraid of something. Or *someone.* His protective instincts roared to the fore, jolting his every sense onto high alert. He abruptly didn't like the press of people around her, didn't like how exposed she was up on this raised dais above the crowd. He needed to be in front of her, between her and the balcony to his left that was a perfect perch for a sniper.

She choked out, "I already have a bodyguard, Father."

"And he's an idiot. Captain Dearing comes highly recommended by a friend of mine. He's the best. After Candace..."

Rothchild trailed off. Silver closed her eyes in pain, obviously understanding her father's veiled reference. Austin's brain kicked into overdrive. Was there more to the Candace Rothchild murder investigation than met the eye? Was the killer targeting other members of the Rothchild family? That would certainly explain daddy bringing in a high-powered bodyguard to protect his most famous child.

Silver seemed to gather herself together. She said more strongly, "I appreciate your concern, Dad, but I don't need another bodyguard. I'm perfectly safe with the one I have."

"What about that incident last week?"

"Brakes fail on cars. And Las Vegas is as flat as a pancake. I coasted to a perfectly safe stop."

"You were supposed to drive up into the mountains that day. What if your brakes had failed then?"

"Well, I didn't go up into the mountains and everything was fine."

Austin had to give the girl credit. Her father was a big, intimidating guy, and she was showing pluck to stand her ground like this.

Brake failure, huh? In his experience, the brakes on any reasonably well-maintained vehicle never, ever failed of their own volition.

Rothchild turned to him. "Ignore her. She needs a decent bodyguard, and I'm signing your paycheck."

Austin glanced over at the singer, who looked more than irritated. For just a second, her wonderfully expressive eyes looked…haunted. What in the hell was going on that had a wild woman like her looking like that? No doubt about it. She put his protective instincts on full combat alert.

He turned back to her father and nodded firmly. "I'll protect her with my life, sir."

"But—" Silver began.

Harold cut her off. "No buts. Austin Dearing is your bodyguard now. Consider him part of our earlier deal."

Whatever that deal was, Silver subsided immediately. But this time, resentment simmered at the back of her transparent gaze. Didn't like being pushed around by daddy dearest. But she was thirty years old according to the banner over her head. She could tell the guy to go to hell if he was that big a pain.

Rothchild gestured at one of the waiters passing by. "Take Mr. Dearing's bag. Check him into the New Yorker Villa and see to it his gear gets up there." Rothchild glanced over at Austin. "As of now, you're on duty."

For his part, Austin nodded and kept his thoughts to himself. Good thing he'd slept most of the way back from Afghanistan on the various flights that brought him here. Jetlag going east to west wasn't that bad, but he was twelve time zones out of sync at the moment. Of course, Harry Rothchild wasn't in the business of caring about anyone's comfort other than his guests'. For his part, Austin was used to the uncomfortable demands of guarding someone else's life.

Speaking of which, Silver turned away from her father and pushed heedlessly into the crowd. But not before Austin caught the flash of naked fear in her eyes. What was going on with her? The currents of mystery and danger swirling around her were palpable. And it was his job to decipher those currents and deflect them away from her at all costs. Of course, Rothchild hadn't exactly helped him get off on the right foot with his famously willful daughter. Austin sighed. Time for some serious damage control. And to think, he'd been on the job a grand total of thirty seconds.

Chapter 3

Silver glanced over her shoulder as a deep voice growled from behind her, "We need to talk, Miss Rothchild."

At least her father'd had the decency to pick a jailer who was easy on the eyes. He was a big man wrapped in muscle. Good looking in a chiseled, all-American kind of way. Totally not her kind of guy. She liked them dark and dangerous, and always seemed to end up with lean, jaded Europeans. He was all tawny and bronze, with a deep tan and sun-streaked blond streaks. His eyes were dark. Mysterious. Smoking hot, in fact. He looked like a male model for sailing attire.

She *so* wasn't stopping to talk to him. He was the living embodiment of everything she hated about how her father was forever manipulating and controlling her life. If Austin Dearing wanted to play bodyguard, he could darn well keep up with her.

She needed to be alone. To assimilate all that had happened in the past few minutes. To figure out how she was going to juggle her secret pregnancy and this incredible opportunity to perform. And then there was Mark. Now she'd have to string him along for even longer, perhaps most of the way through her pregnancy. It would depend on when the shows were scheduled. Yep, that was the key to pulling this thing off. How pregnant would she be by the time the shows happened? No doubt the promoters would want her half-naked and gyrating like she always had. Might be a teensy bit hard to do that looking like Shamu.

She hurried toward the casino, praying that no one would waylay her so Austin could catch up. Thankfully, she'd grown up in this place and knew every slot machine, every twist and turn, like the back of her hand. She zigzagged across the casino practically at a run and made her way to Saul Morgenstern's office by the Grand Theater. He was the vice president in charge of entertainment and the man who would schedule her gig.

Skipping his anal retentive secretary, Silver used her master key card to let herself directly into his office's private entrance. He looked up, startled, phone to his ear, then waved her to a chair in front of his desk.

He shouted into the phone, "Christ, Nigel! These changes are going to cost me a million bucks. Newsflash, your boys aren't worth it… No I'm not giving them an entire floor of the hotel. Just because your band is British doesn't mean they're the freaking Beatles!…and you can procure your owned damned call girls for them. I'm not a pimp… Yeah, well use the phone book. Prostitution's legal in this state, you moron."

Wow. He didn't often get that worked up. Some band had really crossed the line, apparently.

Saul slammed down the receiver, took off his spectacles and pinched the bridge of his nose before he finally said more calmly, "Silver Girl. I gather your father has sprung his little birthday surprise on you?"

He'd called her Silver Girl since she'd been a child. The two of them used to be as close as a beloved uncle and an adored niece. But that relationship, too, had been a casualty of her wild years. He'd overlooked her atrocious behavior far longer than anyone else, but even his patience had run out eventually. Ever since, he'd maintained a frosty distance from her that she'd respected as her just desserts. But she missed him.

"Hi, Saul. I'm sorry you couldn't make my party. Daddy really went overboard." She added wryly, "I expect he was trying to make the point to me that, like it or not, I'm an adult now."

Saul's mouth twitched, but he didn't crack the smile that had once come so readily for her. She sighed. "Harold told me about the show here at the Grand. I never thought he'd do something like that for me. I mean, it's not like I deserve it or anything."

That sent Saul's gray, shaggy brows up.

It was exceedingly uncomfortable having to maintain the entire conversation by herself like this, but apparently doing this gig was going to involve swallowing a healthy dose of crow, too. She continued doggedly. "He didn't tell me what you had in mind for the shows. Am I penciled in yet?"

Saul studied her inscrutably. "How soon can you be ready to go onstage? You'll need to be in tip-top shape, maybe take a few singing lessons. After all these star search shows, singers today are expected to really blow out a song."

The criticism stung. She'd always had plenty of range and power for any song her record label had given her. She replied evenly, "I've been singing again for a while. And I've been working out. I'm ready now, Saul. The sooner we do this thing, the better."

He leaned back, frowning, and said doubtfully, "You're gonna have to find new material....backup singers...you can use the hotel's band and orchestra, but they'll need arrangements... costumes and choreography..."

Her stomach was quickly filling up with lead. What he was talking about could take *months.* In the past, she'd had an entire crew of handlers who had taken care of all the details of putting together one of her tours. Frankly, she'd done little more than learn the songs and show up for a few costume fittings. But this time, it sounded like Saul expected her to do the bulk of the preparatory work herself. An hour ago, she'd have leaped all over the idea of getting to design her own show. But then she'd found out she was pregnant, and a time bomb—in the form of a looming baby bump—had suddenly started ticking.

She took a deep breath. "Saul, I need to do this show right away. I don't have time to develop big production numbers or manage a cast of thousands."

His bushy eyebrows came together over glaring eyes. "Do you want to *blow* this shot?"

She winced. "No. I really, really want to restart my career, and I fully understand how much is riding on this. But I *can't* spend months and months pulling this thing together."

"Why the hell not, missy?"

She closed her eyes. Much more even than her father, Saul could make or break her comeback based on how he supported her show. The good news was that, in many ways, Saul had been more of a father to her over the years than Harold had been. The bad news was he might very well be out to sabotage her comeback.

As Saul stared down at her hands, she realized she was wringing them until they were an angry red. She stopped. "Saul. I swear I have a life-shattering reason why I have to do this show now. But I can't tell you. I don't have any right at all to ask you, but could you please just trust me on this one?"

Skepticism glittered in his eyes.

She sighed. "I've changed. I've grown up. I'm not that spoiled, snot-nosed brat I was a few years ago." Did he remember the night he'd called her that? When she'd called him to bail her out of jail before the paparazzi got wind of it, and he'd come down to the police station and told her she could rot in the slammer for all he cared?

The memory of that night gleamed in his gaze, too. "You're so grown up and committed to your career that you won't sacrifice your personal plans to do this show right?" he bit out sarcastically.

Desperation made her throat tight. "I hear what you're saying. You're absolutely right. But I can't work around this one. I'd give up anything—everything in the world—except one thing, to perform again. And that one thing makes it necessary for me to do this show in the next few months."

Saul stared at her long and hard. If he'd figured out what she was making veiled reference to, he didn't comment on it. Finally, he reached into his desk and pulled out a leather day planner. Saul was old school. No computers or PDAs for him. He did everything on paper. "Lemme take a look at the schedule."

She exhaled on a massive sigh of relief. This could work if he'd cooperate with her.

"You're booked for Valentine's Day next year."

She did the math fast. Good Lord, she'd be over eight months pregnant by then. "What have you got that's sooner?"

He thumbed through the pages. "I always book a year or more in advance. But there is one possibility..." He trailed off as he turned to a page near the front of the planner. She peeked across his desk and saw June in block print at the top of the page. That was next month. Hope sprang through her.

"That phone call you walked in on was the manager for Metal Head Dead."

They were a rock band currently topping the charts. Their reputation was already worse than hers had ever been. And yet, because they were guys, they got away with all the rotten stunts that had deep-sixed her career. In fact, their careers were helped by their wild antics. She put aside her bitterness. The double standard was just part of the business.

Saul was talking again, mumbling to himself. "...would put their knickers in a twist if I canceled their leather-clad butts. And tickets for their show are set to go on sale in three days... We could call a press conference...make a big announcement about your comeback...tickets could go on sale immediately and we could capitalize on the buzz..."

He looked up at her. "You'd have only six weeks to pull the

entire thing together. You won't be able to scrimp on anything… it's going to have to be a top-notch production or you'll be a worse has-been than you are now."

Ouch.

He continued, "I'm telling you, I think it's impossible to get a decent show together by then. Plus, June isn't the big tourist season on the strip."

She replied hopefully, "But it's hot enough that everyone who is in town is inside and going to shows."

He shrugged. "I can't promise sellout crowds with only a few weeks to promote the gig. But if you're hell-bent on doing this thing right away, I can book you for June."

She darted around his desk to lay a big hug on him, just like the old days. The tears of gratitude that came to her eyes seemed to surprise him as much as they surprised her. She whispered, too choked up to speak any louder, "Thanks, Uncle Saul. I promise I won't let you down this time."

For just a moment, he returned the hug. Then he cleared his throat and set her away from him. "Now. About music," he said briskly. "I'd better be the one to make the call to your old label. The way I hear it, you didn't part on the best of terms."

Silver grimaced. Now there was an understatement. She'd been fired and escorted out of the record company's building by armed guards. In retrospect, she'd probably deserved worse. As she recalled—vaguely—she'd been stoned out of her head at the time.

She took a deep breath. "Actually, Saul, I've been writing some of my own stuff. Maybe we could use some of that—"

He cut her off with a slashing hand through the air. "Nobody ever builds a decent career on their own stuff. Three or four big-name, girl pop singers have taken time off recently. There'll be plenty of good songs lying around waiting for a big, sexy voice."

"But—"

"No buts. Your father told me to launch your second career, and that's what I aim to do. You leave the music to me, baby doll."

She wanted to tell him she wasn't a baby doll anymore. She was a grown woman, dammit, and she didn't want to do the same old music she'd sung the last time around. She wanted to do something new. Something more soulful, more…grown up. But Saul was first and foremost her father's man. And, he'd been a dear about the scheduling problem. He'd canceled a huge act for her. Like it or not, she was probably going to have to go along with him on the music thing.

She sighed. Time for more of that maturity stuff.

"…stop by tomorrow, and I'll show you the stage. We've made quite a few changes to it since you last were on it."

She winced again. The last time she'd sung on the Grand stage seven years ago, she'd been too fried to hit a note, had forgotten lyrics left and right and had topped off the disaster by being booed offstage. Not one of her more stellar moments in her meteoric fall from grace.

"I'll be here first thing tomorrow. And Saul…thanks. For everything. This means the world to me."

He gave her his first genuine smile. "I'm counting on it, Silver Girl. If you don't fill the house every night, I'm gonna lose a fortune. Those British prima donnas would've sold a lot of tickets."

"Gee. No pressure there."

He quirked a pragmatic brow. "Music's a tough business. Art be damned—this is about dollar signs. You sure you want back in the game?"

She took a deep breath and answered, certain for the first time in a long time about something. "Yes. I'm sure. This is exactly what I want to do." The only thing in the world she wanted to do as much as be a mother was sing. Good Lord willing, she'd find a way to do both.

She let herself out of Saul's office, blissfully happy, and ran smack dab into a living wall of muscle. "Whoa, I'm sor—" she started. And then she looked up. *Austin Dearing.* "—Oh. It's you."

"If you want to play games with me, Miss Rothchild, I'm telling you now you're going to lose. Please don't try to ditch me again."

"I didn't try to—"

He cut her off. "I'd highly recommend never fibbing to me. I have an alarming tendency to turn into a serious bastard when I get lied to."

She muttered under her breath, "You're already there." Rather than stand around arguing with this mountain of a man, she turned and stalked back toward the casino. If he wanted to tag along, that was fine with her.

Austin tagged along all right. He was half tempted to jack her up against a wall by the shirt front and explain a thing or two to Miss Fancy Pants. She didn't seem to grasp that it was not part of his job description to chase around after his subjects like a puppy on a leash. She might be a celebrity, but her life now rested in his hands…not the other way around.

She barged out into the explosion of color and sound that was the casino's gambling floor, and his irritation intensified. The place was a security nightmare. Cut-throughs and niches were *everywhere,* and an assailant could be lurking in any of them. There was so much commotion in here that a guy like him couldn't possibly see a threat coming with his vitally important peripheral vision. Surely there was a way around the casino in a hotel this size. She needed to take an alternate route, dammit!

A low-level hum of panic vibrated in his gut. As a security man, this place made him feel like he'd already failed. Clamping down on the anxiety clawing its way up his spine, he lengthened his stride to catch up to Silver as they neared the front of the place. His impulse was to pick her up, throw her over his shoulder, and get her the hell out of here. Now. He exhaled carefully. *Must go easy on this particular client. Break her in gently to the idea of having a bodyguard, without alienating her if at all possible.*

"Hey, slow down," he murmured casually from just behind her. He needed to get in front of her, pronto!

She blatantly ignored him and continued marching on.

"I mean it, Silver. You need to move more slowly so I can clear the area in front of you for threats."

She spared him an irate glance over her shoulder and didn't even break stride.

His gaze narrowed. Several extremely unkind names for her flashed through his head. Fine. He could play that game, too.

He grabbed her by the arm and swung her around sharply to face him. She was a tiny little thing, and her weight was nothing in his hand. He took an aggressive step closer and glared down at her. "I tried to do this the nice way. But now we're gonna do it my way. I'm heading for the nearest exit and getting you under cover, and you're going with me whether you like it or not. Got that?"

She nervously eyed a cluster of people near the front entrance, most of whom wielded big cameras. "Don't make a fuss," she hissed.

"Too late," he retorted. "I'm making as big a fuss as I damn well feel like. And you are not going anywhere else in this hotel until I say so."

"I have to go see Stella. She's the head costume designer," she insisted. "She's expecting me."

"You're not seeing anybody until you and I get a few things straight," he replied grimly.

Her eyes snapped and sparks all but flew off her, singeing his fingertips.

She bit out, "Let's get *this* straight. I'm the boss. I say where I go and when, and you follow along like a good employee and do as you're told. You *don't* make public scenes in front of tabloid reporters—of which there are a dozen behind me, right now," her voice rose slightly in volume, "and you *don't* do anything to embarrass me. Got that?" She actually had the temerity to poke him in his chest for good measure.

He was so aggravated he could strangle her right then and there. He scowled down at her and loomed even more assertively. "I am *not* your employee. I work for your father. You're under my protection, and you'll damn well do what *I* tell *you* to do when I tell you to do it and how I tell you to do it. Have *you* got *that?*"

She blanched. "You and me—this is never going to work."

His jaw clenched. "I'm *entirely* inclined to agree with you."

If hate at first sight was possible, this was it. The woman drove him crazy, and he'd known her for two minutes.

He became aware of a surge of movement behind her. The paparazzi had apparently noticed their altercation and were closing in like a pack of hungry hyenas. He swore under his breath. Men in his line of work despised the press almost as much as the public figures they protected did. The last thing he needed was to have his face splashed all over the front pages of the tabloids.

"Let's get out of here," he muttered at Silver.

"Ya think?" she snapped back.

"Hey, Silver!" one of the reporters shouted. "Did you hear that the Tears of the Quetzal is in police custody?"

Another piped up. "Yeah. Luke Montgomery's fiancée found it in her purse. Do you believe that story?"

Austin frowned. What were these guys talking about? He opened his mouth to ask Silver, but just then, someone moved forward out of the crowd of reporters, jumping abruptly toward her. Austin registered dark hair and a black, burning gaze, a uniform of some kind. Something about the set of the man's shoulders, the intensity of concentration in his eyes set off warning bells in Austin's head. Time slowed as the guy lunged in Silver's direction, and Austin went into high threat mode. If he'd told his men once, he'd told them a thousand times, don't question your instincts. Act first. Ask questions later.

The guy lowered his shoulder and rammed it into Silver, spinning her around as their bodies collided. Hard. Dear God. The guy had an open shot at stabbing or shooting her at point-blank range in a vital organ! Austin went airborne, flinging himself full length through the air for Silver.

He wrapped his arms around her in a move worthy of the NFL. His momentum knocked her off her feet. While they were still airborne, he twisted to cover her with his much larger body. He released her at the last moment before they hit the floor, catching most of his body weight with his arms so he didn't crush her.

An explosion of flashbulbs went off nearby.

Austin twisted to look for the assailant, and the guy was rushing past, his right shoulder hunched to hide his face from Austin.

And then the strangest thing happened.

A wave of heat passed over Austin, a tangible thing tingling across his skin. He saw flashes of purple and green behind his eyelids, brilliant, jeweled prisms of color momentarily blinding him. His blood rushed, pounding in his ears until frantic thumping was all he heard. Suddenly he became intensely aware of the feminine softness below him, molding to every contour of his body as if she'd been made for him. Oh, yeah. A promise of sex, hot and sweaty enough to boggle the mind, pored off her.

Silver looked up at him, her gorgeous eyes wide with surprise, fear and something else. Something…aware. Of him. As a man.

Their gazes locked and nothing short of unbridled lust roared between them. All that friction of a few seconds ago had abruptly morphed into something so steamy it set him on fire. She looked ready to come apart in his hands. In fact, a moan slipped out of her throat that was all about raging pleasure. Unseen by the press, her hips undulated beneath his, and he realized his male flesh was so hard he was in danger of busting his trouser zipper.

He swore under his breath.

Her pupils dilated until her eyes were nearly black with raw need. He wasn't in any better shape, himself. Small problem: he was the bodyguard, and a whole bunch of cameras were very publicly recording every second of this.

"You okay?" he muttered.

She nodded, looking shell-shocked.

"I'll get up first, then I'll help you to your feet and pull you behind me. Keep my body between you and the photographers, okay?"

She nodded again.

He started a quick push-up when a voice shouted from nearby, "Get the hell off my girlfriend!"

Austin came smoothly to his feet and turned to face this new threat. A beefy guy a little shy of six feet tall was barreling toward them. Austin assessed the threat in an instant. More beer gut than muscle. Had barroom brawled just enough to think he was a hotshot, but lacked the balance of a trained fighter. This guy would use bluster and bullying to hide his actual lack of physical skill. A lot of noise, but not a lot of true threat.

Austin reached down and lifted Silver, as light as a feather, to her feet. He tucked her protectively against his side away from the cameras. The paparazzi had already turned their lenses on the loudmouth, and predictably, he was preening for them.

"Who the hell are you?" Austin growled.

"I'm Mark Sampson." Bluster Boy jabbed a finger toward Silver. "Her boyfriend. And take your hands off her, jerk wad."

Jerk wad? He hadn't been called that since junior high. Austin allowed his amusement to show on his face. Interestingly enough, Silver huddled more closely against his side, making no move to distance herself from him in front of this boyfriend of hers. Most women would be leaping away from another man, especially with a hotheaded idiot like that for a boyfriend.

Sampson bristled. "Get away from her before I make you do it."

A new round of flashes exploded. He could see the headline now. Brawl Over Pop Singer. He sighed. Seemed as if he was getting off on the wrong foot with everyone on this assignment. But Bubba could damned well come and try to make him unwrap his arm from Silver, who was now trembling beneath his protective hug.

"Please," she whispered frantically from beside him. "Don't make a scene."

As if they hadn't already made a big scene? But then he glanced down at her. Abject terror shone in her face. She was really scared. For him? Surely not. For Bubba? Maybe. But that didn't feel right, either. What then? Did this have to do with her sister's murder and the unspoken reasons he'd been hired to protect her in the first place?

He murmured under his breath, "For you, I won't kick this guy's ass right now. Let's get out of here, though."

"That'd be great," she murmured back gratefully.

He guided her toward the lobby. Or at least he started to guide her. Sampson stepped forward aggressively and blocked their way before they'd gone two steps. "Get your hands off my girl!"

Austin gave the guy a withering stare but spoke calmly enough. "I've been hired to protect Miss Rothchild. I'm not making a move on your lady, so relax already. You're making a scene and you're making Miss Rothchild uncomfortable."

If anything, Sampson got even redder in the face and swelled up into an even bigger bullfrog. "*I'm* her bodyguard! Now, for the last time, get away from her!"

Sampson reached up and grabbed Austin's hand, physically throwing it off Silver's shoulder. Were it not for the paparazzi eating this whole thing up, Austin would've ripped the guy's arm off then and there. But as it was, Silver threw him a panicked look, and he didn't have the heart to make her any more miserable than she already was.

He took a step away from her. But not before murmuring, "I'm going to go talk to the hotel security guys for a few minutes, and then I'll meet you at the costume lady's office. Don't leave the hotel without me, okay?"

She nodded, trust shining in her eyes. He didn't question it, nor did he examine too closely the surge of protectiveness that bubbled up in his chest. He just knew that something big had happened between them, lying together on the floor a few moments ago.

Sampson elbowed him aside, and Austin stepped back readily, without giving the guy the satisfaction of a response. The paparazzi closed in on Silver and Sampson like a pack of sharks in a feeding frenzy. Austin frowned. Sampson ought to be doing something to keep them back. It was a blatant breach of personal security to let that many strangers surround a subject so closely. But the guy seemed more interested in getting his own arm around Silver's shoulders and posing for pictures than in keeping his girlfriend safe. The pair stepped out onto the front steps of the casino and paused again for another round of pictures. Sampson seemed acutely aware of the best lighting and camera angles for the paparazzi and more than happy to give the press exactly what it needed.

Austin shook his head. Surely guarding celebrities wasn't that different from guarding heads of state. No matter how famous and camera-worthy a subject was, no self-respecting bodyguard let would their principal stand still in an exposed position like those steps for this long.

And why wasn't the guy's gaze scanning the area in search of possible threats at a minimum? Bubba was supposed to be her bodyguard! Silver actually looked eager to go…and if he wasn't mistaken, it was Sampson holding her back. No bodyguard would physically stop their subject to pose for the press! It was insane! What kind of training had this guy—

A fast-moving target hurtled out of the shadows off to one side of the lobby toward the front door.

Silver and Sampson had their backs to the attacker!

Austin lurched into motion, sprinting for all he was worth. But his heart sank even as his thighs churned frantically, propelling him forward. *He was too far away to save her.* Time slowed as the horror of an attack on his principal unfolded before him. He couldn't get between her and the attacker in time. Her beautiful eyes, her smile, her soft body beneath his flashed helplessly through his mind's eye.

He opened his mouth to scream at Sampson to throw himself on top of her.

But it was too late.

The deafening report of a gunshot exploded in the lobby.

Chapter 4

Silver froze as the world went mad around her. She registered a flash of motion. A shout of warning from behind. And then an explosion of noise so loud it made her teeth hurt. A giant sheet of glass crashed down a few feet behind her, showering her with shards of exploding glass.

People screamed and were running and ducking and falling everywhere. She didn't know what to do. Everyone around her melted away, leaving her standing all by herself in a sea of glass, marble and glittering chrome. The torrent of crystal prisms fell like rain around her, each with its own rainbow of slivered light trapped within it. *So pretty.* The thought floated through her head, completely detached from reality.

Mark was a dozen feet away, cursing at the top of his lungs. He was turning in circles, as if he was looking for somewhere to run and hide but couldn't decide which way to go.

And then something hit her from behind. It felt like a freight train had just slammed into her at seventy miles per hour. It drove her to the ground, face first, crushing her in darkness and suffocating weight. Panic struck her then. She couldn't breathe! She had to run! To get out of here, away from this insanity. To protect her baby!

"Let me up!" she tried to scream. It came out no more than a breathy gasp devoid of sound.

"Are you hit?" a deep voice asked sharply in her ear.

Austin. A wave of relief washed over her, so powerful and warm it nearly made her faint. "I don't think so."

He shouted from above her, "Sampson! Clear the lobby! Set up suppression around the exterior perimeter so the subject can be evacuated!"

"Huh?" Mark obviously didn't have the slightest idea what Austin had just told him to do.

Violent swearing erupted in her left ear, much of it dealing with Mark's questionably human parentage and complete lack of training. Then Austin was giving her instructions, urgent and low. "We're getting up and running like hell. We're gonna zigzag back and forth so the gunman has less of a shot at you."

Gunman? *Gunman?* Was that what that noise had been? A gunshot? Ohmigod.

"Let's go!" Austin bit out.

All of a sudden his bulk was gone, replaced by light and air and an awful sense of exposure that made her want to curl up in a little ball with her hands over her head and never move again. But then Austin was pulling at her, yanking her to her feet. She managed to stay vertical and keep up with his zigzagging run until they burst out from under the covered overhang into the blistering late afternoon sun. Austin paused, looking around quickly.

"Hey! Let go of her!"

Mark again.

"Give it up, Bubba. You don't know a damn thing about being a bodyguard. Get out of my way before you get your girlfriend killed. Let me do my job." Austin sounded like he'd about had it with Mark.

Austin was dragging her forward again, toward a long, black stretch limo parked on the far side of the sweeping circular drive.

"That's it, pretty boy!" Mark shouted. "You and me, right here, right now—"

"Shut the hell up, Sampson." And with that, Austin yanked open the back door of the limo and surprisingly gently pushed her inside. Her heel caught on the thick carpet and she stumbled, landing on her knees on the carpeted floor as something big blocked the light behind her. The door slammed shut, and yet again, Austin banged into her.

"Oomph," she grunted as she went down on her side.

The glass panel between them and the driver was sliding down. A pale, shocked face stared at them from under a chauffeur's cap.

"Get this car moving if you don't want to get shot!" Austin ordered the driver in a tone of command that brooked no disobedience. The vehicle lurched into motion violently, dumping Austin on the carpet beside her. Tires screeched, and the vehicle made a sharp turn before accelerating powerfully.

She blinked over at Austin, lying no more than a foot away from her. His eyes were green, a deep, shadowy shade like the darkest part of a forest. She said dryly, "We have to stop meeting on floors like this."

He grinned back at her. "I haven't been horizontal this many times with a woman without being in bed with her since…ever."

In bed with him? Whoa. Now there was a thought. A tingle of that same electric attraction that had about jolted her out of skin the first time he'd tackled her shot through her now.

His pupils dilated hard and fast. All of a sudden, his gaze went so black and hot she could hardly bear to look at him. Other details started to register. His arm, heavy and muscular, lay across the indentation of her waist. And his leg was thrown across hers. If she leaned forward just a little bit, she could cuddle up against that big, brawny chest of his. Her face would fit in the strong curve of his neck, and his shoulder would make a perfect pillow for her head. A lock of his hair had fallen across his forehead, and her fingers itched to reach up and push it away.

"Are you okay?" he asked so tenderly it made her heart ache a little.

"Yeah." And then an awful thought hit her. "Are *you* okay?" she blurted, alarmed. Her hands splayed across his chest of their own volition, searching frantically for injuries.

He grinned then, a lopsided thing oozing so much charm it ought to be illegal. "I'm fine. I'd have been glad to take that bullet for you but no, I'm not hit. Thanks for asking, though."

Her hands stopped, somewhere in the middle of all those acres of muscle. "Take a bullet for me?" she repeated blankly.

"Yes. I'm a bodyguard. It's what I do."

"Get shot?"

Another one of those lethal grins. "Well, the idea is to avoid either one of us getting shot in the first place, but if it comes down to you or me, it's my job to take the hit."

She shuddered at the thought of deadly lead slamming into this man and erasing that smile forever. "Don't take a bullet for me, okay?"

He drew her closer against him, and funny thing, she had no desire whatsoever to resist. That volcano of heat and lust that had erupted between them back in the casino exploded again, spewing steam and fire and molten images of sex with him all over the back of the limo. She'd been no saint in her day and had certainly partaken of meaningless sex just for the sake of it now and then. But never, ever, had she been bowled over by an attraction to any guy this instantaneous and this incendiary.

Her entire body felt liquid, flowing over and around him, seeking to engulf every inch of him. His arms tightened around her like tempered steel bands, and his desire rose to meet hers, towering every bit as powerfully as hers. For an instant, fear flooded through her. What had she unleashed between them? It was so big, so overwhelming, she wasn't entirely sure she could handle it. She looked up, and Austin was staring down at her, looking every bit as stunned as she felt. Well, that was something, at least. Somehow, the idea of him being blown away, too, calmed her.

She relaxed once more in his arms, her trust restored. This was not ops normal for him, either. Something gigantic *had* happened between them. She hadn't imagined it.

Wonder filling his dark gaze, he murmured, "I'll do my level best not to have to take a bullet for you. But rest assured, I will do it if necessary. I'll die for you."

The import of those simple words slammed into her like a boulder. She stared at him for a long time, trying to absorb what it truly meant. Finally she managed to mumble, "Nobody's ever said anything like that to me. Ever. Do you really mean it?"

His gaze locked with hers, as he clearly weighed what she'd just said. Was he trying to figure out if she was talking about other bodyguards, or about more? Much more. All of a sudden, she wasn't sure, herself, just how much she'd meant by the question.

He answered so low she almost didn't hear him over the sound of pavement beneath the tires. "Yeah. I *do* mean it."

Now, that definitely sounded as if he was talking about more than keeping her alive. And darned if her pulse didn't race even faster, her heart pounding even harder against her ribs.

He reached up to push a strand of white-blond hair out of her face. He whispered, "You're even more beautiful in person. And I've always secretly thought you were a knockout. Are you really real?"

Her breath caught in her throat. "I'm just a normal girl who's been lucky enough to live an extraordinary life."

He smiled as if he didn't quite believe her. If she didn't know better, she'd swear the guy was a little starstruck. "How 'bout you? Are you real? I thought superheroes only live in comic books."

His grin was a little unbalanced. "I'm just a regular guy who's been lucky enough to get some extraordinary training."

"I think there's more to you than that, Austin Dearing. A whole lot more."

"I could say the same of you, Silver Rothchild."

She gazed deep into his eyes. Shockingly, she didn't see deception. Not an iota of greed or social climbing or self-interest. Was this guy for real? Everyone always wanted something from her—money or fame or a leg up on an entertainment career. Was it possible that he liked her just for her? That all those sparks zinging back and forth between them were real?

A rumble of laughter vibrated deep in his chest. "I have a sinking feeling that you're going to lead me on a merry chase before this is all said and done."

She grinned up at him. "Sounds like fun."

He sighed, but the smile didn't quite leave his eyes. "If I'm going to do my job, we need to get a few things straight between us."

She couldn't resist. She snuggled her hips against his—and gasped at the feel of him, huge and hard between her thighs. "Everything feels straight to me."

He closed his eyes tightly for a moment. When he opened them, she was disappointed to see that he'd shifted into business mode. "I was trying to talk to you about the rules of engagement we're going to operate under when you kept running away from me."

"I wasn't running away from you!"

He quirked an all-too-knowing brow. "What would you call it?"

She replied defiantly, "Creative avoidance."

His crack of laughter inexplicably warmed her heart. She liked making this man happy. Wanted to get to know him better. To explore this thing between them. What was up with that? He was her father's lackey. She ought to hate his guts. But somewhere in the past five minutes, in the midst of their heated argument and diving for cover, something had changed between them. Radically. It was almost as if someone had waved a magic wand and cast a spell over the two of them. Talk about going from zero to sixty in two seconds flat…

Weird.

His arm lifted away from her waist. The movement felt reluctant, like he didn't want to let her go. That was lovely. He sat up and helped her twist around and sit up without coming out of her dress. And that was lovely, too. Considerate. Far too few people in her life showed her simple courtesy not because she was a rock star but because she was a human being.

She scowled at her dress as she gave the dowdy thing one last tug. It figured that she'd meet the man of her dreams the one day she was wearing something this goofy looking—her, the ultimate fashion diva, who never appeared anywhere without looking like the cover of the latest pop culture magazine. But her father had a cow whenever she wore anything even remotely sexy, and she hadn't wanted a fight with him at her birthday party. So she'd chosen this high-necked, long-hemmed, multilayered affair in a demure shade of pink.

"Shall we go for the gusto and actually try using the seats?" he asked wryly.

She felt her dimples pucker up. "If we're gonna hijack a limo, we may as well enjoy it before we go to jail."

He grinned. "Good point." He knocked on the glass partition, which had closed sometime during their exchange on the floor.

The chauffeur looked back at them in his rearview mirror. "We safe now?" the guy asked.

Austin nodded. "Yes, thanks to you. Mr. Rothchild's going to be very grateful that you saved his daughter's life."

The guy snorted. "Mr. Coddington's going to be very *not* grateful that I took off with his limo."

Silver knew Albert Coddington. She jumped in, waving a casual hand. "Albert's a dear. Once he knows what happened, he'll be delighted to have helped."

The driver muttered, "Maybe. But Mrs. Coddington sure won't like having to wait for her ride."

Silver laughed. "I give Mrs. Coddington-Number-Five six more months before she's outta there. No need to worry about her. Albert's determined to be just like Henry VIII, and he has one more wife to go."

Austin's gaze swiveled to hers. "The man's had five wives? What's wrong with him?"

She grinned at him. "He has a weakness for gold diggers and gets suckered, like clockwork, every ten years. But give the guy credit for style. The current Mrs. Coddington is younger than I am. By a lot."

"You're not exactly an old lady."

She shrugged. "It's not like I can lie to you about my age. After all, you met me at my birthday party."

"You'll like being thirty—"

She cut him off. "Don't tell me my thirties will be my best decade yet. I made a pact with myself that I'd murder the next person who said that to me."

He shrugged. "Okay, how 'bout this? My thirties have been great to me so far. Wouldn't trade 'em for the world. I hope yours are the same for you."

"I'll let you know in six weeks," she replied ruefully.

"What happens in six weeks?"

She opened her mouth to tell him about her upcoming gig at the Grand, when the driver spoke from up front. "Sir, when do you want me to head back to town? We're gonna have to turn around now or go straight for about a fifty miles and get gas before we turn around."

Austin frowned. "Let's head back to town. Does the Grand have a private entrance?"

Silver and the driver answered simultaneously, "Yes."

Austin looked over at her. "I forgot. You grew up there, didn't you?"

Indeed, she had. She was plenty familiar with the underground loading dock for the many deliveries it took to keep the Grand running. Rather than have trucks constantly clog the busy streets around the hotel, they unloaded underneath it, out of sight and out of the way. Which also made for an ideal entry for celebrities in search of privacy—or safety.

"We'll have to call ahead to use it. Security's very tight down there," she said. "Particularly in the late afternoon. The casino gets its shipments of cash in at about this time of day."

Austin pulled out his cell phone. "What's your dad's personal phone number?"

She rattled off the number and Austin dialed it quickly. She listened unabashedly.

"Hi, sir. This is Austin Dearing. I wanted to report that your daughter is unhurt and with me…that's correct…what are the police saying about the shooting? Any trace of the gunman?" Austin listened a long time, then commented dryly, "With all due respect, sir, that Bubba who calls himself her bodyguard doesn't know his nose from his ass. You made an exceedingly wise decision to hire me."

Silver's jaw dropped. Mark would go ballistic if he heard Austin say something like that! Everybody knew to tiptoe around his hair-trigger temper. She thought she heard tinny laughter emanating from Austin's phone.

"We'll be arriving at the underground entrance of your hotel in…driver, how long till we're back at the Grand?"

"Twenty minutes, sir."

"…in twenty minutes. Right. Thanks. No sweat." Austin pocketed his phone.

She liked to think of it as healthy inquisitiveness, but nosiness was one of her greatest weaknesses. She liked to know everything that was going on around her. When Austin made no comment, her curiosity quickly got the best of her. "So, what did my father say?"

"He'll have someone waiting at the gate for us."

She huffed. "No. About the shooting? Did the police catch the guy?"

"No."

"Who was he shooting at? Was anyone hurt? C'mon, Austin. Gimme the scoop."

Amusement glinted in his green gaze. "I don't need the police to tell me the gunman was shooting at you. I saw the guy make his move. And, no, no one was seriously hurt. Some guests and staff have cuts and bruises from twisted ankles and falling glass."

She was still stuck on his first sentence. "The gunman was shooting at *me?* Are you sure?"

That earned her an annoyed look. "Yes, I'm sure. It's what I do, remember?"

"How do you know?"

He sighed. "I saw the gunman dart out of hiding and pull out his weapon. He timed his move for when Bubba had stepped away from you to give the cameras his best profile. He really is a jerk, you know."

"The shooter or Mark?"

Austin grinned. "Both of them."

She rolled her eyes. The guy was trying very hard not to be informative with her. She prompted him again. "Then what did the gunman do?"

Austin crossed his arms. "He took aim at you with a large-caliber handgun and fired. One thing we know about him—he's a crappy shot. He should have nailed you cold. Any eighteen-year-old raw recruit could make that kill."

"Well, thank God for small favors," she replied dryly.

He glanced over at her. "Seriously. It tells us a lot about the guy. If he were a professional hit man you'd be dead. This guy's an amateur with something personal against you. Can you think of anyone who might want to kill you? Maybe get revenge for some past wrong?"

She frowned hard, not liking the turn this conversation was taking one little bit.

"Any old boyfriends you had ugly breakups with? Anyone you crossed swords with during your career? Anyone who might feel slighted by your success?"

She gifted him with an annoyed look of her own. "Yes to all of the above. Times about a hundred. In case you didn't know it, my former singing career was…slightly tumultuous."

He laughed. "The way I hear it, that's an extreme understatement."

Sometimes it got really old having a public past like hers to live down. With a long-suffering sigh, she replied, "There you have it. The list of people who want to see me dead is long and distinguished. Take your pick of who the gunman could be."

For a moment sympathy shone in his eyes. But then his gaze went flinty hard. "Never fear, honey. I'll figure out who he is and take the bastard out. Nobody shoots at someone I'm responsible for and lives to tell about it."

She sank deeper into the plush seat, taken aback at his abrupt shift of mood. Maybe Mark was the one who ought to be worrying about ticking this man off, and not the other way around.

"What's the Tears of the Quetzal?" he asked abruptly.

"It's a diamond. It's set into a ring, and my father calls it his most prized possession." As Austin quirked a skeptical eyebrow, she added, "It's a super-rare stone that changes color. It's called a chameleon diamond. When you heat it up it changes from violet to green."

"Cool." A pause. "Why do the police have it?"

She sighed. "Candace borrowed or stole it—depending on who you talk to—the night she was murdered. The ring was gone when her body was found."

Austin's face lit up. "So if the cops have the ring, maybe that means they've got a lead on her killer."

Silver replied fervently, "I hope so. That would be great news."

"Yeah, but if the police are closing in on her killer, the guy's probably hiding or on the run."

His question sobered her sharply. "I dunno."

"No idea at all?" he asked.

"Nope. None."

Austin went silent, tugging absently at his left ear and staring out the window broodingly. She didn't interrupt his thoughts, whatever they might be. She'd like to think a little of his steely resolve to keep her safe had to do with their two intimate exchanges, but that was probably wishful thinking. Now that she was sitting up in her own seat, not in physical contact with him, the crazy attraction of before seemed a little hard to believe. She'd been scared and high on adrenaline and had overreacted. Yeah, that was it. Her temporarily heightened senses explained it.

But they didn't explain the thick sludge of disappointment that abruptly chugged through her veins. It had been an amazing feeling while it lasted.

A few minutes later the driver swung smoothly past the Grand's acres of swimming pool and tennis courts and into the black maw of a gated entrance that looked like it led to a parking garage.

Before their rear fender had barely cleared the entrance, a reinforced steel gate was already sliding closed behind them. Darkness closed in. The limo spiraled down a long ramp, and then light flared ahead. She spied a familiar silhouette and started. Her father was down here personally to meet them? Either she was in big trouble for her display to the press, or Austin was about to get fired.

Reluctantly she reached for her door handle. Time to face the music.

A big, warm palm clamped down lightly over her hand. "Lesson number one in being a good protectee. Never get out of the car first. I will always get out before you and have a look around. Please don't come out until I tell you it's safe. Ever. Got it?"

She looked up at him, startled. Mark had never made her go through any routine like that. "So you're pretty much always going to be a gentleman and get my door for me? I think I can get used to that."

That killer grin of his flashed briefly, then was replaced by an expression more akin to sympathy. He seemed to understand that she was joking about this security procedure to hide her dismay at the seriousness of the situation.

His finger brushed her temple, pushing back that pesky strand of hair again, and then the quick, light touch was gone. But the earthquake it left behind continued to shudder through her for several long seconds. Whoa. No adrenaline heightened senses could explain away that.

Eventually her breathing restarted as she stared at the back of his head. Who was this guy whose casual touch made her all but orgasmic?

"Here we go," he muttered.

As advertised, Austin stepped out of the vehicle and paused directly in front of the door. Heck, she couldn't have gotten out even if she'd wanted to. It did, however, give her an excellent and isolated view of his buns. Tight. Muscular. Made for driving into a woman strongly enough to know she was with a man—

Good grief! She had to get control of herself! Heat climbed her cheeks just as he murmured, "Okay, you can come out."

Her heart all but palpitating, she took the hand he offered and climbed out of the limo. Sheesh. She was a mess.

Her father exclaimed, "How'd you get her to do what she's told like that? I've been trying for twenty years and never got her to behave."

Without stopping to think, she snapped, "He said please."

She wasn't in the habit of sassing her father—she never won and it wasn't worth the hassles to follow. But it had been a rough day. She braced herself, waiting for his explosion. But today Harold made no comment at all. Which was testament to just how upset he must be over the shooting.

She was stunned when he merely turned to Austin and said quietly, "I suppose it goes without saying that I'm grateful to you for pulling my little girl out of there."

Her jaw dropped. Her father never said things like that! She frequently wasn't at all sure he actually felt softer emotions like love or concern for his family.

Harold passed a small white object to Austin. "Your room key."

Austin nodded his thanks. "You understand that nobody is to

know that she's with me. Nobody. The staff can just think that I eat like a horse and like to make my own bed for a few days."

Harold nodded. "It's taken care of."

"And maybe you could thank Mr. Coddington for letting us commandeer his limo like that."

Harold grinned. "I know just the thing. I'll give the guy a fat stack of thousand dollar chips, which he'll promptly lose back to me at the tables."

Silver snorted. That was vintage Harold. Give someone a generous gift that he knew was going to come right back to him. But then he did surprise her by pulling out his wallet, extracting a thick wad of hundred dollar bills and handing them to the limo driver. "Here's a small token of my appreciation for helping save my daughter's life."

Silver stared as the driver stammered his thanks. Well, knock her over with a feather!

Austin said, "Oh, and one more thing, Mr. Rothchild," Austin said. "Fire that Sampson guy. He's worthless as a bodyguard."

Harold grimaced. "Believe me, I'd get rid of him if I could. But I don't employ the guy. You'll have to take that up with Silver. He works for her."

Austin's eyebrows shot up, but he made no comment to her. She got the distinct feeling they were going to converse more on the subject very soon, however.

While Austin steered her toward the elevator, she chewed on her father's vehement comment about Mark. She'd had no idea Harold disliked him that much. Why hadn't her father said something to her about it before now? Although, to be brutally honest with herself, if she'd known it would tick off her father, she might have made the relationship with Mark real just to get her father's goat.

Maybe Harold wasn't as dense as she thought he was. Maybe he'd finally learned not to push on the subject of her boyfriends and let her discover their schmuck-like qualities for herself. And they always turned out to be schmucks in the end. The sad fact was she had terrible taste in men. It was why she'd taken the drastic measures she had to have a baby.

As the elevator door slid shut, Austin called, "Thank you for your help, Mr. Rothchild." Examining both sides of his plastic key, he asked, "Where's my room?"

"Lemme see." She took the card and turned it over. Wow. The New Yorker villa. It was one of the Grand's four incredibly swanky penthouses that shared the roof of the forty story tall hotel. "You've got one of the penthouses. You put your key card in this slot to activate the elevator to the top floor." She demonstrated, and then passed the key back to him. With a quiet, powerful whoosh, the elevator shot upward.

The metal encased space took on a heavy silence she had no interest in disturbing. At some point, Austin was going to start asking her questions—lots of them—and not a one of them was going to be easy to address.

The door opened on a quiet, oak paneled hallway lit by lamps on console tables. Fresh flower arrangements and thickly padded carpeting added to the overall ambience of European style.

"Let me guess. You want to get out of the elevator first, too," she mused.

"Fast learner," he murmured as he stepped out and took a hard look around.

"Your suite's the one to the left."

He nodded and gestured for her to follow. He all but ran down the hall, and for a man as tall as him, that was really moving. She had to break into a jog to keep up. Note to self: wear flats around this guy. She would only come up to his armpit that way, but at least she wouldn't be forced to run in heels.

Austin hustled her into the suite and closed the door quickly behind them. His mental sigh of relief was nearly audible. She knew the feeling. The last hour had been a heck of a ride. Literally. Man, she was getting old. There was a time when this amount of excitement wouldn't have fazed her. But now, the danger and racing around in fear for her life were simply exhausting.

A single thought exploded across her mind. *I'm pregnant.*

She really shouldn't be doing crazy stuff like getting shot at anymore. Her wild days were, indeed, officially over. Now, they just had to convince an unnamed gunman of that fact.

"You hungry?" Austin called from the far side of the living room. He'd been looking carefully out of each of the floor to ceiling windows—probably checking for snipers or something.

Actually, she was vaguely nauseous. "Not really. You?"

"Starving. Adrenaline always makes me hungry."

"Typical man."

"Honey, I'm a lot of things, but typical isn't one of them."

She grinned over at him. "I gather modesty isn't on your list of major attributes, either."

He shrugged. "I call it as I see it, darlin'."

"Want me to order up a steak for you from Room Service? The prime rib here is to die for if you're a carnivore." She started to reach for the phone, and Austin moved to her side so fast he was practically a blur.

He snatched the phone out of her hand. "*Nobody's* to know you're here. As of now, you're officially in hiding."

A moment's relief at the idea of being safe gave way to dawning horror. "Small problem, big guy. I don't have *time* to hide. I have only six weeks to pull together the show of my life."

He scowled down at her. "Sorry. Not happening. What part of 'someone just tried to kill you' didn't you get?"

Chapter 5

Silver stared up defiantly at him. Taking temporary precautions in case her sister's killer tried to harm her was one thing but screwing up the rest of her life by ruining her comeback was another thing entirely.

He had to be wrong about someone from her past coming after her. Sure, she'd stepped on a lot of toes in her early days. But that had been a long time ago. Anyone who'd had it in for her had had more than enough time to get even with her before now. And as for Candace's killer? Her stepsister had made plenty of her own enemies through hard and selfish living. Besides, the past several years her path and Candace's had barely crossed. Silver had a very hard time believing that she and Candace shared any enemy in common. Yeah, there'd been a shooting downstairs, but incidents like that weren't unheard of in this town. Gambling did funny things to people.

Austin pulled at his ear again, looking impatient. But he said evenly enough, "What exactly do you think happened in the lobby?"

"We were in the wrong place at the wrong time. Nothing more. Somebody snapped under heavy gambling losses or got ditched by one of our showgirls."

"Silver, I'm not just your run-of-the-mill bodyguard. I guard heads of state. I train the people who guard heads of state. I'm one of the top personal security experts in the entire world. And I'm telling you that shooter was aiming for you."

She sat down heavily on the nearest sofa as she reluctantly acknowledged the possibility that he might be right. "But… why?"

"That's what you and I are going to figure out."

"How?" she pressed.

"You're going to tell me everything about your life, and I'm going to develop a list of people who might want to see you dead."

Everything? She had no intention of telling this man everything about herself! She said lightly, "If you want to know *everything,* it's going to take a while."

He looked around the suite. "We've got nothing but time, kiddo. You and I aren't going anywhere anytime soon."

"About that. I've got things I have to do. Urgent, time sensitive things that can't wait."

"Like what?"

"Well, I never made it to Stella's office today."

"The costume lady?"

"Don't let her hear you call her that. Her client list is a who's who of the entertainment industry."

He looked unimpressed. "I suppose I can arrange a meeting for you with her in the next few days. I'll scout out a secure route to get you down to see her. What other meetings were you hoping to have?"

"I told Saul I'd take a look at the stage tomorrow morning. Then, I'll have to meet with executives from my old record label, the set designer, choreographers, the Grand's band leader. I need to audition and hire backup singers and dancers, start rehearsals, do costume fittings, press conferences, publicity appearances—"

"Whoa, whoa, whoa. What are you talking about?"

"My father gave me a one-week headliner gig here at the Grand for my birthday. The show's in six weeks. It's going to take scrambling every waking minute between now and then to get it ready."

"I'm sorry. I can't approve it."

She stared. Closed her hanging jaw. And then laughed in patent disbelief. "I'm not asking for your permission, Austin."

His dark gaze drilled into her. "That's good, because you don't have it."

"I don't need it. I turned thirty years old today, remember? I'm an adult. I can do what I want."

"I am responsible for your safety. And that gives me the final say over what you do and don't do."

Outrage at his high-handedness surged through her. "Do you tell the president of the United States what to do like this?"

"I'm not in the Secret Service. But if I were assigned to his security detail, I most certainly could—and would—tell him what to do regarding his security. I tell foreign princes and prime ministers what to do all the time."

Panic threatened to choke her. He had to stay out of her way! This show was incredibly important. Everything rode on it! If she got her career going again, she'd never have to worry about financial security for herself or her child, let alone the fact that singing was in her blood. She couldn't imagine her life without it.

"Why don't you go back to work for some foreign dignitary and quit bugging me?" she snapped.

A pained shadow crossed his features. "Sorry. You're stuck with me."

"I'll call my father and have him fire you."

"By all means, make the call. I have no interest in working with someone who's got a death wish. With this attitude, you won't last a week—even with me here to guard you. You're dead already."

The stark words stopped her cold. Dead? Her? But…she was going to have a baby! She finally had something truly important to live for! Her fury drained away as suddenly as it had exploded. She wandered over to the plate glass windows and, hugging herself, gazed out at the glittering skyline. Night was falling. How could a place as hot as Las Vegas look so cold? And why did this have to be so bloody hard?

She took a deep breath and let it out slowly. Without turning around, she said, "I'm sorry I snapped at you. I'm under a lot of pressure, but I have no right to take it out on you." She would have in the old days. Heck, maybe she was finally growing up a little, after all. She continued doggedly, "There has to be a way for me to get my work done and still let you do your job. What do I have to do to make that happen?"

He spoke from so close behind her she about leaped out of her skin. "Have dinner with me, and let's talk it over."

She ventured a glance back at him. His jaw rippled as he stared out over her shoulder into the night, his gaze roving constantly, always seeking, always testing for threats. Lord, he was attractive. There was something incredibly sexy about having a man like him—a warrior in his prime—totally focused on her and her well-being.

Behind them, a quiet knock sounded on the hallway door.

"Into the bedroom," he ordered her under his breath.

As Austin closed the door on her, she murmured, "Have the waiter lay out supper by the pool. It's beautiful out there, and there's a privacy wall so you can skinny-dip."

Her last sight of him before the door shut was his eyebrows quirking. It dawned on her what she'd said, and her face exploded with heat.

"You can come out now."

That was Austin's rich baritone. If he put his diaphragm behind that voice, she'd bet he wasn't a half-bad singer. The door opened, and his tall silhouette completely filled the door frame. She breathed a sigh of relief. Since when had she turned into such a thunder chicken? Oh, yeah. When she heard she was going to have a baby and someone tried to kill her.

She followed him outside onto the elegant, Zen-inspired pool deck. The simple granite block walls, oiled teak decking and spare bamboo plantings soothed her. The pool sparkled like a turquoise jewel beneath the descending blanket of night. It was still close to ninety degrees, but the temperature was dropping fast. In another hour, she'd need a sweater.

Austin frowned down at the linen-covered table. "There's only one place setting."

She shrugged. "I'll take the salad fork and the dessert spoon, and you can have the rest."

He grinned. "All I really need is a sharp knife. If you know your way around a blade, you can skin and carve just about anything."

She shuddered in mock horror. "That sounds so…carnivorous."

"You wimp."

She nodded firmly. "Yup, that's me. I like a steak well enough, but I don't need any reminder of where it came from."

He shrugged. "I can't tell you how many times I've had to hunt and kill my supper. You get used to it if the alternative is starving."

She examined him closely. "You don't look like a cold-blooded killer."

Without comment, Austin fetched a second dining chair from inside and held it for her. Smiling up at him, she sank down into it. For an instant, his eyes glowed back with a heat that was anything but restrained and gentlemanly. She blinked, and the look was gone. Had she imagined that?

Still standing over her, he asked quietly, "So tell me, Silver. What exactly does a cold-blooded killer look like?"

"I dunno. Just…not you."

"In my experience, the sheep and the wolves all look pretty much the same. The key is to trust no one. Then nobody can sucker you."

"That's a pretty cynical view of the world," she murmured.

"Call me cautious. Comes with the job."

Wow. That was a pessimistic take on life. It was completely

unlike her own positive and generally trusting opinion of her fellow man. "How do you manage to make friends or have faith in anyone with an attitude like that?"

"I trust the guys in my unit."

"No one else?" she probed.

"My boss. The support team for my unit."

"And?"

He frowned down at her. "Who else do I need?"

"What about women? Do you have any girlfriends or just simple female friends?"

"There aren't many women in my field."

"Don't you have *any* friends or social acquaintances outside of your work? Family that you're close to?"

He frowned. "No. And no, I don't feel I'm lacking anything in my life because of it."

As exasperating as her own big, messy, extended family could be, she couldn't imagine life without them. And although admittedly fewer these days, she couldn't imagine life without her friends' laughter and gossip…acceptance and understanding. "You're missing out on what makes life most worth living."

He crossed his arms defensively. "You have your measure of worth in life, and I have mine. I believe in honor, duty and country. I serve those three things above all else. And before you accuse me of being brainwashed, let me add that I do it freely and derive deep satisfaction from it."

"You're an odd duck, Austin Dearing." She'd never met a man who actually put something like honor above his own well-being. Oh, she'd met plenty of guys who talked the talk, but this guy walked the walk. She didn't know whether to eye him with new caution or new respect. Either way, he was an anomaly in her experience with men.

As he slid into his seat, his knee rubbed intimately against hers. Her breath hitched as his leg jerked away. *Drat.* She'd rather liked the contact, and it was disappointing that he didn't seem to share her attraction.

"Sorry," he mumbled.

"Don't apologize," she replied quickly. In a desperate bid not to sound quite so desperate, she added lamely, "It's nice of you to share your supper with me."

He shot her a sidelong grin that all but melted her insides. "In my experience, hungry women are grumpy women. When in doubt, feed 'em, I say."

She laughed and reached for a fork. And immediately encountered a problem. Neither the steak nor the lobster was cut into bite-sized pieces, and he'd already picked up the only knife.

Austin grinned down at her. "Need me to cut up your meat, oh squeamish female consumer of meat products?"

"It's either that or I'm picking up the whole steak and gnawing at it with my teeth. This squeamish girl is *hungry*." It had hit her all of a sudden, but she'd gone from nauseous to ravenous sometime in the last sixty seconds or so.

He cut off a bite-sized chunk of the juicy, pink beef and held it toward her with his fork. She realized he was waiting for her to open her mouth. He fed her the succulent prime rib, and flaming heat reddened her cheeks. Next, he held out a piece of lobster. She had no choice but to open her mouth quickly or else drip butter all over her dress. There was something so personal about him feeding her supper like this. So…intimate.

A little freaked out by how fast they were becoming so *involved* with each other, she slid her chair around to the far side of the table to face him. A pair of candles flickered between them, casting a dance of light and shadow across his rugged features. It struck her yet again what a handsome man he was. Exasperating in the extreme at times, but definitely easy on the eye.

He glanced up at her. As if he'd captured her very thought, he murmured, "The candlelight is good to you."

Son of a gun if her face didn't get even hotter. She mumbled, "Candles hide a multitude of flaws. They're good to all women."

"Trust me, you didn't need the help to begin with. Maybe you should do your show by candlelight. You wouldn't have to worry about what the stage looks like that way."

She laughed. "That's a great idea."

"Why not do something simple? Maybe just you and a spotlight."

"I'm known for big productions. Elaborate stage sets, a bunch of dancers, fireworks."

He shrugged. "I mostly listen to my favorite singers over the radio. I never see 'em. Seems to me a concert should be about great music and not all that other stuff."

She gave him a thoughtful look. It actually was an interesting concept. A one-woman show. Just her and the music. No bells and whistles. One thing she knew for sure—it would be a complete departure from her past image.

"Want some of this cake?" Austin asked. "It looks like German chocolate."

Usually, she loved the Grand's version of the smooth milk chocolate cake, smothered in a rich butter frosting crammed with fresh-grated coconut. But tonight, the idea of all that gooey, über-sweet richness made her stomach churn. Great. Did she have to start feeling pregnant already? She reminded herself quickly to embrace the burbling nausea. It was all part and parcel of the miracle growing inside her.

"What were you just thinking about?" Austin asked.

She glanced up, startled. "Why do you ask?"

"Your face…glowed…all of a sudden."

Yikes. She was going to have to be careful around other people if she was going to keep her secret. "Uh, nothing. I'm just relieved you're willing to work with me. This show means the world to me."

"Why?"

"Are you by any chance familiar with any of my past?"

"I've seen what was in the newspapers," he answered noncommittally.

"You mean the tabloids?"

"Well, yeah. For a few years there, you were hard to miss in the grocery checkout line."

She sighed. "I wasn't nearly as wild as the tabloids said, but the things they published weren't entirely lies, either. I did a real number on my career and my life when I was too young and stupid to know what I had. I've been laying low for the past seven years, trying to regain a little privacy."

"It didn't look like that was going too well today in the casino. The paparazzi were all over you."

"They heard us arguing and smelled a story. And then when Mark showed up, they saw a love triangle and went into a feeding frenzy."

"Speaking of Bubba, what possessed you to hire him as your bodyguard? He's an idiot."

She chewed on her lower lip. Privately, she had to agree with him. But Mark was supposed to be her boyfriend, and she couldn't very well admit he was an idiot. She settled for mumbling, "He had a résumé."

"He lied."

"Why do you say that?"

"He didn't have the faintest clue what to do today when bullets started flying. Then, he committed the mortal bodyguarding sin. He left your side. Failed to use his body to protect you. He should've stuck to you like glue. Instead he ran around screaming like a woman."

"Okay, so he probably doesn't have any formal training. Truth be told, my sister, Candace, recommended him to me."

"And she was some sort of security expert, I gather? That's why she's dead, right?"

Silver flinched at that.

He swore under his breath. "I'm sorry. That was out of line." He reached over and laid his hand on top of hers. "I've been out in the field with a bunch of soldiers for way too long. I don't stop and think about what I say like I should. I'm sorry your sister died. I shouldn't have spoken ill of her."

Silver shrugged. "Why not? She was mostly a bitch and a bully. Being dead doesn't change that."

Austin blinked, clearly taken aback. Then he said noncommittally, "I've always wondered about people's tendency not to be honest about the dead, no matter how flawed they were in life."

She sighed. "Apparently, it's time to air some of that past history you're dying to hear all about. Candace and Natalie are my twin stepsisters. Well, they were until Candace died."

"How are you related to them?"

"Their mother was Harold's first wife. She died from complications during their younger sister Jenna's birth. My mother was his second wife. Mom and Harold got married when I was about ten years old."

Austin nodded. "And how did they feel about you coming into their lives?"

"They were jealous of the attention Harold paid to me. I wasn't his blood daughter and they were. It only got worse as we got older. Sometimes I wonder if he played us off against each other. It would be his style."

"Why do you say that?"

"He believes in jungle rules. Survival of the fittest. He wouldn't hesitate to pit his daughters against each other to see who came out standing and who buckled under the pressure."

"Who blinked first among you three?"

She sighed. "I did."

"But you're the rich and famous celebrity of the three of you."

"I was well down the road to self-destruction when I bailed out on the fast life. Natalie bailed out next. But Candace never slowed down. She was wild till the end. She'd use anyone or anything to get her way. You should have seen how she used her kids…"

Faced with the prospect of becoming a mother herself, she didn't understand how Candace could've treated her sons the way she had, ignoring them when they were inconvenient and using them like pawns to squeeze money from her father.

"Tell me more about how it was between you and your sisters."

"When Harold put a lot of money and backing behind my career, they resented that. In retrospect, I see how Candace in particular set out to sabotage me. She led me into the heavy Hollywood party scene, introduced me to booze and drugs and hooked me up with a whole lot of people who were lousy for both me and my career."

Austin's expression was unreadable. But at least it didn't contain outright condemnation.

"In my sister's defense, I was gullible. I didn't have to go along with any of it. At the end of the day, what happened to my career—to my life—was my fault."

He made a sound of acknowledgment. Leave it to a military man like him not to make any attempt to let her off the hook. She appreciated his forthright worldview, even if it did sting her in the crossfire.

She continued grimly, "If you're looking for people I pissed off with my success in all fairness, you'd have to put those two at the top of the list."

"Except now Candace is dead."

"Yeah, and Natalie's totally past her resentment of me. In fact, we've grown a lot closer since Candace's death." She smiled proudly. "She's a cop now, you know."

That made Austin start. "How does Harold feel about that?"

"About like you'd think. That it's too blue-collar for his daughter and it's beneath a Rothchild. But she seems to really like it, and she's good at it." Silver stirred her ice water with her finger, chasing a stray cube around the glass. "Matt—he's her fiancé—was a godsend. He really helped center her. But truth be told, since Candace died, she's changed. It's as if losing Candace was a wake-up call for her to truly appreciate her life and her family."

"Are you positive Natalie's not behind the attacks on you? As a cop, she certainly has access to resources and people who could come after you."

Her gaze jerked up in surprise. "Not a chance. Not Nat. We're sisters, blood kinship or not. And besides, she's too direct for all these sneak attacks. They're not her style." She added ruefully, "If Natalie wanted to kill someone, she'd do it herself."

Austin nodded. "I have to agree. Tampered brakes…shooting ambush…those don't feel like sibling rivalry gone bad."

"Mark thinks it's a stalker fan."

"Wow. An intelligent thought from the Neanderthal. Who'd have guessed he had one in him?"

She sighed. "At least he's good at keeping the photographers away."

Austin snorted. "Like today? Hell, he was posing for them more than you were. He did his damnedest to draw them to you."

She blinked, surprised. "He did not—"

"Think about it. Who shouted and turned the whole thing into a big scene? Who made threats and slapped my hand off your shoulder?"

She studied him in the dim light. "You could just be saying that to cover your butt for your part in the incident."

He took a slow, appreciative sip from his glass of wine. She noted with interest that, although he'd been sipping at the wine steadily through the meal, the level of the liquid in his glass had only gone down by about an inch. "Are you always this suspicious?" he asked.

"You get a little jaded when you've lived a life like mine."

He studied her for a long moment. "Fair enough. And for the record, I have no reason to push blame onto Bubba. I'm man enough to fess up if I screw up."

She believed him on that one. He'd been much more restrained than she'd expected him to be in the face of Mark's truculence. Speaking of Mark. It was strange that he hadn't been trying like crazy to call her. He was fond of micromanaging every last detail of her life if she let him.

She pulled out her cell phone to see if it was turned on. Yup, and the battery indicator said it was fully charged. That was really strange. Not that she minded the break from him, though. She hadn't realized what a relief it would be to be away from his overbearing presence until he was gone.

No way could she ever actually get involved with him the way he was pushing her to do. The guy drove her around the bend. He actually had the temerity to tell her that a 'little woman' like her couldn't raise a baby on her own. The rugrat needed a daddy. Like him. As if he was actually a viable candidate for parenthood. The very thought made her cringe.

When she'd asked him to help her out with her baby plan, she hadn't known him like she did now. Candace had said he was "cool" and "knew the score." And fool that she was, she'd believed her stepsister. Candace said he was the kind of guy who would scratch your back if you scratched his. Except he'd decided that he wanted to scratch her back literally, and he'd been furious when Silver refused to enter into a real relationship with him.

She'd been crystal clear in her requirements, and he'd agreed to them up front. It was only later that he'd tried to change the rules of the game on her. She could smell a gold digger at a hundred paces, and he was double-dog, big time after a piece of her fame and fortune.

She sipped at a club soda in silence while Austin took his time finishing the cake.

With a satisfied sound, he laid down his fork. "For what it's worth, I did my best to avoid provoking Bubba this afternoon. Not that I didn't want to deck him. He really is a deserving jerk. But you were already upset, and I didn't want to make it any worse for you."

Austin had been worried about her feelings? That was a first for the men in her life. Most of the people who surrounded her were takers, always asking what she could do for them, not the other way around. Unfamiliar warmth suffused her at his consideration.

Her gaze faltered as he looked back at her steadily. Good

Lord. He'd see right through her to the ridiculous crush she was fast developing on him. Abashed, she mumbled awkwardly, "Call him Bubba to his face and he'll deck you."

Austin let out a snort that spoke volumes. "He can try to lay a hand on me, but he'll fail. Besides, Bubba's a far sight better than the other names I've come up with for him. Wanna hear a few?"

"No," she laughed. Frankly, Bubba fit him just fine. She dared not voice the opinion aloud, though. After all, Bub—Mark—was supposed to be her boyfriend.

"What can I say to convince you to fire him?" Austin asked seriously.

"Nothing. I'm not going to fire him."

"Why the hell not?" Austin sounded ready to get all worked up again.

She laid her napkin beside her plate and stood up. Stars dusted the sky overhead, and the silence was deep and dark around her. She wandered over to the edge of the pool. On impulse, she kicked off her shoes and sat down on the rough granite coping, dangling her feet in the inviting water.

"Wanna go for a swim?" Austin asked.

"I don't have a bathing suit."

A chuckle. "Don't let that stop you. You were right. This is a perfect spot for skinny-dipping."

The old Silver—or rather the young Silver—would've taken him up on that dare in a second. She missed that girl. She'd lived life with gusto and hadn't second-guessed her decisions, hadn't lived in fear of paparazzi or headlines. She'd done what made her feel good. Over the years, she'd learned to have a care for hurting other people with her impulses, and that was probably a good thing. But somewhere along the way, all the fun had been ground right out of her. Darn it, she wanted some of it back before her fortieth birthday snuck up on her in shades of gray and boring.

She stared at Austin in one last second of indecision. And then she grinned at him…and slid into the water.

Its pleasantly cool embrace felt amazing against her skin. The spontaneity of it felt even better. She hadn't done anything remotely like this in years. Her skirt floated around her like a pink lily pad. She submerged, dragging it down with her until it was a sodden mess around her legs.

She'd done it. She'd taken back a tiny piece of herself. And she had Austin Dearing to thank for it. He challenged her like no man she'd met in a very long time. Challenged her to do more. To *be* more.

She saw a dark shape looming by the edge of the pool and surfaced for air, laughing, pushing her seaweed-hair out of her face. "Come on in. The water's great."

He scowled. "Unlike some people, I don't jump into swimming pools fully clothed."

She grinned up at him. "Then take off your clothes and go for that skinny-dip."

He stared down at her for several endless, heart-stopping seconds. Then he stunned her by saying evenly, "All right."

She gaped up at him. He was going to strip and jump in with her? Ho. Lee. Cow.

All of a sudden she felt in way over her head, and she wasn't talking about the swimming pool.

Chapter 6

This is madness. But in spite of his misgivings, Austin's fingers moved to the hem of his shirt. He stripped the soft cotton off over his head.

It's totally unprofessional. The bare night air felt cool on his skin. Liberating. He was completely out of line to get in the pool with her. He reached for his belt buckle.

But who would see? It was just the two of them up here on top of one of the tallest buildings in the city. There wasn't a sight line anywhere for a sniper to get an angle on her. She was safe. They both were. He started to push his pants down his muscular thighs.

She gasped.

One corner of his mouth curled in amusement. She didn't know yet that he had on Lycra biking shorts beneath his pants. Interesting that she didn't ask him to stop, though. A bit of the old wild child peeking through her newly pious and mature exterior, perhaps? He liked the hint of daring in her. She wore it well.

He particularly liked throwing her off balance. She was less…guarded…when she wasn't on familiar ground. It was good for her. She was entirely too predictable and bland in this persona her family—specifically her father—had forced on her. While the rebellious, twenty-two-year-old diva no doubt would've driven him crazy, he would almost prefer that version of Silver to the strangled version of her that remained.

Fame sure had done a number on her. It seemed to have driven all the spontaneity out of her. She took no risks lest a cameraman jump out of the nearest potted palm and capture her humiliation for all the world to see. A need to challenge her, to shake her up, coursed through him. Being with her was like being around a puppy that didn't know how to play. It was sad and somehow not natural. A desire to teach her how to chase her tail again overcame him. And hell, he wouldn't mind chasing her tail, either.

Jumping into a swimming pool with their clothes on was a good start on waking her playful side. Except his cell phone, earpieces, gun and various other gadgets were all in his pockets. It was easier to just strip off his clothes, the contents of his pockets intact.

He knifed cleanly into the water. He hadn't been swimming in several years—it wasn't a favored pastime in the remote parts of Afghanistan. Not to mention water was too scarce over there for anyone to even contemplate swimming in giant vats of it. He stroked toward the far end of the pool, relishing the slide of water over his skin, the muffling silence and weight of it. Damn, he'd forgotten how much he loved to swim.

The water was cool but did little to dissipate the heat that woman stirred up in him. She'd be irritating if she weren't so damned interesting. And sexy. And funny. And…cute. She sure was a little thing, all sparkly and bright, like a shiny new coin. Her name fit her.

He surfaced beside her. "You gonna just hang onto the edge or are you coming swimming with me?"

She laughed and took off for the far end of the pool. He caught up and passed her easily. Not only was he trained to swim for hours on end in rough oceans but that dress of hers added serious drag to her hydrodynamics. She ought to take it off—

Slow down, there. No trying to get the client to strip. Although she'd look hot in just her bra and panties. *Stop that!*

She reached the far end and surfaced beside him, panting. "Man, you're fast. Are you some sort of Navy SEAL or something?"

He grinned. "Something like that."

"Seriously?"

"Yeah. I'm part of an Army unit called Special Operations Detachment Delta. We specialize in urban counterterrorism, surveillance, indigenous recruitment and liaison work, establishing and running intelligence networks…" Her eyes had glazed over somewhere around the word *surveillance*. He amended, "Would it be clearer if I just said I do scary stuff involving guns?"

"Much."

She gazed up at him with something akin to awe gleaming in her ethereal eyes. For the first time, he understood how his men could enjoy the groupies who chased after them with this combination of admiration and adoration. It almost made a guy feel like a hero.

Except he knew what a real hero was. They were forged and tested and proven on the battlefield. Under fire and in the face of death. He'd been privileged to serve with more than a few of them.

At a loss for what to say to her, he mumbled, "I can't believe you jumped into the pool in that dress."

"I never liked it anyway. I was happy to ruin it."

"It's not so bad. You look nice in it."

She huffed. "Let's just say it's not me, okay?"

"How so?"

"It's too…pink. Too frilly."

"You're not exactly an old lady."

"I'm not a little girl, either."

He grinned at her. "As a man, may I say—with gratitude—that's an absolutely true statement."

He thought he caught her cheeks reddening as she dived under and swam away from him. He knocked out a mile or so in laps while she mostly floated on her back and stayed out of his way, smiling up at the stars. He wondered as he pulled strongly through the water what put that dreamy expression on her face. It was the kind of look a guy would love to put on a woman's face. The kind of look he'd love to put on *her* face.

High up above Las Vegas like this and isolated behind the thick glass panels that made up the walls of the courtyard, most of the city's noise stayed well below. Of course, with his busted eardrum, he wasn't hearing all that well anyway. At least not in his left ear. Only a faint ringing came from it right now. The doctor said the tinnitus ought to clear up and the hearing recover. Eventually. Maybe.

He ground his teeth together and swam harder. He hated words like *eventually* and *maybe.* He wanted to be in control of his life, dammit! It was hell waiting around like this to see if his ear healed up well enough for him to go back to his unit or not. If not…

He forced himself to finish the thought. If not, his career was over.

It was Silver who climbed out of the pool first, pale silk clinging revealingly to her body. He probably shouldn't have looked, but he did. Had there been any question about her having a dancer's body, fit and toned and sleek, that dress erased any doubts.

He tore his gaze away, climbed out of the pool and went inside to towel off and change into dry clothes. He grabbed a couple towels and his largest T-shirt and handed them to Silver, shivering in a chaise lounge by the pool.

She stared at the garment for a moment. "Aren't we going back to my place to get some of my clothes?"

"Not a chance. Anyone who's out to hurt you will have your apartment staked out."

She sighed and took the sloppy T-shirt. "Can we at least go shopping tomorrow?"

"As long as we don't go to any of your usual stores."

She nodded, a fearful look back on her face. Damn. He said, "Why don't you go take a hot shower? The blue tint to your lips does nothing for your coloring."

Laughing, she disappeared into one of the guest bathrooms.

While she was showering, he ordered up a pot of hot chocolate. It arrived just as the blow-dryer in the bathroom cut off. Good timing.

In short order, he installed her on one of the matching leather couches in the living room with a cup of steaming cocoa. When she was settled in, her bare feet tucked beneath her and all but purring in contentment, he succumbed to envy of his T-shirt and how it rubbed intimately against her rosy body.

"So, Silver, why did your father hire me? Why does he think you're in danger?"

She frowned. "According to you, someone shot at me today. Doesn't that say it all?"

"Harold hired me before that. Why did he think you were in danger a week ago?"

Her normally expressive features shut down, taking on a stubborn cast. Before she could refuse to talk or, more likely, lie to him, he commented, "I'm as close to a priest or a lawyer as you can get without me actually being one. Nothing you say to me will go any farther than this room, I swear. But to do my job, I have to know what's going on."

She studied him for a long time, obviously weighing what to tell him. Finally, she said quietly, "You know my sister was murdered, right?"

"Affirmative. That's not exactly breaking news since the story has been splashed all over the tabloids for weeks now."

Silver nodded. "When it became obvious there'd been foul play, my father and the police initially tried to keep that out of the news. But that didn't last long. And then the threats started—"

She broke off as if she'd said too much.

"What threats?" he asked quickly.

A sigh. Then, "The usual for rich, powerful men. Vague,

anonymous threats. Some crazy guy claiming the Rothchilds wronged his family and vowing revenge."

"Who's investigating this threat?" Austin asked.

She shrugged. "Natalie knows about it. Problem is it could be practically anyone. Do you have any idea how many people my family has walked on or over to get to where it is today? Las Vegas doesn't exactly have the most savory past…particularly the casino industry. Back in the day, it was a rough business."

"What exactly is this person threatening to do?"

"To kill every member of my family one-by-one. He didn't specify how. "

"Has anybody else been shot at or had any attempts made on their lives?"

"My sister, Natalie, was ambushed and nearly shot. But her attacker turned out to be her fiancé's crazy aunt and not Candace's killer."

"Is this crazy aunt in police custody?"

"She's undergoing psychiatric treatment in a facility right now. The police and her doctors say she's not a danger to anyone anymore."

Austin frowned. "Is today the first time you were shot at?"

"Shot at? Yes."

"But…" he prompted.

She continued reluctantly, "But there've been a couple other incidents in the past few weeks. Nothing this serious, though. My car's been sideswiped, and the brakes failed—but you knew that. My apartment was ransacked—"

Austin cut her off. "Anything taken?"

She shuddered over her hot chocolate. "Yes. Some of my sexiest underwear."

A frisson of apprehension and possessive fury rippled down his spine. The would-be killer was a pervert, too? That was never a good combination. But it did help explain why Silver and her sister were the first targets. It also gave him a better idea of what kinds of attacks to expect. This assailant would try to isolate

Silver. Terrorize her before he killed her. Maybe sexually assault her, which involved restraint and imprisonment. The guy would want her to suffer before she died. It also told Austin this guy was capable of long-term planning and complex organization. This was no garden-variety stalker.

"I'm afraid that until this guy is caught, you and I are going to be spending a whole lot of time together," he said quietly.

Her eyes went wide, but he didn't know how to interpret the expression. Hopefully, that was pleasure at the idea of being with him and not dismay.

A cell phone vibrating on the coffee table startled them both. Silver started to reach for it, but Austin said quickly, "I'll get it."

"It could be Mark."

He replied grimly, "Then I'll definitely get it."

"No!" Silver retorted sharply. "You'd be rude to him!" She looked at the face of her phone, and the color drained from her face. As much as he wanted to snatch that phone away from her, he restrained himself. What in the hell did she see in that cretin, anyway?

"Hi, Mark. How are—"

The guy had obviously cut her off. Austin heard shouting as she held the phone slightly away from her ear. His urge to grab the phone and tell the guy where to go grew even stronger.

When the jerk eventually paused for breath, Silver interjected hastily, "I'm so glad to know you're all right. I was worried about you."

That sent Austin's eyebrows up. She hadn't acted worried that he'd seen. She hadn't even attempted to call the guy. If anything, she'd acted relieved not to have to deal with the bastard for a while.

She did sound sincere, though, when she said she'd been worried about Sampson. Although Austin couldn't for the life of him figure out why. She must just be a soft touch when it came to undeserving sons of bitches. No wonder she was throwing out interested vibes in his direction, then.

And what was up with that if she was so involved with this

Sampson character? Something was definitely off in this relationship of hers. Did she actually perceive him like Sampson? A down on his luck bastard in need of being thrown a bone in the love department? It tasted bitter in his mouth to think that she might actually include him in the same class of man as Mark Sampson.

More screaming emanated from her cell phone before she managed to interject, "How about tomorrow morning? Saul's giving me a tour of the Grand Theater stage at ten—"

That was as far as she got, because Austin snatched the phone out of her hands. Unceremoniously, he cut off the call without a single word of explanation.

"What did you go and do that for?" she exclaimed. "Now he'll be *really* mad!"

He growled back at her, "What part of no one is to know where you are didn't you get?"

"He's my bodyguard, for goodness' sake—"

"He's not fit to guard a smelly Dumpster full of week-old trash," Austin snapped. "I'm your bodyguard, now. I'm responsible for your life, and you'll follow my instructions and no one else's from here on out. Got it?"

That earned a glare out of her. Ignoring her, he powered down her phone, which gave a trilling note of warning and went black.

"What are you doing?" Silver cried. "I need to be available in case Saul or someone associated with my show calls me."

"It's ten o'clock at night. They can call you tomorrow."

"The music business doesn't observe normal working hours."

"If folks in the biz want you bad enough, they will from now on."

"But that's the problem," she half-whispered. "I don't think they want me that bad."

"Don't sell yourself short. You were a hell of a singer. For what it's worth, I liked your songs."

She looked up at him sharply. "You're just saying that to be nice."

"Do I look like the kind of guy who'd admit to liking a teeny-bopper pop princess just to be nice?"

"I wasn't a teenybopper!"

"Fine. You were a teenaged bad girl."

She subsided, grinning. "Guilty as charged."

"I don't know about you, but I'm beat. I flew twenty hours to get here. What say we hit the sack?"

"Now that you mention it, this *has* been a big day." She stood up, starting across the living room toward the second bedroom.

"Where are you going?" he asked.

"To bed?" she replied questioningly.

"Bed's that way," he said, pointing at the master bedroom on the other side of the suite.

"That's the master suite. You take it. I'll take one of the other bedrooms."

"Didn't you hear me earlier? I said you don't get to be out of my sight for a while. That's a 'round the clock proposition, darlin'."

She turned and stared at him. "You want me to *sleep* with you?"

"In the same room, at any rate. You can have the bed. I'll take the recliner."

"That's ridiculous. I'll be fine in my own room."

He crossed his arms and stared at her implacably. "You wanna die, be my guest."

Her gaze wavered. Fell. Her hand stole to her abdomen, and she reluctantly nodded her acquiescence at him. He said more gently, "It's just for a few weeks. Until the cops catch this guy. The police have been notified of the attacks on you, right?"

"I suppose so. Mark said he'd take care of it."

Austin grunted skeptically. "Great. In that case, I'll call the LVMPD first thing in the morning to make sure they're aware you've got a stalker."

"Mark's not that awful. You just caught him having a bad moment today."

Austin snorted. "He had a number of bad moments today. And a couple of them could have cost you your life."

Silver walked away from him across the expanse of plush carpet. Her legs were surprisingly long in proportion to her diminutive height. She might be small, but everything was emphatically in exactly the right place.

Without warning, she glanced back over her shoulder and caught him red-handed staring at her juicy little tush and made-for-sex legs. Damned if the corner of her mouth didn't tilt up knowingly. *Little flirt.* If he wasn't mistaken, there was an extra sashay to her hips as she continued on into his bedroom.

While she climbed into the king-sized bed and snuggled in under the down comforter, he pulled the heavy drapes across both walls of floor-to-ceiling windows. He had a great view down the Strip from here, but that represented danger. If he could see all those other hotel windows, it meant a whole lot of people could look back at him. Or at Silver.

He grabbed a blanket and pillow out of the closet and stretched out in the large leather recliner next to the window. It might not be the luxury bed Silver was enjoying but compared to a canvas camp cot or the cold, rocky ground of Afghanistan's harsh mountains, this chair was heaven on earth.

Silver's voice came out of the darkness. "I feel bad about this. You ought to be sleeping in your own bed."

"Honey, I haven't been this comfortable in two years."

"All the more reason you ought to be over here."

"With you?" Why the words popped out of his mouth, he had no idea. Silver went dead silent, and the darkness lay heavy between them all of a sudden. He sighed. "I'm sorry. That was out of line."

Her voice floated thoughtfully out of the dark. "No, it wasn't. And in answer to your question, why not with me? We're both adults, and this bed could sleep six. Heck, given some of the parties that have happened up here, it probably *has* slept six."

He chuckled, grateful for an excuse to cover his shock at the invitation to join her. Surely she didn't have a long night of hot sex in mind. Even he wasn't that lucky.

"I'm serious, Austin. If my life depends on you, I want you to be well-rested and ready to go in the morning. You're a big man, and you're not going to be comfortable in that chair all night. Come stretch out in bed. I trust you."

Ahh. Well-rested. She was interested in him *sleeping* with her and nothing more. He mumbled under his breath, "Maybe you shouldn't trust me."

"I beg your pardon?"

"Nothing," he replied quickly.

"Don't make me get up and come over there to drag you to bed."

He laughed at that. "A little whisper of a thing like you? You couldn't budge me if you tried."

"Is that a dare?"

"What if it is?"

His sharp eyesight made out her shape rising out of the bed, and if he wasn't mistaken, that was a mischievous grin on her face. Uh-oh.

Her legs were pale in the dark, and he focused on them as she prowled toward him, catlike. It was either that or look at the way the soft cotton of his T-shirt clung to her high, firm breasts and skimmed across her narrow waist and lush hips. Nope, the legs were a better bet. But damned if he didn't wonder what they'd feel like wrapped around his hips, clinging tightly to him, urging him deeper into her—

She stopped beside the chair, and he stared up at her warily, hardly daring to breathe.

She purred, "So, if you won't get out of the chair, I guess I'm getting into it with you."

"But there's no room—"

"Wanna bet?" She flung one leg across his lap and straddled his hips, her knees sinking into the cushions on either side of him.

"Uh, okay then. So I lose that bet."

She reached down and used one finger to trace a random design on his chest through his T-shirt. "I dunno. From where I'm sitting, it looks like you might just have won the bet."

He grinned up at her until her realized his hands had come to rest on her hips. He jerked them away. But where to put them?

The armrests put his hands perilously close to her rear end. Frankly, he feared for what she'd do next if he simply let his arms drag along the sides of the chair.

She solved his problem by leaning forward until she fell against his chest and his arms shot up reflexively to catch her.

New problem. Soft parts of her were rubbing against hard parts of him that really didn't need that kind of encouragement at the moment. "Ready to come over to the bed and join me yet?" she murmured.

"You're not fighting fair!" he protested.

"Is there a rule in the bodyguard handbook that says I have to fight fair? Because I distinctly recall in the single girl's guide to men that it says the girl doesn't have to fight fair."

"Where is this guide? I think I need to study up on it."

She laughed up at him. "That's not how it works. We women know the rules we play by, and it's your job as a man to figure them out for yourself."

Her laughter rocked her against him in ways and in places that *seriously* didn't need to be rocked against. He groaned under his breath. "I'm getting a real good idea of the rules of engagement you're operating under."

"Excellent." And then the minx kissed him.

Not a first, chaste getting-to-know-you kiss, not even a flirty, slightly-drunk-and-you're-cute kiss. Nope. This was a check-out-your-tonsils, hot-sex-to-follow, I'm-gonna-eat-you-alive kiss. And having not been kissed in far, far too long, it was more kiss than he could handle and manage to stay calm.

His entire body temperature spiked, and his hands suddenly developed a mind of their own, roaming up her back restlessly. They slipped under her T-shirt, and silky flesh slid beneath his palms so smooth and sleek it stole his breath away.

And her mouth…oh my, her mouth. She sucked on his lower lip, her tongue playing across his flesh, all wet and slick and hot. He about shot out of the chair, it turned him on so intensely. And then her hands were on either side of his head, and she angled her head so she could plunge that clever tongue of hers into every nook and cranny of his starving mouth.

He was absolutely prepared to devour her whole and not think twice about it. Not that the lady seemed to find that an unpleasant idea. She was squirming all over him, making little sighing and moaning sounds that were going to cause him to embarrass himself if she didn't slow down a bit here. After all, it had been a *very* long time since he'd been with a woman.

She breathed his name on a note of wonder. "Austin. Who'd have guessed a man like you could kiss like this!"

"What do you mean, a man like me?"

Her smile flashed down at him. "You know. Straightlaced. Square."

"Square? I'm not square. I'm as wild as the next guy." Besides. Who was she to talk about being straightlaced?

Her laughter tinkled around him like silver bells. "You are not wild. You're Mr. Law-and-Order, do-the-right-thing guy. I bet you sort your socks by color and fold your underwear in perfect squares. You're the epitome of not-wild."

"Hey!"

She shrugged, and the movement made his breath catch as her breasts rubbed tantalizingly against his chest. "Trust me. I know wild. And you're not it."

If only she knew some of the things he'd done in his life. He could tell her about missions so daring they'd curl her toes. He couldn't count the number of times he'd dived into death defying stunts without a second thought. He murmured. "You think messing around with fast cars and dabbling in a few drugs makes a guy wild? You have no idea what wild really is, little girl."

"Oh, yeah? And are you gonna show me?"

Man, he was tempted. Really, really tempted. But from somewhere way deep inside him, a kernel of the self-control she'd accused him of reared its ugly head. He answered her lightly, "Honey, you couldn't handle it."

"Hah! Chicken!"

He smiled up at her knowingly. "I'm not going to bother responding to that because even you know I'm no coward."

Her expression softened, and her gaze grew serious. Aww, jeez. Did she have to go all feminine and sweet on him? That was so much harder to resist than the brazen hussy. "You're right," she murmured. "You're no coward, Austin Dearing."

He couldn't help it. He tugged her close. He had to kiss his name on her lips.

It tasted sweet, like peach ice cream on a lazy summer day. And he was lost.

Chapter 7

Silver's breath hitched as Austin looked up at her like she was some kind of goddess—whom he was about to devour for lunch. It was a heady thing to be looked at like that. Maybe he was right. Maybe she had underestimated him. A thrill of trepidation raced through her. She'd thought all those guys in her youth were wild and dangerous…but suddenly, she wondered. Maybe they'd been the pretenders. Maybe she'd finally found the real deal.

A struggle broke out on Austin's shadowed face and she watched it play across his features in fascination. "What?" she murmured.

He blinked up at her. "I beg your pardon?"

"Ever the gentleman, my dangerous Austin. What's wrong?"

"Wrong?" He sounded startled. "Nothing's wrong."

She smoothed her fingertips across his furrowed brow. "A word of advice. You can't lie for squat."

He lurched between her knees. "I can, too. I'm highly trained in the art of dissembling. I know all the body language that conveys sincerity. I know how to hide the signals of a lie. I even know how to fool a lie detector machine."

"Sorry. I'm not buying it. So give. What's wrong?"

He sighed. "I can think of several things wrong with this scenario."

She felt him pulling away from her, and panic erupted in her gut. Not him, too! He wouldn't leave her, would he? Her fingers tightened convulsively on his shoulders.

"Easy, honey," he murmured low. "I'm not going anywhere. You're safe with me."

As her death grip on him relaxed, it belatedly occurred to her to wonder how he'd known why she'd panicked. She became aware of his big hand stroking down her spine like he was gentling a skittish wild animal. In spite of herself, the tension drained from her under his soothing touch.

"What's so wrong with this…scenario?" she asked.

He sighed. "First, I work for you. It's not ethical to fool around with you."

"You work for my father," she countered. "I figure that means you and I can do whatever we want."

He ignored her argument and pressed on. "Second, I'm only here for a few months, and then I'll go back to my job overseas."

Darn it! She'd finally plunged in and dared to take a chance, and now he was rejecting her? He was the guy who'd emboldened her to do something like this in the first place. She just couldn't win for losing. Especially when it came to love.

Trying—and failing—to keep desperation out of her voice, she replied, "All the more reason not to waste time tap-dancing around each other and just do what feels good."

Doggedly, he continued. "You're a celebrity. I've spent the past decade watching your life unfold in the tabloids. I look at you and I see this face I know, but I have no idea who the person underneath is. It's like you're not even a real person. I've gotta say, I'm not interested in being with a plastic pop star."

That made her pull back. Plastic? Her? She was a lot of

things, but that was *not* one of them. "So because you've seen my face before, you don't want a relationship with me?"

He scowled. "That's not what I said."

"Is it because I'm famous? I can't help being Silver Rothchild. I belong to a rich, notorious family. So sue me. I happen to be a halfway decent singer, and I happen to be successful. So sue me again."

"But that's the point. I don't want to be with the surface image of you. I want to know the real person beneath."

"I am a real person! Right here. I'm me. Silver. I have thoughts and opinions and feelings and dreams in here."

He replied gently, "And I need to know those parts of you before I jump into bed with you. I'm not interested in sleeping with a Rothchild heir or a famous pop singer. I want a real woman."

The arrogance of the man! She was a real woman, dammit! She climbed off him angrily. "I offered myself to you, and all you can say is I'm not a real woman? Well, to hell with you, Austin Dearing. I don't care how dangerous and wild you are. You have no idea what you're missing out on!"

She stormed out into the living room, too furious to stay in the same room with him.

His voice came from directly behind her, and she about jumped out of her skin. "Honey, I know exactly what I'm missing out on."

She whirled to face him, hurt coursing through her. "Then why are you turning me down?"

"What about Bubba?"

She stared at Austin, frustrated. *Mark again.*

"Our relationship is less serious than the press portrays it. And," she added with a certain desperation, "neither of us thinks of it as exclusive." She crossed her fingers and prayed Austin bought her explanation.

His hands came up as if to gather her into his arms but fell away without touching her. "I told you. I'm only here for a little while and then I'll go back to my real life. You're a pop star and I'm a soldier. This thing between us—it would never work."

"You *are* a coward, Austin. We'll never know if it could've worked between us or not because you're too afraid to take a chance on us. That's a shame because I happen to think we could've been dynamite together." Tears clogged the back of her throat all of a sudden. She finished lightly, "Your loss, big guy."

"Silver…"

She turned away from him. She didn't want to hear anything he had to say right now.

Thankfully, he fell silent. She padded over to the refrigerator and pulled out a can of tomato juice. She slugged down its thick tartness, and her stomach gave an ominous rumble. "Ugh." She grabbed the edge of the wet bar to distract herself from the burgeoning urge to run for the bathroom.

Austin was beside her in an instant. "You okay?" He did touch her then, his hands skimming up her arms in concern.

She closed her eyes in pain. This was what she'd sacrificed by choosing to go this pregnancy alone—a partner and lover to share these moments with. The magnitude of doing the whole parenthood thing solo struck her full force in that moment of Austin's quiet concern.

"No," she mumbled, "I'm not okay." As Austin took a step closer, preparatory to wrapping her in his arms, she stepped away hastily. "But I will be okay." She straightened her spine determinedly. "I'll be just fine on my own."

She moved away from the comfort of his big, warm hands and marched back toward the bedroom. She'd made her choice, and now she had to live with it. She didn't need any man's help, thank you very much. They all ended up bailing out on her anyway.

At least Austin had been decent enough to tell her up front that he'd be abandoning her. She probably ought to be grateful to him for sparing her the pain when he just disappeared one day. He was right. They weren't meant for one another. Falling for him would be a very, very bad idea.

But did he have to be such a damned gentleman about it?

Didn't he understand that it would've been so much easier to hate him if he'd been a bastard?

Rather than start another fight, she climbed back into his big bed. Predictably, Austin was right behind her, gliding into the master bedroom on silent bare feet. Except instead of settling in the recliner, he moved over to one of the windows and pulled the curtains back just enough to be able to look down on the Strip. He lounged against the wall and stared out into the night for a long time, his jaw hard and his gaze harder.

For once, she was a little afraid of him and what he might be thinking. She'd been an idiot to throw herself at him. She couldn't blame him for thinking the worst of her. Not to mention, he thought she'd thrown herself at him even though she was involved with Mark Sampson. He must think she was the lowest form of slut.

She sighed and rolled over, turning her back to him. She tried her darnedest to go to sleep, but it wasn't happening. The realization that she was pregnant loomed huge in her mind. Was it a boy or a girl? What color hair would he or she have? Would he or she be small like her, or built more like his or her father? All of a sudden, she understood all those expectant parents who, when asked if they wanted a boy or a girl, fervently answered that they just wanted their baby to be healthy.

And then there was the show to think about. She'd love to do some of the songs she'd written. They were completely different than anything she'd ever sung, more soulful, more meaningful than the pop tunes she'd belted out a decade ago. But Saul was undoubtedly right. If she was going to make a comeback, she had to do what people expected of her. And that was the old Silver, hot and hip and naughty.

To think she'd spent the past seven years doing her level best to shed that image. And now she had to pick it back up again. How was she supposed to do that at the ripe old age of thirty? Heck, even Austin wouldn't jump into the sack with her, and he hadn't been near a woman in two years! She was never going to pull this off. It would be Harold's last and greatest revenge on her for all the crap she'd pulled on him and that he'd never really forgiven her for. He was going to ruin her career once and for all.

She sighed. It was a mean thing to think of him. But she'd seen him exact worse vengeance on people who wronged him far less than she had. She honestly wouldn't put it past him. Not unless he'd changed a whole lot recently. Was it possible that Candace's death really had changed him that much? She had a hard time believing it.

Her thoughts in turmoil, she finally drifted off into restless sleep.

The sound of a baby—her baby—crying in terror jerked her harshly from her dreams, disoriented and frightened. She sat up wildly, looking around in the dark in panic. Where was her baby? Where was she? This pitch black room was not hers. The bed was too hard, the pillows too soft. And, good grief, someone was breathing smoothly beside her! Please God, let it not be Mark! She squinted down at the large form sleeping beside her.

Austin.

She sagged in relief.

And then it all came back to her. This was his bed. His suite. He was protecting her from whoever was trying to kill her. One man against unseen and unknown forces of unknown strength. She couldn't die! Her baby deserved a chance at life!

So much for being relieved.

"Bad dream?" Austin murmured from beside her.

She exhaled slowly. "Yeah."

She looked down at him, and he gazed back up at her sympathetically. "I'm not surprised. You had a rough day."

He had no idea.

"Breathe nice and slowly. Concentrate on long, even exhalations."

Following his soothing instructions, her heartbeat slowed and her breathing returned to a semblance of normal. But the idea of lying down and going back to sleep, back to that horrible sound of a desperate baby, kept her sitting upright.

The bed shifted slightly beside her, and she glanced over at him. Wordlessly, he held out his arms to her. And without a second thought, she went to him, cuddling against his warm, solid, *naked* chest. She didn't dare move any closer and find out if he was wearing another pair of those biking shorts of his—or not. The idea of 'or not' made her pulse pound. Hesitantly, she draped an arm across his broad rib cage. Springy chest hairs tickled her nose. She nuzzled her face against him, enjoying the sensation.

Man. It had been a long time since she'd been with a man like this. She really had withered and dried into a prune of her former self in the past few years.

"Comfortable?" he murmured.

"Uh, yeah. You?"

"Not particularly."

She started. "Why not? Am I poking you?"

He sighed. "I've been in the field a long time, honey, and you're not exactly chopped liver."

"Gee, thanks," she laughed. "That's the nicest thing anyone's called me in years."

"What do you want me to say? That you're possibly the sexiest woman I've ever met, and I can't help thinking all kinds of dirty thoughts about you and wondering what you'd feel like underneath me? That I've been lying awake here all night fighting like hell to keep my hands off you and wishing like crazy that you'd roll over and have your way with me?"

Something in the timbre of his voice told her he was being dead honest with her. Whoa. "Uh, that's better. Much better," she stammered.

Silence fell between them. What was she supposed to do now? Roll back over like she ought to and go to sleep? Crawl up his chest like she wanted to and kiss him senseless? He'd already told her that it wouldn't work between the two of them. And he was absolutely right. But dang, she got tired of being alone, sometimes. She had so much on her plate right now and not a soul in the world to share it with. The least she could do was allow herself to scratch this particular itch.

They were both grown-ups. They knew the rules for these things. One night. Hot sex with no promises of anything more. Mutual pleasure. Mutual release. No more, no less.

A sigh rattled in Austin's chest beneath her ear. "It's late. You need your sleep."

Desperation erupted in her gut. Their moment was slipping away. Like the coward she'd become sometime in the past seven years, she was turning away from going after what she wanted… from really living…again. "No!" she blurted.

Austin started beneath her. "I beg your pardon?"

God, she was an idiot. She was messing this all up. "I…I don't want to sleep."

"Uh, okay. You wanna talk? Or I can make you some hot tea?"

She squeezed her eyes shut in mortification. Where had the aggressive, confident young woman she used to be gone? She hadn't even known that other Silver had disappeared until this man had barged into her life, challenging her at every turn. Heck, it wasn't like he was daring her to bungee jump off a cliff. It was just the two of them. Mostly naked in bed already, and she still couldn't bring herself to go for what she wanted.

He shifted beneath her, partially sitting up. "What's the matter? Talk to me."

A simple request. Just tell him what she wanted.

"I…I…" she forced it out all in an awkward, jumbled rush. "I want to do more than just sleep here with you. I want to get naked and feel your skin against mine. I want to be alive again. To take risks. To be brave. To grab what I want and not always be looking over my shoulder for someone to catch me or disapprove of me. I don't want to care what they all think anymore. I…"

She sat up, looking down at him miserably. "I'm not making any sense at all, am I?"

"If I'm not mistaken, I think you're asking me to make love to you."

She exclaimed in abject relief. "Exactly!"

"All the reasons I stated before not to do that are still in place."

"I know. I'm not asking for a long-term relationship. Heck, I'm not asking for any relationship at all. Don't you ever…" she paused, searching for words "…just need to feel alive?"

"Yeah. I know the feeling. More than you know."

The sigh that escaped her came directly from her heart. "Thank God." She draped her arms over his shoulders and her body over his chest. "You're gorgeous, you know."

His hands roamed up her back, under his T-shirt she was wearing, neatly slipping it over her head. He sighed in satisfaction as her naked breasts came into contact with his chest. Profound relief flooded her. Maybe she wasn't on the verge of dead and buried after all.

"You're not so bad yourself," he murmured.

She kissed her way across his chest, tickling her nose with his chest hairs again. "I've wondered what being with you would be like since the moment I met you."

His hands came under her armpits and he commenced dragging her ever so slowly up his chest until his mouth nearly touched her breast. His breath was a tantalizing caress on her skin as he rasped out, "Ditto, darlin'."

That made her laugh. "Really? Even in that stupid pink dress?"

"You could wear a nun's habit and still be sexy. Demure isn't a bad look on you. Not that much of anything could be a bad look on you."

And then his mouth closed on her flesh, and she lost all capacity to form words. Wave after wave of sensation broke across her as his mouth traveled from one breast to the other, via the valley between, all of it thoroughly explored with his tongue and teeth.

When he surged beneath her she rolled with him, glorying in his weight as his lower body pressed her deep into the feather ticking over the firmer mattress below.

"You sure you want to do this?" he muttered as he trapped her wrists over her head and inserted a knee between hers.

She'd never been more certain of anything in her life. She ached for him from a place deep inside her, from a dry well of desire that desperately needed him to fill her, to replenish her. "If you don't ravish me pretty soon, I'm gonna ravish you."

He laughed richly. "Next time, you get to be on top. Time after that, I want to go back into that swimming pool with you. And that sofa by the windows looked about the right height to bend you over—"

She heaved beneath him, dislodging his knee and capturing the length of his male member between her thighs. She simultaneously squeezed and undulated, drawing forth a hearty groan of pleasure from him. He turned her hands loose and reached between them to skim a hand down her body, following the curve of her belly to where she held his flesh.

"Open for me, Silver. Let me pleasure you, too."

Her thighs fell apart as she pulled his mouth down to hers. He tasted like cinnamon, spicy and hot on her tongue. His teeth clicked against hers, and she tilted her head, fitting herself more comfortably to his voracious need. She grasped at his mile-wide shoulders, reveling in the power of the muscles flexing beneath her palms. His control hung by a thin thread, and she reveled in her power to snap it.

But then his finger took a long, intimate stroke across her swollen, slick flesh, and she all but unraveled on the spot. There was no need to pretend pleasure with this man, no need to live up to her reputation as a wild child, no need to force the sex to meet some celebrity standard. This was *real.*

Shock broke across her awareness. After all those guys, all those casual flings, had she never found real sexual pleasure before?

His fingers danced across her skin, rubbing in maddening, wet circles that drove her out of her mind with need. His knee was back, anchoring her to the mattress, holding her in place for his explorations.

His blunt fingertip slipped inside her and her internal muscle clenched convulsively around him. The pad of his finger pressed forward, rocking against the wall of her passage, and sudden, hot wetness flowed within her. Her limbs went liquid, and her entire being narrowed down to needing him inside her. Now. Filling her with his size and heat. Riding her into oblivion.

She gasped, "What are you doing to me, Austin?"

He murmured against her mouth, "Pleasuring you, I hope."

This pulsing desire, this building torrent of electric sensations dancing across her skin, this sense of impending explosion were unlike anything she'd ever experienced before. How could Silver Rothchild, bad girl extraordinaire, have failed to discover *this* for all those years?

"Do it some more," she begged. "I want…"

His finger drove deeper within her, sliding in and out until she could hardly form words. "What do you want?"

"I want you inside me. I want you to feel this, too. I want to share this with you. It's incredible!"

He rolled away for a moment, his finger never leaving her, never breaking that mesmerizing rhythm that had her shamelessly riding his hand, seeking more and more of that incredible pleasure building deep in her core. His chuckle mostly masked the sound of latex, and then he was back, using his knees to lever her thighs apart.

"Sing for me, Silver."

And then he was over her and in her and around her, filling her so full she thought she might burst. Smelling of man and pleasure, gloriously heavy on her, Austin was all heat and muscle, driving into her with just enough violence to match her surging hips.

And sing she did. She cried out as an explosion of intense

ecstasy such as she'd never dreamed of broke over her. Her vision went black as he transported her out of herself for a moment, and she keened her pleasure on a long, shuddering note he wrung from her very soul.

He froze, his eyes closed in a cross between bliss and agony as her muscles pulsed around him. And then he began to move again, his fingers reaching between them to rub the swollen nub of her overly sensitive flesh. In a matter of seconds, another orgasm clawed at her, flinging her against him in an excess of abandon in her search for release.

And this time, when it broke, he went over the edge with her, his shout mingling with hers, his flesh pulsing as hard and long as hers, his awed collapse into a state of complete, boneless satiation as thorough as hers.

Her mind was blown. Totally, irrevocably blown. His heart thumped like a series of sonic booms beneath her ear, and her own pulse raced double-time in sync with his.

He found his voice first. "Wow."

"Yeah," she managed to breathe. "Wow."

"Did I hurt you?"

That made her laugh. "If that was pain, I want to be tortured to death just like that."

"I think you killed me."

That made her lift her head—a monumental task—to stare at him in the dark. "I'm sorry. I didn't mean to—"

He laid a finger across her lips. "I meant that as a compliment of the highest order."

"Oh." She let that sink in for a moment. "Do all guys get that much pleasure whenever they have sex?"

"I dunno. In my experience, there are degrees of enjoyment. On a scale of one to ten, most sex is somewhere between a five and an eight. But this..." A smile crinkled the corners of his eyes. "This was a twenty-two."

Relief made her feel even weaker. Thank goodness. It wasn't just her. She would've felt like a huge idiot if she'd experienced her first ever orgasm—and her second—and it had turned out to be only average sex for him.

"Only a twenty-two?" she asked lightly. "Next time I'm aiming for a thirty in honor of my birthday."

His chest vibrated with a chuckle. "I hereby place myself at your disposal for the effort."

"Such a noble guy."

A shadow crossed his face. "I'm not so noble. I needed the reminder that I'm still alive. Thanks for giving it to me."

She stared down at him. "What happened?"

He didn't answer right away. She wasn't sure he would at all, in fact. But then he spoke quietly. "A couple weeks back I was guarding a guy. A would-be assassin wired with explosives blew himself up, and I barely got between my guy and the bomber. I thought I was a goner."

The thought of Austin blown to smithereens made her shiver in horror. She wrapped her arms tightly around him. "Thank God you're all right."

He shrugged beneath her cheek. "It's all part of the job."

Suddenly, vividly, she understood exactly what it was he did. He threw himself in the path of *death* for a living. "How can you do that?" she exclaimed.

"Do what?"

"Throw yourself in front of bombs? That's insane!" She lifted her head to stare down at him, to communicate to him the absurdity of such behavior. He had to stop. She couldn't lose him! Not like that.

He stared up at her, a perplexed look on his face. "Somebody's got to do the job."

"But it doesn't have to be you. Let someone else do it!"

"I've got the training and I'm the best."

"Stop being the best, then. Can't you retire or something?"

He dumped her on her back and loomed over her, leaning on one elbow and staring down at her. "What's gotten into you?"

She couldn't exactly tell him he was the first guy who'd ever given her an orgasm and she was desperate for him to stick around and do that some more. A lot more. She stammered, "I don't want anything bad to happen to you."

He smiled broadly. "Thanks."

She swatted his upper arm. "It's not a joke."

"You're right. It's not. And I've got a busted eardrum to show for it."

Ahh. The left ear he was prone to tugging on.

"Why don't you quit?" she asked reasonably.

"I like what I do."

"You *like* it?"

"Yeah. I give people peace of mind. Safety. Hell, I give them their lives. That's a pretty cool gift to give someone, don't you think?"

Almost as cool as multiple orgasms. All right. More cool, dammit. She was being selfish. But in her defense, her motives weren't all self-centered. He was an incredible man, and it would be a tragedy if something bad happened to him.

He interrupted her turbulent thoughts. "And I'll keep you safe and alive, too. I promise."

That's what she was afraid of. How could she ever live with herself if he came to harm on her watch? "Don't you dare die on me. I'll never forgive you if you do."

"If I die, I'm not likely to much care whether or not you forgive me."

"I'll haunt you," she threatened.

"Well, then." Chuckling, he leaned down until his mouth nearly touched hers. "By all means, I'll do my best not to die on you. Not tonight, at least. You still owe me a skinny-dip."

"And the couch," she added sternly.

His laughter rose into the night, balm to her troubled soul. "And the couch."

And then, as much as it was going to kill her to do it, she had to find a way to send him away from her.

Chapter 8

Austin stared at Silver in disbelief in the early morning light. So much for intimate morning-after pillow talk. He could not believe she'd just tried to fire him! "We've already been over this. Your father hired me and pays me. You can't fire me," he replied in a clipped tone.

"But you said it yourself," she argued. "We're too involved for you to do your job effectively."

She might be right, but it wasn't the real reason she was trying to dump him. He was dead certain of it. He'd come to know a thing or two about her last night, and it was clear that she was using a smaller truth to hide a bigger truth.

Not that the smaller truth wasn't a problem in and of itself. How in the hell was he supposed to stand in front of Harold Rothchild and explain that he had to quit this job because he'd leaped into the sack with the guy's daughter at the first opportunity? Plus, he'd have to face General Sarkin. And wasn't that going to be a fun ass chewing? The hell of it was that he knew better. He'd *told* Silver they had no business getting involved.

But had that stopped him when she poured out her heart to him so sweetly and innocently last night? Oh, no. It had turned him on like a raging bull to think that she—Silver Rothchild—wanted and needed him that bad.

So much for the notion of her as a plastic pop star. She'd turned out to be a flesh-and-blood woman who'd made him laugh one minute and stole his breath away with her passion and honesty the next. He'd even gotten comfortable enough with her to bare his soul over the whole business of nearly dying. And that wasn't the sort of thing he talked about with anybody. Ever. Men in his line of work couldn't afford to dwell on such thoughts, let alone admit to having them.

He'd even spilled his guts about his worry that he might not get to go back out into the field if his eardrum didn't heal. To her credit, Silver had been sympathetic about that. She'd already begged him to stop being a bodyguard, but she'd understood him well enough to grasp that his job was more than what he did. It was who he was.

She really was a hell of a woman. Not many like her came along in any guy's life. Especially his, where he spent months on end in the field with his social life drastically curtailed. She was the kind of woman who made a guy think about foreign concepts like commitment. Settling down. Hell, engagement rings.

If Silver were his woman, he'd get a ring on her finger so fast it would make her head spin.

But she wasn't his. As much as it set his teeth on edge to remember it in the light of day, Mark Sampson had first claim on her. Except…

He studied her speculatively across his scrambled eggs, bacon and mixed berries, minus the toast, which she'd snagged and was nibbling on cautiously at the moment.

She did not strike him as the kind of woman who jumped into the sack with one guy while she was involved with another one. Her loyal streak ran a mile wide if he judged her correctly.

If she and Sampson truly had anything at all going on—which he was beginning to be seriously skeptical of—she clearly didn't consider it to be much of a relationship with Bubba.

Silver startled him by pushing her chair back abruptly. "I've got to go get ready," she announced, making a beeline for the second bathroom.

He poured himself a cup of coffee and strolled out to the pool to drink it in the clear, sharp morning light. If she and Bubba weren't an official and exclusive item, then that meant the field of battle was open to other players. He'd be a damned fool to pursue her for himself…but he might just be a bigger fool not to.

The porcelain bottom of his coffee mug gleamed white, and still no solution to his quandary presented itself to him. However, he'd come to the reluctant conclusion that his problem was actually very simple. He wanted Silver for himself. He could absolutely take her away from Bubba if he tried. But the thing was, should he? Was it the best thing for her, or was it grossly selfish of him to go after her?

"Ready to go?"

Silver's voice startled him. He'd been so lost in his thoughts that he hadn't heard her approach him from behind. "Uh. Yeah. Let me go get my SIG Sauer."

"Your what?"

"My SIG Sauer. My sidearm." As incomprehension remained on her face, he added, "My pistol."

Comprehension dawned. Either that or a random shadow had just obscured the brilliant azure of her gaze. "I'm serious. Austin. I'm going to talk to my father today and ask him to remove you from my protection."

Pain and frustration slammed into him. "What flimsy reason are you going to give me next? The fact that I carry a gun? Why don't you just come clean and admit you want me off this case because you're embarrassed about last night and want to get rid of me?"

She murmured in a husky half whisper that sent shivers up and down his spine, "I don't want to get rid of you. Exactly the opposite, in fact."

Huh? He stared at her, confused.

She continued. "Isn't it obvious why I want you off my security? Austin, I'd die if something bad happened to you because of me."

Beneath his exasperation, a kernel of something warm and…and happy…sprouted. She cared about him? Enough to push him away to see him safe? Son of a gun.

More calmly, he responded, "If you send me away, I'll just go back to another bodyguarding job. Most likely someone in a hell of a lot more dangerous situation than you're in. My odds of dying will go up dramatically."

"Yes, but then it wouldn't be my fault. Like I said last night, I couldn't live with it if you died for me."

He shrugged. "This life is my choice. I'm responsible for the results of my job. No one else. Me. Not you."

"Sorry. Not buying it. In my mind, it would be my fault—no matter what you say."

"Stubborn woman."

"Mule-headed man."

"Wench."

"Jerk."

He did a quick flip with his hands to toss her grip off his forearms and pulled her against him too fast for her to protest. "I love you, too, darlin'."

He closed his eyes and kissed her before she could reply. Before he could see if she took his words at face value or treated them as a joke. Hell, he didn't know if he meant them or not. They'd just slipped out. Lord knew, she was the kind of woman he'd have no trouble loving. None at all.

She relaxed into him, melting against him, her mouth opening under his. Welcoming him in, her tongue coaxing him to come and play in their own private garden of sensual delight.

And maybe that was answer enough for now. She definitely enjoyed being with him and was clearly hungry for more of what they'd shared through most of last night. It didn't take a rocket scientist to read the little sounds she was making in the back of her throat. She'd be all kinds of amenable to turning their one-night stand into a two-nighter…or more.

That did it. Mark Sampson was history. This woman was entirely too special, too spectacular for a guy like Sampson. Silver Rothchild was his, effective now.

They'd figure out the details later. She'd get used to his work once she realized how good he was at it. He'd take more time off and be with her every chance he got. He was all over coming home on leave if he had someone like her to come home to.

Exultation filled his heart as he gave in to the inevitable. The two of them were meant to be. She might not have realized it in her head yet, but her body recognized him as her true mate. It was only a matter of time until her conscious caught up with her subconscious.

He could be patient. He'd give her time to adjust to the idea of the two of them. Plus, it would give him time to show Sampson the score and run him off—far, far away from Silver. The worst of it was going to be restraining his protective impulses enough not to drive Silver crazy. She was no big fan of restrictions on her life. Not that he blamed her after having met Harold Rothchild and having seen firsthand how the press hounded her.

He lifted his mouth away from hers and gazed down at her. "Have I told you this morning how beautiful and special you are?" She blinked up at him rapidly. If he wasn't mistaken, those were tears pooling in her eyes. "Hey, why the tears?"

She batted away the moisture, smiling up at him. "You're the most amazing man."

He dropped a kiss on the tip of her nose. "And don't you forget it, either."

"Amazingly arrogant."

"Amazingly confident," he corrected.

She gazed up at him, emotions racing through her eyes too

quickly to name. But most of them looked good for the home team. Hope spiraled through him. By golly, the two of them might just pull off this miracle together.

His voice inexplicably gruff, he muttered, "C'mon. Let's get going. You don't want to be late to your first day of work."

She shook herself out of her thoughts and nodded. "You're right. The new Silver is responsible and on time."

"I like you just the way you are, darlin'. Don't change a thing."

As he paused in front of the door to peer out the peephole, she murmured behind him, "Keep telling me that, and I might just believe you one of these days."

He glanced over his shoulder and grinned broadly. "You've got it."

Silver stared thoughtfully at Austin's back as he led the way down the hall to the elevator. What had gotten into him this morning? He'd been so quiet. And so thoughtful toward her. Not that she was complaining. Thoughtful was almost as new an experience for her as multiple orgasms—of which she was now a proud veteran of several. Yes, it had been a long and informative night.

It was darned hard not to be more than a little shocked by him and what he'd taught her about pleasure and about her body. She literally felt like a new woman this morning.

The elevator door slid open, and after checking to be sure it was empty, he held it for her to step inside. She moved to the back automatically, and he took his place in front of her, a veritable wall of muscle. She couldn't resist. She reached out and ran her hands down the long, powerful V of his back, every contour of the expanse as familiar to her now as her own body.

"Silver—" he rumbled warningly. "I'm working."

"So stop working for a minute. We're alone in an elevator. What can possibly happen to me in here?"

"It's about being alert. In the moment. I have to be ready for anything."

"Mmm. I like the sound of that."

He threw a glare over his shoulder at her that lacked any real heat. "You're incorrigible."

She grinned up at him. "I've been called worse."

He grinned back at her reluctantly. She thought he might have started to turn toward her with a kiss on his mind, but the elevator dinged just then to announce its arrival on Subfloor 1. He whipped back around to face the door, danger abruptly pouring off of him as he stepped outside.

"Clear," he announced briskly.

She slipped in close behind him as he walked swiftly down the basement hallway. They used the orchestra entrance to the Grand Theater, winding through various practice rooms for the musicians and out to the actual pit where they sat unseen during shows. Austin moved up the narrow steps to the main stage and she followed him, admiring the view.

"*There* you are, snookums. I've been *waiting* for you."

She winced at both the nickname and the aggravated tone. Bub—Mark. "Good morning to you, too," she replied evenly.

"What the hell have you been doing all this time? Where were you? Were you with *him?*" Mark's whining was quickly giving way to strident jealousy.

She answered vaguely, "Austin took me someplace safe while the police sorted out what happened yesterday."

"Did they catch the shooter?" Mark asked urgently. She couldn't tell if it was just a case of his usual nosiness or if that was fear vibrating in his voice.

She shrugged. "I don't know. Austin took care of everything." Speaking of Austin, she smiled over at him, and his eyes lit with an answering smile.

Mark looked back and forth between the two of them and thunder gathered on his brow. It didn't take long for the storm to break. About a second-and-a-half. For some reason, this morning his tirade bugged the living heck out of her. She usually let it roll off her back. But today, she saw Mark through Austin's eyes—and the view was not pleasant.

What was she going to do with him? She couldn't get rid of him, but she couldn't stand being around him, either. How much would it cost to just buy him off? He was desperate to get his hands on wealth and fame, and if she gauged him correctly, he didn't care how he got either.

His initial plan had clearly been to marry her. She'd been stunned when he'd proposed to her barely two weeks into their arrangement. That was the day he'd popped the 'little lady couldn't raise a rugrat by herself' line on her, in fact. It had also been the day she'd made it crystal clear that she never intended to become romantically involved with him.

Would a million dollars do the trick?

She wasn't made entirely of money, and that was no small sum to her, but if it would make him quietly disappear, it might be worth it.

Usually Mark ran out of things to yell at her about by now, but this morning, he seemed inspired to new heights of ranting and raving by Austin's presence. She had to give Mark credit. He had being a bastard down to a fine science. Absently, she gazed around the stage, estimating its dimensions and playing with various possibilities for using the space in her show.

Mark continued to yell, and she registered the various stage-hands and technicians drifting off to places unseen. Which was just as well. It was embarrassing having to stand here and take this.

If he'd been mad at her for worrying him sick or for not letting him know right away that she was okay, she might have had more sympathy for his tantrum. But as it was, he was chewing her out for choosing the other bodyguard over him and making him look bad. She was appalled when the phrase "selfish pig" actually floated through her head.

What on God's green Earth had she been thinking to choose him to be the father of her baby?

Speaking of the other bodyguard, Austin stood in the wings of the theater, his arms crossed. At first, he'd seemed amused, possibly even pleased, by Mark's truculent behavior. He probably got a kick out of Mark showing his true stripes to her. Not that she needed the demonstration to know that Austin was exactly right about Sampson.

But now, as Bubba's tantrum wore on, a black scowl had settled on Austin's brow. Apparently, his patience had its limits, too. She knew the feeling.

She noted that in spite of his apparent irritation, Austin's gaze still roved everywhere, never settling in any one place for more than a few seconds. She got the distinct impression he wasn't missing a thing that was going on in every last corner of the cavernous theater. At least one of her bodyguards was doing his job.

A few stagehands still milled around, repairing and touching up the current stage set—part of a traditional Vegas production with lines of showgirls and a vaguely over-the-hill headliner act. Would that be her fate? To do occasional gigs in Vegas for her aging fans? She was so sick of all the phony glitz and glamour. Why couldn't she just do what Austin suggested and come out on stage and sing her songs?

"Silver? Are you listening to me?" Mark snapped.

"Yes, Mark. I'm listening," she replied dryly. "I believe you left off at 'what the hell do I see in that arrogant bastard?'"

Out of the corner of her eye, she caught the upward quirk of Austin's mouth. He was certainly chipper this morning, especially given how little sleep he'd gotten last night after a very long journey the day before. At least he'd gotten to eat and enjoy a hearty breakfast this morning. She hadn't managed to get down more than a slice of dry toast, and even that had come right back up. It had been a close thing to make it to the bathroom before she'd turned green and started heaving.

Speaking of her non-breakfast, all of a sudden, she was ravenously hungry—light-headedly so. Mark could really quit yelling at her any time now. The beginning of a headache commenced throbbing in her temples.

Thankfully, Saul bustled out on stage just then, and the

number of visible stagehands suddenly picked up considerably. And even more thankfully, Mark finally shut up.

Saul glanced down at his watch and she did the same. Hah. She was not only on time, but she'd gotten here a few minutes early. He sounded faintly surprised when he said, "Silver Girl. Glad you could make it."

"I said I'd be here. I keep my word these days," she replied evenly.

That earned her a thoughtful look. Then, without further comment, he launched into a tour of the upgraded features the stage had acquired in the past few years. She'd be interested to see what the lighting guys could do with that digital laser system when it came time to design that part of the show.

Mark tagged along, making snarky comments, until Silver finally turned to him and snapped, "Mark, this is my job. If you can't keep your nose out of it, go somewhere else."

He puffed up, offended, but shut his mouth and disappeared for the remainder of the tour. Unfortunately, when she stepped out to center stage once more, walking through various options for dance numbers and staging with Saul, he reappeared and started up again.

"Let's get out of here, babycakes. You've got the money to hire other folks to do all this work for you. There's no need for you to stand around here all day. You've seen it, now let's go. I made a reservation for us at La Bamba for lunch."

That got her attention. La Bamba Cantina was paparazzi central, with big windows that gave ridiculously easy access to photographers with telephoto lenses. More to the point, a sniper would have a clear shot at her anywhere in the place, too.

"Mark, I don't think it's a good idea to go someplace that public to eat. After the attack yesterday—"

He cut her off. "Nothing's gonna happen today. I guarantee it."

"What? You had a little talk with my stalker and told him to take the day off?"

He went beet-red. "I'm the bodyguard, and I say it's all right, dammit—" His voice was rising quickly to a bellow, and she winced. Dumb, dumb, dumb. She knew better than to set off his temper by being sarcastic.

All of a sudden, a large, menacing presence loomed beside her. Austin. Hovering protectively over her, perfectly still. Poised. Waiting. Threat rolled off of him in palpable waves. "Is there a problem here, Maynard?"

Mark shouted, "My name's Mark, you son of a—"

"Perhaps you should step outside and collect yourself until you can focus enough to do your job. I'll take over protecting the lady until you've calmed down."

Amusement flared in Silver's gut. She didn't for a moment doubt that Austin knew how infuriating his calm and reasonable advice would be to Mark. Sure enough, Mark turned several shades closer to purple and took an aggressive step forward.

Reluctantly, she tamped down her amusement and stepped between the two men. "Mark, it's okay. I'll go to lunch with you."

"You will not—" Austin started behind her.

She whirled to face him. "Stay out of this. Mark's waiting here until I'm done looking at the stage, and then he can guard me at lunch. It'll give you a little time off to rest and eat yourself. After all, you didn't get much sleep last night—" She broke off. Whoops. Probably shouldn't have said that.

"*Whaaat?*" Mark squawked. "What the hell?"

Oh no. Not good. Mark would rush Austin any second now, and in turn, Austin would break Mark in half. The press would find out about her feuding bodyguards and have a field day with it. And Harold would kill her show before it ever got off the ground. Must do damage control. Now!

She spun to face Mark quickly. "Never mind. He told me he was having trouble with jet lag." It wasn't working. A vein throbbed in his temple, and he looked apoplectic. His fists came up and he all but pawed the ground like a bull.

Crud. Time for drastic measures. She raced forward, plastered herself against Mark's beer gut and wrapped her arms around his vaguely rounded shoulders. After Austin, he felt…flabby. Distaste coursed through her. She forced herself to keep her arms around him, though. Nothing distracted him like a display of affection from her. Sure enough, she caught the smug leer he threw over her shoulder at Austin. She braced herself as he squeezed her too tight and tried to kiss her.

She simply couldn't bring herself to tolerate his wet, foul-tasting mouth on hers. She turned away as subtly as she could but feared he'd noticed anyway, given how his arms tightened cruelly around her.

"You're crushing me," she managed to gasp.

As much as she tried to stand it, she had to pull away from him. She wriggled free of Mark's reluctant arms and sighed in relief. She got the distinct impression that had Austin not been there, he wouldn't have let her go and might even have forced himself upon her further. A frisson of alarm skittered down her spine.

She turned and was just in time to catch Austin's tall form fading silently into the shadows of the velvet folds of curtains. Damn, damn, damn. It was all she could do not to run after him. To explain why she'd had to put up with Mark's pawing. To tell him about the secret arrangement, about why it was necessary to keep Mark happy, at least until after her show. It wasn't forever. Just six weeks.

Then she'd be in the clear to tell the whole world how she felt about Austin Dearing. She'd shout it to the rooftops. She just had to get through the show without a scandal. And to pull that off, she dared not alienate Mark. She needed him. Even if it meant pushing away Austin and hurting him. Unfortunately, it felt like she'd just buried a knife in her own heart, too.

Saul broke the tense silence that had fallen over the stage when Mark started to blow. "Silver, do you remember any of your old songs? I had the sound boys cue up the instrumental tracks from a few of your hits so you could try out the speaker system."

Halfheartedly, she smiled at the older man. His timing

always had been impeccable. "That'd be great. Have you got a mike for me?"

In no time, she was wired up with a barely there earpiece and mouthpiece attached to a wireless battery pack in the back pocket of her jeans. The familiar chords of one of her biggest hits started, and she closed her eyes, trying to imagine herself back in the good old days. The dance moves came back to her effortlessly, and she fell into the sequences. The sound system was great, with practically no feedback on the stage.

But there was something missing.

She didn't feel this music anymore. It didn't speak to who she was or what she thought about. She wasn't nineteen and only worried about having fun and dancing till she dropped. Who'd written those lyrics, anyway?

The next song started, an even more upbeat piece. Automatically, she started into the choreography. By the second verse, she was starting to feel nauseous. By the third chorus, the lights were spinning, and the rows of seats were wavering like a roller coaster. She launched into the last big dance sequence, and the entire stage heaved beneath her. And then everything went black.

Chapter 9

Austin lurked in the darkest shadows just offstage, watching in disgust as Sampson leered lewdly at Silver. What *did* she see in him? She was so out of that guy's league. She had more class in her pinkie finger than Sampson would amass in his entire life.

Her energetic dance number brought her over to this side of the stage, and Austin took advantage of his training to make himself invisible behind the various curtains, ropes and pulleys clustered beside him. He frowned. Silver looked pale, and that fine sheen of perspiration on her face didn't look like the honest sweat of exertion.

She finished singing the chorus and danced her way up a ramp and onto a raised platform. She squinted out at the theater, like she was having trouble making out the rows of seats. A hum of alarm low in his gut had him frowning as she wobbled and then took a definite misstep.

His protective instincts fired, and he didn't hesitate. He darted forward, out onto the stage. He peripherally registered Sampson, standing at the other side of the stage, his tongue all but hanging out with lust. But Austin's focus was on Silver. Time slowed as she staggered toward the edge of the platform. Not good.

He put on an extra burst of speed and reached the front of the raised stage just as she toppled over in a dead faint. She collapsed to her knees and then pitched forward into his arms. He grunted beneath her weight but caught her safely.

Sampson was just now getting his butt in gear to move forward. Lousy reflexes—must've had way too much beer over the years to be that dull.

"Hey, Dearing—"

"Not now," Austin snapped, turning to Saul. "Is there a dressing room I can lay her down in?"

"This way, son."

While Sampson blustered behind him, Austin hustled offstage, carrying Silver limp in his arms. Panic made him preternaturally strong, and she felt featherlight. His mind raced frantically. Please, don't be anything serious. Had he missed something yesterday? Had someone poisoned her? Had she eaten anything he hadn't?

They wound their way to a row of closed doors, and Saul opened the first one on the right. Austin brushed past him and into the cluttered space. A chaise lounge in the corner was covered with sequined costumes, which he pushed onto the floor with his foot before laying Silver down.

He glanced up just in time to see Saul slam the door shut in Sampson's face. "Thanks," Austin bit out.

Saul nodded grimly as he locked the door for good measure. "How is she?"

"I think she just fainted." He took her pulse quickly and pressed his ear to her chest. "I hope," he muttered.

Saul volunteered, "She has a history of high blood pressure, but as far as I know, she's always been good about taking her medicine."

Austin commenced chafing her wrists. "Call the hotel doctor. I want a blood pressure cuff on her *now*."

The older man pulled out his cell phone and made a quick call. As he hung up, a god-awful pounding started on the dressing room door, accompanied by Sampson bellowing unintelligibly outside.

Silver's eyes fluttered but didn't open.

He glanced over at Saul, who was looking worriedly at the rattling panel. Austin sighed. "I'll take care of him." He stood up and moved swiftly to the door. He yanked it open. "Quit making a fool of yourself, Mick. The doctor's on his way. Go be useful and show the guy back here when he arrives."

"My name's *Mark*—"

Austin cut him off. "Go get the doctor and quit making so much noise. My four-year-old nephew has more control of himself than you do." And on that note, Austin closed the door—firmly—in the guy's face.

Saul was grinning when he turned around. Grinning himself, he headed back to Silver's side. Her eyes fluttered again, opening partially this time. She asked vaguely, "Did you just call Mark a four-year-old?"

She was conscious. Relief flooded him. It might have been a simple faint, but he'd still been sick with fear. "Actually, I called him worse than a four-year-old."

A hint of a smile crossed her ghostly pale features as her eyes drifted closed.

He knelt beside her and asked gently, "Honey, have you taken your blood pressure meds for the past several days?"

She opened her eyes again, their delicate blue piercing him straight through the heart. "Yes. Like clockwork. Especially now…"

"Why now?" he prompted when she didn't continue.

Her gaze slid away from his. "Especially now that I've got this show to do. Can't afford to mess it up." She lurched in alarm. "Saul, there weren't any reporters around, were there?"

"The theater's closed and locked. We were alone. Just my staff. And they know better than to blab to the press if they want to keep their jobs."

Austin frowned. What was he missing here?

He glanced up at Saul, who obligingly explained. "Tabloids eat up stuff like this. Pop star collapses while attempting comeback." He got a thoughtful look on his face. "But maybe we ought to let it leak. You know what they say. Any publicity is good publicity."

Silver lurched on the couch and blurted, "No!"

Both men looked down at her questioningly.

Reluctantly, she explained, "Harold said he'd cancel the gig if I show up in the tabloids again."

Austin and Saul "ahhed" simultaneously, and then abruptly exchanged alarmed looks. *Sampson.* "I'll go take care of it," Austin murmured.

"You're a good boy," Saul murmured back as Austin headed for the door.

"Where are you going?" Silver cried. "Don't leave me!"

He paused, his hand on the doorknob. She looked as frantic and scared as a kid who'd just lost her puppy. "I'll be back in a minute, honey." When her expression didn't ease, he added, "I promise."

The frown on her brow smoothed out a little, and he stepped out into the narrow hall. It didn't take long to find Sampson. The guy was in the middle of the stage throwing a hissy fit over what was taking the doctor so long.

Austin strode out to have a private word with the man.

Sampson turned to face him and drew a breath, but Austin cut him off before he could utter a word. "Don't get started with me, Mack. Nobody's here to stop me from smashing you into a million pieces this time."

Interestingly enough, Sampson clammed up. Give the boy credit for having a sliver of self-preservation at any rate.

Austin continued, "So here's the thing. Silver really doesn't want this little episode to show up in the newspaper. Saul assures me his staff won't spill the beans, which means, if I catch wind anywhere outside this room of her fainting, it's your ass I'm kicking into last week. Got it?"

"Are you threatening me, Dearing?"

Austin considered Sampson like he might a mildly interesting insect. He reached out to flick an imaginary piece of lint off Sampson's shoulder. Then he answered evenly, "No, my friend, I'm not threatening you. I'm merely telling you what's going to happen if you don't keep your mouth shut."

"I'll press charges. I'll get you tossed in jail, and they'll throw away the key! I have contacts in this town, you know—"

Austin took a gliding step forward, casually invading the guy's personal space even more. "Do you seriously think I'd be stupid enough to leave behind any evidence of your existence? I have friends, too, Sampson. The kind who can and will make you disappear so your remains are never found. You catch my drift?"

The guy's eyes went wide. He took a step back. But when Austin didn't follow, he seemed to regain some of his bluster. "This isn't over, Dearing. I'll show you. I'll show you all. I'll get the girl and laugh all the way to the bank, and you'll be wondering what the hell happened."

A chill chattered down Austin's spine. What did this guy have on Silver? Surely he was holding something over her to be this confident. Certainty that Sampson was blackmailing her washed over him. And if she hadn't come clean and run screaming from this guy yet, it was something big. Something she didn't want to face.

Determination to help her washed over him. But first, he'd have to get her to confess her secret to him. Austin spoke grimly. "Stay away from her, Sampson. If I catch you around her again, I'm going to hurt you. Bad. And that's a promise."

One of the theater's doors opened, spilling a shaft of bright light into the huge, dim space. A man carrying a leather bag hurried down the center aisle.

"Are you the doctor?" Austin called.

"Yes."

"She's backstage. This way." Sampson forgotten, Austin led the doctor quickly to Silver.

She'd regained a little color, which was to say she'd gone from gray to ghostly pale, but she still looked terribly weak. Nonetheless, she waved a wan hand at him and Saul. "Go away, you two."

Reluctantly, he left her to the doctor's care. Saul grinned at him as he paced the hall outside. "She'll be okay, young man. She's stronger than she looks."

Worried, Austin turned on the man. "How do you know that?"

"She holds her own with her father and that boyfriend of hers, doesn't she? She's tough, I tell you."

"Yeah, well, she shouldn't have to be. She should have someone who gives a damn to look out for her and take care of her."

"Like you?"

Yeah. Exactly like him. Thing was, he got the distinct impression that Silver valued her privacy above just about all else. He'd be no better than Sampson if he announced to Saul that he intended to make her his at the first available opportunity. Austin mumbled, "No, not me. I'm only here for a few months, and then I'm going back to my real job."

Saul's gaze narrowed almost threateningly. "Don't you break my girl's heart, you hear? She's had a lot of bad luck in her life, and she's working hard to make a new start. Don't you mess this up for her."

Austin stopped pacing. Stared at Saul, who looked as fierce as a bear at the moment. "You're really worried about her, aren't you?"

"She's like my own daughter."

Austin nodded respectfully. "I won't do anything to hurt her." Except he already had. He'd taken her to bed despite it being foolish and selfish in the extreme. He'd never forget that wounded look on her face last night when he'd called her a plastic pop star. He hadn't meant it the way she'd taken it, but he hadn't thought about how it might sound to her. And then there'd been the blow to her when he'd reminded her he'd be leaving in a few months; he'd seen that flash of *knowing* in her eyes. Men had left her before. Probably without warning and without a goodbye if that look was any indication.

She deserved better than him.

And that was the thought uppermost in his mind when the dressing room door opened a minute later, to reveal the doctor, with Silver standing behind him.

His eyes never leaving her lovely face, Austin asked lightly, "Is she going to live, Doc?"

"I think she might pull through. It was just a combination of fatigue, lack of food and a little stress. Nothing to worry about."

Silver murmured her thanks to the doctor and Austin added his as well.

As they stepped out into the hallway, she asked, "Where's Mark?"

She might as well have punched him in the gut. Sampson was so freaking lucky to have a woman like this give a damn about him. "If he knows what's good for him, he's not here," Austin growled.

"Please tell me you didn't pick a fight with him."

He snorted. "If I pick a fight with him, you'll know it from the blood and Sampson body parts strewn all over the place."

"Did you two argue?" she pressed.

"We had a…conversation. Came to…an understanding."

Alarm blossomed on her face. "Did you make him mad?"

"Kinda hard to talk to him and not make him mad, it seems."

"What did you say to him?" she asked urgently.

Austin frowned. "I told him to stay away from you."

Silver wrung her hands in agitation. "I told you to stay out of it! Oh, Lord. There's no telling what he'll do now."

"He'll do nothing now, or else he'll answer to me." Austin retorted.

"You have no idea what you've done!" she wailed.

Heads were starting to turn among the stagehands, and Saul and the doctor were looking uncomfortable. He said quietly, "Why don't we go someplace a little more private and you can explain it to me."

She looked around suddenly, as if she'd become aware of their audience. She nodded, abruptly silent. Sheesh. What a way to live. Always having to look over her shoulder for journalists or people who'd sell her out to one. He was already craving a little anonymous privacy, and he'd only been living her life for a single day.

Of course, in his line of work, it was all about being invisible. Unnoticed. Sliding in and sliding out unseen and unheard. It was the polar opposite of her existence. She could have this fame and celebrity stuff. He'd take the obscurity and complete absence of recognition of his work over her life.

"Let's blow this joint," he muttered.

"I need to swing by my dressing room and pick up my purse first."

He nodded and led the way backstage, stopping outside the room she'd changed in earlier. She stepped in to fetch her bag.

A muffled scream had him shooting through the door before he was hardly aware of moving.

She stood frozen in front of her dressing table, her hands pressed to her mouth, a look of horror on her face. He glanced up and swore. Scrawled across the mirror in some red, greasy substance were, "YOU DIE NEXT."

He moved around the space fast, checking it for intruders. Thankfully, there weren't any hidey-holes that could conceal a person. He turned to Silver and gathered her trembling form in his arms.

"I've got you, baby. You're safe. Nobody's gonna touch you on my watch."

She shuddered and burrowed against his chest, her face buried in his shirt.

He muttered, "Let's go. I'll call the police and have them come check this out. Can you walk or do you need me to carry you?"

She leaned back far enough to stare up at him. "You'd carry me?"

"If that's what it takes to get you out of here."

"You're in luck. I can walk."

He kept his arm tightly around her shoulders, her body tucked against his side as he turned for the door. He saw Saul standing there, gaping at the scrawled threat. "Lock this door and don't let anyone in until the police get here. Tell the cops to come in plain clothes, through a back entrance," Austin ordered quietly. "If you can manage to keep hotel security out of this for a day or two, that'd be helpful. LVMPD will appreciate having the breathing space to do their job before Harold crawls up their—" He broke off. "Well, you get the idea."

Saul nodded knowingly and pulled out his cell phone. As Austin whisked Silver out of the room, the older man was already on the horn to the police.

He rushed her out a backstage exit, emerging into a service hallway leading to the hotel's laundry. She directed him to a service elevator, and he ushered her inside with a quick look in either direction down the deserted hall. He randomly punched a button and the elevator whooshed upward quickly.

"Are you okay?" he asked in concern.

She nodded, but she still looked badly shaken.

"I gather writings on your mirror are not common occurrences?"

She smiled halfheartedly at him. "Not so much."

"You're not gonna faint on me again, are you?"

She replied bravely. "Thanks for worrying about me, but I'll be fine. Everything's proceeding as it should."

He frowned. Strange way to describe her health. She looked momentarily alarmed, then asked quickly, "What's on the twentieth floor?"

"Huh?" He glanced over at the elevator's control panel. "Oh. We'll transfer to an elevator that will take us up to the penthouse. Nothing special about twenty. I just punched any old button. Odds of someone being there waiting for us are close to zero."

"You really take this security stuff seriously, don't you?"

Surprised he glanced down at her. "I spend most of my life around people who will die if I don't do my job to perfection. I don't get assigned to the popular guys who are beloved by their people. I guard the guys everyone wants to kill."

She shuddered. "That sounds *so* dangerous."

He shrugged. In point of fact, it was more dangerous than she knew. Daily, he lived in real danger of being shot or blown up in an assassination attempt. The fact that he was only sporting a busted eardrum after the latest attempt to kill one of his principals was a minor miracle.

"Have you actually come close to dying before?" she asked curiously.

He snorted. "You're joking, right?"

She looked up at him innocently. What must it be like to be that unaware of how deadly the world could truly be? A need to protect her naiveté surged through him, to keep her just like this—sweet, trusting and sheltered from life's harsh realities.

Except this was Silver Rothchild he was talking about. The way he heard it, she'd seen a whole lot of life's harsh realities already.

He blurted, "How did you stay so innocent through all the stuff you did?"

She stared up at him, saved from answering by the elevator door opening. He stepped out quickly, cleared the empty halls and gestured for her to follow him. It was a short jaunt down a hallway to a guest elevator. He swiped his key card and the elevator leaped upward toward the penthouse level.

He turned to look down expectantly at Silver. For her part, she looked disappointed that he hadn't forgotten his question.

Finally she answered. "What makes you think I'm innocent? I've done some pretty wild things in my day."

He frowned. "Then how do you maintain your positive outlook on life?"

Her hand drifted to her stomach as she laughed shortly. "The alternative is to slit my wrists. And I'm too much of an optimist to give up that easily."

The elevator jerked faintly beneath his feet, but it was nothing compared to the jolt coursing through him. "Is your life really that bad?" he asked. "You have wealth and fame and a family that cares about you."

"My family meddles in everything I do. Living with the press hounding you 24/7 sucks. My career is dead, my personal life is nonexistent and money isn't everything. Next argument for how great my life is?"

He laughed. "Ahh. There's the cynicism I expected out of you."

She sighed as he opened his door and ushered her into his villa. "I'm sorry. I try not to go there if I can help it."

"Why not?"

"It's toxic to my soul. I have a ton of things to be grateful for, and I'm not about to whine about my life. It's no more perfect than anybody else's life, though. Everyone's got problems of their own—rich or poor, old or young, the problems may be different, but we all have garbage to deal with."

"True. So what garbage fills your plate?"

"Nothing you'd care to hear about, I'm sure."

"On the contrary. I want to know everything about you, Silver Rothchild."

She threw him a startled look. Then the expression cleared. "Oh. So you can figure out who's trying to kill me."

No, because he was fascinated by her and becoming more so by the minute. But he bloody well wasn't about to admit that to her. Not yet. She was still far too distant from him to hand her a weapon like that. The first order of business was to test her interest in him to see if she reciprocated any of his desire to take this relationship further.

He commented, "You're gonna have to cancel your lunch date with Bubba. No public places for you today. Not after that message on your mirror."

"Gee. Darn."

He frowned over at her. "What the hell's going on between you two? You've got no chemistry, you've obviously got nothing in common and, if you have a lick of sense, the guy has to drive you crazy."

She sighed. "No comment."

Maybe not now. But he'd get her to tell him the truth sooner or later.

"Speaking of meals, I've got dinner with my family tonight. But never fear. It's at my dad's house. Do you think you can handle the whole Rothchild clan?"

"If you can, I can, darlin'."

She rolled her eyes. "Sometimes they're too much for me."

"If you need to bail out, just give me the signal, and I'll pull you out of there."

She blinked up at him. "What signal?"

He grinned back at her. "Just throw me one of those come-hither looks of yours that I can't resist, and we'll be out of there before you know it."

"You mean like this?"

He squeezed his eyes shut. That had been a mistake. A *major* tactical mistake to admit she had that kind of effect on him. He gathered her in his arms, ignoring the startled look she gave. "Yeah. That look, little minx."

She looked up at him, gazing through her thick lashes, blatantly flirting with him.

That was better. He couldn't stand that haunted look of terror lurking in her eyes. "What am I going to do with you?" he murmured.

She mumbled against his chest, "Keep me safe and never let me go."

If only he could do both.

If only.

Chapter 10

Silver gazed up at the Rothchild estate as Austin whistled under his breath beside her. The mansion was daunting even to her, and she'd spent a good chunk of her childhood there. Not that she'd ever felt that she truly belonged in the place. Candace and Natalie had seen to that. When her mother had married their father, they'd made sure she felt like the ugly stepsister she in fact was. In her opinion, it was a vast karmic joke that she'd grown up to have the striking looks and talent that she had.

To Austin she murmured, "It's just a house."

He grinned over at her. "Yeah. Twenty thousand gaudy square feet of just house."

She shrugged. "There is that." They walked up the front steps to the columned, Italianate half circle of the front porch. "I never can quite shake the feeling of being an intruder here."

Austin looked over at her in quick surprise. "Why do you say that?"

"Harold's not my biological father. When he married my mom,

he adopted me and I changed my name to Rothchild. He said it would serve me better in life than my father's name would have."

"What happened to your father?"

"He made some bad business decisions. Couldn't face the music and killed himself when I was little."

Austin swore quietly, then said, "I'm sorry, Silver."

"I don't remember him much. Harold's as close to a father as I've ever had."

"Then I'm doubly sorry for you."

Startled, she started to ask him why he'd said that, but the front door opened just then to reveal Harold himself. She blinked, stunned. Since when did he open his own doors? It was almost as if he'd been waiting for them!

And then, over the next few minutes, Harold was shockingly cordial to Austin. Usually her father treated the hired help like, well, hired help. But he fawned on Austin as if the guy was some kind of rock star. Which was ironic, because she actually was a rock star and merited only an absent kiss on the cheek.

Most of the clan was already assembled in the billiard room, sipping on cocktails and snacking on canapés before supper. The shrimp salad and curried-something petit fours did nothing for her, and she opted for a club soda while the others arrived.

Jenna Rothchild, Natalie and Candace's younger sister, drifted over to say hello. She was yet another tall, gorgeous female with the capacity to make Silver feel like an inadequate midget. But in Jenna's defense, she had always been kind to Silver. Although they were several years apart in age, they'd been good friends over the years and throughout their various antics.

As a blissfully happy-looking couple strolled toward them, Austin's hand came to rest possessively on the small of her back. His familiar touch ruffled and soothed her at the same time, and she was abruptly aware of how good he smelled. It wasn't the sort of thing she usually noticed in a man. But then, there wasn't much about Austin Dearing that she didn't notice. The guy completely filled her senses, commanding every bit of her attention.

"Austin, this is my sister, Natalie, and her fiancé, Matt Schaffer. He's in charge of security for a major casino chain, which I might add is a competitor of The Grand's. But we forgive him because he makes my sister so glowingly, obnoxiously happy. Nat...Matt, this is Austin Dearing—my new bodyguard compliments of Daddy dearest. He's some sort of military officer."

The two men nodded in mutual recognition like a pair of fellow warriors.

Eyeing Austin appreciatively, Natalie commented, "I gotta say, sis, this model's a vast improvement over the last one."

Silver tensed at the jab at Mark but forced herself to relax under Austin's all-too-perceptive hand. Okay, so it hadn't been the smartest thing she'd ever done to recruit Mark to help her with the whole secret-baby thing. But the deed was done. There was no backing out on their deal, whether she liked it or not.

Desperate to change the subject, she asked Matt, "Any progress on the investigation of Candace's murder?"

Austin went on full alert beside her. Mission accomplished. The boy was officially distracted from the subject of Mark Sampson.

Matt frowned. "The FBI forensics folks are certain from the angle of impact that Candace was pushed forcefully to have sustained her head injuries. But as for who did it, there's not much to go on."

"Are there any suspects?" Austin asked quickly.

Matt shrugged. "Since my Aunt Lydia was ruled out as a prime suspect, our best lead is whoever wrote those letters to Harold."

"What letters?" Austin asked ominously, looking pointedly at Silver.

She winced. "The threatening ones Dad got recently saying that all of the Rothchilds are going to die one by one."

Austin's jaw clenched. "That's the sort of thing guys like me need to know about, Silver. Have you got any more juicy little tidbits along those lines that you haven't shared with me yet?"

Like, oh, she was pregnant and he was guarding two lives, not one? Aloud, she replied, "Nope, that's it."

"You're positive?"

The significant undertone in his voice didn't escape her. What was he hinting at? Surely he didn't know…

She sighed. "Yes, I'm positive."

Thankfully, Matt laughed, breaking the tension between her and Austin. "You gotta be on your toes with these Rothchild women, buddy. They'll lead you on a merry chase."

Austin glanced down at her wryly. "So I've noticed."

She muttered in an undertone pitched for his ears alone, "Good thing you're not chasing me, then." It was a petty thing to say, but it really bugged her that he'd made such a point of telling her he had no intention of getting involved with her. It was apparently all well and good to have wild bunny sex with her but only as long as she knew up front that he was going back to his military life at the first possible opportunity.

He replied teasingly, "Don't knock it. You probably couldn't handle me, anyway."

Hah. She darned well could handle him! He'd loved it when she'd handled him last night, thank you very much. She stuck her tongue out at him and held out her empty glass. "Make yourself useful, and get me another club soda while I catch up with my sister."

Austin took her glass without comment, but he did cast a thoughtful look down at it and back up at her before he turned away. His being so observant might be a good thing when he was looking for bad guys, but it was a pain in the rear when he was nosing into her personal life.

"Wow, Silver. He's a hunk. Where can I get a bodyguard like that?"

"Hey," Matt protested. "What about me?"

Silver laughed along with her sister. It felt good to be getting along with her like this. For too long, she'd been at odds with Natalie. In retrospect, it had been mostly Candace leading the way with Natalie following her forceful twin's lead. Now that Candace was gone, Natalie seemed to have settled down considerably. Candace had always portrayed Nat as the instigator, but Silver had recently revised her opinion on the subject. Now that Natalie was operating on her own, it had become clear that Candace had been stirring the pot all along to sabotage Silver's career and reputation.

Of course, she'd long ago accepted her own part of the blame in letting Candace get away with it. Ever since they'd been children, she'd secretly wanted to be like her flamboyant sister, and it had been her enduring Achilles' heel. Candace had always been the center of attention and the center of the action. So cool. So hip. Funny how, even at the height of her own fame and popularity, she'd always felt like a fraud compared to Candace.

Maybe all that time she'd been chasing Candace's idea of the perfect life and not hers. In a flash of insight it occurred to her that maybe that was why Candace had always been so jealous and vindictive toward her. So, if being a rock star had been Candace's dream, why was *she* diving back into the pop music game again? Guilt over her sister's death, maybe?

She rolled the idea over in her head. *Nah.* She was sorry Candace was dead, but she didn't feel any lingering debts or regrets toward her.

Her hand crept to her as yet flat belly. If she'd learned nothing else from watching how Candace had lived, always hovering on the edge of broke, living off of nothing more than the notoriety of being a Rothchild, using and abusing everything and everyone around her, it was that she was not going to follow Candace down that path.

She'd do the shows at the Grand out of respect for the generous gift that they were. But that was where her obligation to Harold—or anyone else—it ended. She'd do the shows her way, with her music. She made a silent promise to herself. From here on out, her career—her *life*—would go forward strictly on her terms and no one else's.

"Earth to Silver, come in," a voice said laughingly nearby.

She looked up, startled, at her sister. "Sorry." She added quietly, "You look good, Nat. You seem at peace with yourself."

"I am. I wish you the same happiness I've found." She glanced adoringly at Matt.

Simultaneously, Silver and Natalie stepped forward and hugged each other. Silver couldn't remember the last time they'd been so close. It was a shame that it had taken Candace's death to finally bring them together like this.

They drew back, and awkwardness settled between them. There was so much to say, but Silver had no idea where or how to get started. Finally she asked, "How are Candace's boys? I keep meaning to drop by Jack's place and see them." Jack Cortland was Candace's ex-husband and the boys' father.

Natalie sighed. "They're confused. They don't understand why Mommy won't come play with them. But thankfully they're too young to really understand what happened. Maybe it was a blessing in disguise that she didn't spend all that much time with them."

Silver nodded on cue, but she made another silent vow. No way was her baby growing up with an absentee mother too caught up in partying and living large to spend time with him or her. She was going to change diapers and do 2 a.m. feedings and pace the floors with colic…the whole nine yards. She was going to be there for her baby. It was a tragedy that Candace's toddler boys would never know their mother—no matter how flawed and distant she might have been.

Before she could wax any more maudlin and start boo-hooing, Austin returned with her club soda. She sipped at it while Austin and Matt sorted out exactly what sort of military man Austin was and then made small talk about their favorite guns. She was saved from the technical details of some newfangled pistol that both men were excited over by the butler stepping into the billiard room to announce that dinner was served.

Rebecca, looking stunning in emerald satin next to Harold, said dramatically, "Oh dear. Conner's not back from the police station with the Tears of the Quetzal yet. But dinner mustn't get cold."

Harold solved her dilemma brusquely. "If he can't fetch a simple ring in two hours, that irresponsible boy can eat his supper cold."

Silver's mouth twitched. Conner was thirty-four years old and a highly regarded criminal attorney. Hardly a boy, and definitely not irresponsible. Of all her various Rothchild cousins, he was perhaps her favorite.

Austin murmured sotto voce in her ear, "You do realize I'm never going to get everyone in your family straight, don't you?"

Her pulse leapt at the intimacy of his nearness, familiar and protective at the same time. She was tempted to crawl inside his shirt then and there. Whatever woman this man eventually gave his heart to was going to be one lucky lady, indeed. She sighed. What she wouldn't give to be that woman. She'd never met another man even remotely like him.

"Never fear. I can barely keep them all straight, and I've lived with them for twenty years," she muttered back.

The smile he flashed her all but melted her shoes off her feet. Lord, that man was sexy. Sheesh. He had to stop doing that or she'd never make it through supper.

"Doing what?" he murmured as the family commenced heading toward the exit.

She jolted. Had she said that aloud? Apparently. In a millisecond, panic flashed through her head. Should she play it safe or throw caution to the wind? What the heck.

She replied under her breath. "You have to stop smiling at me. Just think how scandalized the family will be if I have to throw you down on the dining room table and have my way with you between the main course and dessert?"

A grin spread across his handsome face. "I dunno. They look like they could use some shaking up."

She suppressed a laugh. "Believe me. You don't want to be around when Harold gets wound up. His temper is legendary."

"Being ravished by you would be worth it."

Her jaw dropped.

Austin pasted on a bland look, offered her his elbow formally and proceeded to decorously lead her into the dining room. Not a single decorous thought rattled around in her head as they filed down the long hall.

The grandkids and nieces and nephews materialized noisily from upstairs, and the entire bunch trooped into the dining room.

Silver was pleased to see Austin's place card beside hers. She started to reach for her chair but caught the glare Austin threw her and let her hands drop. As he stepped forward to pull it out for her, his hand came to rest on the small of her back, a fraction lower than was polite. His fingertips hovered just above the crevice of her buttocks, scorching her through the thin silk of her dress.

As she sank into her chair, grateful that her legs hadn't given out before she was seated, her father glanced down the long table and made eye contact with her. She smiled carefully, doing her darnedest to hide just how flustered she was.

No matter how hard she tried to stay mad at Austin for announcing that he would eventually leave her, she couldn't do it. His mere touch had her all but hyperventilating with lust. She glanced sideways at him as he took his place beside her.

A private smile for her glowed in his rich, green eyes as he glanced back at her. Almost as if he knew and relished the effect he had on her.

Oh, yes. A girl could definitely get used to having a man like him around. Too bad that was the one thing he'd promised he couldn't give her. The whole falling for someone just in time to get dumped bit sucked rocks. And she ought to know. She was the queen of getting dumped.

She made it through the salad course okay, but when the butler served her a plate of lamb chops, quivering green mint jelly and baby vegetables smothered in some kind of sauce, her stomach gave an ominous heave. She picked up her knife and fork and commenced picking at the sumptuous meal in a halfhearted effort to look like she was actually eating the too-rich food.

Her father boomed from the end of the table, "So, Silver, I hear you visited the Grand Theater today."

Oh, God. What else had he heard? Had someone felt obliged to tell him about her fainting episode? The last thing she needed was for him to decide she wasn't up to doing a show. She gulped and replied, "Uh, that's right. I love the improvements you've made to the stage. The digital lighting system is incredible."

"It ought to be. It cost me a bloody fortune. Saul said you ran through a few of your old tunes. How did that go?"

With an apologetic glance at Austin, Silver opened her mouth to utter a bald-faced lie, but a commotion in the doorway distracted everyone. Her cousin, Conner, burst into the room like a minor tornado.

"It was stolen! Right out of the police evidence locker! The Tears of the Quetzal!"

Silver's jaw dropped as her gaze skittered to her father. The Tears of the Quetzal was Harold's pride and joy. Her father swelled up like an angry puffer fish before he finally bellowed, "Whaaat?"

Conner continued, agitated, "They said a man in a police uniform signed it out of the evidence locker earlier today. It was signed back in just a few minutes before I got there to pick it up. Except a paste copy got left in its place."

Silver started as Conner dropped a heavy ring onto the table in front of Harold. Her father picked it up and examined it closely.

Conner went on. "They're reviewing the security videos to see if they can get an image of the guy. But it's gone. The Tears of the Quetzal has been stolen *again*."

Harold swore violently and flung the piece of jewelry the length of the dining room. Thankfully, his aim was true and he didn't bean any of the children seated at the far end of the table with it. The heavy ring slammed into a delicate porcelain vase, which toppled off the buffet and crashed to the floor, exploding into a hundred pieces.

Heavy silence fell over the room.

Rebecca finally broke the frozen vignette, suggesting in a soothing voice, "Why don't we retire to the library and discuss this more calmly."

Silver was surprised. Normally, Rebecca wasn't exactly the Rothchild she'd expect to be a pillar of strength in a crisis. But her stepmother's uncharacteristic calm seemed to penetrate Harold's rage, and he simmered down enough to shove back his chair and storm out of the room. Conner followed on Harold's heels, while the others trickled out more reluctantly. Austin gestured her subtly to remain seated until most of the others had left the room. As a result, the two of them were the last to leave.

Austin paused beside the shattered vase, bending down and scooping up the fake ring out of the shards of porcelain. "How did Harold recognize that this is a copy?"

"I don't know. Lemme see."

He handed her the piece, which had similar heft and weight to the original. The chameleon stone was priceless, shifting in color from purple to green and back again based on its temperature. It was the largest of its type in the world, a one-of-a-kind piece. She turned the stone, studying as it threw off the same peculiar lavender light of the original diamond.

"It's really quite a good copy. It captures the resting color of the original to a tee."

"Resting color?"

"Yes. When this stone is heated up, it turns a brilliant green for several hours. In that state, it's slightly darker than a typical emerald, close to…say…a green tourmaline in color. They're ferociously rare. Hence their value."

"And hence the reason it was stolen, I gather?"

She shrugged. "I don't know why someone would steal it. The stone's so unique you'd have a heck of a time fencing it without getting caught. And I can't imagine too many collectors wanting to risk the wrath of Harold Rothchild to possess the thing for themselves. If Dad ever found out anyone had it…"

Austin nodded and finished for her. "They'd wish they'd never laid eyes on the rock. Never steal from a man with the means and capacity to make you pay for it in blood."

"You've got it." She slipped the ring on and held it out to study it at arm's length. She frowned at a faint roughness against her flesh. She took it off to peer inside the band. "See this jeweler's mark inside the band? The original's band is completely smooth and has no markings inside it."

Examining the jeweler's mark closely, Austin murmured, "Do you know if Harold had a copy made of the ring at some point?"

She nodded. "I believe there is one. My father kept the original under lock and key, refusing any of us access to it."

"How come?" he asked curiously.

She rolled her eyes. "He believes there's some crazy curse attached to it."

"Excuse me?" he asked, his right eyebrow creeping up.

"According to Mayan legend, the Tears of the Quetzal is supposed to bring true love to anyone who possesses it."

"Doesn't sound like much of a curse to me," he mused wryly.

"There's more to it than that," Silver explained. "You see, if the ring falls into the wrong hands, misfortune is sure to follow." She took a deep breath. "Two months ago Candace was wearing the Tears when she was killed. The killer stole it." She sighed. "So of course my father now believes that the curse came true."

Austin stared at her, suddenly comprehending. "So that's why your family suspected right away that she was murdered. Let me guess. You've kept this theft from the press to help the police investigation, too?"

She nodded. "But I can't imagine Harold cooperating too much more now that the police have lost the ring again. He's going to have a stroke if the police don't get it back. He went completely nuts when it was stolen the first time. When he wasn't ranting about catching Candace's killer, he was raving about getting the diamond back."

Austin peered inside the ring's band again, before passing it back to Silver. "Whoever made this fake sure knew what they were doing. Is this perchance the copy your father had made?"

"I don't know. You'd have to ask Rebecca. I expect the copy would be in her jewelry box, or maybe in the safe upstairs." She studied the stone again. "It really is a remarkable copy. If all of the Rothchilds hadn't grown up knowing every intricate detail about the original ring, we wouldn't have known the difference."

"That's probably what the thief was counting on," he said. "He probably won't expect the copy to be discovered for several days at a minimum, which would give him plenty of time to get away with the real one."

She shivered. "I guess we're not dealing with your run-of-the-mill jewel thief."

"You've got that right." Austin's eyes darkened. "Call me paranoid, but the timing of the murder, theft and that threatening letter your father got seem suspicious to me. There's no doubt in my mind that someone's out to get ole Harold."

"But why do you believe that he's the specific target?"

Austin stared down at her grimly. "Correct me if I'm wrong, but wouldn't his daughter and this fabled diamond be two of his greatest treasures?"

She gulped, realizing where his logic was leading. "You think Candace's death and the theft of the diamond were acts of vengeance against my father?"

Austin shrugged. "Or acts of rage." He escorted her out of the dining room and into the hallway where Natalie and Matt, last in the line of family members, were just disappearing into the library. He looked down at her thoughtfully. "Why did you mention vengeance specifically?"

"The letters said the writer was going to get even with the Rothchilds for wronging his family."

He nodded slowly. "It fits. And now, according to our lunatic killer's message in your dressing room, you're next on the list of precious things he's planning to take from Harold."

The thought that Austin was right shuddered through her.

"Did you have to remind me? Now I'll never get to sleep tonight!"

His mouth quirked into that boyish smile that made her toes want to wiggle. "One of the rules in my unit is that if you cause a problem, you're in charge of fixing it. I guess I'll have to help you get to sleep tonight, then."

Okay, that tied her toes right up in tight little knots of anticipation. She could *so* go for more of the same from last night. She could go for more of that every night for a long time to come. But it wasn't in the cards for her. He was leaving, and she'd be an idiot to get more attached to him than she already was. As it was, she couldn't imagine how empty her life was going to seem without him at her side around the clock.

Reluctantly, she replied, "Thanks, but no thanks."

The light left his gaze abruptly. She physically felt his emotional withdrawal from her, as sharp as a knife to her own gut.

She was *such* an idiot. She should've thought before she blurted out a flat refusal of his offer. He deserved an explanation at the least, but she couldn't exactly give him one in front of her assembled family. She tried to stop in the hall where they still had a modicum of privacy. Tried to tell him why she was turning him down. But he put a firm hand in the middle of her back and bodily propelled her forward. Obviously, the man didn't want to talk.

With her heels all but skidding along the marble floor, they rounded the corner into the library, a vaulted space filled with carved stone and floor-to-ceiling shelves of leather-bound books no one had ever read. Austin might be stronger than her, darn it, but he wasn't more stubborn. She owed him an explanation, and he was going to get it whether he wanted it or not. Now.

"Austin—"

"Not now."

"But—"

"No." She had no idea how he managed to make a single whispered syllable into a sharp command she had no desire to disobey.

Irritated enough to draw a little blood, she muttered, "Fine. Be that way. But if Mark found out we spent another night together, he'd kill you."

Austin sighed as if he knew it for the taunt it was and finally looked down fully at her. "And how would he find out? I bloody well wouldn't tell him. I told you. Your secrets are safe with me. Would *you* tell him about us?"

Her female instincts fired strong and clear. He was testing her. Checking to see if she'd slept with him because she liked him or just to get Mark's goat. So Austin was human after all. Sometimes she wondered.

In response to his question, she snorted. "Why would I say anything to Mark about us? It's none of his business. Besides, I'm not in the habit of waving red flags in front of bulls. His temper scares me."

Austin stopped dead in his tracks. He stared down at her in what she would swear was satisfaction tinged with relief.

Then he leaned in so close that her breath caught in her throat and he whispered in her ear, "Don't worry anymore about Mark blowing up. If Bubba ever tries to tangle with you again, he'll have me to answer to. And I promise you, he'll be so dead so fast he'll never know what hit him."

The sexy heat of his breath on her skin distracted her so completely that she barely registered his words. But then she jerked back, stunned by the casual threat in Austin's voice. "You can't kill him!"

Austin straightened up, a fake smile pasted on his face as a few heads turned their way. Behind it he growled, "Why the hell not? I've never met a guy more deserving, if for no other reason than the good of the human gene pool."

Panic climbed the walls of her stomach. "I'm serious, Austin. Don't you hurt him. I need him—" She broke off, appalled at what she'd almost revealed.

"What the hell for?" Austin burst out, abruptly drawing the attention of the rest of her family.

"Hush," she muttered urgently. "Can we talk about this later? *Not* here?"

"Promise?"

"Sure. I promise. Just *please* smile nicely and change the subject."

"All right." He added darkly under his breath, "But I'm holding you to that."

The next hour was a trial, listening to her father bluster about what he planned to do if he ever caught up with the bastard who'd stolen the Tears of the Quetzal not once but twice.

Austin and Matt agreed that the thief in both cases was probably the same guy. And that idea made her intensely nervous. What thief robbed the same victim twice? That spoke of the rage and vengeance Austin had mentioned earlier. Surely, any sane thief would cut his losses and run after losing the ring the first time.

Thankfully, Austin didn't bring up the scrawled message on her dressing room mirror, and word of it seemed—miraculously—not to have reached Harold's ears yet. Of course, it was only a matter of time before her father found out about it from the hotel security staff and had a conniption. She'd just have to convince him that Austin was good enough at his job so she could go on with her show anyway. Piece of cake. *Not.*

"Will Harold be mad if we slip out of here early?" Austin murmured.

Gratitude flooded through her. He seemed to anticipate her needs before she was hardly aware of them, herself. "He's so upset by the theft, he'll hardly notice. Let me just go say goodbye. I'll claim that I have to get up early to rehearse."

"Early rehearsal. Got it."

She grinned up at him as his green eyes twinkled down at her. "I don't make a habit of lying, I'll have you know. But sometimes with Harold, it's so much less complicated to just gloss things over a little."

"I completely understand. Go do your thing with Daddy. I want to have a quick word with Rebecca. And Matt."

It felt weird to step away from Austin. Like part of her was suddenly missing. She'd become so accustomed to his big, safe presence plastered to her side that she felt naked without him. How was she going to manage without him once he went back to whatever war zone he'd come from? The thought was too awful to contemplate. She forcefully pushed it out of her mind.

And then Harold was looming before her, still blustering and cranky.

Taking a cue from her surprisingly adept stepmother as she hugged him goodbye, she murmured sweetly, "Thanks for arranging to have Austin guard me, Daddy. He's wonderful. You're the best."

Harold fussed and acted gruff, but she could tell he was pleased. Hmm. Who'd have guessed that he would be susceptible to feminine flattery? Apparently, old dogs could learn new tricks after all. Or at least they could when a madman was threatening them and all they held dear. But then she caught the calculating gleam in Harold's eye as he glanced back and forth between her and Austin.

No. He wouldn't.

He would.

Could he really be scheming to throw her and Austin together? The idea sent a jolt of exultation through her.

Whoa, there. No Silver and Austin sitting in a tree, K-I-S-S-I-N-G. Austin had made it perfectly clear he wanted nothing to do with a relationship with her.

But dang, it would be nice if he were interested in her. He was a heck of a catch, the kind of man she could see herself being happy with forever.

Sighing, she turned to join him. And her pulse raced. Austin was looking straight at her. Studying her intently, in fact. Her skin warmed and her insides felt mushy all of a sudden. And what was that look in his eyes? Was that actually a spark of desire, calculation even, that she'd glimpsed before he carefully masked his expression?

Could it be?

Was it possible?

No way.

Were Harold and Austin in cahoots to tear her away from Mark? If so, what did that say about the night she'd spent with Austin?

Chapter 11

Austin watched Silver in the shadows of the limousine's interior. An evening with her family had been good for her. She seemed more relaxed, more open, in spite of the drama over the stolen ring. The Rothchilds hadn't been what he'd expected. He hadn't expected them to be that…nice…in the midst of the opulence they lived in. Silver suddenly seemed much more like a regular girl to him. Approachable. Hell, touchable. His life would've been a whole lot less complicated if the Rothchilds were snooty, pretentious socialites and Silver one of them. But no such luck.

At least he'd had a stroke of luck with Rebecca. Sure enough, her paste copy of the Tears of the Quetzal had disappeared not long before Candace's murder. She hadn't thought anything of it when it came up missing; apparently the Rothchild jewelry collection was extensive, and it wasn't uncommon for a piece to be removed from the safe for cleaning or appraisal. It did explain how Candace's appropriation of the original was spotted so quickly, however. With both pieces gone, their absence was perfectly obvious.

And wasn't that an interesting little tidbit about Candace? Not too many women would waltz into their father's safe and help themselves to a priceless ring. Ballsy woman. Rule breaker. Make that a dead rule breaker.

When he'd asked Rebecca about where and when the copy of the ring had been made, he'd struck out. It predated her marriage to Harold, and that was all Rebecca could tell him about it. At least he'd made out the name of the jeweler stamped inside the band. Delvecchio's. If he was lucky, that would turn out to be a local outfit. And just maybe the thief had inquired about the Tears of the Quetzal there.

He knocked on the blacked-out glass partition behind his head and it lowered immediately. "How long until we reach the Grand?"

"Fifteen minutes, sir."

"Thanks. And don't sir, me. I'm hired help, too."

The driver grinned at him, and the partition started back up.

"Wait!" Silver called out, startling Austin. "Turn up the radio!"

The driver did as she asked, and she closed her eyes, listening intently to the now blaring country music tune.

Austin didn't recognize the song. Unfortunately, the remote corners of Afghanistan didn't offer much by way of American country music radio stations. Silver began to hum and then to sing along, her eyes still closed. As she gained confidence with the tune, her voice grew in strength and volume. She began ad-libbing harmonies in a pure, clear tone that soared above the melody, weaving in and around the male artist's voice as seamlessly as if the song had been meant to be recorded that way.

Austin was stunned. He'd known she was a good singer, but he had no idea how good until hearing her in person like this. She didn't sound the slightest bit like the pop star he knew her to be. Gone was the street slang, the riffs, the urban rasp. Her voice seemed tailor-made for this unapologetically mournful ballad of love and loss.

The song ended, and her singing trailed away to humming and then to silence. Her eyes fluttered open and she didn't look like she knew exactly where she was. The glass quietly slid closed, and they were alone again.

"Wow," he said in awe. "That was gorgeous. You ought to record a duet with whoever was singing on the radio."

She smiled ruefully. "Nobody who listens to country music has the faintest idea who I am. Besides, a star that big would never record with me."

"Methinks you underestimate how famous you were in your day."

She shrugged. "'Were' being the operative word. The music business moves fast. You're last week's news in a year or two. I've been out of the game for a lifetime."

"All the more reason you could get away with going in a new direction," he countered.

She laughed lightly. "I can't exactly picture myself prancing around the Grand Ole Opry mostly naked, doing vulgar hip thrusts all over the stage."

"I dunno. It worked pretty well for Elvis. Although the white jumpsuits would be a radical change of image for you. But you do sound like you were born to sing love songs to a twangy guitar in the back of a pickup truck."

"I don't even own a pair of cowboy boots!"

"We're in Nevada for God's sake. A girl has to be able to get a decent pair of boots around here, somewhere. And aren't we going shopping in the morning anyway?"

She shook a playful finger at him. "You're a bad influence, Austin Dearing. My record label and Saul would kill me if I did something that different. My fans wouldn't stand for it, either."

"I'm not so sure of that. They're all seven years older, too. They've gotten married and started having kids and are holding down mortgages and real jobs, now. You might be surprised at the kind of music they're listening to these days."

"Good grief, you make me sound ready for the Lawrence Welk show."

He laughed. "Hardly. I'm just saying I think you could get away with growing up. Your fans have."

She studied him intently, as if the concept were intriguing.

And then it dawned on him what he'd just said. He'd just made another plastic pop star gaff. "Hey, I'm sorry. I didn't mean that the way it came out. You're plenty grown up. I was talking purely about your performing image."

She nodded. "I caught that. But thanks for clarifying. Most thirty-year-old women wouldn't be too thrilled at being told to grow up."

He huffed. "I'm a man of action, not words."

One of her graceful eyebrows arched humorously. "I'm not so sure about that. I haven't gotten all that much action out of you today."

His jaw dropped for a moment before he realized she was intentionally baiting him, then his gaze narrowed threateningly. "You're not challenging my manhood, are you?"

"If the shoe fits..."

"You are a brave woman. Or else a very foolish one."

She waved a breezy hand at him. "I dare say I'm the latter."

Whether he slid forward off his seat first or she slid off hers first, he couldn't rightly say. But before he knew it, they'd met in the middle of the cavernous vehicle on their knees—hands plunging into each other's hair and tearing at each other's clothes, heads tilting for a voracious kiss.

Damn, he couldn't get enough of this woman. His body was already hard and ready. Of course, it didn't hurt that she was crawling all over him like she couldn't get enough of him, either. One of her legs wrapped around his waist, and he growled deep in his throat as her heated core scalded him through his slacks. The smell of her desire, spicy and sweet filled his nostrils, and then her hands slipped around his waist, joining her leg in urging him closer.

"Honey, we're in a car…"

"You've been rolling around on floors with me ever since we met," she murmured back, laughing. "You gonna do something about it or are you wimping out on me?"

He conceded reluctantly. "I've never met another woman who'd bait a man capable of the things I'm capable of like you do."

"I'm not afraid of you," she laughed. But then she lifted her mouth away from his to gaze up at him seriously in what could only be interpreted as adoration. "Seriously. I've never felt as safe as when I'm with you. I love that about you."

He was such a sucker for those soulful eyes of hers. One look like that from them and he was putty in her hands. "The floor, huh?"

Her mouth curved into a vixen's smile. "Actually, I was thinking more in terms of you on the floor and me on you."

"Come here, baby. Show me what you had in mind."

He carried her down to the carpet with him, stripping her out of her panties as he went. He guided her knee across him, relishing the sight of her panting lightly over him, her eyes glowing with desire.

But then she took over, unzipping his pants and catching his flesh as it sprang forth from its confinement. Her eyes took on a look of sleepy anticipation that all but undid him. Smiling down at him, she stroked him into a frenzy of red-hued lust that all but drove him out of his mind. Brazen and beautiful, sexy and innocent all at once, she literally stole his breath away.

As she continued squeezing and stroking him, his pleasure turned to torture of the best possible kind. Gritting his teeth, he hung onto control by the most fragile of threads. And then he begged. Shamelessly. Laughing, she positioned herself over him, her moist heat lapping at the tip of his throbbing flesh.

In a blinding and truly painful burst of belated rational thought, he swore violently under his breath.

"What?" she asked, alarmed.

"I don't have any protection with me."

She laughed. "Not to worry. I've got the birth control angle completely covered. You don't have any diseases, do you?"

"After two years in the field without a woman? Nope. You?"

"I don't get enough action these days for it to be an issue, but no, I just had a physical. I'm good."

And with that, she slid him home. He gasped as sensation exploded all through him. He released his breath on a long, low groan of pleasure. Her dress pooled around them as she began to rock, a slow lullaby at first, building gradually to a frenzied ride that had her clapping both of her hands over her mouth to muffle the cries.

He grabbed onto her hips and hung on for dear life, thrusting helplessly into her, his body desperate to touch the very core of her. She met every thrust with one of her own, her internal muscles gripping him until he thought he was going to die from the pleasure of it. And when his release came upon him, her body milked him relentlessly, drawing out the exquisite agony of bliss until he actually did black out for an instant.

And then light and heat…and joy…came crashing back in on him all in a rush that was almost too much to stand—almost better than the orgasm itself.

Damn, that woman was something else.

She lay collapsed on his chest, breathing hard, her delicate skin flushed with sex and bursting pleasure, a smile of satiation radiant on her face. *And he'd put it there.* Soul-deep satisfaction flowed up from someplace deep within him, filling him with a sense of undeniable *rightness.* No doubt about it. She was The One.

She murmured lazily, "Am I squishing you?"

Hardly. He opened his mouth to tease her about weighing a ton, but the words died in his throat as her cell phone trilled in her purse.

Both of them went tense.

It would be just like Sampson to ruin this moment of delicious afterglow for them.

Silver sighed reluctantly and sat up. She swung her leg over his hips and went digging for her phone in her purse.

Reluctantly he sat up, setting his clothes to rights. He lounged back, still sitting on the floor, and watched her with hooded eyes. How was it that he felt like he was cheating on Mark Sampson with the guy's girl? Silver had made it crystal clear that whatever was between her and Mark wasn't meaningful to her.

And Lord knew, she couldn't keep her hands off of him any more than he could keep his hands off of her.

Sampson was a pig and treated Silver like dirt. The guy didn't deserve to wipe her shoes, let alone date her. Austin swore under his breath. To hell with scruples and keeping his hands off another man's woman. Any man who treated his woman that lousy deserved to lose her.

"Hello?" Silver all but whispered into the phone. A pause, then her voice rose to a normal tone. "Oh. Hi, Conner. Is there news on the ring?"

She listened for a minute, a frown gathering steam on her brow the longer he talked. Finally she replied tartly, "Just because I used to hang out with Darla St. Giles doesn't mean I still do. In case you haven't noticed, Conner, I haven't been arrested or peeled off a sidewalk drunk off my butt in years." She shook her head. "Candace and Darla stayed close, but not me. I haven't even spoken to Darla for a couple of years."

Another silence while Conner spoke, followed by a sigh out of Silver. "Last I knew, she lived over on the west side of town in the Mountain View Villas. Number 24."

Conner got off the phone fast after that, and Silver disconnected the call pensively.

"Everything okay?" Austin asked.

"I don't know. Conner thought he saw an old acquaintance of mine, Darla St. Giles, hanging out across the street from the police station when he came out of it. He thinks she might know something about the theft of the Tears of the Quetzal. He wanted to know where she lives."

Austin nodded, immensely relieved that the call hadn't had

anything to do with Sampson. He held out his hand. "May I have your phone for a minute?"

She passed it to him and he flipped it open and started rapidly pushing buttons.

"What are you doing to my phone?"

He looked up grimly. "I'm blocking Sampson's phone number."

Her eyebrows shot up. "Why?"

"So I don't have to sit through you talking to him." And so he didn't have to see that haunted look on her face every time her damn phone rang. Sampson was holding something over her as sure as the sun rose and set. The trick with blackmail victims was to get them to realize that no exposed truth was as bad as a secret eating out their guts.

Really. How bad could it be? Some pretty nasty things had been revealed about her in the tabloids over the years, and he was still crazy for her. In his line of work, he saw some seriously eyebrow-raising stuff. He was damned hard to shock. Now he just had to convince her of that.

The limo turned into the private, underground entrance to the Grand and commenced winding down the ramp. He couldn't make out her expression in the sudden dark. First order of business—get her to admit that Sampson was blackmailing her. "Tell me what you see in him. Please," he said quietly. "I'm completely at a loss to explain you two."

She shook her head. "I can't."

"Can't because you don't know yourself, or won't because there's no good reason for it?"

"Oh, there's an excellent reason for it. It's just none of your business."

He sat back, frowning. It wasn't exactly an admission that she was being blackmailed, but he could work with the tiny opening she'd given him.

As the limo pulled to a smooth stop, he said, "Honey, everything about you is my business. There's no corner of your life that isn't my business if you expect me to keep you alive. I've already told you I'll keep your deepest, darkest secrets, and I mean it. But you can't hold out on me if you expect me to do my job."

Looking dismayed, she stared him down, finally breaking the stalemate by murmuring, "Aren't you supposed to get out of the car first?"

Damn. He'd almost had her there. Scowling, he climbed out of the vehicle and looked around carefully. Just because he was frustrated didn't mean he got to be sloppy or lazy. After trading nods with the hotel security man standing at the hotel door, Austin spoke over his shoulder. "It's clear, Silver. You can come out."

She stepped out of the limo lightly, her movements elegant. Classy. No sign of their recent sex or their more recent conversation showed on her face. She merely said politely, "Thank you, Austin."

They walked inside, where another security man held an elevator door open for them. Austin whisked her into the small space and scanned his room card. The elevator jumped upward into the night. What the hell. Time to go for the jugular.

"What's Sampson got on you, Silver? The guy's got to be blackmailing you because there's no way you would voluntarily spend two minutes in the same room with him otherwise."

She stared blankly at him, her face a perfect mask that revealed nothing.

"Talk to me. I can help you, Silver."

A sardonic smile finally flitted across her features. "You can't fix everything, Austin."

"Maybe not, but I can damn well try. And I do succeed a whole lot more often than I fail."

She replied wistfully, "That must be a nice way to live life. I have a knack for screwing up most of the things I try."

"That's ridiculous. You had a massively successful career once, and you will again. You have a terrific family, and you're a kind and decent person. I'd say you've gotten more right than most people manage to."

She shrugged as the door slid open. He stepped out, did his security thing and walked her down to his suite. They stepped inside and he froze, his hand on the light switch. Silver bumped into him from behind.

"What?" she breathed. "What's wrong?"

"Someone's been in here."

"Of course someone has. This is a hotel. The cleaning staff goes in and out of all the rooms."

His instinct said it was something else. He pushed her back into the hall and bit out, "Stay here unless that elevator door opens. In that case, dive into the suite and close and lock the door as fast as you can." God, he wished he weren't working this detail solo. He could really use a couple more guys to cover her from an attack coming down the hall while he cleared this place.

Cautiously, he flipped on the lights and spun inside low and fast. He took a quick look around. No one moved. He practically sprinted around the room, checking in closets, under the bar and behind the sofas. A quick check of the bedrooms and bathrooms, a quick circuit around the pool and then back to the front door.

"Okay, you can come in." He all but ripped her arm off pulling her into the room, but he was tense as hell at leaving her outside alone like that. "I've got to show you some self-defense moves," he muttered. "Soon."

"You can relax, now, Austin. We're in your room safe and sound, and no one tried to kill me." She walked farther into the living room. "Oooh, look! Flowers!"

He hadn't noticed the elaborate arrangement other than to note that nobody had been hiding behind it when he swept the room.

She went over and pulled out the small white envelope tucked under a lily the size of his palm. "Let's see who it's from." She opened the envelope, then muffled a cry as she dropped the card onto the table.

He darted forward, scooping up the card in the same movement that wrapped her in his arms protectively.

Over her shoulder, he flipped the card over and read the scrawled words, "I'm coming for her. You can't keep her safe from me."

He swore foully and, keeping Silver tucked under his arm, yanked out his cell phone. He punched out the number of the florist printed on the bottom of the card, but there was no answer. He'd have to wait until morning to find out what they could tell him about who'd sent these flowers. He studied the card more closely. The neat handwriting looked exceedingly feminine. Either Silver's stalker was female, or most likely, a clerk at the florist's shop had written the note for a phone-in client.

"Why is this happening to me?" she wailed into his chest.

"Because you had the misfortune of becoming a Rothchild. Just remember, all this stuff seems aimed at Harold. Whoever's doing it hates him, not you. It's nothing personal."

"Gee. That's comforting."

"Believe me, it's better than someone having a vendetta against you directly."

Not that hearing something like that did a damned bit of good to stop her from shaking like a leaf in his arms. He suggested gently, "Why don't you go take a nice hot bath while I make a few phone calls?"

"To whom?"

"The police for one. The bell captain's station for another. Maybe they can tell me something about who delivered these flowers. It's a long shot, but you never know."

"Could you keep the hotel staff out of it? Daddy hears about everything that's going on around here, and if he knew I was getting these threats, he'd cancel my show for sure."

Austin grunted. "It's not like it's any surprise to Harold that someone's gunning for you, darlin'."

"Why do you say that? You yourself said he believes the shooting in the lobby yesterday was the random act of a deranged gambler."

His reply was somber. "I'm here with you, aren't I?"

She studied him a long time. "Are you really as good as you say you are?"

He looked her dead in the eye. "I'm the very best there is, and no amount of modesty is going to make that any less true. Your father knew exactly the caliber of bodyguard he was getting when he hired me. Believe me, with what I charge for civilian jobs, he knows he's paying for the best of the best."

He hated to be the one to put that haunted look back in her eyes after she'd finally lost it. But there it was again, and it was all his fault. "Go run yourself that bath. I've got your back, honey. You're safe."

"Keep telling me that, and maybe in a decade or so I'll believe you."

That was sounding better and better to him. The more time he spent with her, the more tempting she was. Tempting enough to pull him out of the field, though? Away from his men? His mission? His duty?

Twenty-four hours ago, he'd have said there wasn't a chance she'd manage that. But now? Guns or the girl? The scales looked pretty even from where he stood.

He waited until she'd retreated to the master bath to go for a swim in the giant tub there, and then he made his calls. As he'd expected, the bell captain said a local delivery service had dropped off the flowers using its usual delivery driver. The stalker was careful to cover his tracks. Which meant the flowers were no doubt going to turn out to be a dead end.

And that made him jumpy. Thwarting a psycho killer was one thing. Thwarting a *smart* psycho killer was another entirely.

Following his earlier hunch, he fished the Las Vegas yellow pages out of a desk drawer. No listing for a Delvecchio's Jewelers.

He looked up other jewelers who advertised making paste replicas of jewelry. The first store didn't answer, nor the second. But a man at the third store did. It turned out this very store, now part of a national chain, used to be known as Delvecchio's. When Mr. Delvecchio passed away a few years back, his widow had sold the place. Hot damn.

Even better, the clerk remembered someone coming into the store recently and asking about a copy of a big purple diamond. The clerk didn't know the name of the customer, but maybe the store's goldsmith would know it. He'd be in tomorrow morning. Bingo. Not a home run, but it was a lead. At a minimum, he ought to be able to get some sort of general physical description of the suspect.

Pleased, Austin hung up the phone. And now, to go extract from Silver whatever secret Sampson was using to force her to pretend to be his girlfriend. She wasn't avoiding him this time. He was going to get answers out of her and get to the bottom of whatever was going on between them, and that was that.

The water had turned off a while ago. She ought to be dressed by now. He tested the doorknob to the master suite, and it was unlocked. Perfect. He took a deep breath. Here went nothing. Mentally girded for battle, he turned the knob and stepped inside.

Curled up in a shaft of moonlight like a contented kitten, Silver lay sleeping in the middle of his bed. He swore under his breath.

He moved quietly over to her side to look down at her. Her beauty stole his breath clean away. She was one of those women whom it was hard to believe really looked like she did until you got close to her and saw her like this, with no makeup, no fancy hairdo, no artifice. Just the pure, lovely lines of her face kissed by moonbeams.

As beautiful as she was, lying there, disappointment coursed through him. He really was ready to get to the bottom of this mystery with her.

Man, she'd crashed fast. Poor kid must be exhausted after all the morning's excitement and then facing dinner in the lion's den. Except she was young and healthy…the day hadn't been that strenuous. Unless she was finally sleeping well after days or weeks of sleeping poorly. Sampson really did deserve to be run over by a locomotive or two.

Tomorrow.

Come hell or high water, Silver would tell him what was going on tomorrow.

Chapter 12

Silver was in heaven as she walked down the sidewalk. She was out of the hotel, she was going shopping and best of all, she was with Austin. It was a beautiful, cool morning, likely the last one of the year before the furnace-heat of summer packed in for the next four months. She hadn't felt sick at breakfast and had chowed down a substantial chunk of Austin's omelet, which was a relief.

He'd tried to bring up Mark, but she'd deflected him by gulping down a glass of orange juice, grabbing her purse and announcing that it was time to go. No matter that he was sulking now. Austin could get over it. It was too gorgeous a day to spoil it by thinking about Mark.

And then there was the shopping. She had the perfect excuse to buy a whole new wardrobe—her upcoming show and renewed public image—and she got to go shopping for it with a gorgeous hunk who couldn't take his eyes off her. Oh sure, Austin's assessing gaze moved all over the place like it always did, but every time she stepped out of a dressing room to model something new, his gaze snapped to her and he drank in the sight of her hungrily. It was sweet balm for a girl's ego.

"What do you think of this one, Austin? Is it country enough for you?"

He frowned. "You're actually planning to pay for a pair of jeans that beat up? Those have more holes than cloth."

"Aren't they great?"

He studied her legs intently. "Turn around. Let me see what they do for your caboose."

She turned around, the part in question burning at the idea of him blatantly ogling it. She seriously hoped he liked what he saw. All those hours at the gym had to be good for something, after all.

"Buy them," he said decisively. "But lose that shirt. I like the white one you had on two shirts ago better. It's sexier."

The shirt he liked was a sheer cotton knit so fine you could all but see through it. It buttoned up to a high collar but then fell in soft, figure flattering drapes. Now that he mentioned it, the shirt's very demureness had added to its overall sexiness. It was more understated than she was used to but with the right belt, and paired with these edgy jeans…

She nodded to the clerk who scurried off to fetch the shirt in question out of the reject pile.

Silver studied Austin curiously. "Any other recommendations, oh great guru of fashion?"

He shrugged. "I'm only the bag-schlepping guy today."

"And a fine job you're doing hauling around my bags, too," she laughed. "But you are a guy. You know what looks good on a woman, right?"

One corner of his mouth turned up. "I know what looks good on you."

"Do tell."

She listened in amusement and growing respect as he shredded her fashion choices with painfully accurate comments about what looked good—and not good—on her and why. Before he was done, she'd exchanged nearly half of her original choices for other ones. It wasn't that she blindly bought what he told her to. It was the fact that he made such sensible arguments for what complimented her and what fit the image of a hip, but definitely grown up, star.

At the end of the spree, she stood back and took a hard look at the hanging rack of clothes that had passed muster with him. She had to admit that he'd done well. She'd wear anything on that rack with pride and know she looked not only hot in it but also mature. Chic. That was the difference. She'd tried to duplicate her pop-star, early twenties clothes, and he'd chosen things fitting not for a girl but for a woman. A sexy one, thankfully.

"You know, Austin, if you ever get tired of throwing yourself in front of bullets, you'd make a fine fashion stylist."

He laughed heartily at that. "The only fashion I can fit folks out in is the latest bulletproof vest."

"You did great with me."

He shrugged. "That's different. I've made a thorough study of your body, and I happen to give a damn about how you look."

That made her stare. "Why?"

A hint of red climbed his neck. He harrumphed uncomfortably before finally coming back with, "Hey, I have a rep to maintain. Any woman I'm seen with in public, client or otherwise, has to uphold my usual standards."

She rolled her eyes, amused. "That is such a lie. But I'm having fun and you're behaving nicely for a man dragged along on a shopping trip, so I'll let you off the hook this time."

He rolled his eyes back at her as she pulled out her wallet to pay for her latest additions to the haul.

She vaguely heard some sort of commotion behind her and felt Austin slip into place at her back as she signed the credit card receipt. As the clerk separated the copies and thanked her profusely for the business, Silver murmured without turning around, "Everything okay back there?"

"Looks like we've been spotted. Either that or a whole bunch of skanky guys with cameras are out for a morning stroll and just happen to be mobbing the sidewalk in front of this store."

She peeked around him. "What do they want with me today? I'm just out shopping for some clothes. That's hardly tabloid-worthy news." She punctuated her disgust with a muttered oath.

He glanced back at her, grinning. "I didn't know you knew that word. Shame on you, Miss Rothchild."

"I know worse words, and they all apply to that pack of hyenas out there." She looked over at the clerk. "Is there a back way out of here?"

"No, I'm sorry. That's the only exit."

"Great," she muttered. "Looks like we get to go swimming with the sharks."

"How aggressive do you want me to be with these guys?" Austin asked.

"What are the options?"

"We can pose nicely and let them have their pictures, then we invite them to let us through, so we can clear out as quickly as we can. Then there's the jacket-over-your-head, no-pictures-today-please approach. Which gets a picture of you with your coat over your head printed on the front of a tabloid anyway. Then there's the one where I go out first and threaten to start cracking skulls if they don't back off. They'll use their telephoto lenses and get their pictures anyway, but they won't be directly in your face about it."

She sighed. "What do you recommend?"

"Do you recognize any of those guys?"

She studied the crowd of photographers and tipsters. "Actually, I know most of them. It's the usual gang."

He winced. "As much as I hate to say it, given that your father doesn't want you to get splashed all over the tabloid headlines, you probably ought to take the polite and cooperative approach. And at least that way they'll choose the more complimentary pictures of you to publish. Good Lord willing, some other poor schmuck celebrity will land in a scandal this week and you won't get the tabloid covers."

She appreciated his feeble attempt at humor. It was a kind gesture. "You'll stick close to me?"

"Wouldn't have it any other way, darlin'. And a word of warning. If I see anything that looks remotely like a threat out of any of them, I'm going to pull you out of there at lightning speed."

"Got it," she said with a smile.

"Your hair and makeup perfect?" he murmured.

She checked herself over in one of the many mirrors placed around the boutique and made a few adjustments. This was just like the good old days. Except back then, Candace would've barged out, started a brawl, blamed Silver for it and enjoyed watching Silver get accused all over the tabloids of throwing a tantrum at the press.

Eternally grateful for Austin's level head, she nodded her readiness at him.

He nodded back. "Let's do this, then. I'll go first. Stick close behind me while I talk to them."

Resolutely, she followed him to the front door.

Austin gestured for her to stay in the shadows while he addressed the reporters. "Miss Rothchild will be happy to pose for you for five minutes, but then she's got an appointment. Is that fair, guys?"

A murmur of surprise passed through the crowd. Poor guys weren't used to her cooperating with them. She hoped it took every last bit of fun out of them doing their jobs.

She took a single step forward, and the paparazzi immediately started pushing and shoving one another, all the while snapping pictures of her. What was up with that? They acted like they were in a full feeding frenzy. She hadn't done anything to merit this kind of enthusiasm! They acted like a million-dollar sale rode on them getting the best shot of her.

And then they started to shout out questions. "Is it true? Are you pregnant? How far along are you, Silver? Show us your baby bump!"

They shouted other questions about yesterday's shooting and

the Tears of the Quetzal, but all of those faded away in the face of her shock.

How in the world…

A vaguely familiar face leered at her—swarthy, dark haired and dark eyed, his gaze burning with maniacal enjoyment at this attack on her. Was he the guy who'd jumped at her in the casino two days ago?

He shouted maliciously, "Who's the father of your baby, Silver?"

Her brain shut down. Completely.

An overwhelming urge to flee overtook her. She looked left and right in panic. Nowhere to go. Bodies and camera lenses and flashbulbs hemmed her in on all sides, pressing closer and closer to her. She was cornered. Trapped!

"No. No, it's not true!" she cried. This was exactly the sort of scandal her father had forbidden her to fall into. Her scheme with Mark would be exposed. Harold would yank the gig out from under her. She'd lose everything and everyone who'd given her this second chance. Even Austin. Especially Austin.

Her gaze locked on his back in horror. She watched as, in extreme slow motion, he half-turned and looked over his shoulder at her, accusation written in every line of his face. Terrified, she lifted her gaze to look him in the eyes.

The crowd was shouting too loud for her to hear a thing, but as clear as day, she saw him mouth the words, "It *is* true, isn't it?"

Dear God.

Now what was she supposed to do?

Panicked, she mouthed back to him, "Help."

Thank God, he appeared to put aside his personal fury and nodded grimly at her. Squaring his shoulders, he turned briskly and faced the crowd, the picture of the professional he was. Politely, but firmly, he announced, "Picture time's over boys. Let us through."

When the wall of cameras didn't budge, and the din of shouted questions only got louder, Austin called to her over the din, "Grab my shirt and don't let go!"

She barely managed to catch the soft polo knit before he plunged into the crowd, his hands moving in a blur in front of him. She caught only glimpses of whatever he was doing, but the paparazzi fell back from him like magic, forming a narrow passageway that Austin wasted no time diving through. Flash-bulbs exploded inches from her face, but she put her head down and hung on grimly as Austin dragged her through the gauntlet. Then, all of a sudden, his back dipped down and strong, familiar hands reached out to drag her into the dark interior of their limousine.

"Go, Jimmy!" Austin called.

The car lurched into motion beneath her. It took her a couple of minutes to catch her breath and collect herself. Her brain whirled in frenzied circles as she tried to make sense of what had just happened.

How in the world had the press gotten wind of her pregnancy? Dr. Harris had sworn his staff was the soul of discretion and had promised her that professional medical ethics prohibited him or his staff from speaking about her pregnancy to anyone without her permission. Who then? Nobody else knew!

"Here. You look like you need this."

Austin shoved a can of orange juice from the limo's tiny refrigerator into her hand. She opened it gratefully and sipped its contents. Thankfully, her stomach was still behaving itself, and the juice went down without problem.

"We need to talk," Austin announced gruffly.

She squeezed her eyes shut in dismay. Oh, God. Here it came. He was going to blow his stack at her and dump her the way they all did. Her heart felt as if it was breaking in two already. And suddenly she was terribly sick to her stomach, but it had nothing whatsoever to do with her pregnancy.

Aiming for a flippant tone and failing miserably, she said, "Gee. It seems like I've heard that line out of you before."

"Yeah, it does seem to be a recurring theme with us, doesn't it?" he replied dryly.

She risked a glance up at him. His expression was completely unreadable. "Can we at least wait until we get back to your place? Privacy for this conversation would be a good thing."

He glanced in surprise at the closed partition behind him. No way was she talking where anyone else had even a chance of overhearing them. Not for this talk. He glanced back at her and must've caught the stubborn tilt of her jaw, because he nodded tersely and sat back, his arms folded across his chest.

The limo rolled along for several minutes in stony silence.

Too nervous to stand the strain of the tense silence any longer, she ventured, "Thanks for getting me out of there. You're really good at clearing a path through a crowd."

He didn't bother to reply. Rather he threw her a look that communicated a loud and clear, "Duh."

Okay, so she'd stated the obvious. The least he could do was acknowledge her attempt at breaking the ice between them. She tried two or three other innocuous comments, but he steadfastly refused to bite on any of them and maintained his silence. Harold would've been screaming his head off by now. Which, by comparison, would've been easier to put up with than this.

Betrayal and anger emanating off of Austin was made all the more palpable by his refusal to give vent to either. Maybe control wasn't always all it was cracked up to be. At least once Harold blew his stack he usually calmed down relatively quickly. She had no idea what to expect out of Austin. And that scared her to death.

So terrified she could hardly walk, she followed him through the usual routine up to his suite, waiting just inside the front door while he checked the place out. But this time he added a twist. He went into his room and emerged with some sort of handheld electronic device about the size of a cell phone. He ran it quickly over the walls and furniture before finally speaking.

"No bugs. We can talk now."

Well, she'd wanted complete privacy. The guy had certainly delivered it in spades. But she wasn't even close to ready to deliver on her end of the deal. How could she ever explain it to him?

"Are you hungry?" she asked in transparent desperation.

"Nope. Talk now. Food later."

Great. He wasn't even communicating in complete sentences with her. In resignation, she trudged over to one of the fawn-colored leather sofas that faced each other on the far side of the room. She sat down glumly, her gaze downcast. She felt him sit down across from her, but as always, he moved in uncanny silence and she heard nothing.

She took a deep breath. The only way to begin was to just start talking. The story would come out one way or another. "You understand that everything I'm about to tell you is in strictest confidence."

One eyebrow cocked at that, as if her saying it aloud was some sort of insult to his honor.

"Okay, fine. I know. You promise not to tell anyone anything." She took a deep breath and plunged ahead. "Yes, it's true. I'm pregnant. But I don't have the faintest idea how the press found out about it. Nobody knows. And I mean *nobody.* Me and my doctor and his nurse."

She flinched, waiting for Austin to blow.

But he merely sat there. And stared at her. Yet another silence grew between them. Stretched to the breaking point. And then, shockingly, he repeated relatively calmly, "You're pregnant?"

She nodded miserably and went back to staring at her toes, bracing herself for the explosion to come.

"Well. That certainly explains a lot."

He sounded almost *relieved.* What was up with that? She looked up quickly. "Like what?"

"Like why you fainted yesterday and why you can't eat any rich foods and why you passed up a glass of the hundred-dollar-a-bottle wine your father served at supper last night."

"I don't usually drink anyway," she retorted to that one.

"You didn't even let the butler pour you any. You didn't want to smell it, did you?"

"Well, no."

All of a sudden Austin lurched up, half off the sofa, before settling back, as if an intensely disturbing possibility had just occurred to him and then been as quickly dismissed from his mind.

"What?" she asked in alarm.

Austin asked, his voice dangerously quiet, "Who's the father?"

"With all due respect, that's not exactly any of your business."

He all but came across the coffee table at that. As she pressed back against the cushions of her sofa, violently startled, he waged a visible struggle with himself before settling back down on his own cushions.

His voice was thin with strain. "It's Sampson, isn't it? This is what he's been blackmailing you with."

There it was. The sixty-four-thousand-dollar question.

She had to say yes. The story was already in place. It was a done deal. Mark would take credit for being the baby's father, and she'd avoid the embarrassment of the real story coming out. Sure, an affair with her hick bodyguard was tawdry, but it would keep the press mostly off her case.

And as soon as she admitted that Mark was the father, Austin would back away from her for good. He'd leave her to Mark, no questions asked. He was too honorable to do anything else. He'd do his job, keep her safe and turn her back over to Sampson safe and sound in a few months. For once, she'd be the one doing the dumping and not the other way around.

Of course, he'd also walk out of her life forever and never look back, just like every guy who'd ever loved her and then left her. Of course, she'd learned not to look back, either. Sometimes pride was all a person had left to cling to. And Austin's formidable pride wouldn't allow him ever to forgive or forget this.

Something in her heart cracked at the thought. Pain shot through her. The kind of intense, emotional agony that few people had ever managed to cause her. In a moment of prescience, absolute certainty came over her that a whole lot of guys might have walked out on her over the years but none had ever hurt like this one was going to.

She and Austin could've had something really special between them, given a chance. Of that she was equally certain. In another place, another time, another set of circumstances…the chemistry was unmistakable. This was a man she could love. Deep and hard and forever.

She took a deep breath, prepared to say the words that would drive him away for good. And then she made the mistake of looking up.

The disappointment gleaming in his eyes was more than she could bear. And she was about to stab him in the gut with another lie. She *so* didn't deserve him.

But then something bubbled up within her. A kernel of hope. Maybe…just maybe…he'd understand if she told him the truth.

But what right did she have to dump the whole sordid story of her pathetic life on him? He hadn't asked for it. It was too much to ask of him.

"Silver?" he prompted. "Is this what Mark's been holding over you? Is he the father?"

She opened her mouth. She couldn't tell the lie. But neither could she bring herself to confess the truth. No sound at all came out.

And then Austin's control snapped. He surged up off the sofa. "Forget it. You're right. It is none of my damned business. I had no right to go after you when I knew you were involved with another man."

He cursed violently as he stalked across the room and back. "You're having his baby, for God's sake. Hell, I'm sorry, Silver. You tried to tell me, and I was so set on having you for myself that I didn't listen." He shoved a distracted hand through his hair, setting it akimbo.

It was the first time she'd seen him anything other than perfectly turned out—a measure of just how upset he must be.

"I thought we—" He broke off. "Hell, I didn't think. I'm sorry."

He whirled and strode toward the door.

"Austin! Wait! It's not what you think! I—"

But then the door closed behind him.

He was gone.

He'd walked out on her after all.

Chapter 13

She hadn't been wrong. Nothing in her life even began to compare to the pain of Austin's leaving. With the closing of a single door, her life became bleak and colorless, a sawdust-dry existence she walked through numbly.

Sometimes it sucked being right.

A tall, taciturn man named Warren showed up at the penthouse door late that evening. She was so distraught that she'd thoughtlessly opened the door to his quiet knock without even checking to see who it was. She already knew it wouldn't be the one person she desperately wanted it to be.

"Miss Silver Rothchild?"

"That's me," she'd answered dully.

"My name is Warren Bochco. Captain Dearing sent me. I'll be taking over your protection detail…"

And that had been when her heart well and truly broke. He'd left her for good. Of course, he'd never shirk a responsibility. He'd promised to keep her safe, and he'd see that promise through. But if he'd sent this tall, silent man to guard her, he had no intention of ever seeing her again.

Warren was speaking. "…briefed me on your upcoming show and the problems your family's been having. He said you knew the drill. I'll stay out of your way as much as I can as long as you let me do my job."

Warren was built like Austin, tall and crazy fit, but where Austin had been all tawny and bronze and smiling, Warren was a study in black. Black hair, black eyes, black clothing. Quintessential bodyguard material. And the guy had all the personality of a telephone pole.

The next month passed by in a blur. Grief and going through the motions of preparing for her show were all she registered.

She went along with every song Saul and her newly re-signed record label fed her. The mindless drivel they chose for her was right up her alley; she had no heart left to put into her music. A couple of the songs inspired a certain spurned-female anger in her and were pronounced her likely next hits. Probably because they were the only songs she could find any spark of emotion to relate to.

Interestingly enough, Mark dropped completely off the radar. He never contacted her, although she made no effort to unblock his cell phone number from her own cell phone, either. But he never showed up at any of her rehearsals or planned public appearances. For the first several press junkets she kept an eye out for him, waiting for him to pop up and announce that he was the father of her rumored baby. Why he hadn't done that already, she had no idea.

At first she wondered if maybe Austin had gotten to the guy and managed to apply a little blackmail of his own. It would've been like the old Austin—the one who had looked at her like he wanted her for himself and who'd been fiercely protective of her. But the Austin who'd turned his back on her and walked out—would he bother to shut Mark up to protect her reputation and her privacy? Somehow, she thought not.

Her morning sickness got worse but thankfully settled down to a predictable routine. She didn't eat before 10 a.m., scheduled her rehearsals for the afternoon, avoided all rich foods and she muddled by.

The prospect of a baby was still a miracle to her that she anticipated with immense joy, but her child's actual arrival was still such a distant event that her current agony greatly overshadowed it.

Warren followed her around like a grim shadow, muttering occasional orders that she followed woodenly. Every time he did or said something bodyguard-like, it inevitably reminded her of Austin and piercing pain would stab through her all over again.

The one anomaly to her stoic bodyguard was the daily cell phone call he got. It had a custom ring tone that was more of a subliminal rumble than an actual ring. It usually came in the early evening, and it always made him take a quick look to clear the area around her and then turn his back on her. He'd plaster his hand over his wireless earpiece and mutter in a near whisper into his collar microphone. It was all very secretive and spooky.

It took her a few days to sidle close enough to hear what he was saying without him noticing, and she was stunned to hear him give a quick report on her day's activities and security concerns.

Austin.

She knew it in her gut with absolute certainty. She didn't even have to ask Warren if she was right or not. She *knew.*

At first she clung to desperate hope that his calls meant there was still hope for them. But after a few weeks and still no word from him whatsoever, her hope died. Eventually it turned to anger and then from anger to grief to dry-eyed acceptance.

People began to fret over her losing too much weight, but she didn't have the energy to fake caring about anything.

She slept terribly, and Austin constantly haunted her dreams, but that was her secret. She'd moved into the spare bedroom in the San Antonio suite, where she'd asked to be moved with Warren.

Thankfully, the man didn't insist on keeping watch on her through the night. She heard him get up conscientiously each night to prowl the suite—Austin had sent the very best to protect her—but Warren never intruded upon her privacy in any way.

The threats against her tapered off. Either that or Warren was very good at keeping them from her. And knowing the guy, that would be exactly his style. He was extremely stingy when it came to sharing information of any kind with her.

About a week before her show, there was some kind of a flap over her dressing room, and Warren hustled her out of the theater in the middle of a full dress rehearsal for no apparent reason. She spent a tense hour huddled in the hot laundry room with him until a man she didn't recognize came and declared the scene clear. *Whatever that meant.* Then Warren had whisked her to a regular hotel room on the twenty-third floor and told her curtly not to leave the room.

He'd come back a few minutes later with a haphazardly packed overnight bag of clothes and toiletries for her and had offered no further explanations.

In a better frame of mind, she'd have bedeviled him mercilessly until he spilled the beans and told her what the heck was going on. But as it was, she crawled into one of the two double beds, pulled the blankets up over her head and went to sleep. She didn't hear whether or not Austin called to check on her that night.

Two days before her premiere, Saul was waiting for her in the theater when she arrived to do a last run-through of the dance sequences and a final costume change rehearsal. "Good news, Silver Girl!" he announced jovially.

"What's that?" she asked with no great interest.

"Every show is sold out. You did it! You filled the biggest theater on the Strip for seven nights!"

She nodded. That was good news. "Now all I have to do is keep them in the seats all the way through the show."

"Stop being such a worrywart. Your show is fantastic. You're going to be back on top of the industry in no time."

She gave him the smile he expected but didn't feel it in her heart.

"Have you decided on your encore songs?" Saul asked. "If the media buzz is any indication, you'd better have several songs picked out. Maybe an old one or two. Your fans are coming out in force to see you again."

That was going to be weird. All those stoned college kids who'd screamed their way through mosh pits at the front of her audiences were going to be here? She wondered if they had receding hairlines and office-cubicle paunches yet. Would they bring their kids? She hoped not, because her show was distinctly R-rated. It was definitely more grown up than her early material. But the record label had interpreted her request for more mature content to mean that she would do more explicit material now than she used to.

The songs they had given her weren't that bad, really. The problem was with her. Only long years on the road, doing nightly shows when she'd been drunk and wasted and burned out, saved her now. Somewhere along the way, she'd apparently picked up enough professional savvy to deliver a decent show even if her heart was not in it. Who'd have guessed her misspent youth could some in so handy after all?

The day of the show dawned, and she slept in late, praying that she'd sleep through her regularly scheduled bout of breakfast hurling. She would have a busy afternoon. She had a surprisingly large list of things to do, from a quick press conference to last-minute appointments for hair and nails, a massage and stretch by her trainer and then a hearty meal. She never could eat less than four hours before a show. The nerves usually started about then, and she didn't stand a chance of keeping anything solid down once she started getting keyed up.

Warren was as he always was—vigilant, silent and completely disinterested in her state of mind.

She really missed Austin today of all days. She was half tempted to snatch Warren's phone out of his hand when Austin's daily check-in call arrived. She desperately needed to hear his voice. There was nobody else she wanted to share this moment with but him.

She was pathetic, moping over a man who'd probably already forgotten what she looked like. As soon as his three-month promise to keep her safe expired, he would no doubt cut her totally out of his life. And here she was, mooning over him like some lovesick moron.

Oh, wait. She *was* a lovesick moron.

Austin stepped off the private jet, pausing for a moment to get over the shock of the afternoon heat slamming into him. It felt like he'd stepped into hell's oven. Damn, Las Vegas was hot in the summer.

He checked his watch quickly. He only had a few hours before Silver was scheduled to perform. Warren's team of investigators had finally gotten a lead on the elusive Mr. Mark Sampson, and Austin was personally running the guy down before Silver's show started. It was the least he could do for her.

Hell, it wasn't hardly enough.

He'd gone over to Sampson's place the day he walked out on her to have a little man-to-man chat with the guy about stepping up to his obligations and being a man for Silver's sake. But Sampson had been gone. Not as in out on an errand. As in cleared out. Fled the scene for good.

The Tears of the Quetzal and its thief had disappeared, as well. The goldsmith didn't remember anything about the man who'd asked for information on the diamond other than having told the guy that he wasn't allowed to share information about clients' pieces. The florist shop had received the order for flowers online. Despite getting his own support team's best computer guys on the trail, they weren't able to discover anything about the sender. All the trails to Sampson and the diamond went cold all at once. Which was suspicious in and of itself.

Despite Harold's protests, Austin had gone to the local police and the FBI with everything he'd had. Natalie continued to work on the case as much as she could, but because of conflict of interest issues, her hands were largely tied. A guy named Lex Duncan in the FBI's jewelry/gem theft division had been brought in on the case, too, and he seemed sharp.

But Austin had an unshakeable, niggling feeling in the back of his mind that it wasn't enough. His gut said Mark Sampson wasn't done messing with Silver yet. He snorted. Where she was concerned, though, his instincts hadn't proven to be worth a hill of beans.

How could he have missed the fact that she and Mark were not only involved but expecting a *baby* together?

A stab of piercing regret—hell, of uncontrolled jealousy—tore through his gut. It did every time he thought of her holding a baby in her arms. She'd be a beautiful mother. A good one, too. She was funny and fierce and loyal and loving…everything a mother ought to be.

Everything a woman ought to be.

Everything a wife ought to be.

And he'd walked out on her.

But what else could he have done? She was having another man's baby, for crying out loud. He had no right to encroach on Sampson's turf like that. It flat out wasn't honorable to put a move on a pregnant woman. No matter how much he'd wanted Silver for himself, he wouldn't stoop that low. It was beneath him—and beneath her. She deserved better than that.

But damn, losing her had been like ripping his heart out with a spoon. A dull one. With rust on it.

He'd never been a man who gave his friendship or loyalty easily, let alone his love. But once given, he'd always been the most steadfast of companions, never wavering in his support. But not so with Silver. He hadn't been strong enough to stand by her in her time of need. He'd been too hurt, too angry, too betrayed to handle being with her.

He'd failed her.

Sure, he'd brought in Warren Bochco, who was arguably the finest bodyguard in the business, so technically he'd kept her safe.

But if he didn't miss his guess, he'd done a real number on her heart and her head. The woman Warren described to him daily was quiet, withdrawn and impassively cooperative with everyone around her. That wasn't the sexy firecracker he'd fallen for like a ton of bricks.

He didn't doubt for a second that her change was all his fault.

He nearly broke down and went to her the day there was a bomb scare at the theater. An anonymous caller said there was a bomb in her dressing room and that she was going to die in a blaze of glory.

If it had been the stalker who'd murdered Candace, it made no sense for the guy to call and warn his intended victim to get out of harm's way. But what if it had been Sampson? It sounded just like his style. Make a fuss so he could rush in and be the hero.

Austin had played and replayed that first day he'd met Silver over and over in his mind, examining every remembered detail for some evidence of who the stalker was. He had the sneaking feeling he'd seen the guy but not known at the time who he was looking at. This stalker was brazen enough to show himself to the Rothchilds and their would-be protectors.

While the mental exercise had revealed no hint of the stalker's identity, something else significant eventually had come to him. Sampson had not been alarmed when the first attack had happened on Silver—the guy who'd jumped her out of the blue. Sampson's only real reaction had been fury that he hadn't been the guy at her side to heroically protect her.

Bubba knew the attack was going to happen.

Given Sampson's comments about getting the girl and laughing all the way to the bank and given that Silver clearly hadn't agreed to marry the guy even though she was carrying his baby, his guess was that Sampson had decided to apply a little extracurricular pressure to get her to turn to him for protection.

Except Sampson's plan had backfired. Harold had thrown the guy a nasty curveball and hired Austin to protect Silver. When she felt threatened, she'd turned to him and not to Sampson.

But it had been more than that between them, dammit. There'd been something special there. They'd almost had it all.

Swearing under his breath, Austin took the suitcase the copilot handed down to him. He headed across the sweltering ramp for the car he'd arranged to have meet the plane.

That second attack in the hotel lobby—the shooting—had scared the living hell out of Sampson. The guy had flatly panicked. He clearly hadn't been expecting that attack. Austin was convinced the shooting had been the work of the real stalker.

The only question that remained to be answered was whether or not Sampson and the shooter were in league with each other. More than one partnership-in-crime had suffered a case of crossed wires before. It was possible that Sampson's crone wasn't supposed to take that shot, or not at that time and place.

The fastest way to find that out was to go to the source directly. And that meant finding and talking to Sampson. Forcefully, if necessary.

Austin's gut said the guy hadn't left the local area. Silver was the guy's golden goose, and he didn't see Sampson walking away from her without making one last effort to get his hooks into her.

The one silver lining to the whole mess—pun intended—was that she hadn't made any attempt as far as Warren could tell to contact the guy. She hadn't even mentioned Sampson, in fact.

While Austin was privately relieved that the scum bucket was apparently out of her life, intellectually he wished for her sake that the guy would've stepped up to the plate and been there for her. Lord knew, she had a lot to deal with right now, and she could've used a strong shoulder to lean on.

Like his.

Damn, damn, damn.

He punched the address Warren's guys had obtained for Sampson into the car's GPS system. It was supposedly a dive on the unlucky side of town where a guy matching Sampson's description had been spotted entering and exiting over the past few days. If Austin got lucky, he could have this whole mess quietly cleaned up and out of the way before Silver's big night.

Some parting gift. But it wasn't like he could do any more for her. He'd pretty much cut off his chances of that when he'd walked away from her. For the thousandth time, he reminded himself it had been the right and noble thing to do. And for the thousand-and-first time, he thought grimly that if losing the woman he loved was the price of his honor...*it wasn't worth it.*

Silver looked up hopefully as her dressing room door opened. Her hopes wilted when it was only Saul and her mother. Harold, Natalie, Conner and various other relatives had stopped by to wish her luck.

"Ready, Silver Girl?"

"As I'll ever be."

"Break a leg, kiddo," her mother added.

"I thought that only applied to actors."

Anna grinned. "I dunno. Just don't actually do it, eh? You've got six more shows to do."

After those, she looked forward to sharing her baby news with her mother. Recently, she'd been feeling a deeper bond with Anna as becoming a mother herself became more real in her mind.

Silver turned back to the makeup artist who was just finishing applying the heavy-duty, waterproof makeup she needed so as not to sweat it off during the first dance number.

Saul continued to hover. "How are you feeling?"

She frowned at his reflection in the mirror. There was no way he knew she was pregnant. But it almost sounded like..."I'm fine. Nervous. Okay. Sick to my stomach and thinking about bolting. My hands won't stop shaking, my knees are knocking, and my teeth are about to start chattering. But I always get that way before a show."

He nodded sagely. "I recall. But I see you're not taking chemical measures to calm yourself this time."

She laughed. "I keep telling you—I'm not that irresponsible kid anymore."

He came over and rested a hand on her shoulder. "Believe me, I've noticed. And the change suits you. I've put the word out in the biz that you were an angel to work with on this show. I made sure your label knows it, too."

She blinked up at him through sudden tears. Whether it was stray eyeliner or emotion putting them in her eyes, she wasn't sure. Either way, she murmured, "Thanks, Saul." A pause, then she asked quietly, "Are we square, then?"

He gave her a long, considering look. "Yeah. We're square."

Well, at least one relationship in her life was back on track. Speaking of which, she asked, "Any messages for me? Any visitors?"

"Your father tried to come backstage again. I told him you were too busy getting ready."

"Bless you, Saul."

The older man grinned at her knowingly.

"Anyone else?"

"Like that young man of yours? No."

She didn't have the guts to ask him which young man he was referring to—Mark or Austin. The one she could do without. The other…

A stagehand poked his head in the open door. "Ten minutes, Miss Rothchild."

She couldn't do this. Not without Austin. He was her strength. She was weak and frightened and incomplete without him.

"Where's Warren?" she called out suddenly. "I need Warren!"

The tall man stepped inside her room immediately. He must've been standing guard just outside. "What's the problem, ma'am?" he bit out.

"Everyone else, out. I need to speak to my bodyguard alone."

The crowded space emptied quickly, leaving behind an island of quiet amidst the last-minute chaos.

"What's up, Miss Rothchild?"

"I need your cell phone."

He blinked at that and actually looked faintly surprised. "May I ask why?"

"I need to make a phone call."

He glanced at her crystal encrusted cell phone, sparkling conspicuously on the corner of her dressing table. "What's wrong with your phone?"

"Please, Warren. I've never asked you for anything before. Do me this favor."

Frowning, he pulled it out and handed it to her. She stared down at its unfamiliar face in dismay. "How do I retrieve your recently received calls?"

Comprehension broke across his face. And then a grin. "'Bout damn time you two got over what's been going on between you."

Her jaw dropped. In the first place, Warren never smiled. And in the second place, he *knew* about the two of them?

In answer to her unspoken question he rolled his eyes. "It doesn't take a rocket scientist to see how miserable you two are apart. You've been moping around like a zombie ever since I took over for him, and he's not in much better shape."

Okay, that put her jaw on the floor. "He's upset?"

Warren actually laughed. A rumbling sound from deep in his chest. "He's a bloody wreck. Gimme that phone. I'll get him on the horn for you."

Thank God. She was actually light-headed with relief at the idea of finally getting to talk to Austin again. Whatever it took—pleading, begging, crawling on her hands and knees—she had to get him back. She couldn't live without him.

The revelation broke over her, cool and refreshing, and as inevitable as spring following winter. She loved him.

And that was exactly what she was going to tell him.

The apartment door opened, and Austin went on full battle alert behind the wheel of his car. His hand drifted to the door handle. The guy looked like Sampson. Maybe a little slimmer than before. If he took off that baseball hat, Austin could be sure. As soon as Bubba turned back to the door to lock it, Austin slid out of the vehicle quietly. He moved fast and low across the parking lot toward his target, ducking between cars and using a tall cactus for cover.

Sampson turned and walked the opposite direction. Perfect. Austin put on a burst of speed to close the final gap. It would've been a piece of cake, except his cell phone rang just then. Sampson threw a startled look over his shoulder and took off like a jackrabbit.

Swearing, Austin ignored his phone and gave chase. The bastard wasn't getting away from him this time, no sir. With Silver's face firmly in mind, Austin gave chase. It really wasn't much of a chase. His superior fitness, training and motivation made short work of the distance between them. Austin made a flying leap and tackled Sampson in a move his high school football coach would have been proud of. In short order, he straddled Sampson, who was facedown in a patch of dried-out grass with one arm cranked up high between his shoulder blades.

Swearing erupted beneath him as Sampson struggled against the restraint. The baseball hat flew off, and Austin looked down grimly at the profile, half-ground into the grass.

It was not Sampson.

"Who the hell are you?" Austin burst out.

"Who the hell are *you?*" the guy snarled back.

"Name's Dearing. What's yours?"

"Call me Dingo."

Austin let up a little on the guy's twisted arm. "I'm looking for a guy named Mark Sampson. Ever heard of him, Dingo?"

"That son of a bitch. I'll kill him myself if I ever catch up with him…" The guy devolved into a spate of angry curses.

Surprised, Austin demanded, "What did he do to you?"

"Stiffed me on a deal. I did some…jobs…for him, and he was gonna pay me ten grand for the package. I came over here to his place to collect, but the bastard's skipped out on me again."

Austin squeezed his eyelids shut in frustration. "Any idea where he's gone?"

"You think I'd be here if I did?"

"What kind of job did you do for him?" Austin asked.

The guy's chattiness evaporated in an instant. "Just a job," he muttered.

Something illegal, obviously. Ten grand worth of illegal. Which meant it was something major. Possibly dangerous. Like, oh, stalking Silver? "Ever heard of a girl named Silver Rothchild?" Austin asked darkly.

Dingo lurched violently beneath him, struggling frantically to free himself. Austin nodded to himself. Uh-huh. Exactly what he'd thought.

"Sampson paid you to harass her, didn't he?"

Dingo went perfectly still this time. Like a deer in a hunter's headlights.

Oh yeah. He'd nailed this one spot on. Given some time and some…gentle…persuasion, this guy would no doubt sing and give him all he needed to put Sampson away for a good long time. But time was the one thing Austin didn't have right now. "I'll pay you ten grand to tell me where he is."

The guy sighed. "Man, I'd tell you in a second if I knew."

Austin reached into his jacket and pulled out a plastic strip. He looped it deftly around the guy's wrists and gave a yank.

"Oww! What are you doing?"

Austin pushed to his feet and quickly gave the same treatment to the guy's ankles. "I'm making sure you're still here when the cops get here."

"Aww, man. I swear. I don't know where Sampson is."

This guy didn't strike Austin as being sophisticated enough to be the stalker who'd murdered Candace, stolen the Tears of the Quetzal and shot at Silver. But that wasn't up to him to decide.

"Ask to speak to a cop named Natalie Rothchild," he advised grimly. "Tell her how Sampson hired you to stalk Silver and cooperate your ass off with her, and maybe she'll cut you a break."

"What the hell did Sampson do to bring all this heat down on him?"

"He messed with the wrong girl."

"Looks to me like he messed with the wrong guy," Dingo grumbled.

Austin laughed shortly. "That, too."

He turned and headed for his car. He pulled out his cell phone and called the LVMPD to tell them about the little fish he'd caught and left all tied up with a bow for them to come collect. That done, he climbed into his car. What the hell was he supposed to do now? The idea had been to catch Sampson before he hassled Silver again.

Silver.

Austin swore violently. Her show was about to start. And Sampson was still on the loose. Three guesses where the bastard would be right now, and the first two didn't count.

Austin gunned the engine and pointed it toward the Strip. As he drove, he checked his cell phone to see who'd called him earlier and nearly screwed up his ambush. This was a work phone, and he didn't get social calls on it.

Warren? What was Bochco doing calling him?

Panic leaped in his gut. Oh, crap. Had something happened to Silver?

He punched out Warren's number fast and plastered the phone to his ear. It rang. And rang. And rang, dammit. Warren either couldn't hear the damned thing…or worse, he was too occupied to answer it.

Austin stood on the gas pedal. Hard.

His thoughts devolved into complete turmoil. What would he do if something happened to Silver? He couldn't lose her!

Hang on baby, I'm coming.

Chapter 14

Through the scaffolding and the fireworks, Silver made out the cheering crowd. The lift had about eight feet to go and then she'd begin to rise out of the top of the stage set. The violins started on cue, buzzing like a swarm of hornets. Six feet to go. The guitars wailed a chord. The audience cheered even louder, all but drowning out the drums. Four feet to go. The hiss of Roman candles all around her started up, their heat enveloping her. And then her head cleared the floor. Her claustrophobia subsided and a single thought filled her head.

Showtime.

She spread her arms, welcoming the wildly screaming mass of humanity below her. It was a heady moment. Silver, the rock star, was back.

Too bad Austin wasn't here to share it with her. It would've been perfect then.

Get your head back in the game!

On cue, she stepped off her mark and commenced the dangerous race down a narrow set of steel stairs in her high stilettos. The backup singers laid down the introduction, and Silver launched into the first song.

She reached the stage and danced over toward stage right. Quickly, she scanned the faces backstage. Maybe she did it out of habit, or maybe desperation. But there was no sign of Austin's familiar features.

Singing gustily, she and the dancers spun their way across the stage so she could wave at the left side of the audience. No Austin in the front rows of the crowd.

Stop that.

Throughout the entire song, she searched for him. She'd been so sure he'd be here. After Warren admitted how unhappy Austin had been after their split, certainty had lodged in her gut that he would come. He knew how important this night was to her. He'd be here for her, to share her big moment with her.

The second song came and went with no sign of him.

Then the third.

And something went out of her. Her enthusiasm drained in a slow leak she was powerless to stop. She forced herself to keep going through the motions of the show, but it just wasn't the same. The lovesick moron in her head had misled her heart yet again. When *was* she going to learn? Austin was done with her.

And something in her was irrevocably broken.

Hmm. That would be her heart.

After the fifth song, she slipped offstage while the dancers and backup singers finished the last chorus to one of her old songs with the audience bellowing it out in a giant sing-along moment. Saul had decided that instead of a traditional intermission she'd take breaks every half dozen songs or so to make quick costume changes and keep the show going in a continuous flow. It was ambitious and strenuous, but it kept the show's energy sky-high.

She raced for the changing area, where Stella and her two assistants stripped off the first costume and crammed her into the second one. She had one minute and forty seconds to make the change, assuming the band didn't speed up the chorus like they had a tendency to do.

Saul poked his head around the screen after she was decent again. "Pick up the energy, Silver. You started out great, but you're losing steam."

He was right. But she just couldn't find it in herself to care. She closed her eyes. She could do this. If not for herself, for her baby. For his or her future.

Stella ordered, "Turn around, honey. Time to curl your hair."

They'd rehearsed this until they had it down to a fine science, and Silver made the required one-eighty spin.

And that was when she saw him.

Standing way back in the darkest shadows at the back of the stage. Staring at her fixedly. His arms crossed, his face as potently handsome as ever. When they made eye contact, some turbulent emotion passed across his face. What was that? Anger? Relief? Anguish? Or maybe it was just the shadows and her imagination.

She jerked free of the curling irons and lurched toward him.

Stella squawked behind her, "We've only got fifty-five seconds left!"

She called back over her shoulder, "So my hair'll be straight! This is more important!"

She screeched to a stop in front of him. And just looked up at him. Her vocal cords tangled in hope and fear until she couldn't speak. Please let him be glad to see her. Please let this not be just business. Please let him forgive her. Please let this not be a lovely hallucination.

"Hey." His voice sounded abnormally tight. Could it be? Was Warren right? Had Austin missed her, too?"

"Hey," she murmured back.

Time stopped, and it was as if a cone of silence descended around them.

He jammed his hands into his pockets. "How've you been?" he finally asked roughly.

She reached out to touch his chest. He drew in a sharp breath but didn't move away from her touch. Yup, he was real, all right. Warm and strong and as solid as ever. "I've been okay—" She broke off. Tried again. "No, strike that. I've been terrible."

"Is the baby all right?" he asked quickly.

She blinked, startled at the depth of concern in his voice. "Junior's fine. Still making me sick every morning."

A frown flickered across his face. "What's wrong, then?"

Shouting from behind her penetrated the fog that shrouded her brain. "Thirty seconds!"

She gazed up at him, hungrily drinking in the sight of his features. Lord, she'd missed him. She answered simply. "You were gone."

The old fire leaped in his eyes, fierce and protective, for just a moment. He opened his mouth to say something.

"Silver! Let's go! You'll miss your mark!" She scowled as the stage manager rushed up to her and took her by the arm. She started to resist his urgent tug.

"Go," Austin bit out.

She let the stage manager drag her away but called back over her shoulder, "Hold that thought! I'll be back in six songs and I want to hear it!"

She knocked the next set of songs out of the park. Not a person in the house was sitting down, the crowd screamed wildly after every song and even Saul was beaming and tapping his foot with the music in the wings offstage.

Her feet barely touched the floor, and she rode a wave of exhilaration that she could hardly contain. He'd come back. He still had feelings for her. He hadn't said anything yet, but it was written on his face as clear as day. The only problem with her show now was that it was taking too blessed long to get to the next costume change.

But finally it came.

She jumped down a hidden hatch in the stage floor to the screams of the crowd and slid down the short slide, landing on a crash pad. She'd barely stopped moving before Stella and her girls went to work. She got decent, the privacy screen went down—

—and Austin was standing there, looking almost as impatient as she felt.

Stella looked back and forth between the two of them. "Straight hair again?" the costumer asked in resignation.

Silver answered briskly, "Yup." To Austin, she said, "Come with me."

She grabbed his hand and pulled him toward the tiny lift that would reposition her for her next entrance. They stepped into the cramped space, and the doors closed behind them. Oh, God. He still smelled as good as ever. She hit the stop button. In deference to the show in progress on stage, the elevator had no alarm bell, and relative silence enveloped them.

They both started to speak simultaneously. Then they both laughed, which cut a little of the heavy tension between them.

"You go first," he said.

"That day when you walked out—"

He interrupted in a rush. "About that. I'm sorry, Silver. It was selfish of me. I couldn't handle it and I bailed out on you—"

She reached up quickly and pressed her fingers against his lips. "I've only got a few seconds. Let me get this out. I was trying to tell you when you left that Mark isn't the father of my baby."

Austin stared at her, stunned.

Urgently she pressed on. If only there was more time to explain it all. To break this to him more gently.

"I used artificial insemination. I wanted a baby, but I didn't have a man in my life. At least, not the right man. I used an anonymous donor. But to avoid ending up in the tabloids over it, I asked Mark to pose as the father of my child." She exhaled sharply. "I swear, I didn't know him at all when I asked him to do it or I never would have chosen him. Candace told me he was…different…than he turned out to be. She was good at sabotaging me that way—" Silver broke off. That didn't matter anymore.

She heard faint voices outside yelling through the elevator door, asking if she was okay and announcing ten seconds until her next mark. Reluctantly she took her finger off the stop button. The lift lurched into motion.

Austin was nodding. "So that's what he had on you."

She shrugged. "It wasn't one of my more brilliant moments."

"It wasn't a bad plan. You just didn't have the right man for the job."

Her gaze snapped up at the sexy timbre abruptly vibrating in his voice. Austin was staring down at her. The elevator stopped and the doors started to open.

"So you never were romantically involved with Sampson?"

She snorted. "Hardly."

The screams of the audience burst in on them and Austin lurched around, startled. Apparently he hadn't realized they were riding up to the back of the stage proper. The scaffolding of the set was a steel jumble directly in front of them.

Austin swore quietly beside her. Whether he was reacting to the news that she'd never been involved with Sampson or the fact that he was practically on stage with her, she couldn't tell.

"Gotta go," she told him quickly. "Promise me you won't leave again until we talk more."

"I promise."

Her cue sounded, and she raced forward into the lights through a shower of sparks.

Austin watched her go, dumbfounded. Son of a gun. Sampson had never been her boyfriend. Relief and exultation all but knocked his legs out from underneath him. A stagehand dressed in all black slipped into the elevator and started almost as violently as he did to find Austin in the lift.

"I'm Silver's bodyguard," Austin said quickly.

The guy nodded and punched the down button. Austin stepped out below. Stella and her girls were packing up. "How do I get up to the stage?" he asked the woman.

She gave him directions, and he made his way to the staircase and up into the wings of stage right. Silver was on fire out there, and he relished watching her lithe form as she performed. The music wasn't half-bad, either. He still preferred her singing a soulful ballad, but she had a great voice no matter how she used it.

He scanned what he could see of the audience carefully. No sign of Sampson. His gut said that if the guy was still in town, he was here tonight. And furthermore, his gut said Sampson's bag of tricks wasn't quite empty yet.

Austin's jaw rippled. Now that he'd found his way back to Silver, he wasn't letting her out of his sight for any length of time. Not until Sampson was caught and his role in the Rothchild stalkings uncovered.

Had the guy actually been smarter than he seemed? Was Sampson capable of murder? Of the clever theft of the Tears of the Quetzal from a police lockup? Of the calculated and well-planned moves of the stalker?

Was Sampson so smart that he'd successfully pulled the wool over people's eyes and convinced everyone he was a dimwit? The thought chilled Austin to the core.

He spied Warren across the stage, and the two men made brief eye contact before going back to their respective scans for threats.

Silver was a free agent. Available for the taking. He *so* wanted her for himself. And a baby? Did he want an instant family, too? What about his job? Was it fair to Silver and the baby to go back out in the field for months on end? To put himself in harm's way day in and day out? How was he supposed to choose between his career—which was more than a career, more like his identity—and love? Did he have to choose? Could he have both? Possibly, but was it fair to Silver to ask that of her?

The questions continued to roll through his head, and damned few answers were forthcoming. He clenched the bulky rope beside him in frustration. He knew for sure that he didn't want to lose Silver again. And she seemed pretty intent on not losing him, either. They'd find a way to make things work between them. They *had* to. He'd burn up from the inside out if they didn't, leaving behind only a hollow shell of his former self. He'd lived that way for the past six weeks, and he couldn't do it for a lifetime.

The rope vibrated faintly in his hand, and he frowned. Nothing had happened on stage to explain it. He looked up, following the rope into the darkest recesses of the black-painted ceiling overhead. It led to the lighting system. Each of those big spotlights up there weighed several hundred pounds, and there were dozens of them. What was heavy enough to jiggle all of that tonnage? Elaborate scaffolding suspended the entire lighting system from the ceiling, a massive affair that stretched all the way across the stage. All the way across the stage—

Ohdamnohdamnohdamn…

He looked around frantically for a way up there. He spied a narrow ladder and dived for it, swearing in a steady stream around his sudden, choking certainty. He knew exactly where Mark Sampson was planning to make his final strike at Silver.

Question was, would he get there in time to stop it or not?

Chapter 15

Silver fell backward into the arms of her dancers. They turned her in a slow circle while she gazed up at the ceiling, catching her breath. Something moved overhead, and she started. That was odd. It looked like someone was up there. One of the stage-hands, no doubt. There must be a problem, because all the light sequencing was done digitally. Even the spotlights were operated by remote joystick.

The dancers put her down and she sashayed off, keeping one eye peeled on the lights to make sure she didn't need to make any on-the-fly adjustments.

The song ended, and she made her way to the front of the stage to introduce the next song. It was actually a scheduled pause to let all the performers catch their breath after that last number. She asked the audience if they were having fun and got a gratifying scream of approval back.

She turned to face the band and cue up the next piece. As she strode to the back of the stage, she glanced up.

And did a double take. There was definitely someone crawling around up there. More than one someone.

She spun to face forward and took one more look up into the rafters.

Oh. My. God.

That was Austin up there. And that could mean only one thing. He'd spotted a threat.

"Silver!" the drummer hissed.

Crud. She'd missed the cue. The band did a smooth repeat of the last few bars of the music, and she started the song on time this time. It was an effort to remember the lyrics and stop herself from looking up every two seconds. But the audience would figure out that something was wrong if she did, and it would take them out of the show.

She ran to stage left and up the ramp to the second platform and took the moment to see what was going on above. She spotted Austin immediately…and he was grappling with someone else. *So not good.* He was a good three stories above the stage. If he overbalanced the slightest bit, both men would crash down. And there was no safety net.

She pasted a smile on her face, prayed the audience was far enough away not to see the panic in her eyes and pressed on with the show.

Above, Austin hung on fiercely, trying futilely to get enough purchase to subdue his opponent. Sampson was fighting like a crazy man, and that made him a great deal more dangerous than he'd otherwise be. He seemed to understand that the jig was up and this was the end for him. The guy acted prepared to make a suicidal last stand.

A seam on Sampson's shirt gave way and the bastard tore out of his grip, spurting away down a narrow catwalk. Austin gave chase, swearing. He didn't much like how the heavy scaffold was wobbling under the force of their gymnastics up here. The planks under foot were maybe eight inches wide, and he pounded after

Sampson's fleeing form carefully. At least if Sampson was occupied getting away from him, the guy wouldn't have time to harm Silver.

Sampson dodged to the right, down one of the side access walks. Austin skidded around the corner and accelerated hard. Time to put an end to this foolishness. Sampson reached the end of the planks and paused momentarily in indecision, looking right and left. And that was his fatal mistake.

Austin went airborne, laying himself out flat. His arms wrapped around Sampson's waist, and his momentum carried both men straight forward, down to the very end of the plank they stood on. He felt himself tilting to the left. Air loomed under his left side. In a survival reflex, he wrapped his legs tightly around the narrow catwalk he straddled.

Sampson started to fall, and as strong as Austin was, he wasn't powerful enough to stop the guy's body weight. Nonetheless, he hung onto Sampson's waist with all his strength. The guy flung out his arms and managed to snag the perpendicular catwalk. With Austin's help, the other man dragged himself back up onto the planks.

"Give it up, Sampson," Austin grunted. "You're gonna kill yourself up here."

"If I can't have Silver, who cares?"

"Get over it. You never gave a damn about her. You just wanted her fame and fortune."

"Go to hell, Dearing."

"Your life's not over. You still have a lot of years to score the big one and get rich. Don't throw it away."

"You've got nothing on me. Back off!"

"Ever hear of a guy named Dingo? He and I had a little chat earlier today. He's in the custody of Las Vegas's finest as we speak, singing his heart out."

That took the remaining starch out of Sampson.

"If you make a full confession, maybe the district attorney

will go easy on you. Come quietly with me now, and I'll put in a good word for you."

"I didn't shoot at her that day," Sampson blurted. "I had nothing to do with that."

"You willing to say that hooked up to a lie detector?"

"Yeah, I'm telling you. It wasn't me!"

Somehow, he believed the guy's whining. But he wasn't about to give Sampson the weapon of that knowledge. "Tell it to the cops. You and Dingo cut her brakes. You had Dingo assault her. You sent her threatening notes—"

He broke off as Sampson frowned, perplexed. So he hadn't been behind the bouquet and the death threat that came with it? Damn. Aloud, he commented, "It doesn't matter. With what Dingo's telling the cops, they'll still nail you cold. You're hosed."

Sampson uttered another foul suggestion for what he could do to himself. Time for a little reverse psychology.

Austin shrugged. "If that's the way you feel, there's no sense in my trying to save you. You should go ahead and jump. The publicity for Silver will be spectacular. She'll make global headlines. You'll make her millions of dollars in record sales."

Sampson snarled something about not giving her a red damned cent. Austin didn't catch the rest of what the guy called Silver, which was probably just as well. He would've hated to have to toss Sampson off the scaffold himself.

Austin loosened his grip slightly and glanced below. "I'd recommend you go off the back of that plank you're on. It's a longer fall on that side, and there's some sound equipment down there. The combination ought to kill you nicely." He gave Sampson a little push in that direction.

"Are you crazy?" Sampson hollered.

Austin's voice dripped with anger when he replied coldly, "Buddy, I'm stone-cold sane. But I am getting you out of Silver's life for good one way or another tonight."

Sampson's eyes widened fractionally as he realized that Austin meant business.

Austin continued emphatically. "I really don't give a damn if you climb down from here or fly down. But you're done stalking Silver. As of now. It's over. What's it gonna be? Stairs or airborne?"

Silver looked up yet again, watching in horror at the drama unfolding over her head. She had to do something! Mark was volatile and unpredictable, and Austin could get hurt or killed up there!

She stumbled and missed a couple steps but did her best to cover it.

She couldn't lose Austin now, just when she'd finally found him again. She sang through the song's chorus, and as the last verse approached, the words didn't come to her. Damn. What came next?

She looked up again. And gasped. Austin dived for Sampson and both men crashed down onto the scaffold, which started to swing ominously. She missed the first line of the verse, but thankfully the backup singers were also belting it out at the same moment, neatly covering her gaff.

The two men looked to be struggling. She couldn't make out who was winning, but she had to believe Austin had the upper hand, given his fitness and training. Assuming Mark didn't pull them off the scaffold and kill them both. He was vindictive enough to do it.

She searched frantically off to her left. There. Warren was still lurking offstage. In the guise of waving at the audience, she desperately gestured at the bodyguard until he glanced her way. She made frantic eye contact with him.

He started to move forward, but she shook her head. He stopped, looking confused. She pointed up, looking up as she did so. It wasn't the choreographed movement for the song, but fortunately she was the star of the show, and she could deviate from the routine the backup dancers were grinding out without looking strange.

Warren, thank goodness, correctly interpreted her movements. Frowning, he looked up, peering into the blackness of the stage ceiling. Suddenly he jolted and reached into his jacket for his pistol. He must've spotted the two men. He spun and took off running into the bowels of the theater.

She executed a couple of spins across the stage, glanced at the dancers to see what they were doing, got in front of them where she belonged and picked up the routine again. An urgent prayer for Austin's safety ran through her head in a continuous loop of near panic as she continued the performance. It was the best she could do.

Austin waited tensely while Sampson blustered for a few more seconds, but then the guy went limp.

All the fight went out of Bubba and sullen defeat entered his eyes. "Stairs, you son of a bitch," Sampson snarled.

Austin laughed shortly, without humor, a hard sound even to his ears. "Your misfortune was to run into a son of a bitch who wanted the girl just a little bit more than you. Let's go."

He dragged the guy to his feet and, as much as was possible in the narrow, dangerous confines up here, goose-stepped him to the ladder that led offstage.

Sampson stopped abruptly at the top of the ladder and muttered, "Who the hell's that?"

Austin glanced down. Praise the Lord. Warren. His worry about how to maneuver Sampson down the ladder without the guy pulling something stupid evaporated. He answered, "That's my partner. And if you think I'm a badass, you ought to tangle with him. He'd kill his own mother to get the job done."

Sampson grumbled under his breath. Uh huh. As Austin had thought. The guy had been planning to do something on the way down.

"Here's how this is gonna work, Mike. You're gonna go down in first, and my buddy down there's going to keep his gun on you. Try anything and he'll shoot you off the ladder like a juicy little pig in a shooting gallery."

"My name is Mark, dammit," Sampson ground out.

Austin leaned close and murmured in the guy's ear. "I've got a friend named Mark. Good man. Saved my life a few times. You don't deserve the same name as him, you slimeball. Now get moving." He gave Sampson's arm a sharp twist that drove the guy to his knees.

For the first time, true fear entered Sampson's gaze. Was the jerk just now starting to figure out how dangerous a man he really was? Austin snorted. *Gee, Maynard. A little slow on the uptake there.*

On stage, Silver spied Austin standing at the top of the ladder with Sampson kneeling in front of him and nearly sobbed her relief into her microphone. Thankfully, she was due for her last costume change before the grand finale, a medley of her greatest hits. She was supposed to exit stage left, but there wasn't a chance she was going anywhere but stage right to meet Austin.

She all but ran off the stage at the end of the song, while the lead guitarist held a "Which side of the theater can cheer louder?" contest.

Across the stage, she spotted Saul and Stella flapping in consternation like a pair of wet chickens, and a flurry of activity as they tried to pack up, no doubt, with the intent to race over with the last costume. Whatever. She so didn't give a darn about any old outfit right now.

She raced behind the big velvet curtain to where Warren was just finishing slapping handcuffs on Mark. With a wordless cry she flung herself at Austin. He heard her coming in enough time to turn around before she barreled into him, which was probably what saved them both from tumbling to the floor.

"Oh my God," she cried. "Are you okay?"

"Easy, darlin'. I'm fine. I spotted me a rat up in the light rig and went on a little hunting expedition."

She twisted in Austin's arms to stare at Mark. "What did I ever do to you to make you want to hurt me?"

The guy opened his mouth, but Austin cut him off. "Don't answer that, Sampson. In fact, don't say anything at all. You scared Silver tonight, and that's all the reason I need to break your neck." He added in disgust, "Get him out of here, Warren, before I hurt him or worse."

The other bodyguard nodded tersely and dragged Sampson away.

Silver buried her face against Austin's chest and let out the sob she'd been desperately holding in ever since she'd realized what was going on overhead.

"Hey, sweetheart. Why the tears? Everything's okay now."

She sniffed, smiling up at him damply. "That's why I'm crying, you big oaf. I thought I was going to lose you again, and I flipped out."

He pulled her close and buried his face in her hair, murmuring unintelligibly beneath the roar of the crowd. But she didn't need to hear the words. She felt his relief that she was okay in the way he crushed her against him, felt his caring in the way he nuzzled her hair with his nose, felt his emotion in the way his heart pounded against hers.

She'd almost lost him tonight. The realization flowed through her like a glacier, freezing everything in its path with stark terror. Suddenly, nothing else mattered. Not some stupid costume change, not her career, nothing. She'd been out there shimmying around and he'd been overhead, putting his life on the line for her. It made what she did seem so blessed shallow.

Heck, she'd spent all these weeks assuming he'd left her for some selfish reason of his own. He probably had some noble reason for doing that, too! "Why did you leave?" she blurted.

He lifted his head to look down at her solemnly. "You were having another man's baby. A man you were involved with. What kind of lowlife would I be to break the two of you up? I cared about you too much to do that to you. I had to leave. It was the only right thing to do."

Yup. Noble to the core. And she'd been too blind to see it. She'd been busy thinking all kinds of terrible things about him, and he'd done it all for her. She *so* didn't deserve him. How was she ever going to live up to his sense of honor and decency?

She'd sold out on him. Given up on him—and on them. She'd sold out on her career. Sold out on everything. She'd just rolled over and done what everyone around her told her to, whining all the while about how miserable she was. Meanwhile, he'd made a giant sacrifice for her, an ultimate gesture of caring, without a word of complaint. How could she possibly make that up to him?

And then what he'd just said truly registered on her overwrought brain. He'd cared for her enough to leave. Cared.

Past tense.

It was too late. He'd come back to nab Sampson, not to be with her. She was in the middle of her big show, and he was gentleman enough not to dump her until it was over. But his return had nothing to do with her. She'd truly blown it.

The floor might just as well have opened up and swallowed her whole at that moment. Apparently, somewhere deep in her subconscious, she'd been holding out some small hope that they'd get back together, for that spark just blinked out of existence. And her world went black. All desire to go back out on that stage drained away.

She had to leave. Go somewhere far, far away from here, and never come back.

Austin frowned down at her, and all of a sudden, the light disappeared from his gaze, too. He knew. He'd realized that she'd figured out why he was here and that he could drop the pretense now. She spun away. "I've…I've got to…go," she mumbled. Where to, she had no idea. Just away. Now.

Vaguely, she became aware of her name being repeated over and over. "Silver! Silver! Silver!" It was the crowd chanting—screaming at the top of its lungs, actually—for her return.

Austin gave her a push toward the stage. "Go. Your fans are waiting for you."

Blindly, she stumbled forward. And realized the spotlights had picked her up. She was back on stage. She stared out at the audience numbly. *Sing. She was supposed to sing.* But she had no idea what song came next. She didn't care what song came next.

One of the guitarists whispered urgently to her, prompting her with the line for the beginning of the final medley.

She heard Saul behind her, asking Austin urgently what the hell he'd just said to her. Austin murmured back that he hadn't said anything at all. *And that was the problem. He had nothing to say.*

Nothing to say.

That was the title of the song she'd written right after Austin left. It talked about how there weren't words to describe her love and loss.

"Sing, Silver!" Saul hissed at her angrily.

Sing. Right. As if coming out of a trance, she walked out to the center of the stage and reached behind her waist to flip on her microphone pack. "Everybody, with your indulgence, I'm going to change up the pace, now."

She gazed up toward the back of the theater where the lighting director and his men sat in a concealed booth. She couldn't see them, but she knew they were there. "Gentleman, if you could cut all the lights and give me a single white down-spot, center stage?"

The party atmosphere in the audience faded as the lights went down, and the crowd buzzed, clearly perplexed.

She glanced back at the band. "Jerry, may I borrow your acoustic Gibson?"

The lead guitarist looked stunned but nodded and turned to the stand behind him. He picked up the plain, wooden guitar and passed it to her.

She looked offstage. "Is there a stool around, by any chance?"

After a few seconds, a stagehand ran out with a bar stool. She directed the kid to place it in the wash of light shining down from the spotlight above. She glanced over the wings of stage right. Saul mouthed furiously something to the effect of "What in the hell are you doing?"

And Austin—he had faded back into the shadows, but she still recognized his tall form, nearly invisible behind Saul. Already pulling away from her, huh? Her heart broke a little more. Well, at least she was now in approximately the same frame of mind she'd been in when she wrote the song.

She perched on the stool and gave the guitar an experimental strum. She looked up at the audience but couldn't see even the front rows in the blackness now enveloping the theater.

"You know, folks, a lot of time has passed since I was last onstage. And I've done some growing up since then. To pass the time, I've been trying my hand at a little songwriting. If you don't mind, I'd like to play one of my songs for you now. It fits my mood better than what was up next on the playlist. I hope you like it."

And with that, she closed her eyes, strummed the opening chords, and began to sing. It wasn't so much a song as a confession. The ballad told the story of her long search for and finally finding the right man. It told how she'd taken him for granted and how she'd lied to him and lost him. She sang of her loss and pain but also of her regret and sorrow. She poured out all the anguish in her soul into the music, her voice soaring into the silent void all around her.

And then the song was over. The audience was dead silent. The moment stretched out eerily as she opened her eyes in slow motion and looked up. And then the spellbound quiet broke as thunderous applause erupted, shocking her out of her reverie. The applause swelled to cheering, then to screaming and to a standing ovation that was deafening.

But that din was nothing compared to what came next. A massive explosion slammed into her, throwing her off the stool, flattening her on the stage. It was so loud that the impact of the noise ripped the air from her lungs. Sharp pain burst in her ears, ringing through her head until she couldn't see.

She registered screams. Then a crunching, creaking sound of metal tearing.

And then the entire lighting scaffold crashed down on top of her.

Chapter 16

The explosion sent ice picks of agony stabbing into Austin's left ear, driving him to the floor along with the concussion of the blast. *Holy—* Before he could finish the thought, his instincts took over and he rolled back to his feet all in one lightning fast motion. *Silver. Must get to Silver.*

He jumped for the stage just as the light system came crashing down before his eyes, burying Silver somewhere beneath tons of lights and wires and steel beams.

Right then and there his life flashed before his eyes. Except it wasn't his past scrolling through his mind's eye…it was the future they could've had together. Laughter and fireworks and sweet memories. The exciting roller coaster of her career. Laid-back retirement for him. Kids playing in the backyard. Fourth of July picnics with sparklers and burnt hot dogs. Lazy moments together in bed. And the love.

Oh, God. The love.

Oblivious to the screams and chaos around him, he leaped

onto the twisted pile of steel, thinking frantically. She'd been sitting slightly forward of where he was now. He shifted over that way, searching furiously. He threw pieces of twisted metal in all directions, dodged bundles of wires that might or might not be hot, all the while bellowing, "Silver! Silver! Where are you?"

The noise in the theater was deafening. People screamed, feet stampeded and the roaring aftereffects of the explosion still echoed in his skull.

Quickly, he was waist deep in the pile. Still, there was no sign of her. What was she wearing? He cast his mind back frantically. Pink. Hot pink. He looked around in the deep shadows cast by the emergency lighting system across the stage.

"Light! I need light over here!" he shouted. No telling if anyone heard him or would respond if they did.

He grabbed the lip of a mangled spotlight and laboriously rolled the thing, weighing easily two hundred pounds, to the side. It crashed off the stage, causing squeals and more localized panic. He didn't care. Silver was under here somewhere, hurt, maybe dying. Please God, not already dead.

He jumped down into the new opening. Squatting, he was finally able to catch glimpses of the stage under the overarching pile. He looked around carefully, squinting to make out something, anything, resembling a human being.

Over there. Could it be—

He crawled to his right, snagged his trouser leg on something and ripped it free impatiently. He looked again. A hint of color caught his eye in the gloom. Studying the pick-up-sticks pile above him, he carefully pulled free a long metal pipe. The pile shifted slightly above him, then settled again. He released his breath.

He crawled another few feet. Oh, yes. That was definitely a splash of pink.

"Silver! Can you hear me?"

Nothing. The inert pile of cloth didn't move. It looked like she was lying in a pocket surrounded by stacked railings and girders. But she didn't look crushed.

He managed to draw a breath. Now, if she only hadn't taken a blow to the head or neck. He ought to wait for firemen to get here. They had extraction training for collapsed structures. But what if she was seriously injured? Dying? He couldn't afford to wait.

Eyeballing the stack overhead and doing his best not to bump or dislodge anything, he slithered mostly on his belly under the worst of the pile and toward where she lay, still and silent.

Finally, a lifetime later, he reached hcr.

He plastered a hand to her throat. Nothing. Oh, God. He moved his hand slightly to the side and something jumped under his fingertip. He held his breath. Come on. Be a pulse. Another thump beneath his finger. *Yes.* She was alive.

It was awkward checking her over for injuries because of a pair of steel poles between them, but he managed. Her limbs seemed intact. The floor beneath her felt dry. No bad bleeding, then. Carefully, he ran his hand down her spine, checking for any bends or bumps that shouldn't be there. It felt all right.

It was a risk to move her, but did he dare leave her under here, where the pile could shift and crush her at any time? And what about the baby? What if it was in distress?

That decided it for him. He maneuvered around to the left, positioning himself above Silver's head. Sitting on his behind, he leaned forward, hooked her armpits and eased her toward him. As petite as she was, he was only able to move her a few inches at a time, lest her clothing snagged on something and brought the house of cards tumbling down upon them both.

Finally, she was lying mostly in his lap. He scooted backward, pulling her along with him. He didn't come out the way he'd come in, for he'd spotted a clearer route out the back of the pile. It still took him several minutes to work his way to the edge of the mess.

As he neared the light now shining down on the stage, he heard male voices shouting. "Austin, Silver, can you hear us?"

"We're here!" he called back. "I've got her. She's alive but unconscious. Get an ambulance!"

"One's already here," somebody called back. "Wave your hand if you can. I think I've spotted you."

He lifted his hand through a small gap overhead and waved it back and forth.

"Gotcha. Sit still. There's an unstable area between us and you. We're shoring it up now."

He acknowledged the instruction and used the pause to catch his breath and to stroke the tangled hair off of Silver's face. She looked surprisingly peaceful and unscathed. "Wake up, honey," he murmured. "You're scaring me. I need to know how you are. If anything hurts."

Maybe it was a trick of the flashlights playing across the pile from behind him, but he could swear her eyelids fluttered. He called her name more urgently, but she didn't respond.

In a matter of minutes, a big guy in a canvas jacket and fireman's hard hat put a hand on his shoulder from behind. "Lemme carry her out, buddy. You crawl behind me."

Austin didn't want to give her up, but the fireman was best qualified to evacuate Silver from this mess. Reluctantly, he laid down on his back and dragged her up and over his body to the fireman behind him.

In moments, he was free of the hellish nightmare of the pile. Silver was just being laid on a gurney by a pair of medics. Austin leaped to his feet and rushed over to her.

"I'm coming with you," he announced to the EMT.

"Are you family?"

"Yes," he lied. "Her fiancé and father of her baby." He registered gasps of surprise around him but ignored them. They could split hairs with him about his relationship status with Silver later.

"C'mon," the paramedic said without ceremony.

Austin sprinted down the hall beside the racing gurney and climbed into the back of the ambulance outside. It was a fast, noisy ride to the hospital and another sprint into the emergency room, which was filling up fast with frantic Rothchilds. The bad news was Silver was still unconscious. The good news was the medic had found a heartbeat on the baby using the sonogram in the ambulance.

Anna and Harold closed in on him to grill him about the baby, but he put them off by telling them to ask her when she woke up.

Austin was not allowed to accompany her into the trauma unit, however, and was relegated to the waiting room to pace impatiently. It was the longest half hour of his life. And then a nurse came out. "Mr. Dearing?"

He whirled quickly. "That's me. How is she?"

"Come with me."

The nurse smiled. That was good news, right? She wouldn't smile if something terrible had happened, would she? He all but ran the poor woman down as they headed down the hall.

He turned into a room full of electronics and monitors and skidded to a halt. Silver was sitting up in the bed…smiling at him. Swear to God, he went light-headed. His knees went weak and he felt crazy hot all of a sudden. He grabbed the door frame to steady himself until his vision cleared and he could breathe again.

"Hey, beautiful," he managed to murmur.

"Hey, you," Silver murmured back. "I hear you saved my life."

He shrugged and moved over to the bed, almost not daring to believe that she was okay. "Nah, I just dragged you out from under the lighting scaffold." He took her hand gently. "How're you feeling?"

"Woozy."

"Woozy? What the hell is that? Weak? Sick? Or is that some kind of pregnancy thing?"

She laughed and then winced. "It means I'm a little nauseous and my head's swimming a little. And I have a headache, too."

"And the baby? Junior's fine?" he asked in concern.

Silver glanced over at the doctor, and Austin's heart skipped a beat. Oh, God. Not the baby…

"Her baby's fine, Mr. Dearing," the doctor said soothingly.

He about fainted again. Big, tough him, who faced down assassins without blinking and leaped in front of bullets for fun. This business of being in love was hard on a guy. *Being in...*

Son of a gun.

Sure enough, he was slam-dunk, out-for-the-count, no-doubt-about-it, in love with Silver Rothchild. His heart did a flip.

"Sir," the doctor said firmly, "where is that blood on your collar coming from?"

Blood? What blood? He cranked his chin down and noticed a bright red stain along his left shoulder seam and running down the front of his shirt. "No idea. I'm fine."

"Sit down on this stool and let me have a look."

He sat. The doctor did a quick examination of his head and neck but stopped abruptly after he stuck a light in Austin's ear and elicited a sharp yelp from his patient.

"Nurse, call in Dr. Whitney." To Austin, the doctor said, "He's the best ear, nose and throat guy we've got around here."

Austin frowned. And then comprehension dawned. Oh no. His bum eardrum. Had he busted it again? It had bled the last time he ruptured it, too. This could delay his return to the field for weeks or even months, dammit. Although, on the upside, it would give him more time to spend with Silver and convince her to marry him. *Marry...*

Damn! His brain had to quit throwing these heart-stopping thoughts at him like this!

Marriage? To Silver?

Oh, yeah.

No doubt about it.

Now to do a better job of convincing her to go along with his plan than Mark Sampson had...

Another doctor interrupted his strategy planning, whisking him out of the room over Silver's protests and taking him upstairs to an office full of more equipment, most of it designed to poke him in the ear and cause as much excruciating pain as possible.

After about fifteen minutes, the doctor quit poking and took a seat on a stool in front of Austin. The guy had just opened his mouth to speak when a knock sounded on the door. A nurse stuck her head in.

"I tried to keep her downstairs, but the E.R. doc said we'd better let her come up here or she was going to cause a riot. She insists on seeing Mr. Dearing right away."

The woman stepped aside, and Silver barged into the room, her eyes blazing and her arms akimbo. She looked like a minor tornado.

Austin came up off the table. "What's wrong?" he bit out.

"Nothing. I just want to be with you and make sure you're okay. And those tyrants downstairs told me I had to wait there for you. It's been forever, and I got worried—"

He laid his fingertips on her mouth, gently cutting off her babbling. "Dr. Whitney was just about to give me the verdict."

She turned to the doctor. "How bad is it? Can he still be a bodyguard? He's a Special Forces soldier, you know. A captain. He has a team of men and does all kinds of cool things..." She trailed off, glancing over at him, abashed.

Surprised, Austin asked, "How do you know all that about me?"

"I read up about Delta Force on the Internet. You guys do some amazing stuff. It scares me to death to think of you doing it, but if that's what you want to do, I guess I can live with it."

Dr. Whitney cleared his throat, and Silver and Austin turned simultaneously to face him.

"I don't think that's going to be an issue for Captain Dearing, young lady. You see, his eardrum's basically shredded. Best case, I'm estimating that by the time it heals, we're looking at a fifty percent hearing loss. Worst case, it could run up to eighty percent hearing loss in the left ear. I've done some work with the military doctors over at the air force base across town, and my understanding is that this will disqualify Captain Dearing for combat."

Austin heard the words with his good ear. But they failed to register. *No more combat?* "Ever?" he asked in disbelief.

"I'm sorry, son."

Silver gasped beside him and her hand came to rest comfortingly on his shoulder.

Well, hell.

This was certainly not how he'd envisioned ending his career. He'd always thought to go out in a blaze of glory. To do something wildly heroic and go down in the annals of the Delta Force as one of the great ones.

Although, saving the life of the woman he loved wasn't too bad a way to go out.

"Oh, Austin. I'm so sorry. I know how much your job means to you." He heard tears in Silver's voice and looked up in surprise.

"I thought you hated what I do."

"I do. But it makes you happy. Made you happy. I'd never wish for you to lose something that you love."

He gathered her close and buried his face in his hair. "I almost lost the thing I truly love tonight when those lights came down on you."

She froze in his arms. Small hands pushed at his shoulders, backing him up until she could look at him. They were almost eye-to-eye with him sitting on the table like this. She whispered, "What did you say?"

"I said I love you."

"Seriously?" she asked.

He gave her a withering look. "Do you take me for the kind of guy who'd joke around about something like that?"

"Well, no. But…really?"

"Yes, really, you silly vixen. I love you. I love your music. I love your temper. Your smart mouth. Your giant heart. Your laughter. All of you."

"*All* of me? Including the fact that I'm pregnant?" she replied hesitantly.

"Speaking of that." He winced. "Back at the theater, when you were unconscious, I might have let it slip that you're expecting."

Alarm made her jolt. "Who heard you?"

"Uh, I imagine pretty much everyone in the place. I sort of bellowed it at the top of my lungs."

She groaned. "You didn't."

"'Fraid so. The cat's out of the proverbial bag."

She laughed ruefully. "Well, it was bound to happen sooner or later. At least I got the first show under my belt before that bombshell exploded in my face."

"Uh, Silver?"

"Hmm?"

"I, uh, also sort of let it out that I'm, uh, your…" he trailed off.

She frowned down at him. "If I didn't know you better, I'd swear you look a little afraid. What in the world did you say?"

He closed his eyes. Opened them. Took a deep breath. "I claimed to be the, uh, father of your baby."

Her jaw dropped. She stared at him, speechless for several long seconds.

"I swear, honey, I'm not pulling a Sampson on you. I'll recant the statement if you want me to. But I would love to be the father of your baby. I was thinking maybe I could adopt Junior if you'd agree to it…"

Even to his good ear, that sounded too lame for words.

She frowned at him, clearly perplexed. "But to adopt the baby, you and I would have to be married."

"Well, of course we would—" he burst out before stopping abruptly. "Whoops. Got ahead of myself. You do that to me, you know."

He slid off the table, landing on one knee on the floor in front of her. "Silver, would you make the happiest man alive and marry me? I'm hopelessly, helplessly in love with you and can't think of anything I'd rather do than spend the rest of my life with you. And that includes my career." Now he was the one babbling, but he didn't care. "Frankly, I'm glad my eardrum is shot. That way you can't send me back into the field when I drive you crazy. Because I'm sure I will, now and then. I apologize in advance, but I'm just so crazy about you. I want to wrap you up and keep you safe and never see that haunted look in your eyes again. The one you get when you're scared—"

He broke off. "Lord, woman, you make a blubbering idiot out of me. Put me out of my misery and agree to marry me. Please!"

A tinkling sound, like little silver bells ringing, intruded upon his senses. Was it another one of Dr. Whitney's hearing tests?

And then it hit him. It was Silver. Laughing. And crying. And falling to her knees in front of him and flinging her arms around his neck.

"Is that a yes?" he mumbled into her hair.

"Oh, yes. Yes, yes, yes!"

It hit him like a ton of bricks. A wave of joy so damned big and powerful it blasted him plumb off his rocker.

"Hot damn!" he yelled as he jumped up, dragging her with him and spinning her around in joy. He staggered to a halt, dizzy.

Dr. Whitney intruded dryly, "You might want to go easy on the spinning, there, fella. Your sense of balance won't return to normal for a few weeks."

Austin grinned widely. "Doc, with this woman for my wife, I'm not ever gonna regain my balance."

"Hey!" Silver protested, laughing.

He grinned down at her. "Don't get me wrong, honey. I think balance is highly overrated. Marriage to you is going to be more fun than ought to be legal."

She grinned back up at him. "Right back at ya, big guy."

Another nurse poked her head into the now-crowded office. "Miss Rothchild, a man named Saul sent me up here to let you know that, and I quote, 'The entire Rothchild clan is waiting for you downstairs, and there's going to be a revolt if they don't see for themselves pretty soon that you're all right.' I might add that about fifty reporters are also down there. They're asking for a statement regarding rumors of your pregnancy and the identity of the father of your baby."

Silver glanced over at Austin. "You're sure about this?"

He nodded firmly and looped his arm around her shoulders. "Positive. It's you and me, darlin', from now on. You'll never have to face your family, or the press, alone again."

She leaned into him and said softly, "I love the sound of that."

"I love you, Silver."

"Mmm. I love the sound of that, even more. I may even have to write a song about it. A whole bunch of songs." She smiled tenderly at him. "By the way, I love you, too."

He bent down to kiss her sweetly, savoring everything about her as he did so. They hadn't done too bad together, the two of them. They'd survived Mark Sampson, revived her music career, found each other and were on their way to a family of their own. Sure, Candace's killer was still out there, and whoever had written those threatening letters. But together, he and Silver could face anything life threw at him. Endings didn't get too much happier than that.

He asked doubtfully, "Are sappy love ballads allowed to have happy endings?"

She laughed and hooked her arm around his waist. "All that matters to me is that *our* song has a happy ending."

There was only one answer to that. "Amen, honey. Amen.

Epilogue

Silver sighed in contentment and enjoyed the view of Austin's broad shoulders and athletic grace as he strode out of her father's house. He came over to the pool and handed her a tall glass of iced orange juice. She never got tired of looking at him. He claimed the same thing about her, and she was going to hold him to it when she grew to the size of a house over the next few months. She couldn't wait. She thought she'd spied a little swelling in her abdomen this morning when she was getting dressed. Her hand drifted to her belly as she smiled up at him.

"Thanks. What would I do without you, Mr. Dearing?" she said. His retirement from the army had come through a few days ago.

He grinned down at her. "I don't know, and fortunately, you're never going to have to find out. You're stuck with me for good, Mrs. Dearing."

She loved the sound of that. Their wedding had been a quick, quiet affair with just family attending. The hospital that had treated her and Austin after the accident had its own schlocky wedding chapel—gotta love Las Vegas. They'd scheduled it on ten minutes' notice and been married before they walked out of the hospital at midnight the night of her premiere.

The press had loved it. On top of her triumphant comeback to rave reviews, she and Austin had announced to the world that they were married and expecting a baby all in one fell swoop.

Conner was working on the legalities of making Austin the official father of her baby, but it didn't take a piece of paper to make it so in her heart. In the past two weeks Austin had stepped in the to the role of doting daddy-to-be as if he'd been made for it.

"What are you thinking about?" Austin murmured as he sank into the cushioned pool chaise beside her.

"What a great father you're going to make."

The look in his eyes as he gazed over at her was pure love. "Can't wait."

He reached out and she took his hand, their fingers intertwining between their lounges. In quiet companionship they watched the sun set in a kaleidoscope of crimson and purple.

A jovial voice rang out behind them. "There you are, you two lovebirds!"

Silver glanced up as Conner joined them, drink in hand. "How's tricks, cousin?"

He shrugged. "Could be worse. I got a lead on your buddy Darla. Her landlord says she skips town for a couple weeks at a time now and then, but she always turns up again. He told me about a club where I might find her when she shows up. I'm gonna go check it out later tonight."

Silver scowled. "She was Candace's pal, not mine."

Conner raised his glass and grinned. "So noted."

A new voice came from near the back doors. "Rebecca said I could find all of you out here."

Silver looked up to see Natalie stepping outside. She was in her police uniform—she must have just gotten off duty. It was still strange to see her stepsister wearing a gun. "Defending truth, justice and the American Way, are you, sis?"

Natalie smiled, but her gaze remained serious.

Austin went watchful and quiet beside her. He asked quietly, "Any news?"

Natalie nodded. "Today the FBI ran the polygraph tests on Mark Sampson and his buddy Dingo that they agreed to as part of their plea bargains."

Silver went on high alert, but it was nothing compared to the predatory intensity that suddenly enveloped Austin beside her.

Natalie continued, "The polygraph examiner confirms with high certainty what they've been saying all along. Sampson and Dingo had nothing to do with the shooting in front of the casino. According to the test, they're not lying, either, when they claim not to have left that message on Silver's dressing-room mirror, and neither of them had anything to do with the sabotage of the light scaffolding."

Silver frowned. The police had concluded that someone set small explosive charges at key support points all over the big lighting rig over the stage and brought it down on her intentionally. "If not Mark, then who?" she asked in alarm.

Austin and Conner traded grim looks. It was Austin who answered her. "Whoever's targeting the whole Rothchild clan."

She met his gaze worriedly. "What am I supposed to do about it?"

Austin shrugged. "Exactly what you've been doing. Keep working on your next album. We continue to lie low here at the mansion, and I continue to watch over you."

"For how long?" she asked.

"Until the killer is caught."

Conner piped up, "So you're convinced that whoever murdered Candace and stole the ring is behind the attacks on Silver?"

Austin replied, "Makes sense."

Natalie added, "The threatening letter to Harold suggests it's the same guy."

Conner nodded. "Well, then. I guess I'd better head over to that club and see if I can track down Darla. If she can lead me to the ring, maybe she can lead me to the killer."

Natalie murmured, "You want some backup?"

"Nah. I got this one. I'll give you a call if I need you to charge in, guns blazing, and save the day."

Natalie and Conner wandered into the house, arguing good-naturedly about the kind of trouble he was likely to get into without her there to bail him out.

Silver looked at Austin in concern. He held out his arms, and she didn't hesitate. She crawled into his lap and cuddled close as he wrapped his strong, safe arms around her. She laid her head on his shoulder, and they watched the last vestiges of sunset fade from the sky. Venus came into view overhead and the first few stars blinked into sight.

He murmured, "It'll be okay, Silver. I've got your back now."

"Promise?"

"Promise."

And that was enough for her. Enough to build a family on. Enough to build a life on together. Forever.

* * * * *

A sneaky peek at next month…

By Request

RELIVE THE ROMANCE WITH THE BEST OF THE BEST

My wish list for next month's titles…

In stores from 18th April 2014:

- ❑ Indecent Arrangements – Mira Lyn Kelly, Anna Cleary & Julia James
- ❑ The Lost Princes: Darius, Cassius & Monte – Raye Morgan

3 stories in each book - only £5.99!

In stores from 2nd May 2014:

- ❑ Las Vegas: Scandals – Nina Bruhns, Loreth Anne White & Carla Cassidy
- ❑ Single Dad Needs Nanny – Teresa Carpenter, Alison Roberts & Cindy Kirk

Available at WHSmith, Tesco, Asda, Eason, Amazon and Apple

Just can't wait?

Visit us Online

You can buy our books online a month before they hit the shops! **www.millsandboon.co.uk**

0414/05

Special Offers

Every month we put together collections and longer reads written by your favourite authors.

Here are some of next month's highlights—and don't miss our fabulous discount online!

On sale 18th April

On sale 2nd May

On sale 2nd May

Find out more at
www.millsandboon.co.uk/specialreleases

Visit us Online

0514/ST/MB468

Step into

THE ROYAL HOUSE OF KAREDES...

TWO CROWNS, TWO ISLANDS, ONE LEGACY

One royal family, torn apart by pride and its lust for power, reunited by purity and passion

Now available as a complete collection at: www.millsandboon.co.uk

0414/MB467

24 new stories from the leading lights of romantic fiction!

Featuring bestsellers Adele Parks, Katie Fforde, Carole Matthews and many more, *Truly, Madly, Deeply* takes you on an exciting romantic adventure where love really is all you need.

Now available at:

www.millsandboon.co.uk

0514/MB470

Discover more romance at

www.millsandboon.co.uk

- WIN great prizes in our exclusive competitions
- BUY new titles before they hit the shops
- BROWSE new books and REVIEW your favourites
- SAVE on new books with the Mills & Boon® Bookclub™
- DISCOVER new authors

PLUS, to chat about your favourite reads, get the latest news and find special offers:

- Find us on facebook.com/millsandboon
- Follow us on twitter.com/millsandboonuk
- Sign up to our newsletter at millsandboon.co.uk

M&B_WEB

The World of Mills & Boon®

There's a Mills & Boon® series that's perfect for you. We publish ten series and, with new titles every month, you never have to wait long for your favourite to come along.

By Request — *Relive the romance with the best of the best*
12 stories every month

Cherish™ — *Experience the ultimate rush of falling in love*
12 new stories every month

Desire™ — *Passionate and dramatic love stories*
6 new stories every month

nocturne™ — *An exhilarating underworld of dark desires*
Up to 3 new stories every month

For exclusive member offers go to
millsandboon.co.uk/subscribe

M&B/WORLD4a